CWAAA01556

The
Allegation

By the same author

The Baby War
Robbers
Villains
Bandits

The Allegation

Peter Whalley

Ringpull

Published by Ringpull Press 1994

Ringpull Press Limited
Queensway House
London Road South
Poynton
Greater Manchester
SK12 1NJ

Copyright Peter Whalley © 1994

The right of Peter Whalley to be identified as the author of this work of
fiction has been asserted by him in accordance with the Copyright,
Designs and Patents Act 1988

All rights reserved. No reproduction, copy or transmission of this
publication may be made without written permission. No paragraph of
this publication may be reproduced or copied or transmitted save with
written permission or in accordance with the provisions of the Copyright
Act 1956 (as amended). Any person who does any unauthorised act in
relation to this publication may be liable to criminal prosecution and civil
claims for damages.

A CIP catalogue record for this book is available from the British Library

ISBN 1 898051 18 6

Typeset in 11/13pt Baskerville
Filmset by Datix International Ltd, Bungay, Suffolk
Printed and bound in Great Britain by Clays Ltd, St Ives plc

This novel was the basis of the BBC Radio drama serial *Letters Of Introduction*, transmitted on Radio Four during March 1994

'There you are, Mr. Gillow,' said the young woman behind the reception desk, 'room three-forty-seven.'

Melissa remained seated in one of the leather armchairs that were to the side of the desk until he came to her with the room key dangling from his fingers.

'The keys to the kingdom,' he said. 'Shall we go?'

'Oh, I think we should,' she said.

She walked beside him across the foyer to the row of lifts. They let the first go since it was already occupied. Taking the second, they rode up the three floors in silence. He took hold of her hand and threaded his fingers through hers. The lift slowed and stopped and the doors slid open.

Their room was some way along. Releasing her hand, he put an arm around her and pulled her to him so that they had to walk in step. He spoke softly into her ear.

'You know I can never stay in a hotel anymore without thinking of you. As soon as I see corridors like this and bedroom doors with numbers on, I can smell that perfume you're wearing now.'

They came to room three-forty-seven. He had to let go of her in order to take the key from his pocket and open the door. Then he stepped back and waited for her to go in first.

It was a room with a king-size bed, some abstract prints and white-painted furniture. She threw her bag on to a chair and stepped out of her high heels. He was careful to place the Do Not Disturb sign outside the door before closing it.

'You are beautiful,' he said, coming to her and taking her in his arms. He kissed her hard on the mouth. She could taste the whisky he had had at the end of their meal. Then he began to nuzzle into her neck, feeling with his hand for the zip at the back of her dress.

'Wait, let me —' she said. She pulled down the zip and shrugged off the dress. He gave a moan of appreciation and reached out to take hold of her again when the telephone began to ring.

She saw the alarm on his face. 'What the hell . . .?' he muttered. She could only shake her head: no, she had no idea who it could be. He hesitated a moment longer, then picked up the receiver.

'Yes?' he said.

She remained where she was, motionless in her black bra and pants, not wanting to make a sound. She saw him relax as he listened to what was being said. He gave her a reassuring smile, then spoke into the phone. 'If you could just hang onto it for me, yes please. . . . Richard Gillow, yes. . . . Not at all. Thank you very much indeed.'

Replacing the receiver, he began to laugh. 'It's my pen,' he said, coming to take her in his arms again. 'After I signed in, I left my bloody pen down there on the desk!'

'You've got to learn not to be so careless,' she said, teasing. 'Or one day it might get you into all sorts of trouble.'

I

'It is Myott, isn't it?' he enquired.

The assistant turned the jug over in her long fingers and they peered together at its base. 'Myott, Son & Co. England,' she read aloud. 'Hand Painted.' They shared a small laugh of relief that it was what he had taken it to be.

'Wonderful,' he said. 'I'll take it.'

'Would you like me to wrap it?' she asked.

'Yes, please. But before you do . . .' He pulled out the slim jewellery case from his inside pocket. 'Will this go inside?'

'Oh, I'm sure it will,' she said, taking it from him. He saw her check for a moment to read the embossed Regent Street name before she inserted it into the neck of the jug.

'It's for a wedding anniversary,' he said, glad to explain and have the chance to share his pleasure in the sheer extravagance. 'It's to say thank you to my wife for staying married to me for twenty-five years.'

She smiled. 'Congratulations.'

'Thank you.'

He reached into his pocket again, this time for his wallet, twisting slightly as he did so, which was how he came to be looking out through the window of the shop and saw David, his son, passing in the street outside.

What's more, David saw him – of that Richard was certain and would have sworn to it on oath. For a long moment they were looking into one another's eyes. David was the first to react, his look of surprise giving way to something more like horror, then he hastened forward and disappeared beyond the frame of the window.

'Excuse me,' said Richard quickly. 'Somebody there I recognize. I'll be back in a second.'

Without waiting for the assistant's reply, he hurried to the door of the shop, pulled it open and stepped out into the street.

It was lunchtime. The pavement had disappeared beneath a flood of office-workers looking for sandwiches and burger-bars in addition to the shoppers and those who were simply out enjoying the sunshine. He caught a glimpse of what might have been David's shaggy, black hair some twenty yards ahead and ran forward in pursuit as best he could, squeezing between people and sidestepping a woman with a pushchair but then finding that his quarry had disappeared. He continued along the street, jostling people in his haste and calling back apologies but came to the corner without managing another sighting. Uncertain about which direction to take, he stood looking around him but there was no further sign of David. He turned and retraced his steps, peering into the shops that he passed in case David had turned into one of them and even going into a Greek restaurant that was about level with where he had last seen his son. But no, he had disappeared.

It was a mystery, and also disturbing, that David should have fled like that. Richard told himself that it might not have been David at all but simply someone of the same heavy build and dark colouring. But he didn't believe it. For a second there, he had been looking at *his son* and not a mere likeness.

There were other questions, like what could David possibly be doing here in Chiswick anyway, when he was lived in Wales and had always made much of his dislike of London and his avowed intention of avoiding it at all cost? But dwarfing all of them was the question of why he had fled when he had seen Richard and realized, as he must have done, that Richard had seen him?

Richard returned to the antique shop where the assistant had wrapped the jug in brown paper. She looked relieved to see him.

'Sorry about that,' he said, offering her a credit card. 'I thought I saw my son.'

'You only thought?' she said. 'Does that mean it wasn't him?'

'It wasn't, no. I made a mistake.'

It was a lie. But how could he possibly explain to a shop assistant something which he found so utterly baffling?

He had always believed himself a friend to his son, flattering himself that David would have confirmed this, had anyone asked. He had given him what help he could through the wilderness years of adolescence, the low points of which had been an ex-girlfriend's attempted suicide and a court appearance for possession. And the high points . . . well, there had been a host of those, academic and sporting successes as well as family memories to be cherished. And hadn't they spoken on the phone just the other week, with David urging him to visit the cottage in the Brecon Hills where he now lived with Suzanne?

So why, when he spotted his father through a shop window, should he have taken to his heels, like a criminal evading capture?

It remained an unsolved mystery, and a worrying distraction throughout his afternoon of meetings and then during his train journey up the spine of England and towards home.

Claire, his wife, had never minded his regular absences from home. Indeed, had she been invited to draw up a list of the reasons their marriage had remained a happy one while so many around them had declined into relationships of habit or mutual deception, she might well have placed his weekly sojourns in London close to the top.

When he had first begun staying away, sleeping in the flat on Frampton Street which they had inherited from her parents, he had been concerned she would find being alone unsettling or even frightening. Each week before departing he would question her gently: 'You're sure you don't mind?' and 'You would tell me if you weren't happy about this?'

'Of course I would,' she'd insisted. 'I'm perfectly happy, so go on.'

'It's just that nobody's going to take me seriously as a publisher unless I'm available in London.'

'I know. And so off you go to London. Who's stopping you?'

'You really, really don't mind?'

'I'll only mind if you don't come back.'

This affectionate bickering had long since died away. She had so often insisted that she had no qualms about his going that he not no longer questioned her. It had become an established part of their lives together.

Even when Diane, their second child, had taken wing and gone to university and so there were no longer children at home to be considered, it had never been suggested by either of them that Claire might now start to accompany him on these trips. He still went alone. In fact, he noted with amusement how he would apologize profusely if anything cropped up that demanded his presence in Manchester and so forced a postponement of his London trip.

'I'm sorry,' he said, when it had happened twice within a single month, 'but I'll definitely be going next week. Promise.'

'You'd better,' she replied. 'I don't want you hanging around the house, cramping my style.'

Of course, it was a joke. Though, like all the best jokes, it had an element of truth in it, one she felt he also perceived. It was good for both of them to have these brief, two-day respites from their almost-twenty-five-years of marriage together, and then to meet up again refreshed. He would always bring her something back, often wine for their meal together, sometimes a book or art catalogue which he had let upon and thought might interest her.

While she, for her part, always made a particular effort with dinner on the evening of his return, digging out the Rockingham china and the antique Waterford crystal and setting places in the dining-room, rather than the kitchen where they usually had their family meals.

If Diane, their daughter, were home from Cambridge, she would refuse to join them: 'You don't really want me. I'll just make a sandwich.' They would cheerfully agree, pleased that their 'special dinners' had become an event in their children's lives as well as their own.

And so Richard and Claire would eat and drink in the modest grandeur of their dining-room and swop accounts of their time apart. He would tell of authors and agents he had met and the deals he had done on overseas rights and translations. And she would tell him what had been happening in her world of textile design: commissions she'd been offered; shows in Florence or Munich it might be nice to attend, though she seldom did.

She would also feed him the latest village gossip that had come her way via Adele next-door or Moira, her closest friend, who would ring almost every morning with *something* worth passing on. It was tittle-tattle which he absorbed with a seriousness it never quite deserved, even sometimes prompting her: 'So, any major scandals while I've been away?' As though it were his duty to keep up.

Certainly he couldn't be accused of taking much pleasure from what she had to tell him. 'Why do they do these things?' he would cry, horrified by her latest tale of deception and betrayal.

4

He would moan with genuine distress on hearing the consequences of their neighbours' philandering: homes smashed and families divided like spoils of war.

'If they can't be faithful to one another, then why can't they at least learn to forgive?' he asked on one such evening, bewildered by the recent rupture of a family they had both known well and been fond of.

'Because they're stupid,' Claire said, less constrained in her judgements than he was.

But he wasn't to be so easily shaken off. 'You know they're not. In other things they're intelligent, capable people. You can't just dismiss them as stupid.'

'Where sex is concerned, everybody's stupid,' she said. Then, seeing him turn his brown eyes towards her, she wanted to add, 'Except for us,' but stopped for fear of sounding smug or inviting some kind of disaster to befall them too.

She knew there were those among their friends and acquaintances who would welcome such a disaster. Not openly of course; openly they'd be full of sympathy and dismay. But privately they'd be reassured to discover that the Gillow marriage was just as subject to stresses and strains as any. Even more subject than most, others might have thought, what with his frequent trips to London and her swanning about as she pleased.

Besides, the Gillows had enjoyed more than their fair share of life's blessings: wealth, intelligence, beauty; success in the eyes of the world and contentment together; bright and loving children. In fact, more than a fair share: they had somehow managed to acquire several other people's shares along the way.

Natural justice demanded they should sooner or later come unstuck. And, when they did, well, having climbed the highest, they would have the furthest to fall.

These were fears that Claire kept to herself. Richard was more trusting, less cynical than she was. Had she put her fears to him, he would have protested that none of their friends would have harboured such dreadful thoughts.

But she believed she knew better. It was the main reason she kept him up to date on the collapsing marriages that seemed to be everywhere around them. It was a reminder to them both how precious and how fragile was the life they had together.

*

Along with the backlog of gossip, there would be an accumulation of mail awaiting his return. There might be as many as five deliveries while he was away. Claire would rescue each small pile from the doormat and carry it into the kitchen. She then extracted those items that were for her or, a rarity now, for the children, and stock-piled the rest on the mantelpiece above the Aga, ready for Richard's return.

He had once challenged her on this, saying, 'While I'm away, why don't you just open everything, even if it does have my name on?'

She shook her head, resolute. 'I couldn't.'

'But I don't mind,' he urged. 'Then, if there was anything important, you could phone me.'

But she still shook her head, not wanting to open his post nor even to phone him. For part of the game they played – by tacit agreement – was that, while away in London, he was beyond the range of phones or faxes. Barring life-or-death issues, of which there had been none so far, they didn't communicate until his return.

'Anything addressed to you, I'll keep it till you get back,' she said.

He didn't pursue the matter. Why bother? She wanted him to know that she believed he had a right to a private life, even if he didn't wish to exercise it.

Of course, in flicking through each morning's mail in order to separate what was his from what was hers and the children's, she had over the years become adept at recognizing the various communications he habitually received: letters from friends or colleagues, charity circulars, brochures which were specific to publishing and others that were not and offered cut-price holidays or investment offers. Then there were the ones with French stamps on, which were to do with their holiday home and contained either demands for tax or communications from their caretaker on the re-plumbing of the swimming-pool.

But she opened none of them, keeping them in the order in which they had arrived and piling them on the kitchen mantelpiece where they – like she – awaited his return.

Adele had come round from next-door, as she was prone to do during these afternoons of mid-summer. She did her usual apologizing and urged Claire to send her away if she were busy but Claire said, as she always said, that she had been working for long enough and would welcome a break.

They carried their coffees out into the garden and strolled round, admiring the bright beds of flowers. These were largely Claire's responsibility though she would have been the first to admit there was a gardener who came in regularly to do most of the donkey work.

'Your garden always looks so lovely,' said Adele, making it sound more complaint than compliment.

'So does yours,' countered Claire lightly.

'No, it doesn't. It takes me all my time just to keep it tidy.'

Their friendship went back some years, since Adele and husband Lawrence had moved in next door, and Claire had gone round to introduce herself and ask if there were anything she could do to help. She had ended up on her knees, scrubbing the kitchen floor. Barely a day had gone by since without Adele visiting or at least calling out and waving as she passed outside the window of Claire's workroom.

It occasionally struck Claire that there was something Adele wanted from her. Quite what this was she was unable to define but she felt it most strongly on occasions such as this, when a tour of her garden would prompt Adele into denigrating her own. As though she were saying, *Why can't my garden be more like yours?* and wanting an answer that went beyond practical advice on planting and pruning into realms that Claire suspected might best be termed 'spiritual'. Or anyway 'counselling'.

Changing the subject, she asked about Lawrence and whether he was currently involved with any interesting cases. Lawrence was a solicitor with a Manchester practice. He specialised in criminal cases and spent most days in and out of court.

'Oh, the usual sorts of things,' said Adele dismissively. 'Defending a load of dead-beats who'd be better off in prison anyway. But I'll tell you what else he's doing, shall I?'

'What?'

'He's writing a novel.'

Claire gave the reaction of surprise that Adele was clearly expecting. While privately she wondered what tricky questions of etiquette this might raise for Richard – finding that his friendly next-door neighbour might soon be looking for a publisher.

'Really. What sort of novel?'

'He won't tell me. But, knowing him, it'll be about the law.'

'Well, I hope he's going to let Richard have first look at it.'

What else could she say?

'I don't know what he's going to do,' said Adele. 'I'm not even supposed to be mentioning it to you. To tell you the truth, I think he's a bit embarrassed by it. I only found out by accident because he'd forgotten to lock his desk.'

Claire heard the kitchen door opening as someone emerged from the house. She immediately dropped the cigarette she was smoking, thinking it might be Richard returned early.

But no, it was Diane in bare feet and shorts that looked uncomfortably tight. She had come back only last week from France where she'd been spending the long vacation reading Nietzsche and perfecting her tan.

'Oh, hi, Adele,' she said.

'Hello,' said Adele, gazing at her wistfully, as if she were thinking, And it's not only the garden – *why can't I have a lovely daughter like this?*

Diane turned to Claire. 'I'm going over to the stables. And then I probably won't be back, so don't cook for me, OK?'

'But you'll be back tonight, will you?' asked Claire, scrambling for the cigarette, then checking it was still lit.

'I don't know. But I'll take a key so you can lock up anyway.'

And with that she was gone.

'Is she really going around with that *biker?*' asked Adele. 'The one who was here the other day?'

Claire smiled. 'He's only a biker in his spare time. Mostly he looks after the stables his father owns. Then at the end of the summer he'll be going back to Edinburgh where he's studying medicine.'

Adele seemed startled by this, just as she had been startled earlier when Diane had made it clear she might be out for the night. No doubt she would have been even more startled to have learnt that Diane had been on the pill since the age of fourteen, when her mother had discovered a packet of contraceptives at the bottom of her school-bag.

She never would learn it because Claire would never tell her.

This was the one topic – sex – on which the two women had never confided and, Claire felt, never would.

It was only after Adele had gone and she was burying her cigarette-butt among the begonias that she wondered whether Adele believed her as proficient at sex as she was at gardening and whether she might not be looking to her for the secret of that too.

The Gillows' house dated from the 1920s and was constructed in red brick, with a grey slated roof. It was built to deceive, with the modest front lawn and brief driveway giving no inkling of the grounds that stretched away to the rear. There were almost three acres in all. Closest to the house were the formal gardens, then came the orchard and, beyond that, the paddock which now went unused since Diane had gone to university and so the horse she had kept there, an eight-year-old bay gelding called Minstrel, had been sold.

The house had a celebrated architectural quirk, and that was the turret that rose from one end of the roof and went up fifteen feet before being topped with a stone coping and a black, cast-iron weathercock. It was a local landmark, rivalling the church steeple, and made the house visible above its neighbours no matter which approach you took.

When the children were young, it had been a regular competition between them to try and be the first to spot the turret as the family returned home from outings or holidays. The prize for the winner would be the right to unlock the front door and be the first into the house.

Now Richard, returning home in the back of the taxi bringing him from the station, gazed out as keenly as the children had ever done for his first sight of it. He didn't believe himself a sentimental man, or one particularly attached to places; yet this place, where his children had grown up, exercised a gravitational pull on him that he felt afresh on each return.

He paid off the taxi, opened the front door and stepped into the house. 'Hello?' he called as he moved forward and placed his bags at the foot of the stairs. Sometimes he returned to find Claire absent, which was always a small disappointment.

This time though he heard the door to her workroom opening. 'Darling . . .?' she called.

'Hello, yes, I'm here.'

He opened his arms to embrace her as she arrived with her warm, familiar perfumes and her piled auburn hair. It was hair that was always just that one shade brighter than he had remembered it.

'Wonderful to be home,' he said, holding her.

'Wonderful to have you home,' she intoned her usual response, then kissed him. There was a passion to the kiss that he found surprising and distinctly encouraging.

'Where's Diane?' he said softly, his mouth still against hers.

She gave a small shake of the head. 'Out.'

'And Adele's not –'

'No.'

'So there's nobody –'

'No.'

He caught the look of devilment in her eye, which was confirmation enough, and so swept her off her feet and headed for the staircase with her cradled in his arms.

'Help,' she called in mock alarm.

'No use. There's no-one to hear you.'

'I hope not,' she said. But then she became serious as they came to the top of the stairs and onto the landing: 'Oh, but wait. Can I just go and turn my computer off?'

'What?' he laughed. 'You're asking me to play second fiddle to that thing?'

'I just don't want to lose –' she began to protest, but he said, 'It's all right, go on,' as he lowered her to the ground.

Their bedroom, at the back of the house, was still warm from the afternoon sun. He was glad to throw off the clothes in which he had travelled, though he wasn't quick enough for Claire, who came running in after him. 'You not ready yet?' she derided, slipping out of her own clothes in less time than it took him to remove his socks so that she was in the bed first and waiting for him.

Afterwards, when he had showered and dressed, he went downstairs and through into the kitchen. Claire had gone ahead of him, slipping out from beneath the sheet while he was in a post-coital doze. She was hard at work preparing their dinner, trout by the look of it. He kissed the nape of her neck.

'Don't disturb the cook,' she said.

'You want a drink or is it too early?'

'Too early for me. You have one.'

'No, I'll wait for you,' he said and poured himself a coffee. He was in no hurry to advance the evening, wanting to linger in this blissful aftermath of his return.

As always there was a small pile of post on the mantelpiece. He lifted it down and took it to the table.

'Any messages?' he asked.

'Nothing,' she said, her back to him as she prepared the fish. 'Unless there are some on the answerphone.'

He did a quick division of the letters, dealing them into three piles of Bills, Charity Appeals and Others. Then he started on the Others, slitting them open with a convenient kitchen knife.

'Oh, yes, and Adele says Lawrence is writing a novel.'

'He is?'

Wasn't everybody, he thought. Sometimes it seemed there were more people writing novels than reading them.

'Only it's a secret.'

'Well, I'll read it if that's what he wants.'

'I think it probably is since he told Adele not to tell me. Which almost certainly meant she would.'

But Richard's attention had suddenly been wrenched away, claimed by the letter he was reading. It was no more than a half-page, written using a red biro and printed in sloping capitals.

He read it again, still not quite able to believe the words. Or even to believe that he could be sitting here, in his own kitchen, holding such a thing in his hands. He looked at the envelope but yes, it was addressed to him all right and carried a first class stamp.

'Darling . . .?'

He looked up and saw she had turned towards him, waiting for his response to something she must have said.

'Sorry, what?'

'I said what happens if you read this novel of Lawrence's and you don't like it?'

'Then I'll tell him,' he said abruptly.

He cleared his throat, not sure how to inform her what had just happened. He didn't want to alarm her but he could think of no way of avoiding the simple truth of what was there on the paper he was still holding.

He said, 'This letter I've just opened . . .'

'Yes?'

He waited till she turned towards him and he had her full attention, then he said, 'I think I'm being blackmailed.'

2

She stared at him, trying to guess the joke. 'What, you mean by some author . . .?'

'No, I mean . . . Here. Read it.'

He held out the letter but she displayed her fishy and oily hands as the reason she couldn't take it from him.

'Read it to me,' she said.

'Well . . . all right,' he agreed reluctantly. He knew there was no-one to overhear; all the same, he would have preferred if she could have read it herself, silently.

'It's hand-written,' he said. 'That is, printed. Addressed to me. And it says . . .'

He looked up to be sure she was listening. She was, and so he began to read aloud the ludicrous contents of the letter in as matter-of-fact a voice as he could muster.

'Dear Mr Gillow. I have been watching you for some time and know all about your relationship with Melissa. I know when you meet and I have photographs to prove it. I shall write to you again, giving you more details and also telling you how much you must pay to stop me telling your wife and friends about this.'

There was a silence when he came to the end. He saw she was watching him with a faint, tentative smile. She was still waiting for him to give the game away and admit it was a joke, someone he knew playing silly buggers.

'That's all,' he said.

'You can't be serious?'

'Yes.'

'And it's not, you know . . . some sort of joke?'

'Might be. I don't know what it is. Oh, except I should add that I don't know and I have never known anybody called Melissa.'

'Let me see,' she said.

She wiped her hands on a tea-towel, then picked up the half-moon reading-glasses she kept by the clock.

He passed the letter to her and waited while she read. It gave him time to wonder whether he'd been wise even to have shown it to her or whether he shouldn't simply have put it to one side and said nothing. Later he could have destroyed it. But it was too late for that now.

Of course, it could be argued he had already proved his complete and utter innocence by the way he had immediately drawn the letter to her attention. No man with anything to hide would have done that.

'Amazing,' she said, having finished reading.

'Isn't it.'

'And you don't know *any* Melissa?'

'No.'

'I don't mean . . . intimately.'

'I don't know any Melissa, not in any way at all.'

He was pleased to see she didn't seem at all perturbed. If anything, she was entertained by the curious letter. She was questioning him only because she was searching for a clue that might explain how it had come to be written.

'She's not someone you've met, say when you've been in London, and then someone's seen you with her —'

'I have never, ever known anybody called Melissa,' he said, wishing he had and so could help her resolve things.

Melissa was hardly a common name or one he was likely to have forgotten. Besides, this letter made it sound as though his association with her was a recent event, or even one that was on-going.

Claire came and stood beside him and placed the letter on the table so they could look at it together. She smelled of fish. He put an arm around her waist.

'You do believe me?' he said, with a smile.

'Darling, yes! Oh, of course! How could you think I wouldn't?'

She seemed genuinely shocked by his question. It encouraged him to believe he had done the right thing in showing it to her after all.

She went on: 'I just think you're being blackmailed by the world's worst blackmailer. He gets everything wrong. Names, addresses, everything.'

Richard laughed. 'Or else,' he said, taking up the joke, 'he sends out the same letter to a random selection of men, hoping he'll strike lucky somewhere!'

'Yes!'

'He probably makes an overall loss.'

'Oh, and I'll tell you what,' she said, picking up the letter again. 'Yes, look. He says he has *photographs*. Now those I can't wait to see!'

'I think you'd better prepare yourself for a disappointment.'

'You mean there aren't any . . .?'

'Certainly not of me, no.'

She went back to preparing dinner, still chuckling over the notion of the hopelessly confused blackmailer. Richard put the letter aside, deciding not to throw it away yet, if only because of its curiosity value. He went quickly through the rest of his mail, relieved to find it unremarkable.

They ate dinner together in the formal setting of the dining-room, as they always did on his first night home. He told her about his odd experience in Chiswick, when he had seen David through the shop window and gone in pursuit. Though without, of course, admitting just what *he* was doing in Chiswick.

'Well, it couldn't have been David,' Claire protested. 'Just somebody who looked like him.'

'I know, except . . . I'm sure it was.'

'In Chiswick? What would he be doing there?'

'I've no idea. I'll give him a ring over the weekend, see what he has to say.'

'It's been quite a day for mysteries one way and another,' she said, sliding their used plates together and carrying them from the table.

She meant the mystery of the letter of course. Her sudden reference to it when they had talked of so much else made him wonder whether she'd been secretly brooding on it.

Richard Gillow was not a man who believed he knew his wife's every waking thought, far from it. Even after their many years together, she still often surprised him, expressing opinions he would never have expected of her. For a dyed-in-the-wool liberal, she could be suddenly all for capital punishment or newspaper censorship, according to how the mood took her.

On top of which there were days, sometimes several together, when she would become distant and withdrawn. Yet if he taxed her with her mood – 'But what on earth is the matter? Just tell me!' – she would accuse him of imagining it and would then withdraw completely, spending hours at a time in her workroom and then at night lying rigid and untouchable on the far side of the bed. He had trained himself to say nothing and to wait for the moods to lift. He wondered how far they might be a side-effect of her artistic abilities, the dark side of her creative talents.

Certainly he would never have said that he could read her mind. She might well be harbouring doubts about the letter without his being aware. All right, she had earlier laughed at it and made fun of its sender; but she was quite capable of doing that while still privately reserving judgement.

Or perhaps she wasn't even reserving judgement. Perhaps she believed the letter lock, stock and barrel and had already con-demned him as an adulterer? She believed that there did some-where exist a woman called Melissa with whom he was having an affair.

And, if that were so – *if* – then how the hell could he prove otherwise? How could anybody counter accusations made anony-mously and without evidence or witnesses?

It staggered him to realize how, in no time at all, the joke had soured to become a terrible threat he could see no way of combating.

Even the fact that he had shown the letter to Claire proved nothing. Sure, it might be seen as the action of an innocent man. But it could also been seen as the action of a clever liar who wanted to be seen as innocent.

He heard Claire returning from the kitchen and vowed to put these fears to her. Whatever she might say could be no worse than what he was imagining. Better to have it stated and out in the open.

'Sorry I was so long,' she said. 'These weren't quite set.'

She brought their desserts, which were small pots of lemon mousse with a chocolate decoration on each.

'That's OK,' he said. 'It gave me time to think.'

'Oh, dear. That sounds ominous.'

'Look. That letter. It's not worrying you, is it?'

'No, of course not.'

She seemed so at ease in her answer and so quick to give it that he was almost disarmed.

'I really am not having an affair with anybody. And certainly not with anybody called Melissa.'

'Well, I would hope not. I would hope you'd have more taste than to choose someone with a name like that.'

The joke jarred with him. He had been inviting her to respond honestly and tell him what she really felt, not to be smart-arsed about it.

'Please, darling, you would tell me . . .?'

'Tell you what?'

'If you'd any doubts. If you thought I was trying to fool you about the letter.'

'Yes, I *would* tell you. But, in fact, there's nothing to tell because I don't have any doubts.'

Still he couldn't leave it alone. 'You don't?'

'No! Oh, come on, Richard. Do you think I could let you go away every week – well, almost every week – most weeks – if I doubted you? If I were left sitting here picturing you with other women?'

'I know . . . I know,' he said, his fears receding. Though he still felt obliged to make the point: 'It's just that we've have never had a crank letter like this before, have we.'

'We haven't, no. But why should it make any difference? I'm sorry, Richard, I just don't know what it is you're trying to get me to say.'

'I'm not trying to get you to say anything. I just want you to know that I love you and that there's never been anybody else in my life and there never will be.'

'And I love you,' she said. 'And there'll never be anyone else for me either.'

It felt like a renewing of their vows and left them both a little breathless, stuck for something that would follow it. Until Richard smiled and said, 'OK, I'm sorry if I've been going on about it. Forget the letter.'

'Well, I really think we should,' she said in heartfelt agreement.

Though of course it wasn't as simple as that – forgetting it. At least not for her. It remained on the edge of her consciousness over the weekend, a minor irritant that might yet prove malignant.

The letter itself remained on the mantelpiece. Well, she wasn't going to throw it away. After all, it was his letter, addressed to him.

As it turned out, the weekend gave her little time for dwelling on it. The Silver Wedding with everything that was going to entail was no more than seven days away. The children, Diane and David, had insisted on taking responsibility for organizing the celebrations and even for paying for them, though both Claire and Richard were adamant that they shouldn't do so in full since the outside caterers alone were going to cost a bomb. There had even been talk of a jazz band.

Claire had her work too. She could always escape into that, pottering about amid her samples and scraps of fabric and the stacks of drawings that filled her cabinets to bursting. It was a world free of words, where she could feel safe and in control.

And if, putting down her pencils and brushes after a morning's work, she still couldn't completely wipe all thoughts of the letter from her mind, at least it no longer seemed so urgent, a problem that had to be faced up to and solved. It had arrived, been read and put on one side and there for the time being it could stay.

'I had a word with David,' Richard told her.

It was Saturday afternoon. Claire had been into Chester for some bits and pieces while Richard had remained in his study, catching up on letters and phone-calls.

'How is he?' she asked.

'Yes, fine. But I asked him about the other day, that business I told you about when I thought I saw him in London . . .?'

'Yes?'

Richard shrugged. 'Well, he swears it wasn't him. Says he wasn't anywhere near London.'

'So it must have been somebody else then,' she said, drawing the obvious conclusion since he seemed unwilling to draw it for himself.

'I suppose it must.'

'Well, there you are then,' she said, not really understanding why he was making such a fuss about it, unless it were to distract her from the other matter. 'And did they say what time they'd be here next week, David and Suzanne?'

'No. No, sorry, I didn't think to ask.'

Later, when the heat of the afternoon had become less oppressive, Claire went for a walk around the garden and hid among the apple trees in order to have another surreptitious cigarette. It was a habit she had officially kicked nearly two years ago. Richard had been so proud of her, she couldn't bring herself to confess she'd been back-sliding.

She was wondering whether to tell Moira about the letter, since Moira was the friend to whom she told everything – almost everything – and whom she would be seeing that night anyway. The loose arrangement for Saturdays was that at some point in the evening they would all meet up for a drink in the George.

At least the garden was in good order, she observed, wandering back towards the house. She must make sure Tommy did two days this week, ensuring it would be spick and span for the festivities. She would also need him for clearing up afterwards.

She heard the roaring of a motor-cycle away to the side of the house. So Diane had returned. Suppose she had invited Will, her leather-clad companion, to stay for dinner – could she spin out the noisettes of lamb for the four of them?

She stopped at the window to the lounge. Through it she could see Richard, shabby in his old corduroys, sprawled across a sofa and going through the newspapers. She tried picturing him with another woman, a blonde perhaps, taller than she was, and younger too. Of course she had seen him in the company of other women often enough, but they had been friends of theirs, at parties, which didn't count. To picture him making love to another woman . . .

She shook her head to dispel the ugly image. She must resist these disloyal and dangerous thoughts. Remember Othello and the handkerchief and the tears that had led to.

If only Richard hadn't been so persistent in his questioning of her at the end of their welcome-home dinner. It had been almost a cross-examination. The way he had kept on at her, forcing her to say that she believed him. It hadn't been enough that she had *demonstrated* her support by not blowing up when she had first read the letter; no, he had to keep on and on, dragging the words out of her. Content only when she had finally stated that she loved him and would never doubt him.

And, of course, she did love him. She had surely proved that by the sheer bloody hard work she had put into this marriage of theirs. All the same, wouldn't any wife the world over have had just a tiny moment of doubt on seeing such a letter? They might then put it firmly behind them, as she was intent on doing; they might even be ashamed of having harboured such doubts; but only a complete fool or a dewy-eyed innocent could look at such a letter and never even ask herself whether there might not be something behind it.

In the event, when they all landed up at the George and managed to grab a table and the men were elbowing their way through to the bar, she said nothing to Moira.

For one thing, Moira had told her so much − too much really − about the flirtations and the affairs of her own husband and the revenges she had taken and the rows that had ensued. Her husband, Roy, was a dentist, prematurely balding and with a self-deprecating smile. He was generally regarded as a pillar of the community, except by those who had heard Moira's version. 'Randy Roy' was how she habitually referred to him.

She had more than once accused Claire of not playing fair since she had never once passed on similar secrets about her own husband.

'Richard is a very sexy man. I can't believe he's never had a fling with anybody!'

'I know he's a very sexy man. And he's also a very faithful one.'

'You know, I've got to tell you − you look very self-satisfied when you say that.'

No, Moira would seize upon news of the letter; she would be secretly delighted by it. After all these years it would be Claire's turn to play the wronged wife and she, Moira, could at last be the adviser, the shoulder to cry on. And her advice − Claire had no doubt − would be that there was no smoke without fire and so the letter should be taken at face-value.

This would not be because Moira was unduly malicious or because she didn't like Richard, but because that was how things had always been with Roy.

*

20

After a leisurely Saturday, Sunday was hectic, with people dropping in, a Samaritans' fund-raising lunch in the church hall and then the annual Open tennis tournament at the club. Claire didn't play, but Richard had been entered and made the semi-final, which everyone seemed to think was highly creditable for a man of his age.

Meanwhile the phone continued to ring with people saying yes to their invitations to next Saturday's thrash – so many people, in fact, that Claire felt she had to tackle Diane: 'Just how many have you invited?'

'Mother, that's nothing to do with you.'

'Of course it's to do with me. It's my Silver Wedding and my house.'

'It doesn't matter. Just leave everything to me and David, will you please?'

'No, I won't. How many?'

But still Diane wouldn't give her a serious answer. She looked her mother in the eye, said, 'Hundreds and hundreds,' and walked off.

Lawrence stopped by in the evening and took Richard off to the pub for an hour. Then, just as Claire was beginning to draw breath, Adele came round with her sister who was staying with them for the weekend. So that it was quite late before she was able to settle with her *Times* and *Observer*. Even then, she didn't get far before she found herself nodding off to sleep over them.

The bonus to all this activity was that it had allowed neither of them time to speak about the letter. For her part, Claire had barely given it a thought, except to reflect on how something that had loomed so desperately large at the beginning of the weekend was already becoming the stuff of history, and unimportant history at that. It had shrunk back to being a joke, one that she must one day remember to tell Moira about.

The second letter came with the first post on Monday. It was there on the mat when Richard did his tour of unlocking the house and opening the curtains. He recognized it by the printed style of the address and the fact it was done in the same red biro.

Claire was in the kitchen, still in her dressing-gown. She was getting breakfast together – muesli and toast and coffee – when he came through from the hallway. Without a word, he placed the envelope on the table before her.

She looked at it, then at him, and knew immediately what it was. She felt a stab of despair: she wasn't ready for this. She had convinced herself there wouldn't be another one. It would be so much harder now to turn this into a joke or see it as a mistake.

He gave a small, apologetic smile. He also knew that this letter, whatever it contained, couldn't be dismissed so easily.

'Do you want to open it or shall I?' he said.

3

'Why not just throw it away?' she said quickly. 'Then neither of us has to read it.'

'I don't think that would be a good idea.'

'Why not?'

'Because then we'd be trying to guess what it might have said.' He had already taken up a knife and split the envelope.

'Well, you do what you want with it. I don't want even to see it,' she said, and turned her back.

'We can't ignore it,' he said quietly. 'It's arrived and so we have to read it.'

'Well, I don't.'

He took out the paper from inside the envelope. As before, it was a single sheet, hand-printed in that same sloping style.

'Dear Mr Gillow,' he read. 'As I promised, here are some details of your meetings with Melissa. They were all at the Queens Hotel, Duke Street, Manchester, and took place on May 26th, June 9th, June 23rd and July 7th of this year. On each of these occasions you had dinner with her in the restaurant of the hotel, then you took a double room to which you both of you went. I have photographic evidence of this, which I am keeping for the time being. In my next letter I will explain what you must do to prevent this information becoming public. I hope you will take this seriously, because I can assure you that I am very serious indeed.'

He turned the paper over but the back was blank. So that was it then. He felt a sense of relief. He had expected something vaguer but also more sinister. The fact that it was all so *specific*, with dates that could surely be checked, seemed to diminish the threat. The hotel it talked about, the Queens, was one he knew to be in the centre of Manchester but which, so far as he could remember, he had never so much as set foot inside.

Claire was buttering toast, still refusing to take an interest. He held out the letter.

'Darling, you should read it.'

'No, thank you.'

'Well, I honestly think you should. Or I'll read it to you if you like . . .?'

She looked at him as if to say, *well, just remember this was your decision.* Then she sighed and said, 'OK. Give it to me. You want me to read it – I'll read it.'

She left the table and went to the clock to collect her reading-glasses.

'And before you read it –' he began, but she was quick to interrupt.

'No, never mind *before* I read it. You want me to read it and I am doing.'

He said nothing but handed the letter to her as she returned to the table. She put on her glasses and began to read.

He thought: however she reacts, I shall remain calm. We mustn't get into some unseemly squabble about this. When all's said and done, it's just a load of contemptible nonsense, written by someone with a sick mind.

She looked up, essaying a smile. 'To which you both of you went . . .!'

'What?' said Richard, on his guard.

'No, I mean it's not very elegantly put, is it?'

'No . . . no.'

Well, he hadn't expected that, a comment on the style. But then he never knew quite what to expect from her. He had always told himself such uncertainty was one of the joys of their marriage.

He waited patiently while she read the remainder of the letter. Then, as he had done, she looked to check there was nothing more written on the back.

'Wherever I was on those dates, it wasn't at that hotel,' he said. 'Since I've never even set foot in the place.'

'But it does exist?'

'*Exist* . . .?'

'The hotel. I mean there actually is –'

'Oh, yes. Yes, it's in the centre of Manchester.'

'But you've never been there?'

'No.'

She shrugged. 'Fine. So why don't we just throw it away? And the other letter. Throw them both away?'

It was an idea that tempted him. Particularly as it had come from Claire and so she could hardly accuse him later of having done it in order to destroy the evidence. Still, he felt uneasy about just tossing the letters away when there was no knowing whether there might be more to come or what might lie behind them.

'I wish we could,' he said. 'It's just that, if this goes on . . . I mean if the damn things keep on arriving . . . we might want to take them to the police.'

'The *police*? Really?'

'It's a criminal act,' he said. 'You can't just go sending this kind of thing through the post.'

'Perhaps not. I still don't see what the police would be able to do.'

'Neither do I at the moment. I only said we might want to go to them if this goes on.'

'Yes, well, all right,' she conceded. 'Do what you like with them . . . keep them, burn them, anything. I'd just rather talk about something else if you don't mind.'

But he couldn't leave it at that. He was pleased that she didn't seem to be paying much attention to these new accusations. She must have realized how the letter-writer had given himself away by being too specific and so advancing claims that could easily be disproved. It was the fact of there being another letter at all that seemed to have upset her and left her agitated.

'You mustn't let these things get to you,' he urged. 'That's exactly what this lunatic wants –'

'Oh, you know what he wants, do you? That's assuming it is a he.'

'I don't know anything. I'm just assuming that he . . . and all right, let's assume it's a he because they usually are . . . I'm assuming that he wants to make us miserable and set us at one another's throats – as he's very nearly succeeded.'

'Yes, all right,' she said, wincing as though another word on the subject would make her demented.

The letter lay where she'd left it on the table. He glanced through the other items of post that had arrived with it and then, as was his custom, took in first the front page of the newspaper and then the sports pages, finishing off with the cartoon on the back.

'More coffee?' asked Claire.

'No, thank you,' he said. 'Better get going.'

He picked up the letter, re-folded it and placed it back inside its envelope. Claire had now taken up the newspaper and was concentrating doggedly on it. She didn't so much as glance in his direction until he had placed the letter on the mantelpiece beside its predecessor.

'OK, I'm off,' he said. 'See you tonight.'

He had been prepared to leave her sitting there at the table but she suddenly jumped up and came to him.

'Sorry if I've been narky,' she said, putting her arms around him. 'It's really nothing to do with you. It's just that I've a million and one things to do before Saturday.'

Yes, of course! Her words were a revelation. Here he was putting everything down to those damn letters. It had never occurred to him that it might be the arrangements for the Silver Wedding that were weighing on her.

He kissed her forehead and said, 'Is there anything I can do?'

'No, just try and ignore my bad moods, that's all.'

'Get our daughter out of bed. She's supposed to be the one in charge.'

'In *overall* charge. I'm not sure she's quite so strong on detail.'

It pleased him that she seemed to have recovered her good humour. She accompanied him to the front door and kissed him goodbye as he left.

'Ring the hotel,' said Moira.

'And say what?'

'Ask them if they had a Mr Gillow staying with them on whatever those dates are that you just read out.'

'And what if they say why? If they want to know why I'm asking?'

'They won't. Why should they? And if they do, tell them you're his wife. You won't have to say anything else. Just say – this is Mrs Gillow speaking.'

'I just hate the idea of checking up on him. Going behind his back.'

'Then let me ring the hotel.'

'No!'

The minute Richard had gone, she had taken the letters down from the mantelpiece and re-read them. Then she had rung Moira and read them to her over the phone.

Of course it broke all her earlier resolutions but she didn't care. She had to speak to someone, to spill out all her fears and suspicions, and Moira was the one person to whom she could do that. If only because there had been so many confidences passed in the opposite direction.

Moira had listened to her reading of the letters, and then asked, 'And do you believe them?'

It rather put Claire on the spot. 'I ... I don't know. I suppose, on balance, I didn't believe the first letter, no. But now with the second one ... And it's so detailed. I mean with the dates and everything.'

Which was when Moira said, 'Ring the hotel.'

The idea had already occurred to Claire. She had thought of it even before Richard had left, but then it had struck her as sneaky and disloyal, something somebody else might do under similar circumstances but she would prefer not to.

'I've done it before now,' Moira was saying. 'Plenty of times. Normally I've been checking to see whether Roy's actually stayed where he says he's stayed, and nine times out of ten the answer's been no, they've never heard of him.'

'But what would it prove?' said Claire, still unsure.

'Well, if they've never heard of Richard, then you can throw the letters in the bin and make sure you give him a good time when he gets home tonight.'

'And if they say yes, that he was staying on those dates?'

'Then ... I don't know. Let's just say it gets more complicated.'

Claire sighed. She still didn't want to ring the blessed hotel and yet ... to hear them say no, that they had no record of any Richard Gillow ever having stayed there – wouldn't that be wonderful.

'I wouldn't have to tell Richard, would I,' she said, thinking aloud.

'Of course you wouldn't. You'd be a fool if you did.'

'Even if they say that he's never stayed there, I still don't have to tell him that I called them.' She wanted to be sure there were no pitfalls or come-backs to this that she hadn't foreseen.

'He'll never know you've rung unless you want him to,' said Moira firmly. 'You don't have to tell him and the hotel certainly won't.'

It was the clincher. Claire hesitated no longer.

'Put down the phone. I'll ring you back as soon as I've something to report.'

Moira had the phone off its hook before the second ring. 'Yes?'

'Well, I got through to the hotel,' said Claire, watching the smoke from her cigarette climb towards the ceiling.

'And?'

'They were very helpful. They went and checked their records –'

'Yes, but had he been staying there or hadn't he?'

Claire paused, then said carefully: 'They said that they had no record of anyone of that name ever staying at the hotel.'

'That's marvellous,' said Moira quietly. 'I'm very pleased for you.'

'Thanks,' said Claire. She wondered if she sounded as shaky as she was feeling. Now that the lie was told, she wanted only to curtail their conversation before her tears returned.

But Moira was suddenly voluble, and sounding tearful herself: 'Because it's no joke living with somebody you can't trust. Somebody you know can lie to you with a smile on his face. And I know because that's all my marriage has been, right from the start. Even when I find him out in a lie and he promises . . . he swears that that'll be the last time, I know that he's lying again. I sometimes think the only way he'll ever stop lying is when he's dead. So I'm delighted for you. Really I am.'

'Thank you,' said Claire again. It was all she dare trust herself to say.

'Hey, and you remember what we said. You don't have to tell Richard anything, not even that you rang the hotel.'

'No.'

'In fact, it'll be better if you don't. Or else he'll start wondering why you didn't trust him and had to go checking up.'

'Yes,' said Claire. She had to clear her throat. 'I suppose he might.'

'But, God, I'm so pleased for you. You and that lovely husband of yours. You're what I think about, you know?'

Claire closed her eyes, wanting to stop her, wanting to confess her deception. But she couldn't, and so had to sit there and listen as Moira continued.

'When Roy's been up to his tricks and I'm near to losing faith in everything there is – you and Richard, loving one another and being faithful to one another, you're what I think about to help me persevere with the bastard I've got.'

'Gillow Press' inhabited what had once been a Unitarian church, serving the worshippers of South Manchester. Downstairs was now a reception and display area with warehousing tucked away behind. Upstairs, within the steeply pitched roof and reached by a steel staircase, were the offices. These were of equal dimensions but unequal space since some were dissected at head height by thick roof beams.

Richard's office was at the altar end and free of beams. Claire had suggested he displayed the sign 'God' on the door; he had settled for 'Managing Director', and wondered if that wasn't a touch grandiloquent.

When people asked how he'd got into publishing, he always replied that it was as a rugby wing-forward. He had been a regular for the Saracens after his Blue at Oxford, during which time he also collected fourteen caps for England. He had been a member of a solid back row that had been invincible for the best part of three seasons. It was during an after-match reception at Twickenham that he met the managing director of a major British publishing-house, who after only their second drink offered him a post as 'sports consultant'.

'Largely a matter of putting yourself about,' it was explained to him. 'With plenty of time for the rugby.'

He accepted until something better came along.

In fact, what came along was Claire. She was already blazing a trail of her own as a textile designer. Trying to present himself as a prospective husband, Richard became acutely aware of the need to put together a genuine future for himself and end his reliance on past glories. He had already surprised his firm by

29

proving he could read and wasn't a bad judge of copy and now managed to persuade them to make him sports editor instead of the nebulous consultant.

People would then ask, so why did you move from that to running your own company?

He would explain how he had had no choice. The British company were bought out by an American giant who announced on day one that they had no interest in sports books; they intended to sell off that side of the British operation. Richard pondered, spent a sleepless night, then went in and made them an offer that they could well have refused but didn't. Which was how he came to launch his own company, on borrowed money and a good many prayers and, most important, with the unflinching support of his wife.

He was a publisher, though it took him some time before he could fully believe it. Books on hobbies and then gardening and cookery were added to the sports list and then finally, experimentally, some fiction. The firm stayed afloat when times were hard and expanded slowly when they were a little easier. He bought the decaying church in 1982 for £15,000, then spent several times that amount on halting the decay and installing a mixture of high technology and home comforts.

He still got a kick every time he parked up alongside the sand-blasted building and went in through the heavy, studded door which had a stone cross embedded in the wall above it. This particular morning was no different. Any lingering thoughts of blackmail letters were pushed aside as he was greeted by Yvonne at reception and then presented with his schedule for the day by Lynne, who was his secretary, the minute he arrived in his office.

' . . . You've got Philip Neal of Snowden Associates coming in at ten. That's to do with the new covers for the Twenty-First Century Living Series. And at eleven there's this Spanish gentleman whose name I can't pronounce –'

'Senor Tejedor-Cifuentes,' said Richard.

'Him yes. And then I promise Philippa White that you'd give her a ring *some time* this morning . . .'

Before any of that could begin to happen, he had Simon tapping on his door and insinuating himself into the chair on the other side of his desk. Simon was young and eager and was

responsible for contracts, which gave him priority status when it
came to getting into see the boss.

'I need to see you about –'

'Let me guess,' said Richard, feeling the adrenalin beginning
to run. This was all a wonderful release after the dreadful,
claustrophobic weekend at home. 'You need to see me about
Glenda.'

'Yes. She's being impossible. Or her agent is. I mean there's
no give-and-take. They just want everything.'

'Tell me about it.'

They settled to a line-by-line re-drafting of the contract,
distinguishing what might be sacrificed from what was essential.
The phone rang. It was Lynne from the adjoining office. She
apologized for interrupting, but it was his wife on the line and
she had insisted she be put through to him.

'I did something I know I shouldn't have done,' said Claire.

'Well . . . what was that?'

He was puzzled by her manner. She sounded upset and yet
defiant, as if challenging him to dare tell her she was in the
wrong.

'I rang the hotel.'

'Hotel . . .?' But then it came to him. 'The hotel in the
letter?'

'Yes. I just wanted to hear them say that you hadn't stayed
there. I know I shouldn't have needed that but –'

'I don't mind.' Or perhaps he did: he wasn't sure. But there
was something more important that he must know first. 'What
happened? What did they say?'

'They said . . . they said that yes, you had stayed there.'

He didn't know whether to laugh or cry, it was such a
transparent farce. Though he could see that for Claire it must be
assuming the dimensions of a full-blown tragedy. At least he had
the consolation of knowing these ludicrous accusations to be
false, while she – he could hear it in her voice – couldn't help
but believe them.

'Well, it's not true,' he said. 'I mean it's as simple as that. It's
just not true.'

'So why are they saying it?'

'What, they're actually saying that I stayed there?'

'Yes. And not just once, but on all four of those dates that're in the letter.'

'Just a minute,' he said, and reached for his diary. 'What was the first date?'

'May twenty-sixth.'

He riffled through the pages, found the end of May and saw immediately the list of London appointments that covered the twenty-sixth.

'What was the second one?' he said.

'I've already checked them against the calendar here,' she said in a flat, defeated tone.

'And what?' he said. Though he knew already what her answer would be.

'You were away on all of them.'

It was like being Alice on the other side of the Looking-Glass. There was a logic to all this but it wasn't the logic of the normal world. The lies were growing around him, consistent with one another and supporting one another, so that in time he would be totally enmeshed by them.

'Yes, well, I might have been,' he protested. 'I might have been away in London. The one place I wasn't was in that blessed hotel.' Then, fearing that sounded weak, he added, 'For Christ's sake, Claire, believe that, can't you!'

He saw Simon's head come up slightly where he was poring over the contract across the desk.

'Simon, sorry,' he said, with a gesture of helplessness. 'Can you just give me five minutes?'

'Sure,' muttered Simon, and slipped from the room, pulling the door closed behind him.

Meanwhile Claire was talking into his ear: ' . . . And I said no, I think there must be a mistake. Could you please check again. And he said he had the records, the computerized records, there in front –'

'Who?'

'What?'

'Who was it said this? Who did you talk to?'

'The manager. I spoke to some girl and then, when I told her what I wanted, she said she'd put me through to the manager.'

'What was his name?'

'I don't know. I can't remember –'

'It doesn't matter. I'm going to call him. Let me see if I can sort this out.'

'Richard, I'm sorry. I know I had no right to –'

'You had every right,' he said. 'It's just I can't understand why they should tell you I was there when I wasn't. Seriously, Claire, I have never set foot in the damned hotel. I don't care what they've told you – you've got to believe that!'

There was a silence.

'Oh, I see,' he said bitterly.

'So what're you saying?' she countered. 'That the hotel are lying?'

'No, just that –'

'Because it's what *they* said! It's not something I'm making up. It's what they said!'

'I understand that –'

'Well, then –'

'And I'm saying that they're mistaken. I mean maybe somebody's . . . ' He cast around for a solution, couldn't find one and gave up. 'Well, no, I don't know.'

He couldn't begin to explain it. The whole thing was an impenetrable mystery. He could only keep telling her that he was innocent, no matter how heavily the evidence weighed against him.

'Look,' he said, 'I've things I've got to do here, but I'll get away as soon as I can –'

'Why? What's the hurry? What do you think I'm going to do?'

'I don't think you're going to do anything,' he replied patiently. 'I just want to get this thing sorted out before . . . well, before it gets any worse.'

Diane met him in the hallway as he entered. He had the impression she'd been waiting for him, perhaps hoping to catch him before . . . well, before he encountered whatever else was going on in the house.

'Daddy, what's the matter?' she said, keeping her voice low.

'Why, what's –'

'Mummy's been crying.'

'Has she? Oh, dear.' He couldn't decide, in the instant, how

33

much to tell her, and so became evasive. 'It's nothing . . . nothing for you to worry about. Just . . . a stupid mis-understanding.'

'And she's drinking.'

'Drinking . . .?'

It was an odd accusation coming from a young woman who was to be seen nightly in the George drinking pints of lager and who'd grown up in a house that among its other quirks boasted a small but well-stocked wine cellar.

'I mean just . . . sitting there by herself drinking.'

'Yes, all right. Thanks for telling me.'

Diane frowned but said nothing more. She slipped away to the lounge. He couldn't blame her if she'd found his response inadequate. One day he would explain everything to her but only when he understood it himself, when all this mess had been finally cleared away.

Claire was in the kitchen and did have a glass of something, though he couldn't make out what. He also caught a whiff of cigarette smoke but he wasn't going to start challenging her on that just now. Let her smoke and drink all she wanted but let her not doubt him or his love for her.

He closed the kitchen door so that Diane shouldn't overhear. Though, if she were listening, then the closing of the door alone would be confirmation enough that something was seriously amiss. The house had contained them all so happily and for so long that any disruption, however minor, emitted shock-waves they all felt.

Claire looked up at him but said nothing. He sat down across from her.

'How are you?' he asked.

'Fine.'

'Well, no. I'm sure you're not,' he said. He moved briskly on: 'I rang the hotel. And I spoke to the manager . . . the same person you'd spoke to . . . and well yes, he told me exactly the same as he'd told you.'

She nodded. It was just an infinitesimal lowering of the head, as though she had no energy left for anything more.

'And I got him to check the address that was given – as I'm sure you did . . .?'

She nodded again.

'And of course it was this address. Somebody had stayed at that hotel and given my name and this address.'

'On nights when you were away,' she said quietly.

'As it happens, yes. But that's not such a rare event. Almost every week I'm away for one or two nights, yes?'

He waited for another nod of confirmation but this time she didn't seem able to manage even that. Coupled with Diane's warning, it made him wonder whether she was entirely sober.

'What's that you're drinking?'

When she didn't answer, he reached for the glass but she grabbed it before he could pick it up and said, 'Sherry.'

'And how much have you had?'

'Not enough.'

She stood up, suddenly coming back to life, and went to the bottle that stood on the draining-board.

Well, let her drink. All the better if it loosened her tongue so that she would tell him what she was really thinking and not keep it bottled up. It was the silent hostility that he couldn't cope with. He had never been able to cope with it.

She knew this and so used it as her most lethal weapon.

He must persuade her to talk: to talk honestly to him about what she was feeling. How often had they agreed on this: that any amount of pain and suffering, to say nothing of legal fees, would be saved if only people would *talk*. Rant and rave if they had to, call each other all the names under the sun, but *communicate*.

He said: 'I know I've said this before, but I'm going to say it again. I have never known anybody called Melissa. And I have never been to the Queens Hotel.'

'You want a drink?' She was waving the bottle at him.

'No, thank you.'

'So the hotel are lying, are they?'

'No. No, I'm not saying the hotel are lying —'

'Well, somebody is.'

'Yes, I suppose —'

'And it's not the blackmailer. He's the only one whose story checks out.'

She had transformed in an instant from near-comatose drunk to sharp-as-a-razor lawyer, trying to catch him on the hop. Perhaps then she wasn't quite so overwrought as he had supposed

35

or as she was happy to have him believe. Perhaps she was the one calling the tune here.

Even after so many years – now only days short of their twenty-fifth anniversary – he never ceased to be surprised by her intelligence. It was a particular kind of *creative* intelligence, and was no doubt tied to her artistic gifts, her ability to push things around, collapse them and reassemble them so that the pattern remained recognizable yet was different. Where he was methodical, even conventional – he wouldn't deny that – she had a way of slipping past him on the blind side so that, as he advanced slowly, believing her to be behind him, she would be already ahead, waiting for him to catch up.

He decided to challenge her.

'So you believe the letters?'

She flinched, then said, 'It's not a matter of –'

'Do you believe the letters?' he insisted.

A brief pause as their eyes met then, defying him, she said, 'Yes.'

'You do?'

'If you want the simple answer then it's yes. If you want the more complex answer, then it's that I don't *want* to believe the letters. I'd give my right arm *not* to believe the fucking things. But I don't have that choice. Belief . . . belief isn't voluntary.'

He caught a faint, distant echo in that last phrase, one which he couldn't place.

'Belief isn't . . . ?'

'It isn't voluntary. You can't choose whether to believe something or not.'

It came back to him: that early time in their lives together . . . was it when the children were young? or even before they'd been born? . . . anyway, an early time when she'd flung herself into philosophy, reading Kant and Descartes and Gilbert Ryle, and then entertaining him every night over dinner with a distillation of her readings and what she thought about these crafty old men.

'Belief isn't voluntary,' or something of the sort, she had last said to him twenty years or so ago. What he had said in reply then he couldn't remember.

Now he said, 'So what is it?'

'What?'

'If it's not voluntary, then what is it?'

'It's something you're forced into.'

'And you've been forced into believing that I'm having an affair with another woman?'

'Well, yes.'

'Well, no, I think you forced yourself into that. Because you rang the hotel. Nobody forced you to do that, did they?'

He was becoming irrational, he knew. And also angry, which was more dangerous.

She said: 'I only did it because I wanted to hear them tell me that you hadn't been staying there!'

'Only they didn't do that.'

'No. And so now I can only believe what I have evidence for!'

There was a kind of perverse rationality here that irritated him. She was saying she didn't believe him. His wife. She was accusing him of adultery and deception and endless lies; and managing to wrap the whole thing up to make it sound like something beyond her control.

'You need evidence?' he said.

'What?'

'No, I'm just trying to understand what it is you're telling me. You're saying that you can only believe something if you have evidence for it?'

He heard himself and knew the ridiculousness of what he was saying. This was his marriage at stake and here he was logic-chopping across the kitchen table, playing the pedant. But it was the only way he knew to get to her. He knew he must follow her to wherever she retreated and carry the battle to her there.

'It's not just me –'

'No. Anybody.'

'Anybody –'

'Anybody needs evidence before they can believe something?'

'Well . . . yes.'

'OK. So if I can give you evidence –'

'Well, but –'

'Wait. If I can offer you concrete evidence that I am telling the truth, then you'll have no choice, you'll have to believe me, yes?'

He knew that he was bullying her but couldn't stop himself. She stared at him, as though suspecting a trap. But, if there was one, then she couldn't find it was, and so she gave him a cautious answer.

'Yes, of course, I would. And, anyway, I want to believe you. It's just that –'

'You haven't any reason to.'

'Well, no –'

'Then let's go.'

He stood up and gestured towards the front door and the car beyond.

'Where?' she asked, bemused.

'Just let's go. Come on.'

He had the kitchen door open now and was calling out to Diane. Claire had come from behind the table but still unwillingly, asking 'Richard, where are you taking me?'

If he told her, she might not come.

'You'll find out where. I'm going to take you somewhere where you're going to get this proof you keep asking for.'

Diane had come running downstairs and had probably heard the tail-end of that. Never mind: let her make whatever she could of it.

'We're going out,' he told her.

'But when are we eating?' Diane said, turning to Claire, who was coming from the kitchen.

'When we get back,' said Richard, playing the domineering father for once. 'We've something important we have to do first.'

In fact, as he realized, Diane's arrival was to his advantage. Claire evidently had said nothing to her about the letters and didn't want her to know what was going on. It meant she could no longer question Richard, with Diane standing there, but had to follow him from the house.

He held open the passenger door of the car for her and she got in without a word. Coming round to his own side, he looked back and saw Diane watching them from the door.

'We'll be a couple of hours,' he called. 'Three at the most.'

Then he climbed into the driver's seat and started the engine.

'Well, yes, very clever,' said Claire in a low, resigned sort of tone as they pulled away. 'You've got me in here. So now could I ask please – where the hell are we going?'

4

The doorman held open the glass doors for them and they passed through into the foyer of the Queens Hotel. Richard was a step behind her, with his hand just touching her arm as if ready to propel her forward should she falter or perhaps to grab her should she try to escape.

They crossed a wide expanse of blue and gold carpet, passing alcoves in which brown leather sofas were arranged around coffee tables. The reception desk was of mahogany and had huge vases of camellias at intervals along it. A young women in a red, high-shouldered suit emerged from behind one of them and said 'Yes, madam?' Claire didn't answer but left it to Richard to explain that they wished to speak to the manager.

She had protested vehemently when he had finally revealed their destination, insisting he stop the car and let her out. But he would do no such thing, telling her that this was something that must be done and promising they would stay not a minute longer than was necessary.

'But why are we going there?' she had asked.

'I'm going to prove to you that I've never been there.'

'But we've already asked them –'

'I don't mean the hotel records,' he said.

What he did mean he didn't tell her and she had no intention of asking.

Now, as they waited by the reception-desk, Claire stared about her. So this was where he had come with his woman, was it? And had they stood here together, checking in, or had she gone and sat demurely on one of the chairs while he attended to the formalities?

Richard moved close to her and said in a low voice: 'And would I come here? Would this be where I would choose to bring somebody?'

But she wasn't going to allow him such an easy point. 'Perhaps it was Melissa's choice.'

He gave a tired smile at that. 'Perhaps it was.'

The young woman directed them to one of the tables, promising that the duty manager would join them as soon as he was free. They sat, gazing about them. She now had time to notice the chandelier that had been over their heads as they stood before the desk; and the pianist in evening-dress tinkling away in the corner. They were on a stage-set, she thought; and why not, since they had come here to play their parts in her husband's elaborate deception.

The duty manager arrived, and Richard stood to shake his hand. He was a tall, thin man with wavy, brown hair. 'Eamon Nolan,' said the name-badge on his lapel. There was a tinge of Irish to his accent as he greeted them, which Claire hadn't picked up on the phone.

He sat down beside them and listened solemnly, his fingers together as if in prayer, as Richard outlined what had happened and reminded him of their calls earlier in the day, first from Claire then from himself. Yes, Eamon Nolan said, he remembered the calls, and he gave Claire what seemed to her a sympathetic look. She tried to recall how she must have sounded over the phone: upset certainly.

Eamon Nolan had a number of print-outs from the hotel computer and spread them on the low table before him.

'I'm afraid I can only confirm what I said on the telephone,' he said, looking apologetically from one to the other. 'Here's the bookings. Have a look for yourselves.'

I don't want to look, thank you, thought Claire. Nevertheless, she took the papers as Richard passed them on to her.

'Those letters CA,' explained Eamon Nolan, pointing, 'they signify that the gentleman paid cash. And the D – you see it was a double occupancy. Same on each occasion.'

Why am I going through with this charade, she thought. She stood up suddenly. The two men looked at her in surprise.

'I don't think this is getting us anywhere,' she said. 'I mean thank you. It's not your fault. But it's just not, is it?'

'Just one minute,' pleaded Richard.

But she wasn't going to sit down again. She remained standing while Richard turned back to Eamon Nolan.

'Would you have a copy of the signature of this man?'

'Not if he paid in cash, no.'

'But wouldn't he have to sign in?'

'Oh, yes. But that would be on a card, which I'm afraid will have been destroyed by now. The only record we keep is on the computer.'

Richard persevered: 'All right, but when he signed in –'

'Yes?'

'Would he have had to offer any evidence of identity?'

''Fraid not. People come here, they can call themselves anything they like so long as they pay up.'

Claire expected Richard to protest, to put on a show of outrage, that someone could pretend to be him and get away with it. But no, he simply shook his head in dismay, then stood up beside her. Eamon Nolan also stood up, then they all shook hands. Richard thanked him for his time while Eamon Nolan said he was sorry he couldn't do more to help.

'OK, let's try over here,' said Richard, taking her hand so that she had no option but to go with him.

'Over *where*?' she said, but he didn't answer.

She saw that a small queue of people had now formed at the reception desk, waiting to check in. They seemed to her to be businessmen, with perhaps the odd businesswoman. But, so far as she could see, there were no couples.

Perhaps they came later, the adulterers, sneaking in after nightfall.

She realized Richard was questioning her, speaking in that confidential, earnest tone that demanded she agree with him.

'Did he recognize me? The manager? Or any of the girls at reception? Did you notice any sign that they'd ever set eyes on me before?'

'No,' she said dully.

And so was that it? Was that the proof he had brought her all this way to put before her? That the hotel *apparatchik* weren't leaping around at his approach, calling out, *Hi Richard, Where's Melissa?*

He was still leading her by the hand. They went through a doorway and came into what she saw was the restaurant. There were few diners – it was still too early – just empty tables, laid with table-cloths of dusty pink and arrangements of cutlery and glassware.

41

She pulled her hand from his. 'I'm not going to eat here.'

'Neither am I. I just want to ask —'

Now there was a waiter approaching, or perhaps it was the head waiter even. He was wearing a black dinner-suit and had a red carnation in his buttonhole.

'You would like a table, sir? Table for two . . .?'

'No!' hissed Claire desperately.

'No, we don't want to eat,' said Richard. 'All I want to know is — have you ever seen me in your restaurant before?'

So this was the form that his proof would take. They were going to speak to everyone in the hotel, who would all swear they had never seen him before in their lives. The sheer weight of this collective testimony would force her to cave in — or so he thought.

The waiter bit his lip and made an uncertain gesture. 'Difficult to say, sir. We have so many gentlemen who dine here —'

She could have laughed aloud. The man wasn't even trying to give an honest answer but was looking for the diplomatic one. What answer would 'sir' like?

'But you don't *remember* seeing me?' insisted Richard.

'No, sir,' risked the waiter. 'I can't honestly say that I do.'

Richard smiled and nodded his thanks: it was clearly the correct answer.

Would he tip him, wondered Claire. A sly tenner passing from one palm to the other?

If he did, she failed to notice.

And now they were coming out of the restaurant and back into reception. She felt a sudden shame that made her cheeks flush red. It wasn't so much for herself, being dragged along as an unwilling witness, as for Richard, that he should feel the need for it and believe he could allay her suspicions with such a transparent farce.

'I'd like to go home now,' she said.

'Not yet. We're going to have a drink first.'

She stopped, trying to force him to stop too. But he only went on ahead of her so that she had to hurry to catch up.

'Richard . . .?'

'We're just going to have a drink. Then I promise we'll go after this.'

She felt him gripping her elbow. She could do nothing but

allow herself to be led into the bar where faces turned towards them as they entered.

She hated him when he was in this assertive mood, taking decisions for her, physically manoeuvring her through doorways. It was something he did when he was nervous and unsure of himself, over-compensating. She wondered whether he might not be more nervous than he was betraying. After all, hadn't he every reason to be on edge if he had been here, in this very hotel, in this bar, with Melissa? He must be fearful that at every turn they might bump into someone who would recognize and unwittingly expose him.

She allowed him to propel her the bar, vowing that this would be their last port-of-call.

'What would you like?' he asked, when he had attracted the attention of one of the barmen.

'Anything.'

She saw his look of exasperation and added, 'White wine.'

'Sweet or dry, madam?' said the barman.

'Dry.'

'And I'll have a scotch and soda, no ice,' said Richard, then turned to her. 'You see. Have any of these people ever seen me before?'

'How should I know?'

He sighed. 'Well, do they show any sign, the merest flicker, of having ever seen me before?'

'No.'

'Well, then.'

Did he really see her as so naive? The little wife who spent most of her time safely at home and so knew nothing about big city ways?

She kept her voice low and controlled. She knew that he was immune to shouting. The only way through to him was by reasoning.

'What sort of a hotel is this, would you say?'

'Well, you can see for yourself −'

'City centre, four or five star . . .?'

'Yes.'

'A place where businessmen bring their mistresses?'

'Oh −' he began to protest.

'Or businesswomen bring whatever they call it when it's the

other way round? Come on, Richard, you know as well as I do – half the couples in this place are using it for a quick, illicit fuck!'

He looked at her and shook his head, as if despairing of her, though whether of her sanity or her language she didn't know.

She didn't care either and went on, wanting to drive the point home: 'And so the staff in a place like this, well, they're discreet, aren't they. I daresay they're even trained to be. Of course they don't show any sign of recognizing you, but surely you can understand why? It's because *you're here with a different woman!*'

'No –' He began to shake his head.

'All right, you say no, but can I remind you –'

She had to break off as the barman returned with their drinks. He enquired if they wished them charged to their room number. She noticed how Richard avoided her eye as he explained that they weren't guests in the hotel and so he would pay for the drinks there and then.

'Can I remind you that you brought me here?' she said, when the barman had moved away.

'Yes, I know –'

'And why? So you could prove to me –'

'Prove I've never been here before, exactly!'

'But it doesn't prove that. And it never will.' This was the heart of it. She wanted him to see how completely she saw through what he was trying to do. 'We could stay here all night and you could take me round every single member of staff here and they could all swear they've never seen you before but it would all prove absolutely nothing!'

She spoke triumphantly, as if claiming a kind of victory, while what she felt was a bottomless pit opening beneath her. How wonderful it would have been if he could have proved his innocence. She didn't want him guilty. She wasn't his prosecutor; she was his wife.

'So what am I supposed to do?' he asked quietly.

She couldn't answer that. He had already done too much, dragging her against her will to the hotel and mounting his own show-trial, knowing all the time what the verdict would be.

Well, it hadn't worked. Her visit to the Queens Hotel had left her all the more persuaded that the letters were true. Her

44

husband had betrayed her with another woman, and was now betraying her again in subjecting her to these humiliations.

Perhaps where he had been wrong from the start was in imagining himself to be the target of a crank, and a random target at that.

What he had learned at the hotel suggested something quite different. There was nothing random about this. It had been planned way in advance and carefully executed so as to make it impossible to refute the allegations in the letters. Whoever was masterminding this knew him personally and was out to do him damage.

Why, he still had not the slightest idea. But there was organization behind this. It was a planned campaign he was facing, stretching back over several months if the hotel records were to be believed.

The first letter had struck him as a joke. It had come out of a clear blue sky and made not a word of sense. The second had been no different but for the details it offered. It had been designed to tease, to tempt him to check it out. Then, where Claire had done so, the plot against him had finally emerged.

Even then, it could have been easily dismissed. If he had been at home with Claire on only one of those dates – any one – then the attempt at blackmail would have instantly collapsed. What gave it its power was the way in which the dates given for his stays at the hotel were all ones when he had been away from home.

He tried to see it from Claire's point of view. Certainly what evidence there was supported the letters. If you thought of it as a jigsaw, then the picture still incomplete but emerging was of himself and Melissa about to enjoy a night's fornication in the Queens Hotel.

All the same, he was saddened by Claire's stubborn refusal to take him at his word. More than that, it alarmed him to witness the perversity with which she re-interpreted his every effort to demonstrate the truth. At his most depressed, he could even fancy that she and the blackmailer were in league.

They returned home and ate a hasty dinner, for which neither of them had any appetite. Diane had gone out and so they were alone. Claire ate silently, her head down. He wanted desperately to talk about what was happening between them but didn't know what there was that hadn't been said already, more than once.

'Look, I'm sorry. I shouldn't have taken you there,' he said.

'Why? Because what you were trying to do didn't work?'

'I don't know what you mean by *didn't* work. It certainly hasn't helped, I'll admit that.'

'No, it hasn't,' she said shortly. 'And I can't eat any more of this.' She pushed her plate away from her.

Before she could leave the table, he said, 'What would you like me to do? Shall we take the letters to the police, see what they make of them?'

But she only shook her head and insisted: 'I'd rather we never mentioned the awful things again.'

'So would I. So long as I know you don't believe them.'

She said nothing.

'So what do you want me to do?' he insisted.

'Anything!' she said, flaring up. 'Go and see Melissa if you like!'

Then she had gone, almost running from the room. He heard her footsteps through the hallway and then the slam of the front door.

He even tried to blot out his concern for her. You've done all you can, he told himself. If she chooses to believe a writer of anonymous letters rather than her own husband of many years, then on her own head be it.

It was impossible. He couldn't dismiss her so lightly or continue to live alongside her without being acutely aware of her feelings. Their lives had become so intertwined, it required a huge effort on his part simply to be there in the house with her and not say anything.

He wondered if she had said anything to Diane. His daughter still breezed in and out of the house and seemed cheerful enough, yet he believed he detected a new caution in her manner towards them. She was leaving them alone where before she might have lingered and spent time with them, at the end of a meal say. She was careful to close the door as she left, as though making it clear that they were now free to talk.

Or perhaps she'd always closed the door and he'd never

noticed. The trouble was that everything had now become significant of something else. Even the smallest of exchanges between them – about the garden or what time he might be home – couldn't be taken by him at face value. He would recall it and scrutinize it for what its tone might reveal about the rift between them, whether it was widening or healing.

He went to London again but he did not stay overnight. He crammed his appointments into one long day and caught the late train home. He ate in the dining-car and was relieved when the seat opposite remained empty: he was in no mood for chit-chat. He felt tired but it was more than that: for once in his life he was not relishing the sight of that turret and the prospect of arriving back home.

He hoped Claire would be in bed and so he would be spared her polite enquiries about the day. Though, of course, if she were in bed, he would then be haunted by the thought that she had gone to bed deliberately, in order to avoid him.

What they would neither of them be spared was their Silver Wedding, now less than forty-eight hours away. How vain and fate-tempting now seemed their planned celebrations. Why hadn't they kept quiet about it or at least limited things to their close circle?

All right, it had been the children who had argued for a real party. He and Claire hadn't had the heart to disappoint them and so had gone along with it. Now there would be untold hordes arriving to go through the sham of toasting them and their happiness. It was a nightmare fast approaching.

He even wondered about cancelling but that would be to accept defeat. Perhaps it would even bring about a real, terminal defeat where their marriage was concerned. Anyway, he couldn't cancel without giving a reason which, whether a lie or the truth, would only provoke speculation and infect their relatives and friends with the misery which up to now they had kept to themselves.

He drank the last of his wine and watched the darkened landscape rushing past.

What he could do . . . well, he could start by considering how other men might handle this. Men who were less complacent, less confident in their wives' trust than he had been; men who

47

were wiser than he was; even men who were regularly unfaithful and so were accustomed to scheming and lying and would have been more on their guard from the outset.

Roy, for example. What would Roy had done if the letters had gone to him?

He had rung to make an appointment; even so, a young WPC, with her hair tied back in a pony-tail, sent him back to a row of stacking-chairs where two men were already waiting. They eyed him suspiciously as he lowered himself to sit beside them. It made him conscious that, in his suit and with his size, he might well appear to them as more at home on the other side of the counter.

He couldn't remember the last time he had set foot in a police station. There had been the odd occasion when he had had to produce his car insurance and licence as a result of some minor traffic offence. But he couldn't remember calling before to report a real crime – which was how he had decided the letters should properly be viewed. They were no joke, not anymore. He was the victim of a serious attempt at blackmail and so was entitled to seek police assistance.

'Mr Gillow . . .?'

He looked up and saw a stocky, smiling young man with curly, gingerish hair looking in his direction.

'Yes?'

'Would you like to come this way please.'

He followed the square, sports-jacketed shoulders through a security door and into a small, sparsely furnished room. The young man's hair was thinning on top. Seen up close, perhaps he wasn't so young as he'd first appeared. Late thirties at a revised guess.

'I'm Detective Inspector Beresford,' he said, offering his hand.

'Richard Gillow.'

'And what can we do for you then, Mr Gillow?'

'I'm being blackmailed,' said Richard, and produced the two letters, still inside their envelopes. 'I received these two letters. That was the first . . . and that the second.'

'Thank you,' said Beresford, taking them from him.

Like most people, Richard had retained a basic faith in the police, unaffected by false-arrest and corruption scandals. It was not, he hoped, an unrealistic faith. He didn't believe that the uniform automatically elected its wearer to sainthood; just that a majority of those wearing it were doing their best against odds that seemed ever-lengthening.

Detective Inspector Beresford finished reading and placed both letters side by side on the table.

'And you don't know who these are from?' he asked.

'No.'

'You don't recognize the handwriting?'

'No.'

'OK.'

He didn't seem surprised by either answer. He gave Richard a smile, then launched into what sounded like a well-rehearsed routine. The gist of it was that everything Richard might care to tell them would be treated in total confidence. Even if the case eventually came to court, he would be granted anonymity when he came to testify. Nothing would be admitted in evidence that might help identify him.

The other point was basically a legal one. The offence they were discussing was certainly that of blackmail. However, it was likely that the charge brought against Richard's blackmailer, should they ever nail him, would be 'demanding money with menaces'. It was a simpler charge to make stick; and never mind whether the menaces were to do with physical violence or unwanted revelations.

Richard nodded to show that he understood. He was pleased to find that Beresford seemed intelligent and disposed to treat the letters seriously. He hadn't come expecting miracles. It was enough that his complaint should be filed and any routine steps taken.

After all, it was to impress Claire that he was doing this. He wanted to let her see that he had no qualms about involving the police and nothing to fear from any investigation. Then, please God she might begin to realize that he was the innocent victim with nothing to hide.

'A thing we often find with blackmail,' said Beresford, 'is that the victim knows the blackmailer. I mean personally. They work together or they're neighbours or, I don't know, but there's some other connection between them.'

'I'm sure, yes.'

'So what I mean is – can you think of anyone who might have written these letters because they've got some grudge against you?'

Richard sighed. This was something he had tried to do but failed. 'Not really. I mean I'm sure I must have enemies. Who doesn't. But . . .' He shook his head.

'He might not seem like an enemy. He might be someone you count as a friend.'

'I still can't think –'

'Let's face it. Whoever it is knows about the young lady.' He consulted the letters. 'Melissa.'

'There is no young lady,' said Richard quietly. 'The letters are a complete fabrication.'

Beresford looked at him as though disappointed. 'Mr Gillow, it's like I said. Everything you tell me is in complete and utter confidence.'

'I know –'

'Remember the crime is blackmail. It's not having an affair or –'

'I've told you. I don't know any Melissa. I'm not having an affair.'

He had anticipated that the situation would take some explaining and so tried again.

'Inspector, when I received those letters, the first thing I did was show them to my wife.'

'You did?'

Richard sensed that he had scored a first here. Other blackmail victims burned the letters or stored them in the bottom of their wardrobes or perhaps even ate them: anyway, they did not show them to their wives.

'I did, yes. Why shouldn't I? There isn't a word of truth in either of them. I don't know any Melissa and I never have.'

Beresford sat back and smiled. It was a smile that was beginning to lose its charm for Richard, who was finding it irksome having constantly to protest his innocence like this. Even more irksome to feel himself constantly being disbelieved.

'You don't?'

'No.'

'All I can say, Mr Gillow, is that, by shielding this Melissa, it's just possible you might be shielding the blackmailer.'

'Really,' said Richard, suddenly feeling the hopelessness of his situation descend on him like a great weight.

Beresford sounded encouraged, as though he felt he might be getting through. 'Like I said, blackmail usually involves somebody who knows the victim. Now you say you can't think of anybody. Well, OK, so it might be somebody who doesn't know you but who knows Melissa. Yes? You follow my reasoning?'

'I do, yes.'

'So it would help if we could talk to Melissa. She might be able to think of a likely candidate. She might even recognize the handwriting. Have you shown these to her?'

'No, I haven't.'

'Well, then I think –'

'And I can't and never will be able to – because *she doesn't exist*!' said Richard, bringing his hand down on the table.

He could take no more of this. He had come seeking help, not this kind of hard-bitten-cop cynicism. Yes, he could understand that the case was unusual. He had deliberately taken things step by step: the letters first, then the explanation. But he wasn't going to sit there and be told to his face that he was lying.

'She doesn't?' said Beresford.

'No!'

Beresford waited a moment, then said, 'All right. You say she doesn't exist. So I accept – she doesn't exist.'

Richard let the insult pass and waited.

'So let's look at the second letter, the one that gives us these dates . . . how many? . . . four dates.'

'Yes.'

'The letter says you were staying on these dates at the Queens Hotel in Manchester.'

'That's what it says but, in fact, I wasn't staying there.'

'You weren't?'

'No. I've never stayed there.'

Of course he couldn't leave it at that. The detective had to be made to appreciate the extent of this campaign against him.

'But I've been to the hotel. And I've got them to check their records. And there was someone staying there on those nights using my name.'

It sounded, well, like a poor excuse. A poor, weak, emaciated excuse. The sort of excuse that Beresford would relate afterwards to his colleagues in the police canteen and they would guffaw over.

'There was?'

'There was, yes.'

'Somebody using your name but it wasn't you?'

'It wasn't me, no.'

'So how do you explain this? What do you think can have happened?'

His tone now was barely civil. He was toying with him, as he might have with a suspect rather than a complainant. Richard fought against his growing exasperation.

'I think it's pretty clear that someone's been impersonating me.'

'And then blackmailing you?'

'Well, possibly. Or the blackmailer might be somebody else. And, if he is, well then they might be in league with one another or . . . or possibly not.'

The more he said, the more ridiculous he knew he sounded. Would he have believed himself if he'd been in Beresford's shoes?

'I suppose they might, yes,' said Beresford, his expression giving little away. 'OK, so let me ask you something else.'

Richard waited.

'On these four nights when you say you weren't at the hotel – where were you?'

Richard winced. He felt like throwing in his hand there-and-then. What he was about to say would without doubt confirm Beresford's view of him as the bashful adulterer.

'I was staying in London.'

Beresford pounced as though it were a confession.

'In London?'

'Yes.'

'So you weren't at home?'

'No.'

'Was there anyone else with you in London?'

Richard didn't answer. What was the point? Beresford was clearly set on disbelieving him, no matter what. There seemed to be no good reason for prolonging the interview.

He stood up.

'I don't think this is getting us very far.'

Beresford stared in surprise, blinked, then became suddenly

animated, radiating concern. Perhaps he realized he had gone too far in openly displaying his cynicism. He might have had a vision of Richard filing an official complaint and feared he would one day have to explain why he hadn't taken this man's problems more seriously.

'Please sit down, sir. I promise you I am trying to help –'

'That's all right.'

'And this is certainly a serious matter, I do appreciate that –'

'Could I have the letters please? They are mine I think?'

Beresford hesitated, then pushed them towards him. 'Sure.'

'Thank you.'

Richard picked them up, then remained on his feet until Beresford moved unwillingly past him and opened the door. Then he stood back to allow Richard to leave first.

As they came back through into the waiting-area, he said, 'Don't hesitate to call us if you do feel there's anything we can do.'

'Thank you,' said Richard, privately vowing he would be doing no such thing. One such pointless and humiliating encounter had been enough.

Beresford followed him to the outside door, then spoke as Richard was opening it.

'Let's see, there was a gap of what . . . four or five days between the two letters?'

'Something like that, yes.'

Beresford nodded, then gave a small smile.

'So if there's going to be a third one,' he said, 'I suppose you might be expecting it anytime now.'

5

It was Saturday, their twenty-fifth wedding anniversary. Richard awoke with a feeling of despair. He could not see how they could possibly get through a day in the public eye without some dreadful and embarrassing demonstration of the gulf between them. Had it been possible, he would have cancelled the whole grisly event but of course he couldn't: the invitations had gone out and he must stand the course.

Claire's side of the bed was already empty and cold. Was it tact or revulsion that had sent her scuttling downstairs before he was awake, pre-empting the tricky question of whether they should start their big day by making love?

He dragged himself out of bed and peered out through the curtains. It was a clear sky and promised a hot day. Diane, the official hostess, would be mightily relieved. The garden looked immaculate. The gardener had been over the lawn last night and striped it with the precision of a draughtsman.

Richard thought of another such day, when the prospect of public disaster had loomed large – the day of their wedding. He remembered with absolute clarity how he had awakened on that morning, muzzy from the night before's booze and knowing that calamity was about to strike – the end of the world even – knowing it for a fact, because no-one could be allowed to be as happy and fulfilled as he would be once he became the husband of the most delightful girl there had ever been.

Unaccountably the calamity had failed to occur. The taxi had arrived on time to take him and his Best Man to the church. He had stood at the front, facing the altar and not daring to look round, painfully conscious of the guests filling the pews behind him, both sets of parents to the fore.

It was around this point he had realized that it wasn't going to be a calamity of biblical proportions that would foil their plans; it had been arrogant of him to have expected it. No, it was going to be that hoary old farce: the bride would change her mind and he would be left standing at the altar. She was probably already locked in a bathroom somewhere, refusing to come out. He was beginning to wonder how long they should wait before making some sort of announcement, and who should make it, when the organist struck up with the Wedding March. He heard the congregation getting to their feet and risked a glance over his shoulder. There she was coming towards him, a bride as beautiful as any there had ever been. She was clutching her father's arm and looking as terrified as he had been feeling.

Twenty minutes later they were married. There followed a boisterous reception at the Fox And Hounds Hotel, then it was off to the Bahamas, trailing confetti onto the aeroplane.

All of which was now twenty-five years ago to the day. And still the calamity he had expected then had failed to materialize. Their marriage had survived and the world had gone on spinning; though for how much longer it would continue he couldn't say. He had a feeling they might have overdrawn on their balance of happiness and that someone somewhere was about to call in the bailiffs.

He pulled on some clothes and started slowly downstairs towards where he could hear her moving about in the kitchen.

''Morning,' he called, testing the waters.

'Oh, you're up,' she called back. 'I was going to bring you a cup of tea.'

He was encouraged by that. She sounded determined that at least they weren't going to begin the day at loggerheads. He came to the kitchen door and saw that she hadn't dressed yet but was in the Chinese wrap she used as a dressing-gown. There was a smell of coffee and hot rolls.

'Happy anniversary,' he ventured.

'Happy anniversary,' she responded, smiling.

He wondered whether she expected him to go forward and embrace her – or whether she would want him to. Then he remembered that he had another card to play first, one that might help reinforce the promising start to the day.

'I've just got to collect something,' he said. 'Shan't be a minute.'

He turned and headed for the front door, his spirits rising. Perhaps this anniversary might prove timely after all.

Then, as he took his keys from the hall table, he saw the post piled on the doormat, swollen with what he guessed were cards.

Oh no, he pleaded, not today. Spare us today.

But they weren't to be spared. Even as he lifted the pile in both hands, he caught a glimpse of the envelope and the hand-writing on it that told him the third letter had arrived on schedule.

Bastard. Oh, you evil, cruel bastard, he cursed silently.

He looked round but Claire had remained in the kitchen. He pulled the blackmail letter from the rest of the mail and slipped it into the right-hand pocket of his trousers. He would open it later. This time he might not even show it to her. Let him first see what it contained and then decide.

Leaving the heap of cards on the hall table, he went outside to where the cars were parked. The Jaguar was generally referred to as 'his' and so he had thought its boot a safe hiding-place for the art deco jug he had brought back from London. Lifting it out now, he was reminded of the strange event that had accompanied its purchase, when he had caught sight of his son, or anyway someone he had taken to be his son, and gone running after him.

Well, David would be here today so perhaps light would be shed on that little mystery. Though it hardly seemed to matter as much as it had at the time. Its importance had shrunk since their lives had become dominated by the other, greater mystery of the letters.

He carried the wrapped jug, and also the pile of mail, back into the kitchen.

'Rather more post than usual. Can't think why,' he joked. Then he handed her the present. 'Oh, and this is for you.'

'Thank you,' she said and kissed him on the cheek as she took it.

'Can I come in?' said Diane from the doorway.

'Of course you can, darling,' said Claire.

'Happy anniversary, both of you,' said Diane, coming first to him to give him a hug and a kiss. There was an appeal in the look she gave him. Let today be all right, it said, please, for all our sakes.

It will be, he wanted to say to her. If it lies within my power, then I promise you that.

'Oh, it's Myott!' exclaimed Claire, as the wrappings came away.

'And there's something inside,' prompted Richard, pleased by the success of his surprise.

She lifted out the jewellery case, then paused before opening it and looked at him.

'I don't deserve this,' she said quietly.

He took this as referring to the way she had believed the accusations contained in the letters and refused to accept his denials. Though, with Diane there, they were both prevented from saying more.

'Open it,' he urged.

She did so and took out the necklace of antique silver. It had a row of finely-wrought pendants. Seeing it in her hands he knew he had made the right choice. The delicacy and complexity of its working suited her.

'Oh, it's lovely,' she gasped. 'Oh, darling, thank you.'

She came and kissed him again, this time warmly, on the lips. He held her to him, treasuring the feel of her body against his. He was elated, suddenly confident that today would prove a turning-point and they would put the unhappiness of the past week behind them.

'Oh, yes, it is,' enthused Diane, fingering the necklace. 'Oh, daddy, well done!'

'Now it's my turn,' Claire said, pulling away from him.

At the same moment the doorbell began to ring.

'I'll get it,' said Diane, and hurried out.

'Happy anniversary,' said Claire, and handed him what he first took to be a jewellery case similar to the one he had given her, but no: this held a pen, a silver fountain pen, engraved with his name.

'Sorry it's not wrapped properly. I didn't . . . well, with one thing and another, I didn't get round to it.'

'It's lovely,' he said. 'Thank you.'

'And it has been wonderful being married to you.'

'Still isn't too bad I hope . . .?'

She gave a tearful smile. 'It's still wonderful.'

He would have taken her in his arms and kissed her again but now there were voices from the hallway. Adele appeared, calling out her congratulations, and behind her came Lawrence, staggering beneath the weight of a large plant pot which held some kind of sapling supported by canes. It was so tall that he had to bend his knees and dip the pot in order that the thin branches could pass safely under the lintel of the kitchen door.

'Be careful,' instructed Adele.

'I'm being bloody careful,' he gasped.

'Oh, it's a silver birch . . .!' said Claire.

'Well, I'm always pinching cuttings from your garden. And you're so difficult to buy for because you've got everything. And so I thought of this.'

They thanked her and said it was wonderful. Richard opened the patio doors so that Lawrence could stagger on through and deposit it outside. The doorbell was ringing again. Richard went to answer and found that the advance guard of the caterers had arrived. They were seeking admission to the garden so that they could install their barbecues and refrigeration units. Diane took charge of them while Richard fielded a phone-call from David who, speaking quickly from a pay-phone, said they were on their way but had got off to a late start and so not to panic if they didn't arrive till almost lunchtime. A florist appeared on the doorstep with a bouquet from the Martindales, who had the house opposite.

Richard could feel the party gathering momentum beneath his feet. Useless to fight it; still, he was sorry that the moment with Claire when they had exchanged presents and re-discovered something of their old intimacy had been cut short. He sensed they had been on the verge of a reconciliation, one that would now have to wait.

Claire instructed Adele to help herself to coffee, then escaped upstairs to get dressed. Still conscious of the letter unread in his pocket, Richard shouted to Diane that he was going to get ready too.

But he didn't follow his wife into their bedroom. Instead, he went along the landing to the second bathroom, the one used by the children when they were home or by any guests who might be staying. It was there, after he had locked himself in, that he perched on the edge of the bath, took the letter from his pocket and began to read.

It was pretty well what he might have expected. The threats were repeated and money demanded, now a specific amount. But otherwise nothing new.

He cupped the paper in his hands. He would screw it into a ball and then flush it away.

What stopped him was the feeling that he was acting like a guilty man. Why should he destroy it if he were as innocent as he had protested all along?

He flattened the paper, re-folded it and returned it to its envelope.

Claire was standing naked in front of the dressing-table mirror. She was assessing herself, not looking for anything in particular but inspecting her body in the way that she sometimes did before getting dressed. She was startled by the sound of Richard's step outside the door and had to fight her instinct to grab the towel and cover herself. Wasn't this the man who'd seen her waltzing around naked for twenty-five years and more? And hadn't she sworn that today would be as though those poisonous letters had never arrived? So stand here. Don't move. Let him see you.

He came into the bedroom, then stopped as though surprised by the sight of her.

'I'm just checking on how well the bride has lasted,' she said, searching for something light-hearted that would keep things easy between them.

'I'd say she looks even lovelier today than she did then.'

She had begun to smile at that, and had even had the fleeting thought that they might end up back in bed, when she saw the envelope he was holding.

Oh, it couldn't be, she thought. No, surely not today . . .? She had to ask.

'What's that?'

He nodded as if in confirmation. 'It came this morning. I didn't want to open it down there —'

'Not another one?'

''Fraid so. I wasn't going to show it you but . . . well, why should I hide it? The minute I start hiding these things from you, that's the minute I start admitting they're true!'

She said nothing.

'Surely you can understand that?' he pleaded.

'Why can't you understand that I just don't want to see any more of these things?' she said.

'There's nothing new in it. I mean no more dates or anything. Just a demand for the money.'

She reached for her towel and pulled it tight around herself. Why couldn't he have destroyed the blessed thing? Or at least learnt something from all that had happened and kept it to himself? At the very least, why couldn't he have put it aside until today was over, a day on which they had to pretend to be deliriously in love with one another before an invited audience of over a hundred people?

'He wants five thousand pounds.'

'Does he.' She picked up a brush and tugged it through her hair.

'Of course, I don't intend to pay it.'

'No.'

Despite her resolution not to show the slightest interest in this further letter, she couldn't totally shut herself off from what he was saying. So the demand had finally been made. If he didn't pay it, as he was now claiming he wouldn't, what would happen then?

She could hardly blame him for deciding not to pay it. Never pay a blackmailer – wasn't that standard advice in these situations?

Yet there was a nagging voice at the back of her mind reminding her that the first two letters had mentioned something about photographs. Presumably the five thousand was to have been in exchange for those. Was the real reason he was refusing to pay because such photographs, once delivered, would turn out to be of himself and Melissa and so would be evidence that even he wouldn't be able to deny?

'And what'll happen if you don't pay?' she asked.

'According to the letter?'

'Yes.'

'He's going to tell my wife.'

She looked at him. 'He's going to . . .?'

'It's what he says in the letter. If I don't pay, then he's going to tell my wife.'

She had to smile. 'Not much of a threat, is it.'

'Not in this house. Here, have a look at it.'

She recoiled. 'No –'

'Well, it's up to you.'

He placed the envelope on the dressing-table amid the clutter of her jars and make-up and moved away towards the door.

'I'll leave you to get ready. I want to see what these caterers are doing. Then I'll get ready afterwards.'

She didn't try and prevent his leaving. She only wished he had never arrived so that the happiness she had felt might have lasted.

Really his behaviour was sometimes so . . . thoughtless. How he could have been stupid enough to come in and throw this thing at her, today of all days, when it must have been obvious to him that she was making such an effort to put the whole dreadful business behind her?

The letter remained on her dressing-table, impossible to ignore.

Besides, part of her did want to read it. Not in front of him perhaps but, now that he was gone, there could be no harm in taking a peek. She picked up the envelope and pulled out the single sheet of paper from inside. She touched it gingerly, conscious that the blackmailer had also handled it.

'Dear Mr Gillow,' she read, 'You will now have had time to consider my two earlier letters and I hope you will have realized that I am serious. I am sure that you do not want your wife and loved ones to know about this relationship. And in particular about its financial nature. In return for my silence and for the photographs that I have of you in the company of Melissa, I shall require a single payment of five thousand pounds. I will write again telling you how you must pay, but please make sure you have the money in notes that are not new and not too large.'

So she had been right in thinking that it was the photographs that were on offer. It raised the inevitable, unavoidable question. If he were innocent and had never met this Melissa, then why shouldn't he welcome the prospect of getting his hands on evidence that would exonerate him? Surely that would be worth five thousand of anybody's money?

It occurred to her that she might challenge him on this, even offer to pay the money herself and see what he would say then. But not now. Not on the day that had been set aside to celebrate their twenty-five years of marriage. The arrival of the third letter was a set-back but she would prove herself strong enough to withstand it.

Though, before she did finally put the letter aside and concentrated on the day about to unfold, there was just one line in it that she must read again. It had struck an odd, jarring note.

She searched for it, wondering if she had misread. But no, there it was: ' . . . I am sure that you do not want your wife and loved ones to know about this relationship. And in particular about its financial nature.'

'*And in particular about its financial nature.*' Which meant what?

They didn't just screw when they met but there was money involved. Was that it?

And, since it was unlikely that she paid him, it presumably meant that he paid her. Or perhaps even that he was supporting her on a regular basis.

Did he have this Melissa stuck away in some nasty, little flat somewhere? If so, then he probably gave her other money too, so that she could go shopping for kinky underwear or whatever it was that turned him on.

She gave a cry of despair and swept the letter to the floor. That it should come today of all days and that he should place it before her . . . this was a rare and exquisite torture she would not easily forgive.

The rumours about a jazz band proved true. The Choo-Choo Train they were called, seven men in shirt sleeves and straw boaters, one with a handle-bar moustache. They had established themselves in front of the greenhouse and were warming up with a version of 'In The Summertime'.

Diane said, 'Mummy told me you two met in a jazz club.' And she waited for his approval.

'They're wonderful. Thank you, darling,' he said, and kissed her.

Had they really met in a jazz club? He had memories of them falling into conversation in one of the Oxford bars. Perhaps there had been a jazz band playing at the time.

David arrived with girlfriend Suzanne – or *partner* Suzanne was probably the term nowadays – just before midday, as the first of the guests were beginning to congregate. 'I haven't missed it? Don't tell me I'm too late?' he called out, coming through the house, surely larger than ever and with that slightly bewildered, manic air which made those who knew him want to protect and care for him. His hair was still long and he wore his purple silk shirt outside his trousers. Beside him, Suzanne was cropped and lean, a creature from the Poor House.

Seeing him afresh now made Richard more certain than ever that this had been the man passing the shop window in Chiswick, the man he had pursued. It had been later that day that he had returned home and opened the first of the letters. He was struck by the coincidence of the two mysteries and wondered – could there be a connection?

'Dad. Happy anniversary,' David said, after they had hugged and slapped one another on the back. He presented him with a wooden crate in which were six bottles of claret, while instructing him on it: 'I got it from a man who knows. And he says it's the right year, right side of the orchard, *everything*. Unbelievably expensive. Don't let any of this lot you've got here today get their greedy hands on it.'

Richard thanked him, proud of him because he did these things in such a generous fashion, not scrimping. He resolved to put behind him his doubts about Chiswick and whether that might have any connection with the letters. He didn't want such doubts lingering and souring his relationship with his son.

There were more cries of greeting as Claire and Diane joined them, distracted from their dealings with other guests. Richard was glad to see how animated Claire appeared. She had barely spoken to him since their exchange about the newly-arrived letter. He had feared that the ground regained this morning after he had presented her with the Myott jug had somehow been lost again.

But now here she was greeting her son joyfully and looking resplendent.

David had a gift for her too, a glossy volume of modern paintings, which she fell upon excitedly. 'How did you get this? I didn't think it was available except in the States . . . !'

Looking on, Richard silently blessed his son for his display of love towards them, and for his simply being there. He would never know how vital his presence was, lifting the mood and making them feel – making Richard feel anyway – that the last two weeks had been an aberration they would one day look back on and laugh about.

He would not mention the letters to either of his children unless Claire thought it best they be informed.

By two o'clock the gardens at the back of the house had been completely taken over. The invasion of friends and neighbours and some people he didn't even recognize had carried all before it. What they had treasured as their private bit of the world had become a public park into which the world and his wife had blundered.

The caterers were working manfully to give everyone a plateful of chicken legs and salad and garlic bread and a plastic cup of whatever they wanted to drink, short of David's gift of the claret which Richard had locked away in his study. The Choo-Choo Train had had a break for lunch, then restarted with 'Is You Is Or Is You Ain't My Baby?'.

For Richard it wasn't quite like drowning – where the whole of your past life supposedly passes before you. It was more like a fitful series of immersions, where bits of his life floated in and out of vision. There were business colleagues, some present, some decidedly past; as well as people from the village whom he saw every day, and others who'd spent hours on the motorway to get there.

And, of course, there were the guests from their wedding, those whom Diane had managed to trace. Odd ones had totally disappeared or settled overseas while three, it transpired, had died. The survivors posed a continuing challenge to Richard. Having been invited and made the effort to attend, they expected to be recognized, something which, twenty-five years on, he struggled to do.

It was a relief to find himself with Roy. Roy and Moira initially, but then she moved away to seek out Claire and the two men were left together amid the trees of the orchard, watching the heaving throng and hearing the distant strains of 'I Ain't Nobody's Darling But Yours' from The Choo-Choo Train.

'I know we're supposed to be here to celebrate the sanctity of marriage,' said Roy. 'But personally that kind of thing makes me throw up.'

'You didn't have to come,' said Richard, entertained. Roy's honest-to-goodness approach was refreshing after the sanctimonious congratulations he'd been receiving wherever he turned.

'Yes, I did have to come. Or my wife would have crucified me. Besides, I want to ask you a favour.'

'What?'

'I've met this really quite amazing lady –'

'Again,' interposed Richard.

'Again. All right, I don't deny I'm easily led astray. The trouble is – she's allergic to hotels.'

Richard managed a smile. 'Is she.'

'Doesn't like all that business of checking in and having receptionists look at her. She thinks they're wondering why she doesn't have a wedding-ring on her finger. At least I suppose that's it. All she tells me is that she doesn't like hotels. The point is – could I borrow your flat?'

'In London?' said Richard, thrown by the sudden request.

'Well, that's where it is, isn't it?'

'Yes –'

'I don't mind where it is quite frankly. I'm desperate. And I'm hoping she's desperate. But I certainly am.'

Richard hesitated. What Roy got up to was his own business. He seemed to manage these *on-the-side* relationships successfully. His marriage with Moira bumped along as well as most.

Even so, Richard would have preferred not to have been asked. This wasn't the best time for him to be aiding and abetting another man's philandering.

'Well, when exactly – ' he began, searching for an excuse that would let him off the hook.

He was rescued by the arrival of Diane, with Will, her conquest of the summer, trailing behind her.

'Dad, sorry to interrupt but mum wants to talk to you.'

'She does?'

'And I got the impression it's important. So if you wouldn't mind going now –'

'Where is she?'

When they had first bought the house, or perhaps it had even before that – when they had come to view it – they had both been taken by the mouldering delights of the old greenhouse and had promised one another that they would renovate it. It was a wooden construction, some thirty foot by ten, and ran, half-hidden by shrubbery, down one side of the garden.

But other things had come first and the greenhouse remained in a state of cherished neglect: its panes were cracked, the irrigation system had silted up and the ventilation rusted into immobility. In the end they admitted to one another that they preferred it that way.

What plants there were had to fend for themselves and some did: clematis straggled up one wall while a whole colony of egg-plant had established itself along the far side. Elsewhere, pensioned-off lawn-mowers and collapsed wheelbarrows were piled into corners and provided homes for mice and voles. It was to protect them that Claire would never have a cat in the house.

She now stood with a glass of champagne and gazed at the dried-out flowerpots around her. She thought: I should bring Adele in here and tell her, *See, we aren't as good as you think we are.*

The door at the far end creaked open as Richard entered. It thudded closed behind him, its glass tinkling. He looked worried. Well, yes, she could understand that he would be puzzled by her summoning him like this when they were in the middle of such a monster party.

Excellent, she thought, taking another sip of champagne. It was part of her plan that she should catch him unawares and so force him to be honest with her.

'Diane said –' he began.

'Yes, I know. Just sit down . . . anywhere.'

He perched on a decaying wall which had once served to support a bed of tomatoes.

'Wonderful party,' he said, gesturing vaguely.

'Oh, isn't it, yes. I just feel such a fraud. As though we don't deserve it.'

He sighed. 'I know what you mean –'

She realized this wasn't going the way she had intended. 'But listen. Something I want to say.'

'Yes?'

He looked so serious that she had to look away. This was going to be difficult enough without having to meet that soulful gaze.

She took another swig of champagne and began. 'When you first started in publishing. I don't mean working for Marchants. I mean on your own. When you set up on your own –'

'Yes.'

'And it was like a big gamble, a total change –'

'Certainly was.'

She hesitated, losing her thread. Perhaps she'd had more to drink than she'd realized, too much to manage this conversation properly. But then what she had intended to say came back to her.

'And we both knew you'd be away from home quite a lot. Like you always said, you can't be a publisher and not go to London.'

It was with a tremor that she recalled those days when they would hold hands as they discussed – endlessly, into the small hours – whether he should risk this leap into the dark, throwing up his job with the major, big-time publisher and striking out on his own. Afterwards, he had told her that he had been able to do it only because of her encouragement and her support. Knowing that, if he lost everything else, she would still be there for him.

'I remember that,' he said.

'Well, I thought then . . . I honestly did think . . . that sooner or later there'd be the other woman.'

'But there hasn't –'

'I don't intend that as any judgement on you,' she hurried on. 'Or that I doubted you. Because I didn't. Not for one minute. It's just that –' How to explain? 'Well, it seemed to have happened to so many of our friends. I suppose I thought – why should we escape? And I suppose . . . I can't remember, but I suppose I might have lost sleep over it for a night or two, but then . . . well, then I made a sort of resolution.'

He was observing her almost fearfully, trying to anticipate where this might be going but failing.

'What sort of resolution?' he said.

'I resolved that, whenever this other woman came along –'

'But she hasn't,' he interrupted sharply. 'There isn't any other bloody woman!'

'I want you to listen,' she pleaded.

'Sorry,' he said. 'Go on.'

She struggled to shut out her awareness of the crowds outside and the sound of the jazz band and even the thought that they were there in the neglected, long-suffering greenhouse, of all places.

67

'I resolved that if there should ever be another woman –'

She waited for his reaction, but this time, mercifully, he said nothing.

'If there should ever be another woman, then I would see it for what it was and not build it into some great, earth-shattering event.' She hurried on, wanting to capitalize on his silence: 'It's that phrase men use, isn't it. *A bit on the side.* I mean they don't really want to leave their wives. All they want is . . . variety.'

She knew she was pleading with him but she couldn't help herself. She wanted him to see that this was a time for honest confessions from them both. Not despite the party but because of it. Being in the middle of the party meant they would still have to behave well towards one another, no matter what was said.

'Some men, yes. But not me,' he said obstinately.

'Richard, please –'

'All right, let's get this clear. What you're really saying, I mean when it comes down to it . . . is you're asking me to tell you about Melissa.'

'Yes,' she said.

She held her breath in the hope that he was at last going to admit that there was some truth to the allegation contained in the letters. He might not be about to admit to everything. That wouldn't matter. So long as he would admit to *something* and so allow her to forgive him and prepare the way for the barriers between them to fall at last and for them to be able to regain their trust in one another.

'And you could live with that?' he said. 'You really think you could live with the thought of another woman in my life?'

'Yes,' she said firmly. She had thought about this and knew it to be true. 'If she wasn't . . . central to your life, then I could, yes.'

'And you would want me to tell you –'

'Yes! That's exactly it. I want you to tell me. Because what I can't stand is . . . not knowing.'

He slowly shook his head.

'Yes!' she insisted.

But she had misunderstood.

'Melissa doesn't exist,' he said.

'Yes, she does. We both know she does.'

'No, she doesn't. You might believe she does but actually she doesn't exist and she never has.'

He spoke with vehemence. She reeled back. It was as though he had struck her when she had been expecting a caress. Certainly she had failed. He had set himself against her and now would never confess. She felt a sudden lurch of despair. How important was this woman to him that he would go to any lengths to defend her?

'I wish she did exist,' he said, and sighed. 'I really do wish there was somebody called Melissa in my life, because then I could tell you about her and you could forgive me. Or perhaps you wouldn't forgive me, I don't know. But, anyway, that would be an end to it.'

She was angry with him. Hadn't she gone as far as anybody could to let him know that he could tell her *anything?* Hadn't she virtually forgiven him even before she'd heard what he had to confess? And yet here he was, still clinging to the lie – *there is no Melissa; she doesn't even exist.* He had stated it after the arrival of the first letter and had been clinging to it like grim death ever since.

She was going to show him that she didn't believe, and never would believe, a word of it.

'That last letter –' she said.

'Yes?'

'It asked for five thousand pounds. And it said that you'd get the photographs in return.'

'That's what it says, yes.'

'All right, so pay it,' she challenged. 'Pay it and let's see the photographs. In fact, I'll pay it. I'll give you the money.'

He was already shaking his head and wincing as though the very thought was painful.

'Well, why not? I'd have thought you'd have wanted them if they're not photographs of you. Then you'd have some proof!'

'There aren't any photographs,' he stated quietly.

'What?'

'How can there be? I've never been to that hotel. I don't know anybody called Melissa. How the hell can there be any photographs of me with her?'

His logic was irreproachable. She had no answer to it, except to keep repeating that yes, he had been to the hotel and he did know someone called Melissa. But that would lead them only into another barren slanging-match, which was what she had sworn to avoid.

She picked up her glass and walked past him, across the uneven tiles and out through the door, meeting with a brave smile the cries of their guests when they saw her emerging from what they took to be a romantic tryst with her husband.

6

When the children had first insisted on organizing a Silver Wedding party, Richard and Claire had made one stipulation: that there should be no speeches. People could come and have a good time; but they mustn't be forced to stand and listen to eulogies on the wonderful married lives of their hosts.

Both David and Diane had agreed – no speeches.

So why, wondered Richard, were he and Claire now being told by David to stand beside him on the patio? And why were their guests, smiling and whispering, shuffling forward to form a small crowd on the lawn before them?

'What's happening?' demanded Claire, also alarmed. 'David, tell me please. I want to know.'

David beamed. 'You're going to be so embarrassed.'

'No!' She looked ready to flee. 'We said no speeches. Yes, David, we said that and you agreed!'

'I know. And shall I tell you something?'

'What?'

'I was lying.'

'Richard . . .?' she appealed, turning to him.

But now everyone was waiting, faces raised expectantly. He could only shrug helplessly and attempt a feeble joke: 'It can't be more embarrassing than getting married was.'

'Well, *I'm* not making a speech,' she insisted.

'You won't have to,' said David. 'Now calm down.'

He turned to the assembled guests and held up a hand. A hush descended. It was almost a surprise to Richard to hear the birds and realize it was an ordinary summer's afternoon in Cheshire and not some wild carnival night in Rio.

David began to speak, thanking everyone for turning up and, as he put it, 'behaving reasonably well'. For the benefit of those who hadn't yet found the toilets, he pointed out where they were. He then invited everyone there to stay the night if they wanted, or even to stay for several weeks, since the house was clearly far too big for two people.

Richard was surprised by how accomplished the performance was. He had always thought of his son as intense and private; seeing him now playing the public orator, and at ease in the role, was a revelation. He had grown up a lot since leaving them to set up home with Suzanne.

Then suddenly, as David got beyond his opening remarks, a minor mystery was solved.

' . . . The week before last I broke one of my guiding rules of life and I went up to London.' He grinned at Richard. 'And, what's more, I nearly made a total bollocks of it because who should I see in some poncy shop on Chiswick High Road but – my father!'

'Yes,' exclaimed Richard aloud, vindicated in this at least.

David went on: 'Only he must have thought I'd gone ba-nanas because all I could think of doing was to run for it. Sounds stupid now but that's what I did – just charged off down the street and relied on the fact he's not as fast now as he once was. He must have seen me, I know he must have, because he rang me later, asking me about it, and all I could do was deny ever being there.' He turned to Richard. 'Dad, I'm sorry.'

'Never mind being sorry. Are you going to explain?' countered Richard, not minding now being part of the entertainment, the straight man in this cross-talk act with his son. Besides, he still did desperately want to know just what the whole strange episode had been about.

'Of course. I'll explain in one second. If I could first of all ask my glamorous assistant to step forward . . .?'

People were asking one another what he meant and craning their necks. Richard looked round too and saw Diane approach-ing. She was carrying what looked like a framed photograph or picture.

David went on: 'The reason I wanted to avoid my dear father – who's normally a man whose company I enjoy – was that I was coming from the offices of the *West London Echo*, where I'd just been to collect this copy of an article that they had carried exactly twenty-five years ago this week.' He paused, then re-peated in case anyone had missed the significance, 'Twenty-five years ago. I wonder if any of you can guess what that article was about . . .?'

There was laughter and applause. Even Claire was now smiling broadly. Richard placed an arm around her. It would have looked peculiar for them to continue standing side by side without touching. She didn't flinch but nor did she allow herself to sway even an inch towards him.

And now Diane was prevailed upon to read aloud the framed newspaper cutting she'd brought with her. It was, of course, an account of the marriage of Richard Stephen Gillow to Claire Anne Shepherd that had taken place in St Giles' Church twenty-five years ago.

'Given away by her father,' Diane read, 'the bride wore an ivory, embroidered gown, which she had designed herself, and carried a bouquet of red roses.'

It surprised Richard that he could remember nothing of that, not the details regarding the dress or the roses. He remembered only Claire, young and vulnerable, giving herself to him and his own disbelief and joy that it was happening at last and there had been no last-minute hitch.

Diane continued to read and he forced himself to concentrate. There were cheers of recognition when she came to those among the list of bridesmaids and groomsmen who had made the party today.

It had all been carefully and lovingly planned and its intention was to revive cherished memories, Richard knew. And yet he could feel only sadness, recalling how *young* they had been. He felt envy too, for that simple, unquestioning love this young couple had shared.

'And that's it,' announced David, when Diane reached the end of the brief account. 'I'm under strict orders not to say anything embarrassing, like telling you what wonderful parents these two have been and how they're still as much in love with one another today as they were then. So I won't say any of that. All I will say is – congratulations, mum and dad, and here's to the next twenty-five.'

This produced another, even bigger cheer. Richard called out, 'Thank you,' and shook hands with his son. The jazz band struck up a wavering version of 'Congratulations' which petered out after the opening chords. It made everyone laugh and effectively marked an end to the formal part of the proceedings.

Richard looked around him for Claire, but she had gone. Perhaps she had slipped away into the house. Whether she had gone to compose herself or to get away from him he had no idea. For the moment it didn't seem to matter very much. He was only relieved that they had come through the little ceremony that David had devised in their honour without the rift between them being publicly exposed.

Besides, he was now preoccupied by a new idea. It had come to him when he had spotted Roy cheering and applauding along with the rest. This was the same Roy, who had earlier sought the loan of his London flat so that he might use it to seduce some young woman, the latest in a long line of such conquests if half the rumours circulating about him were to be believed.

And what had he said? What reason had he offered?

That the young woman he was lusting after 'was allergic to hotels'.

There was an irony here that had not been lost on Richard: if only the woman haunting him, the mysterious Melissa, had suffered a similar allergy . . .!

She hadn't of course. On the contrary: from what little he knew about her, she had been drawn to hotels, and to the one hotel in particular. He now wondered whether there might not be a reason for hope here, no more than a straw to be clutched at but at least something that might be a first step towards making sense of what up to now had been senseless and so impossible to defend against. Whenever his *doppelganger* and Melissa had got together, they had done so in a hotel – the same hotel, the Queens, in the centre of Manchester.

Why?

Was it because they liked hotels? Or did they have an attachment to this particular one? Or had they gone there for the simple reason that, like many in their situation, they had nowhere else to go?

The answer could be any or all of these. It didn't matter. Whichever it was, there remained a puzzling inconsistency. The fact that they had used the hotel at all sat oddly beside a snippet from the latest letter. It was the passage that Claire had commented on: 'I am sure that you do not want your wife and loved ones to know about this relationship. And in particular about its financial nature.'

'*And in particular about its financial nature.*'

So was he supposed to be keeping this woman? That was the most obvious interpretation of the phrase. It suggested that he was paying her rent or her mortgage, plus a little something extra so she could enjoy a few of life's luxuries.

So why use the hotel?

Or any hotel for that matter. Why weren't they holed up in this cosy, little flat of hers, if that really was what he was paying for? Going to a hotel was a distinctly curious thing to do. It brought with it the risk of their being seen together in public and, in the wake of that, the risk of their being recognized and even, in the most unlikely and extreme of cases, the risk of . . . blackmail.

The phrase giving rise to these questions – '*and in particular about its financial nature*' – might not be capable of having such a weight of interpretation placed on it. It might even be something the blackmailer had invented, a small embellishment. Still, it remained a strange, teasing discrepancy, one Richard felt he could hardly afford to ignore.

A few people were leaving, friends from the tennis club. He shook hands with them and thanked them for coming. They enquired as to the whereabouts of Claire. He was sorry but he wasn't sure just where she'd got to. He would, however, pass on their thanks for the party and their renewed congratulations.

It was Lawrence Nevison he was looking for, his next-door neighbour. He prowled around the garden and finally spotted him talking to a couple of his cronies from the George. He was about to approach him but then an aunt of Claire's materialized and had to be fussed over and escorted to her car.

Coming back into the garden, where things had perceptibly slowed and the jazz band were playing 'Stranger On The Shore', Richard scanned the groups of guests and saw Lawrence detaching himself from his pals. He was setting off across the lawn, holding what looked like an empty glass.

'Just the man,' Richard called, hurrying to catch up.

'Why, what have I done?' smiled Lawrence, as they fell into step. 'By the way, that son of yours knows how to handle a mob. He should have been a politician.'

'Or a lawyer.'

Lawrence clutched at his chest and staggered for a few steps. 'You know where to land a blow, sir, I'll grant you that,' he said.

They came to the bar. The grass before it was trampled and littered with cigarette-ends and crushed plastic cups.

'Now I'd like to offer to buy you a drink, old man,' said Lawrence. 'Except that, as you're paying for all this, there wouldn't be much point.'

'I'll have one with you anyway.'

They were served two beers at the bar, then Richard drew Lawrence away from there and round the corner of the house to a spot where they were shielded a little from the glare of the sun and the raucous noise of the band. It also ensured that no-one could overhear their conversation.

'I know I shouldn't be talking business today,' said Richard, trying to find an approach that wouldn't seem strange. He didn't want Lawrence to go confiding to Adele and so have this get back to Claire, who would be sure to put an unfavourable gloss on it.

'It's your party,' said Lawrence. 'I'd say you have the right to talk about whatever you want.'

'Well, this might be the only chance I get to see you this weekend.' The preliminaries over, he leaned forward and explained in a low, confidential tone: 'I'm trying to trace somebody. I won't bore you with all the details as to why. Business reasons. The trouble is I really haven't much of an idea how to go about it —'

'We do it all the time,' interrupted Lawrence, with a grin.

It was the response Richard had been hoping for. 'I thought you might,' he said.

'Oh, we're always trying to trace somebody or other. Either because we have to serve a summons on them or we need them because they've been a witness to something or it might be . . . I mean half the time we're trying to give them some good news, like they're heirs to a fortune and they don't know it.'

Richard listened patiently. Then he enquired, as casually as he could manage: 'So how do you go about finding them?'

'We employ a private investigator.'

It was what he had expected to hear yet it still seemed a

strange admission: that Lawrence's blue chip law firm relied for part of its work on these shady individuals with their dusty offices and high-collared macs. Or perhaps it wasn't like that. Perhaps that was a world existing only in literature and the reality was, well, something else.

'Is there someone you can recommend?' he asked.

'Yes. Depends on what kind of a job it is though. Is this an individual you're after or some kind of company?'

'An individual.'

'In this country or abroad?'

'In this country,' said Richard, then wondered: he couldn't even be sure whether this person existed. Though it was a reasonable supposition that, if she existed at all, she was more likely to exist in this country than in any other.

Lawrence said: 'OK. Well, then I'd recommend an investigator we've used a lot. Man by the name of Maurice Townsend. Calls himself Townsend Investigations, but it's just him. He's an ex-policeman. Very reliable, very discreet. And if you let him know that I've recommended you then his charges shouldn't be too horrendous.'

'Is he local?'

'His office is in Manchester. I've got his number at home. Look, I'll go and get it now, why not –'

Richard demurred – no, he couldn't send him on an errand like that when he was a guest – but it was difficult to marshal much conviction. In truth, he very much wanted this man's number, and the sooner the better.

In the end, they walked round to Lawrence's next-door house together, drinks in hand. Lawrence unlocked the front door. They went in through the hallway with its display of porcelain figures and into Lawrence's tight, little study. Richard glanced round, wondering where the threatened novel might be hiding while Lawrence found the phone number in his address book and copied it onto a piece of white card.

She mustn't indulge herself like this. She had guests, dozens of them, wandering the garden and no doubt wondering where she was.

'I've got to go out,' she said to Moira, though without moving.

Moira had come with her into the workroom, immediately after David's speech when she had felt an overwhelming need to escape from the party. She had sat listening and making sympathetic noises while Claire had admitted her lie about the hotel and told her everything: how Richard had dragged her there – to the last place on earth where she ever wished to set foot! – and made them trek from reception to restaurant to bar in a fatuous attempt to prove that no-one recognized him.

'All that proves is that he must have tipped them well in the past,' said Moira, taking her side immediately.

Claire told her of the arrival of the third letter and how Richard was still pretending to understand nothing.

Becoming tearful, she found herself saying that she couldn't stand it any longer and would leave him. The letters were upsetting, of course they were with their accusations of his infidelity. But, if he had only confessed – if he had admitted to this casual liaison, or even if it were not so casual, never mind – then she would have forgiven him and they could have faced the consequences together.

But no, he would admit nothing. Instead, he had put her through these ridiculous and increasingly hard-to-bear charades. They were designed to prove his innocence but, in fact, only served to widened the rift between them. She would leave after the party was over, she said. She might have swallowed her pride and forgiven him for taking another woman but she wasn't going to stand for having her intelligence insulted like this.

'No, you mustn't go,' insisted Moira, the old campaigner. 'Whatever you do, you mustn't go, because then you'll have handed him everything on a plate.'

'I don't care. He can have everything.'

'Your house? You want to give up your lovely house?'

'I don't care about the fucking house,' said Claire, lighting another cigarette.

God, talking to Moira was as hard as talking to Richard. Couldn't she understand that this wasn't about possessions? It was about . . . it was about trust. Honesty.

'Well, you should care. You have to care,' insisted Moira. 'Look at me. I could have gone a million times. But I don't. I stay. Because I have a right to stay and I've given up so much else to that man I'm not giving up my fucking rights as well!

78

Now listen, you've got me swearing,' she said. She took up the bottle they had brought with them from the garden and poured more wine into each of their glasses. 'Don't even think about leaving,' she said. 'Because then either you've got to stay away forever or you've got to come back. And, whichever you do, you've lost.'

Claire wondered why she had ever broken her resolve and confided in this woman. Well, no, she knew why: because Moira was her best and dearest friend, one who would stand by her to the death. Even so, she was displaying a remarkable and exasperating talent for missing the point.

'I don't care about the house! I honestly and truly . . . he can have it!'

'You're saying that now. Well, of course you are. But what will you be saying in six months' time, that's what you have to ask yourself.'

Claire told herself: she is talking like this because of everything she'd been through with Roy. She couldn't help but interpret what was happening between Claire and Richard as much the same sort of thing.

Perhaps, after all, she was right and it wasn't so very different. That was the most depressing, debilitating thought of all, that their marriage, which they had believed to be so special and which all these people had assembled to celebrate, was no different to anybody else's. In fact, it was worse. Roy and Moira at least knew the truth and had settled for living with it. Claire couldn't do that: she meant every word of what she had said about leaving Richard.

Outside the party continued relentlessly. Claire could hear the occasional shriek of laughter. The band would come to life and then fall silent again after a couple of numbers.

'I've got to go out,' she said again.

'Promise me you won't do anything drastic without talking to me first,' said Moira.

Claire felt like rebelling against this injunction. On what grounds did Moira make such a demand? Their friendship was close but it hardly allowed her to claim a veto over Claire's future behaviour.

Yet she heard herself saying, 'I'll talk to you, yes. And, anyway, I can hardly do anything with all this lot here, can I?'

What did it matter what she said? When it came to it, she would do what she bloody well liked.

She got to her feet and checked her face in the mirror that hung by the door. Her mascara had smudged from the tears that had briefly appeared. It would mean slipping through the house to her bedroom in order to repair the damage. She looked around her at her workroom, with the glasses and the makeshift tin-lid ashtray and the smoke hanging in the air, and was suddenly ashamed of how she'd fled the party and tried to shut herself away as a child might after being picked on and bullied.

'Are you going to be all right?' enquired Moira.

'Yes, I'm fine.'

She would go back out with a smile on her face and see the day through. She owed her children that, her wonderful and loving son and daughter, who had gone to so much trouble and expense in her honour. Maybe she even owed it to Richard for the twenty-five years, minus a couple of weeks, during which they had been happy.

Though with that thought came the accompanying question – but how many other women had there been during all this time? How far had their much-lauded happy marriage depended on her blindness to his philandering?

How many other tarts, whores and assembled mistresses had there been before Melissa?

Richard's study was on the first floor and its windows over-looked the garden. It was one of the reasons he had chosen it as his study in those far-off days when they had first moved into the house. It had given him a view of a benign, landscaped world to which the changing seasons gave a perpetual interest.

It now meant that, while dialling the number that Lawrence had given him, he was able to look down on those of their guests who remained. Some had sought the shade of the distant trees; others were collapsed about the lawn. The men had their jackets thrown down beside them and their ties pulled loose. The women appeared to have survived the afternoon better. They looked cooler and less flustered in their summer dresses.

Watching this party given in their honour coming to its end, Richard thought of all the parties he had attended with Claire.

Parties given to celebrate Christmas, New Year, birthdays, chris-
tenings, bankruptcies, General Election nights, Bonfire Nights,
book launches, house warmings, decree absolutes, wedding anniversaries . . . difficult to think of anything they hadn't celebrated
over the years.

But no party they had ever attended had been such torture as
this.

Never before had he so desperately wanted an event to be
over. If only he could raise his lawn and shake it to send his
guests flying off into the distance. He wanted to be left alone
again with his wife so that at least they could talk freely and
honestly. They had put on a performance which had just about
got them through and now he longed for it to be over.

The ringing tone had given way to the recorded message of an
answerphone: 'You are through to Townsend Investigations,
Maurice Townsend speaking. The office is closed at the moment
but if you care to leave your name and number I'll get back to
you as soon as possible. Please speak after the bleep.'

Richard cleared his throat, waited for the promised bleep,
then said, 'My name is Richard Gillow. You've been recommended to me by Lawrence Nevison, who I believe you've
worked for in the past. I'd like to make an appointment with
you . . . well, as soon as possible.' He gave his home telephone
number and then, picturing Claire taking the call and wondering
how she might react, he gave his business number as well,
suggesting that Mr Townsend might try that first if he were
calling during office hours.

It was all he could do for the time being. He took a deep
breath and returned to the party. Claire gave him a fierce look
which he couldn't understand as he went to stand beside her.
Now people were leaving in earnest, forming a small queue to
thank them for their hospitality.

Despite everything, he couldn't help but be aware that the
party had been a success. Their departing guests displayed that
unmistakable glow of people who would talk about today for
weeks to come. The band had found a new lease of life and were
playing 'When The Saints Go Marching In'.

Richard tried to console himself with thoughts of the message
he had left on Maurice Townsend's answerphone. It was to
this man that he would put his idea, the one that Roy had

unwittingly prompted with his talk of hotels. Then, hopefully, he could take the first steps towards unmasking his enemies.

The evening was a welcome anti-climax, a winding down. Though it was busy too: there was the clearing up to be done, the returning of the house and garden to normal. Black bin-bags were filled with the rubbish that the caterers had overlooked or couldn't be bothered with. There was even a small collection of lost property: a floral tie, a lady's high-brimmed hat, a paperback novel.

David and Suzanne were staying over, which meant there were five of them sharing the chores in a more or less organized fashion. About eight o'clock, Claire called a halt.

'I'm tired,' she said. 'And I can't stop till you all do. So please, can we just leave the rest till tomorrow.'

They were happy to give in to her. And then miraculously – so it seemed to Richard, walking in – she had produced a cold spread in the dining-room. They all gathered around the large table, bringing cans of beer and more wine, and a silence fell as they ate. Richard was surprised to find how hungry he was. As for drinking, well, he had begun the afternoon on German beer and somewhere along the way had moved onto champagne and from that to French red wine.

Technically he must be well drunk, unfit to drive or even walk; yet he felt capable and clear-headed. If he were a little tired, that was inevitable after the kind of day it had been.

If only it could continue like this, he thought – all of us around the table, content to be filling our bellies and getting quietly pissed, and the outside world that had been invited in and had come in droves now pushed firmly out again into the surrounding darkness. He raised his glass and found he had their attention, even before he knew what it was he wanted to say.

'Er, can I just propose a toast – to our wonderful children who organized this day for us.'

'Hear, hear,' said Claire, though she was looking at David and Diane rather than at him.

'Yes, I think we did a pretty good job,' said David, 'to say it's the first time our parents have had a Silver Wedding so we haven't had much practice.'

Suzanne lent over and whispered something to him.

The Allegation

These are not children, thought Richard, though he had just
that minute used the word to describe them. They are adults
who deserve to be treated with honesty and trust. The time for
emotional barrier-nursing was long since over.

David was speaking. 'Sue wants to tell you something. Well,
no, actually she wants me to tell you something. But I'm not
going to – she's the one who's pregnant, so she can tell you
herself.' Then he went 'Oops!' and put a hand over his mouth in
mimicry of someone realizing too late what he had said.

They all turned to Suzanne, who said, 'I just hope it's not
going to be as stupid as its father.' Though she was smiling,
pleased to be able to share her secret at last.

'Oh, congratulations,' Claire said, going round the table, to
hug first David, then Suzanne.

Diane just said, 'Great, marvellous, hey . . .' as though the
news had stunned her.

Richard said, 'I'm very happy for you both.' He was conscious
of their discretion and was grateful for it. They must have
planned it this way, withholding their news until the Silver
Wedding celebrations were over lest they should seem to be
competing for attention. It made him want to share his own
secret with them.

'Let's tell them about the letters,' he said to Claire.

She stared at him, as though he had said something obscene
or shocking.

'Well, come on,' he urged. 'Why not –'

'You must tell them what you like,' she said, tight-lipped.

So he had said the wrong thing and now it was too late to go
back. Well, too bad. Perhaps he was a little drunk after all, too
drunk to care.

Anyway, he believed he was in the right to bring this whole
business out into the open. These were not children and should
be entrusted with the truth.

He saw David, Diane and Suzanne staring at him, waiting.
Claire was looking the other way, staring out of the window.
The young people appeared baffled and perhaps in Suzanne's
case somewhat miffed that here was some other piece of news to
top her own announcement.

'No, what it is,' Richard said, looking at his unresponsive wife
and praying she would understand why he was doing this, 'I've

had some letters, accusing me of having an affair.' He felt them recoil from the word. 'They're blackmail letters,' he hurried on. 'There's not a word of truth in them. I swear to you all that there isn't. But . . . well, they're upsetting for your mother, as I'm sure you can imagine.'

'What do they say?' said David softly.

Richard looked to Claire but she was keeping her face averted from him. She wanted him to know how painful it was for her to have these wounds re-opened.

Forced to answer his son's question, Richard said, 'They say I'm having an affair with someone. A woman named Melissa apparently.'

'Tell them the rest,' said Claire, without moving.

He was tempted to challenge her. If she wanted them to know more, then why couldn't she tell them herself? Still, he was the one who had begun this and so he supposed he had to see it through.

He said: 'I'm supposed to have met this woman in a hotel. Which is a pack of lies. The trouble is that when we came to check with the hotel . . . well, your mother did . . . we found that there'd been somebody using my name. So I mean yes, the letters were true to that extent but not . . .'

He saw their scared, disbelieving faces and thought – I shouldn't ever have embarked on this. They are children after all.

'Never mind. Forget it,' he said.

Claire shrieked at him in their bedroom, wilder than he had ever known her: 'How dare you involve our children? How dare you try and use them against me?'

Richard backed away, shaking his head: 'Really and truly that was not my intention –'

'Telling them things that should be private to us! Inviting them to choose sides!'

'I was not inviting them to choose –'

'No? And so what were you doing?'

'Like I said, I wanted them to know what was going on –'

'Oh, yes, and why?'

'Why . . .?'

'It's the same as that stunt you tried to pull in the hotel. You dragged me round there and now you're trying to drag the children in. All because you're trying to convince me how innocent you are. Because only an innocent man would show his wife the letters, wouldn't he?'

He tried to stem the torrent of abuse. 'No, that wasn't –'

'Only an innocent man would take her to the hotel where he's supposed to have taken his mistress.'

'Claire –'

'And now –' She became deformed and ugly as she spat the words out at him. 'Now I'm expected to believe that only an innocent man would confess everything to his children!'

'No!' he shouted back. 'No, that wasn't why I did it.'

He wondered if they could be heard by the children who were in their various bedrooms elsewhere.

'Well, yes, I think it was.'

'No,' he said doggedly.

'See, I'm beginning to understand your methods now. You're trying to turn these letters into a joke. Because once they're a joke then . . . well, you'll be off the hook, won't you. Only it won't work. It won't ever work. Because *I know what you're up to*!'

'All right,' he said, 'you want me to leave?'

His sudden offer surprised himself as much as it did her. He hadn't planned to say such a thing and had no idea what he would do if she were to take him up on it. Though at least it had momentarily silenced her.

'You want me to go to Melissa? Go and stay with her in her flat?'

Claire said nothing. She seemed to be holding her breath. She was waiting for whatever confession might be about to follow hard on the heels of that bit of dangerous rhetoric.

'Is that what you want?' he demanded.

'Is that what you're going to do?'

'It's what I'd *like* to do,' he said, not knowing whether he meant it. 'Except that, as I've told you from the start, there is no Melissa. None. Sorry but there is no Melissa!'

Now he was the one yelling at her while she stood unflinching, her silence challenging his every word.

He couldn't remain there in the bedroom with her. After what had been said, it was unthinkable. He could never again take his clothes off and climb into bed beside her.

'I shall go and sleep in the spare room,' he said.

'Yes,' she said. 'I think I'd rather you did.'

He left the room without another word being exchanged. Coming onto the landing, he had to think quickly about just who was sleeping where. David and Suzanne had been allotted David's old room, which was larger than the so-called spare-room, and so which now remained free for Richard.

He made his way towards it, turning out landing lights in his wake. Arriving and closing the door, he sank onto the double bed, trying to pull the bedclothes loose.

Throwing off his clothes and scrambling beneath the sheets, he thought well, that's today over. Let's be grateful.

Yet he knew that things had got immeasurably worse where Claire was concerned. He should never have attempted to tell the children about the letters. She had regarded that as a heinous offence, one she wouldn't quickly forgive. Worse, she saw it as further proof of his guilt since only a guilty man would go to such lengths.

And yet he was innocent. He knew that if no-one else did. So why couldn't he be content in his innocence, indifferent to her accusations?

He began to laugh. He was tired and drunk and in a minute would be asleep. Still, he knew that among the many things he had said to his wife that day, some hurtful, some tender, their last exchange in the bedroom had held a grain of bitter truth. If only there were a Melissa, someone to whom he could go to seek sympathy and a welcoming embrace. How strongly he would then be tempted to go to her, driven from his own home by the mistrust and hostility he now met there at every turn.

7

Townsend Investigations was situated in Cheetham Hill, to the north of the city. Richard drove to it, catching a glimpse of the Queens Hotel as he passed through the city centre. A mile or so beyond came the red-brick bulk of Strangeways prison, and Cheetham Hill after that, with its trading-estates and shops.

The address he'd been given turned out to be a reinforced brown door squeezed in between a greengrocer's and a bookie's. There was a bell at eye level, with an intercom device beside it. It was all precisely as Maurice Townsend had described it when he had rung Richard that morning in his office to say he had received his message and would be happy to see him just as soon as was convenient.

Richard had said, 'Would today be possible?' and been pleasantly surprised to hear that today was certainly possible. They had agreed that Richard should visit the office later that morning.

He pressed hard on the bell but heard nothing. He was about to try again when the intercom crackled into life. A distorted voice said, 'Yes?'

'It's Richard Gillow.'

Another crackle, then: 'Push on the door.'

He pushed and the door clicked open.

Inside was a flight of stairs with a worn, green carpet running up the middle. At the top was another door, which stood open and had the words 'TOWNSEND INVESTIGATIONS' stuck on in black lettering.

'Come on through,' a voice called.

Richard entered a tiny waiting-room, which contained a few wooden chairs and not much else, then went through another door to where, in a larger room full of filing-cabinets and a big, battered desk loaded with phone, PC monitor and fax machine, a man was getting to his feet to greet him.

'Mr Gillow. I'm Maurice Townsend,' he said.

'Pleased to meet you,' said Richard as they shook hands.

First impressions were of a big, shambling man in his fifties, wearing a rather baggy brown suit and a Hawaiian shirt with an open neck. He had a long, bony face, which remained unsmiling as he invited Richard to sit down and then resumed his own seat across from him. He had the solemn manner of someone who knew that his clients were not there on trivial matters.

Most striking was his hair. He had a full head of wavy, grey hair, which was pulled at the back into a pony-tail. It might have been a declaration that he was no longer on the force but was his own man.

'Would you like a coffee?' he said.

'I wouldn't mind, yes, thank you.'

'Do you want caffeinated or de-caf, milk or sugar or neither?'

Richard opted for de-caf with no sugar, then took the opportunity to look around while Maurice Townsend bustled about with a kettle and cups and saucers. Certainly, if files and records were anything to go by, this was a busy man. The tops of the cabinets were piled almost to the ceiling with loose-leafed folders while the open shelving on the other wall was filled with more folders, a few yards of video-cassettes, an assortment of reference books and what looked like a complete set of telephone directories.

'It's good of you to see me so quickly,' said Richard.

'I find that if people want a private investigator, then they want him now, not in two weeks' time.'

Richard might have taken this for a joke had it not been delivered with a monk-like solemnity. Anyway, thinking about it, it struck him as no doubt true. Certainly he had been glad of the quick response.

'Yes, I've done a lot of work for Mr Nevison's firm,' said Maurice Townsend suddenly. 'I should tell you that I've already taken the liberty of contacting Mr Nevison just to confirm what you said, about him recommending you. I hope you don't mind that.'

Did he? There didn't seem any reason to.

'Not at all.'

The coffee was served in a willow pattern cup and saucer. Maurice went and closed the door, which was standing partly open, then returned. He placed his hands on top of the desk, spreading his long fingers which were bedecked with gold rings.

'Now I don't know what it is you wish to consult me on, Mr Gillow, but can I say first of all that anything you tell me will be treated in the strictest confidence.'

Richard nodded. The phrase recalled his fruitless interview with Inspector Beresford, who had made the same promise. He could only hope that this wouldn't prove a similar waste of time. It wasn't just that he needed help now even more than he had then; he now had a more specific idea of what it was he wanted doing.

'So, how may I help you, sir?'

'I'm being blackmailed,' said Richard tersely. 'I've received three letters, which accuse me of having an affair with a woman. The odd thing is I'm not having an affair and I've never heard of the woman. Quite frankly, I can't make head or tail of it.'

Maurice Townsend frowned and brought his hands together as though in prayer.

'Blackmail is a crime,' he said.

'I'm aware of that.'

'And so it should be a matter for the police.'

'I've already been to the police. They were no help. In fact, they were worse than that – they were downright insulting. They insisted on believing the letters rather than me.' He felt a rush of anger even now at the memory of that encounter.

'That's a great pity,' said Maurice Townsend. He seemed genuinely upset that Richard had received such cavalier treatment. 'But I've still got to point out that an agency like this doesn't really have the resources to investigate criminal matters.'

Richard raised a hand. He had foreseen these objections and believed them to be irrelevant. He was sure Maurice Townsend would think the same, once he had heard what it was Richard wanted from him.

'I realize that, yes. Please, would you first like to read the letters and then I'll tell you how it is I think you might be able to help.'

It would also be a test of his theory as to the identity of Melissa. He would put to it this neutral, dispassionate observer and see what he made of it.

He took the letters from their envelopes and passed them across the desk in the order in which he had received them. Since Claire had begun her accusations, he had removed them from the kitchen mantelpiece and locked them away in the small safe that was in his study. He didn't want her destroying them in a fit of rage.

Maurice Townsend read slowly, nodding as he finished each letter and placing it face down to one side. When he had finished the third, he looked up and said, 'I see.'

'As for the Queens Hotel, I have never stayed there, not on those dates or at any other time,' said Richard, wanting everything crystal-clear. 'But I've got to tell you that somebody did stay there on those dates using my name.'

Maurice Townsend took a moment to absorb that. And you'd better believe it, thought Richard, eyeing him. The slightest hint of Inspector Beresford's cynical, come-on-you-can-tell-me-the-truth routine and he would be out of the office and down those stairs in a flash.

But Maurice Townsend's expression suggested only a polite, respectful interest. 'You've checked with the hotel?' he asked.

'I have, yes.'

'And it was your address –'

'The impostor had used my name and my address. But he had paid in cash and there was no phone number so –'

'I see, yes.'

Richard felt himself warming to this man with his quiet, courteous manner, so different to the sneering Inspector. And how wonderful it was, what a change to his recent experiences, to be given a fair hearing without having every word pounced upon and challenged.

Maurice had completed his deliberations and was ready to pronounce.

'I can understand that this is unsettling –'

'Extremely.'

'Even so, why not just throw these letters away? Ignore them? If you do, what's the worst that can happen?'

Richard gave a wry smile. 'I'm afraid the worst has already happened. My wife has read them and she believes them.'

This time Maurice saw the implication immediately. He nodded. 'I understand.'

'That's the reason I'm here. I'm in desperate need of something, anything at all, that'll persuade her I'm telling the truth.'

Maurice thought some more, then said: 'But the letter gives specific dates –'

'Yes.'

'So weren't you at home on any of them?'

Richard sighed. This would be the test of the other man's belief in him.

'No, I wasn't,' he said. 'Though that isn't so remarkable. I'm often away. I have a flat in London, and that's where I was on those dates.'

'And you were . . . on your own?'

'Yes. Well, I mean I might have seen the odd person in the evening for a drink but . . . even if I could recall exactly where I was or what I was doing, I doubt it's the kind of alibi that my wife would any longer accept.'

Maurice Townsend nodded, his expression set. There was no half-smile, no raised eyebrow to call Richard's account into question. It encouraged Richard to hope that this was the ally he needed.

'I can see that it's an unfortunate situation,' said Maurice, 'very unfortunate. But I still don't understand –'

'Where you come into it?' anticipated Richard.

'I was going to say – how I can help you.'

Richard hesitated, wary of exposing the idea he had now been carrying around in his own head since the moment at the party when his conversation with Roy had made him think of hotels and some people's reluctance to use them. Now was the time to put it to the test. He leaned across the desk, picked up the letters and shuffled through them till he came to the third.

'You see what it says here – *and in particular about its financial nature . . .?*'

'Yes.'

'I've been wondering just what that might mean.'

'I wondered that too.'

'I suppose the most obvious interpretation is that this man, whoever he is, is supporting this woman, whoever she is.'

'Right,'

'He's providing her with accommodation and possibly with money to live on.'

Maurice nodded. 'She'd be what's traditionally referred to as a kept woman.'

'She would. But I'm not sure that this is the case. I've been thinking about this, and I don't think he's keeping her at all.'

'No?'

'No. For one thing, why don't they meet in this flat or house or whatever it is he's paying for her to live in? Why do they need a hotel at all?'

He gave Maurice Townsend a moment to consider that, then took the next step.

'Now of course this phrase *its financial nature* could mean something else. It could mean he's paying her for the service she's providing. It could mean she's a prostitute.'

Maurice's brow furrowed as he pondered. Then he gave the thought his blessing. 'Yes,' he said.

Richard warmed to his theme. 'And, you see, the other thing I was thinking about was her name.'

'Melissa . . .?'

'Yes. It's quite an uncommon one. I suppose you might call it exotic. And that made me wonder . . . I mean put together with that reference to money . . . it made me wonder whether Melissa might not be her real name at all but one she uses when she's working.'

'It might,' agreed Maurice. 'Yes, it might.' He seemed rather taken by the idea. 'Most of these young ladies do like to have a name to hide behind, and *Melissa* . . . there's no denying it has the right sort of ring to it.'

Richard was heartened. It was a great encouragement to find that this seasoned private eye and ex-policeman didn't seem to find anything wrong with his interpretation of things. His own conviction was growing.

'See, it's not as though they ever stay together at the hotel for any period of time, say a week or a month,' he said. 'It's just odd nights. So what I think . . . ' Summing up now. 'What I think is that she's a prostitute, he's the customer and this hotel is their regular meeting-place.'

He waited, and was delighted to find that Maurice was still there with him.

'It makes sense to me.'

'Good.'

'I can also tell you something you might not know – that hotel, the Queens, has something of a reputation as a pick-up joint.'

'Really?'

'Always has been. Four star, with prices to match, but a pick-up joint all the same.'

Richard felt like shaking the man's hand. He had at last found someone who was on his side and who didn't see him as a liar and adulterer.

'Well, then that all ties in,' Richard exclaimed. 'They meet there and he pays her for her services.'

'I'd go with that, but, er –'

'You still don't see why I've come to you . . .?'

Maurice gestured at the office around them. 'I'm really in the information business. I don't solve crimes. That's the job of the police.'

'I know, I know,' reassured Richard. 'I don't want you to try and solve it. Or even to stop the blackmail. No, what I would like you to do is one thing and one thing only. I would like you to find Melissa.'

Not a man for quick answers, Maurice deliberated, asked to re-read the letters, deliberated some more and only then finally said that yes, he would accept the commission.

Richard felt an immense relief. Maurice Townsend's willing-ness to take on the case felt like a small victory in itself. It was the beginning of his fight-back.

Maurice handed Richard a printed sheet which explained the basis of his fees and expenses. He asked Richard if he would read it and then sign it as the basis of the contract between them. Richard said he would be happy to and glanced over the list, which seemed reasonable enough. He signed the paper and handed it back.

Maurice explained how normally, with a new client, he would ask for a payment in advance – say, a hundred pounds. On this occasion, however, he would waive such an advance since Rich-ard had come recommended by Lawrence Nevison.

After which they talked some more about Melissa.

They agreed that, if she were a prostitute and working the Queens Hotel, then she was unlikely to be found among the

93

cheap, street-walking end of her profession. She would have to be classier than that, able to pass as the glamorous wife or girlfriend joining her exhausted businessman husband for the evening. More likely then she was either working for herself, from her home or through some accommodation address, or for one of the many saunas and escort agencies that were all over the city and well-advertised.

'Must be a hundred such places,' said Maurice. 'Of course, every week some are closing, others are opening, so it's a moveable feast.'

'But you think you can track her down?' It was beginning to sound like a more difficult task than he had foreseen.

Maurice shrugged. 'I can try. I'm afraid we don't give any guarantees.'

'I wouldn't expect you to,' said Richard. Though he remained curious. 'How will you set about it?' he enquired 'That's if it's not a trade secret.'

Maurice allowed himself a wry smile, the first he had let slip from beneath his solemn mask. 'Did you notice that little news-agent's on the corner?'

'Not really.'

'Well, there's more to that business than meets the eye. Out front he's selling sweets to kiddies and birthday cards. But there's a back room, and that's where he keeps his specialist magazines. A couple of those will provide me with a comprehensive list of every tart in Greater Manchester. Then it'll be a matter of letting my fingers do the walking as they say.' He gestured towards the telephone.

Richard nodded, reassured to know he had hired a man who seemed to know his way around this murky world. 'What do you think the chances are?' he asked.

Maurice pondered. 'I think our chances of finding her are good,' he said gravely, 'if we've guessed right and she is what we think she is. There's always the possibility we're barking up the wrong tree altogether.'

'I understand that.'

'In which case I might find you any number of Melissas but none of them will be the right one.'

'I know but . . . I still think we're right. He's paying her, well, for sex. It's the only thing that makes sense to me.'

'It makes sense to me too. That's why I'm taking the case. No, I think she's a tart. Melissa – it's a tart's name.' He raised a long forefinger as though in warning. 'There is just one other thing I need to know –'

'Yes?'

'When I find her . . . *if* I find her . . . do you want me to approach her in any way? Or do I leave her well alone and simply pass the information on to you so that you know where she is and you can approach her yourself?'

Richard hesitated. He hadn't thought this far ahead. His only aim had been to set the chase in motion. He hadn't considered what would happen when the quarry was sighted.

'No, don't approach her,' he said, making the decision. 'Just tell me where I can find her and then I'll approach her myself.'

Since the arrival of the letters, his life had become a series of moral conundrums. The one he had to face on returning home that evening was whether he should tell Claire what he had done. Would it help things for her to know that he had engaged this private investigator, Maurice Townsend, to track down Melissa?

If he told her, her likely reaction would be to accuse him of playing games again. No doubt she would go through the now familiar litany, reminding him of how he had shown her the letters in the first place, then how he had dragged her to the hotel, how he had gone to the police and, to top it all, how he had insisted on blurting everything out in front of the children.

And so now he had engaged a private investigator? Big deal.

On the other hand, if he *didn't* tell her . . . well, then what was the point of going to Maurice Townsend in the first place? The whole idea of trying to find Melissa was for Claire's benefit. Melissa, if she did exist and could be found, was to be his witness, testifying to his innocence.

The dilemma remained unresolved. He returned home, still not knowing what to do for the best.

Diane came hurrying to intercept him as he entered the front door. She looked serious.

'What's the matter?' he said, alarmed.

'Mum's been crying again,' she said, keeping her voice low.

Richard sighed. He was genuinely sorry for his wife, whom he loved and had lived beside for twenty-five years. He knew how unhappy she must be. Wasn't he also unhappy, brought almost to his knees by this wretched, bloody business?

Still, there was a part of him that blamed Claire even as he sympathized. The blackmailer's letters would have remained a joke, they could have been thrown away and forgotten about, but for her willingness to believe them.

'Did she say anything to you?' he asked Diane.

'No. But I just thought you should know.'

'Yes. Thanks. And, believe me, I am trying to sort this out.'

'I do believe you,' she said, and reached up to kiss him on the cheek. 'Of course I do.'

He felt that, if sides were ever to be taken, his daughter would be on his. At least she wouldn't be against him. She was younger than David, of course, and so still had that childhood longing that everything should stay as it was and nothing should change. Yet he sensed more than that from her: she had a real sympathy with his predicament and was doing what bit she could to help him through it.

Whereas David, leaving on the Sunday morning, had been withdrawn and resentful. It was as though Richard had let him down by getting himself blackmailed after David had gone to so much trouble over the Silver Wedding party and the framed newspaper article. He would be on his mother's side, no doubt about it.

Claire was in the kitchen, bright and brittle. 'Hello. Did you have a good day?'

He made no attempt to approach her or embrace her as he would once have done without a second thought.

'Fine, thanks. And you?'

'Oh, yes.'

He poured himself a glass of wine from the already-open bottle and sat at the table so that he could watch her as she prepared the dinner. Dicing vegetables and adding them to a simmering pan.

Useless to pretend there could be any other topic of conversation, he thought sadly. Where their lives had once seemed filled to overflowing, so that they had sometimes gone out to restaurants simply so that they might be alone for a couple of hours and catch up on one another's news, now there was nothing but the two of them locked in this dreadful conflict. Everything else had withered away, scorched by the heat of their passion.

Yes, he would tell her about his visit to Maurice Townsend, he decided. And bugger the consequences.

'Those letters,' he said.

'What about them?' She began to chop more quickly.

'Well, I daresay you'll only think this is another trick I'm trying to pull . . . another of my stunts.'

'Will I?'

'But what I've done – I've engaged a private detective.'

He saw the curl of her lip. It was the disdain he had expected, her contempt for his every attempt to clear himself.

'A private detective . . .!' she said, as though this were some freakish animal he had produced out of a hat.

'Someone Lawrence recommended,' he said, determined not to be riled.

'I see. And can I ask just what you hope to achieve by that?'

'I hope that we may be able to find Melissa.'

She gave a short laugh.

'Well, you may find that funny,' he said, 'but I think it would be a valuable step forward.'

She had now abandoned all pretence at cooking and had advanced to the table across from him. 'A valuable step forward? That's what it would be, would it?'

'I think so, yes.'

She gave a smile of undisguised contempt. 'But I thought Melissa didn't exist?'

He felt he had been ambushed by her and didn't know what to say. Of course he could be as sardonic as she was being and point out that she had been the one who had insisted that Melissa did exist. He could try and score debating points, as she was doing. But he had hoped for something more, and couldn't afford to abandon that hope.

'As far as I'm concerned, she doesn't exist,' he said. 'And that's still true. She doesn't.'

'So then why –'

'Why am I paying somebody to try and find her if she doesn't exist? Yes, I can see that must seem paradoxical.'

'It seems downright stupid.'

He forced himself to remain calm. He would not be provoked

by her. He tried to explain: 'There was a line in that last letter that talked about the financial nature of the relationship . . .?'

She was gazing at him blankly, as if reluctant to admit she had even set eyes on the blessed letter, let alone that she had read it.

'You remember?' he pleaded. 'It said that the relationship had a financial nature . . .?'

She shrugged. 'No, I don't. But I'll take your word for it. So what?'

'So I think that probably means that this Melissa is some kind of prostitute, some kind of call-girl. And Maurice, this private detective, he agrees with me. And so he's going to try and find her.'

She took a packet of cigarettes from her pocket and lit one. It was the first time she had smoked openly before him since she had publicly kicked the habit, though he had his suspicions that she was sneaking the odd one.

'You're smoking again.'

'So?'

'Nothing.' He regretted having even mentioned it.

She blew a stream of smoke towards the ceiling, then said, 'You've been to a private detective.'

'Yes.'

'And instructed him to do what? To try and find a prostitute called Melissa?'

She made it sound like the act of a madman.

'Well, not just any prostitute,' he replied patiently. 'The one in the letter.'

'And then what?'

He didn't understand. 'What?'

She spoke with an exaggerated slowness, as though explaining to a child. 'What will happen if he succeeds and he does find her?'

Unable to see where her questions were leading, Richard hesitated. 'Well, then I'll talk to her,' he said finally. 'Try and get to the bottom of this.'

'You're planning on bringing her here?' said Claire, with a quietness that he knew belied the vehemence behind the question.

'No –'

'You're planning on bringing her here, some tart, and then you'll expect me to believe her when she tells me that it wasn't you she was with in the hotel?'

'No, I'm not saying that I would expect you to believe her. Just that . . . well, she might be able to tell us something that would shed light on all this!'

He had sworn to remain calm. He had told himself that this would not be another evening when the house would rock from their exchanges, yet here he was raising his voice to her. He could hear himself but couldn't prevent it.

'Why should I expect you to believe her,' he went on, 'when I know that you won't believe me, your own husband? In fact, the only person you will believe is that bastard who's written those damned letters!'

'I won't believe a tart,' she retaliated. 'If she'll let you do anything for money, then she'll say anything for money. Well, isn't that obvious?'

Suddenly Diane was in the doorway. They both turned to her as her voice was raised even above theirs.

'I'm going out! All right? I don't want to eat here and I won't be back tonight, so you've got the house to yourselves and you can shout at one another as much as you like!'

Then she turned and was hurrying away.

'No, darling . . .' called Claire after her, but it was too late. They heard the crash of the front door being slammed closed.

'I can't say I blame her,' said Richard.

'Neither can I,' retorted his wife.

'Because you'd rather blame me.'

'Would I,' she said flatly. She pushed her hand through her hair and turned away. 'I don't think I feel much like eating tonight. I'm sorry but you'll have to fend for yourself.'

'Oh, come on – ,' he began, but then stopped, not knowing what more to say. It was a protest born out of habit. Why should they continue to take their evening meal together when every other component of their married life was self-destructing around them? They were already sleeping apart; from now on they would be eating apart.

He had stayed on in the spare room since the party and its awful aftermath when – unwisely? yes, probably – he had confided everything to the children. He had even moved some of his clothes into the wardrobe there and had taken his shaver and toothbrush out of the en suite bathroom so that Claire would know she was alone and there was no risk of his intruding. Petty manoeuvrings perhaps, but he was sure she was as keen as he was to avoid the nightly farce of their having to climb into their own sides of the same bed – each careful to stay as far apart as possible and lying rigid, determined that there should not be any contact from straying limbs.

Now he watched her go as she left the kitchen without even a glance towards him. Her footsteps went away up the stairs.

So was everything he had done that day a pointless waste of time? What purpose could be served by Maurice Townsend tracking down Melissa if Claire had already rejected her testimony out of hand as the word of a paid whore and therefore worthless? *And this was even before they had found the woman!* Was there anything he could do to exonerate himself or had his wife already condemned him and ruled any further evidence out of court?

Had she simply fallen out of love with him so that evidence of any kind was beside the point?

It was a chilling thought, making him wonder why he was bothering to do anything at all. Shouldn't he simply resign himself to a loveless marriage in which neither would ever again trust the other? It wouldn't be the first such and might yet stagger on to see a few more anniversaries.

He roused himself from the stupor he had fallen into. He went to examine the meal she had been preparing in the faint hope he might salvage something. The vegetables looked as though they were destined for one of her thick soups. There were strips of liver still wrapped in cellophane beside the grill. Abandoning that, he made himself a ham sandwich and poured another glass of wine.

He knew he mustn't give up, if only for the sake of David and Diane. He must fight the temptation to despair.

Wait and see what Maurice Townsend could come up with. What Richard needed more than anything was to understand what was going on here and who his enemies were. He didn't believe himself to be a coward; it was the insidious nature of these attacks on him that had unmanned him and left him helpless.

Please God that Maurice might find Melissa. That was all he asked: that, and the opportunity to talk to her.

Claire had retreated to her workroom. She had to go somewhere and it was ridiculously early for going to bed. All she wanted was to be away from him. She could no longer tolerate his constant attempts to bully her into submission. He seemed to believe that if he went on long enough her opposition would be eroded or she would simply grow tired and let him have his own way.

She was amazed at his tenacity on this, the way nothing could deflect him or shut him up.

And now – his latest manoeuvre – he had employed a private detective. Whose job was to produce some woman, any woman really, who would claim to be the Melissa mentioned in the letters. No doubt she would also claim never to have seen Richard before and so the whole thing must have been a gigantic mistake, and that would be that.

Claire didn't know which distressed her more: the lengths to which her husband seemed prepared to go to protect this other woman or the low opinion in which he evidently held his wife that he could ever imagine she would be placated by such transparent tricks.

She would put up with no more of it. She would leave tomorrow.

And, yes, she knew she had promised Moira that she wouldn't, but then they had been discussing a different kind of leaving. Moira had pictured her rushing to divorce lawyers whereas all she wanted to do was get away.

It wouldn't be the first time. She had often travelled on her own before, taking odd weekends when she had needed to have time to herself. Of course, those weekends had always been with Richard's blessing. This would be different.

She would go without telling him. It was the only way to avoid another almighty row. And she must speak to Diane, their poor, dear daughter, and attempt to explain it all to her. As for Moira, well, it would probably be wise to ring her and let her know she was going – if only to stop her jumping to the conclusion that Richard had killed her and hidden the body.

There would be no rushing to lawyers. If that were ever to come, it was still some distance away.

She would wait till the morning and let him go off to work. Then she would collect a few clothes and be gone. It surprised her and raised her spirits to realize how easy escape would be.

8

The fourth letter was lying on the mat the following morning.

The sight of the cheap envelope and the printed address in red biro stopped Richard in his tracks. He stared at it for a long moment before bending and picking it up along with the rest of the post.

Of course there had to be a fourth letter, he knew that. He had yet to receive any instructions as to how he was to make the five thousand pound payment. This fourth letter would no doubt tell him.

Even so, it was a small shock to find it there. His visit to Maurice Townsend had left him feeling that he had seized the initiative. For the first time he was going onto the attack. And now, even as that attack had barely been launched, here was letter number four arriving on his doormat, as though the blackmailer were out to demonstrate his ability to remain effortlessly one step ahead.

He returned to the kitchen, where he was making an early breakfast in the hope of getting out of the house before Claire descended. It seemed the only sure way of avoiding further confrontation. He took a sip of his coffee then picked up the blackmailer's letter. Even touching it, he felt he was running the risk of contamination, absorbing more of the poison that had already seeped into his marriage. He used a kitchen knife to split the envelope and pulled out a familiar-looking piece of note-paper with printing on one side only.

'Dear Mr Gillow,' he read. 'The address to which you must send the five thousand pounds is as follows. Room 608, 125, Stanmore Road, Manchester. When I receive the money, I will immediately send you the photographs and that will be the last you will hear from me. If I do not receive the money within two weeks then I will be sending the photographs to your wife and to other people who might be interested.'

So that was it. He re-read it, then sat back to consider.

The threat to send photographs to his wife had a hollow ring considering all that had happened. Yes! – he wanted to reply. Yes, please do send all the photographs you have. I will be fascinated to see them.

Though of course there couldn't be any. Since he had never met Melissa, it was impossible there could be photographs of them together. This was a truth he must cling to, lest he should ever begin to be persuaded by the letters and wonder whether he hadn't done these things after all.

There was one thing new in this letter. That was the address to which he was to send the money. 'Room 608, 125, Stanmore Road, Manchester.' It excited him by offering the possibility of an alternative route to the blackmailer if Maurice's attempt to locate Melissa should end in failure.

He re-read the letter a second time but could see nothing else of significance. He wondered about 'Stanmore Road'. Where could that be? Was there an 'A to Z' around the house that he might consult? Claire would know but he wasn't going to ask her. He must be patient until he got into work and could commandeer a copy from somebody.

He heard light footsteps approaching and steeled himself for another cool encounter with his wife. But it was Diane who appeared in the doorway, wearing her college tracksuit and her favourite pair of hedgehog slippers.

'Morning,' he said, relieved.

'Morning.'

She gave him a brief kiss on the forehead, then shuffled off to put some bread in the toaster.

'I promised I'd help Will at the stables this morning,' she said, yawning. 'They're short-staffed.'

'Good for you.' He would rather think of her doing anything than sitting alone in the house. 'And how is Will?'

'Oh, fine, thanks. Says he's in love with me, but then they all say that.'

'Do they?'

'Sooner or later.'

He deliberated for a moment, then pushed the letter across the table towards her. 'I don't want to spoil your breakfast, but another one of those disgusting letters has arrived.'

She looked at it, eyes wide. 'Can I read it?'

'Certainly. It's your mother who wants to keep the whole thing a secret, as if it's something we should be ashamed of. I'm happy for anyone to read it.'

She made no response to that, which made him wish he hadn't said it. No matter how tempting it might be, he must discipline himself not to criticize Claire in front of her.

'Oh, but there's an address!' she exclaimed.

'Yes.'

'Well, then surely . . . I mean can't you just give it to the police?'

'Yes, I could, but I don't think it'd get them very far.'

'Why not? '

'I doubt that's our blackmailer's home address, if that's what you're thinking.'

'So what is it?'

'I would suspect it's some kind of accommodation address. Where you pay somebody to keep your letters for you.'

'OK, so you . . . you . . .' She cast around for an appropriate scenario. 'You send him a parcel full of torn-up newspaper and then you keep a watch on the place until he comes to collect it!'

Well, yes, it might one day come to that. For the moment he said simply, 'Don't worry about it. The important thing is that he is not going to be paid even a single penny piece.' He took the letter from her and tucked it back into its envelope. 'Listen, I don't think I'm going to show this letter to your mother. It'll only upset her again. So if we can just keep this to ourselves . . .?'

'Sure. What do you think I am – stupid?'

She was playing it light, a game between them, but he wasn't fooled. He felt the desperation she was working so hard to hide. 'Come here,' he said. He took her in his arms and give her a hug. It was something he had lost the habit of doing since she had become grown-up. She hugged him back and nuzzled up against him.

'I know it's difficult to believe, but I really don't know what these damned letters are about,' he said.

'I know.' She looked up. He saw a face that might have been Claire twenty years ago, the fine nose and mouth and porcelain blue eyes. 'If you had understood them, then you wouldn't have made such a mess of everything.'

It was an odd vote of confidence but he was grateful for it and gave her another hug before letting her go. She hurried away to collect her toast.

'I hope I wouldn't,' he said. 'But I am trying to put things right, I promise you that.'

He was tempted to say more. Her support made him want to tell her about Maurice Townsend and the search for Melissa, but he checked himself. Since the arrival of the first letter he had been guilty of saying too much altogether. Now he would be more guarded and would bide his time till there was something positive to report and he could tell it to the whole family, Claire included.

In the past, when he had returned from London and they had had their dinner together during which Claire had brought him up-to-date on whichever of their friends' marriages was the latest to collapse, he had wondered at the resilience of the people involved. How did they manage to get up in a morning and get their children to school on time? Even more remarkable, what reserves of strength carried them to the office or to wherever it was they earned their crust and allowed them to function as though nothing untoward was happening?

He had admired such displays of bravery, idly wondering whether how he would react under similar circumstances.

And now here he was, displaying that same *sang-froid* he had found so amazing in others. He arrived at his offices even earlier than usual and managed a cheery greeting for Yvonne on his way through reception.

It wasn't a matter of strength of will, he realized, but of escaping. He noticed the wood-carving of Christ on the cross, a feature that had survived the conversion. He thought, I am here seeking sanctuary from persecution.

Also, and he gave a wry smile at this notion, however much anyone here might despise or distrust him, they were none of them going to say so in the unambiguous terms that he'd had thrown at him by his wife. There was nowhere quite as vicious as home and nobody as brutal as your own spouse when it came to telling you what kind of bastard you were.

Lynne arrived with an armful of post.

'My, we're early today,' she said, looking in.

'I'm trying to set a good example. How are you?'

'Oh, I'm fine. And you?'

'Very well, yes.'

Lynne was nominally his secretary but often assumed effective command during his absence. She was a tall, fair-haired woman, somewhere in her thirties. She was coolly efficient and liable to become impatient with those who weren't.

Richard knew she was protective of him and loyal. On occasions she would become over-zealous, waving his desk-diary over him like a whip. When this happened, he also knew he had to resist her, otherwise she would take over completely.

She had disappeared into her own office but now bobbed back into view. 'Oh, yes, and I need to know when you'll be going to London this week.'

It was a question he had been avoiding asking himself. Of course he would have to resume his weekly visits to London soon, or appoint somebody else to go in his place. He couldn't forget that it was these visits that had lent credence to the letters. And Claire certainly wouldn't have forgotten. With her in her present mood, he didn't want to be away from home if it could be avoided.

'Probably Thursday,' he said. 'But I won't be staying. I'll try and fit everything into one day.'

Lynne looked put out. 'But I've already pencilled in a couple of appointments for Friday.'

'Then you'll have to change them. I'll let you know later.'

She flashed him a look of annoyance, a warning that she expected better behaviour than this, and went out, back to her own desk. He could hear her through the open door, slashing and ripping at the mail.

A good thing the blackmailer hadn't sent his evil, little letters here instead of to his home address. He tried to picture Lynne opening them. How would she have reacted? It would have been a severe test of office etiquette, probably undermining the relationship between them as it had his relationship with his wife.

Lynne returned with the filleted mail and also the appointments book. He put out his hand to take it but no, she was going to read to him from it, spelling out whom he was meeting and when. He said nothing till she had finished.

'Thank you.'

'And you are going to London on Thursday? I can take that as definite?'

He was tempted to rebel but he needed his energies for elsewhere. A wise general avoided fighting on two fronts at the same time.

'You can, yes,' he said, yielding to her.

His first meeting was at ten o'clock, with a freelance designer who had pleased them with his first commission and was now being considered for more. After which, Lynne's briefing had made it sound a full day through into the evening. It occurred to him there was something he must do while he still had the time.

He rang down to reception. 'Yvonne?'

'Yes, Mr Gillow?'

'I'm expecting a call today – from a Mr Townsend. Or the caller might just use the name of the company, which is Townsend Investigations.'

'Yes, Mr Gillow.'

'Can you make sure that call's put straight through to me. It doesn't matter what I'm doing or who I'm with – straight through to me, OK?'

Perhaps he was being optimistic in expecting such quick results. Maurice had talked as though he were giving the case top priority but perhaps he talked that way all the time. Richard's case might have gone to the back of a substantial queue. Even so, if there were anything to report, he wanted to hear it immediately without Lynne having the chance to intercept.

The designer came from Tipperary and turned out to have a passion for rugby. Their meeting over-ran by half an hour as they analysed last season's All Blacks tour and, in particular, the way England had pulled something extra out of the hat and run them ragged in the last Test at Twickenham. It turned out they had both been present at that match. They were enthusiastically re-living England's final try when Lynne phoned through. She apologized for interrupting but thought he should know that Simon was waiting for his scheduled meeting and so could Richard please give her some idea of when he might be available?

He told her five minutes but then was delayed beyond that,

discussing prospects for the present season. It was a long time since he had shown such a passionate interest in that world of rugby he had long forsaken.

It put him in mind of Doctor Crippen.

He had once read how Crippen, the notorious wife-murderer, had taken a keen interest in county cricket scores and had them relayed to him virtually up to the moment when they had put the rope around his neck. Richard had always doubted the truth of it but now he began to see how it might be so. The more tragic your life became, the more you clung on to the trivia, seeking a few minutes' distraction. Though he still doubted whether the news that Gloucester had achieved a first innings lead could ever have quite driven out the image of the gallows.

Simon had joined him and they were putting their heads together over a contract for the next three in a series of cookery books when Yvonne came through on the internal phone.

'I've got that Mr Townsend on the line for you, Mr Gillow. The one you asked me to put straight through.'

Richard's heart raced and he swung his chair away from the desk so that Simon shouldn't detect his excitement. Such a quick response must mean Maurice had found her, found Melissa. Surely? Mustn't it?

'Yes, thank you,' he said to Yvonne. 'Put him on.'

Maurice came through. 'Good morning, Mr Gillow.'

'Good morning. It's nice to hear from you so soon. Does this mean we have a positive result?'

'Well, I can't say for sure, but I think we might have, yes.'

Wonderful, thought Richard, bloody wonderful.

He began to swing his chair back, about to ask Simon if he would mind leaving them for a moment, but Maurice was continuing: 'I don't normally like talking about these things over the phone. I wonder if we could meet somewhere later, say over lunchtime?'

The delay was irritating: Richard wanted to hear everything immediately. But he could see the sense in it. He didn't want to discuss things on the phone either, not right there in his office with God-knows-who listening in.

'Yes, I can do that. Where would you suggest?'

Maurice named a city centre pub and they agreed on one

o'clock. Ringing off, Richard called through to Lynne and told
her he could no longer make his lunch appointment and would
she convey his apologies and re-arrange it. She didn't even try to
disguise her disapproval. Yes, she would do it, of course; but her
tone implied – just this once.

The pub in which he had agreed to meet Maurice was
crowded and noisy. Richard arrived first and bought himself a
scotch-and-soda. He was considering that, when Maurice arrived, he should propose that they went elsewhere but then got
lucky with a small table in a reasonably quiet corner.

He saw Maurice enter and look around. Richard stood and
waved to attract his attention. He could be an ageing rock star,
he thought, watching him coming towards him. Better still, a
jazz musician, with his gaunt, besuited figure and the tied-back
pony-tail of grey hair.

They shook hands. Richard insisted he sit down while he
returned to the bar to buy him a drink. There was an exasperating wait to be served before he could return and they were
sitting down together.

'Your good health,' said Maurice, raising his glass.

'Cheers.'

'I hope you don't think I was being over-cautious, not wanting
to speak on the phone –'

'No. No, I think you were quite right.' He would have agreed
to anything so long as it allowed them to move swiftly to the
heart of the matter – *had he found Melissa or not?*

But Maurice was not to be rushed. He took a long pull at his
beer, then positioned his beer-mat carefully before setting it
down. 'Only I promised you confidentiality,' he said. 'Which I
don't believe anybody can guarantee if they're speaking on the
telephone.'

'No.'

'Right, well, I'll tell you the first thing I discovered, shall I?'

'Yes?'

'Wherever else the recession might have hit, there is one
profession which is booming.' He paused, then repeated for
emphasis, 'Booming.'

'What they call the oldest profession . . .?' hazarded Richard.

Maurice nodded. 'The oldest and the newest. There must be

more young women going into prostitution than there are into the armed forces.'

It was an observation Richard hardly felt qualified to contest. He nodded, not wanting to delay Maurice from coming to the point.

'Anyway, I got the evening papers. And I got the magazines from my friendly local newsagent. And then I spent most of yesterday evening on the phone, being offered more-or-less anything you could think of at prices that went from ten pounds upwards.'

But did you find her? He didn't need this preamble, just a simple answer to the only question that mattered.

'But no Melissas,' said Maurice.

Richard stared in sudden alarm. Could the man be serious? Surely he hadn't been brought here, cancelling meetings and hurrying to this less-than-salubrious watering-hole, only to be told that the search had produced nothing?

Maurice must have seen his alarm. 'Not at first,' he added hurried.

'But then —'

'Then I came across a Melissa, yes.'

Richard breathed again. 'And you think this is the one —'

'Well, as for that I can't say. Your instructions were that I wasn't to contact her but that you would do so yourself and so —'

'Where is she?' asked Richard eagerly. 'How do I find her?'

Maurice produced a torn-out fragment of newspaper from his pocket. He laid it on the table between them and flattened it with his hand. 'Here,' he said, pointing.

Richard looked and saw that an advertisement in the Personal Column had been encircled in blue felt-tip.

'The Star Escort Agency,' he read. The advert was no more than a couple of lines long, offering 'a wide choice of intelligent and lovely girls for evening engagements', and giving a number to ring.

Maurice explained: 'I rang them and I asked them did they have a girl who worked for them who was called Melissa. This was the same question I'd been asking all night, so that I was almost ready to ring off before I'd heard the answer. Except that this time the answer was . . . that yes, they did.'

Richard waited for more. When it didn't seem to be forthcoming, he prompted: 'And so what about this Melissa? Does she have a second name? Did they tell you anything else about her?'

Maurice was already shaking his head. He drained the last of his pint before replying. 'I did ask them what they could tell me about her and they said all the usual things about how beautiful she was. I said yes, I'm sure she is, but could they tell me anything else? And they said no, that was all they could tell me, and anyway why did I want to know?'

'Damn,' said Richard quietly.

'I kept trying but all they said was – why don't you ring us back if you want to meet the young lady. And then they put the phone down.'

'Well, thank you for your efforts. So it seems the only way I'm ever going to talk to this young lady . . . is if I make a date with her via this agency.'

It seemed a bizarre notion, but how else was he to get to her? The agency was their only route and the agency was giving nothing away for free.

'I think it is,' agreed Maurice. 'Unless you want me to do that on your behalf.'

'No, I'll do it,' he said. He had an intense curiosity to meet and talk to this woman, who might have the key to the mystery of all that had been happening to him.

'OK. Well, you've got the number there. Just ring that and tell them you want a night out with Melissa.'

'You don't think I should tell them why?'

Maurice shook his head. 'My advice would be to let them think it's a regular date. Let them think you're like all the others and you just want her for sex. Or even something a bit kinky that involves her dressing up as a nurse or something and whipping you. They won't mind that. They'll be happy with that. Just don't let them know you only want to talk to her.'

'Can I keep this?' asked Richard, placing a finger on the piece of newspaper with its precious number.

'Be my guest.' He raised his glass, then seemed to remember that it was empty and set it down again.

'Let me get you another,' said Richard, taking the hint. Though first there was one more thing on which he had wanted Maurice Townsend's advice. He took from his inside pocket the letter that had arrived that morning and tossed it onto the table. 'Have a look at this. The latest in the series.'

Maurice had read it by the time he returned from the bar. 'Very kind of you,' he said, taking the pint that Richard placed before him. 'As for this letter, I assume you're still determined on not paying?'

'I certainly am,' confirmed Richard with feeling. 'Not one penny. You needn't have any doubts about that.'

'I'm glad to hear it.'

'But I was wondering about the address —'

'So was I, yes. A pound to a penny it's just an accommodation address, a letter-drop. Where it says Room 608 . . .'

'Yes?'

'That's probably a reference number. Six hundred and eight rooms . . .? Don't make me laugh. The place is probably a one-room office. Most of its business will be men who subscribe to magazines they don't want delivered at home.'

'And the odd blackmailer,' said Richard.

'Well, yes. But would you like me to check it out anyway?'

'Please.'

Maurice produced a pen and copied the address into a small notebook. Richard took back the letter.

'Now, if you don't mind, I've got to get back to the office,' he said. No doubt Lynne would always be watching the clock. Besides, he couldn't wait to ring the Star Escort Agency and take his next step towards his meeting with Melissa.

Maurice said: 'Can I just offer you a piece of advice, Mr Gillow?'

Surprised, Richard said, 'Please do.'

'Do be careful when you go and meet this woman, won't you. Whatever you do, don't use your real name. And don't tell her anything about yourself. Remember, if she is mixed up in this blackmailing business then there's probably somebody in the background keeping an eye on her.'

Richard thanked him for his advice, and for the good work he'd done. Maurice said he would contact him again once he had something to report on the address given in the latest letter. They shook hands again before Richard left.

Lynne was still at her lunch. Perhaps she was attempting to

demonstrate that she could be just as irresponsible as he could. The bonus was that he was able to shut himself in his office without fear of interruption and dial out the number for Star Escorts.

The phone rang twice, then was picked up.

'Star Escorts. Julie speaking,' said a woman's voice.

Richard cleared his throat. 'I saw your advertisement –'

'Did you, dear, yes.'

'And I . . . well, I wonder if I could arrange to meet one of your young ladies.'

'Of course you can.' The voice, deep-throated as though wreathed in cigarette smoke, had taken on an oily familiarity, coaxing him along. 'And when would this be for?'

'Well, tonight if possible.'

'Yes. And are you in a hotel, dear?'

It was a question he wasn't prepared for. 'Not, er, not at the moment, no.'

'Well, the meeting would have to be in a hotel. Or possibly a restaurant. Our girls don't go to private addresses.'

'Yes, that's all right. I can arrange to be in a hotel.'

'And I'd better explain the charges to you. There's an agency fee of twenty-five pounds. And then the girl charges another seventy. So that's ninety-five altogether. Will that be all right?'

'Fine, yes.'

'So you'll need to have that with you, either in cash or a cheque with a banker's card, and then you can pay it to the girl when you meet her.'

'I understand.'

She didn't come cheap then, this Melissa. Even before the extras, you were looking at what would be an expensive night out by any standards. It encouraged him to think that this must be the lady he was after. He had always pictured her as expensive, not from the bargain-basement end of her profession.

'Well, we have a number of girls for you to choose from –'

'Ah, no,' interrupted Richard. 'It's one particular girl I'd like to meet.'

'And who's that, dear?'

'She's called Melissa.'

There was a pause.

'You do have a Melissa?' he asked, becoming anxious.

'Yes, we do, dear.' She sounded as though she would have preferred it had he named someone else.

'And is she available?'

'To be honest, I can't answer you that straightaway. Do you have a number where I can ring you back?'

He said yes and gave the firm's number, thinking as he did so that here was a problem he hadn't foreseen. He had expected all arrangements to be concluded immediately, not for there to be this need for further calls. For Julie's return call to get through to him, he would have to give her his name, something he was reluctant to do.

Salvation came from the label insert of his telephone which gave the extension number, never used in normal circumstances but a godsend now.

'And ask for extension 21,' he told her.

'Extension 21, yes. Now, if Melissa isn't available, we do have several other girls who're all —'

'No,' he insisted. 'I'm sorry but it has to be Melissa. If she can't make it tonight, then tomorrow night. But it has to be her.'

'Yes, all right, dear. Well, I'll see what I can do.'

'Yvonne?'

'Yes, Mr Gillow?'

'There may be someone calling me this afternoon, asking for extension twenty-one.'

'Yes.'

'That's all they'll say. Extension twenty-one.'

'Extension twenty-one.'

'Can you put them through directly to me. It doesn't matter who I'm with, just put them straight through please.'

'Certainly, Mr Gillow.'

She sounded puzzled, as though, like Lynne, she couldn't understand what had got into him today. Never mind that. He could concentrate on nothing else until he received a return call confirming his meeting with Melissa.

It was like being a love-sick teenager, this waiting for the phone to ring. He should have been going out in the afternoon, to take his invited place on a panel gathering in Manchester Town Hall to discuss 'Manchester And The Arts.'

'Tell them I'm very sorry but I can't be there,' he instructed Lynne.

'And shall I give any reason?' she asked, disapproving.

'Yes, give whatever reason you want.'

Except the truth, he thought – which was that he was waiting for an escort agency to phone him back with news of his date for tonight.

Lynne stared at him, taken aback by the casual response. Clearly she considered that he had taken leave of his senses. She turned and stalked out of the office.

Still the phone refused to ring.

Seeking to kill time, he took up a manuscript that had been recently received from one of the authors on their small fiction list. He read the title and the dedication and then began to read page one. He got to the page three before realizing that he had taken none of it in, not a word. He gave up, closed the manuscript and sat staring at the phone, willing it to ring or bleep or go up in smoke but at least to do *something*.

When finally it did ring, it was a disappointment. He grabbed for the receiver, only to hear Yvonne saying: 'It's a Mr Townsend for you, Mr Gillow. You told me this morning that I was to put him through if –'

'Yes, that's all right. Put him through now.'

Maurice came on the line. Richard had an image of him back in his office, behind his big, gnarled desk. Though why he should be ringing now, so soon after they had spoken in the pub, he couldn't imagine.

'Mr Gillow?'

'Hello.'

'I hope I'm not interrupting anything.'

'Nothing, no.'

'Only I ran some checks on that address, the one in the letter.'

Of course – the address to which he was supposed to deliver the five thousand. He had invested so much hope in his planned meeting with Melissa that it took a real effort for him to respond to this other matter.

'Yes? And did you find anything –'

'It's what we thought. An accommodation address. And not inclined to be very helpful by the sound of things.'

'Well, never mind. Perhaps we'll try them again if I don't get anywhere with this escort agency.'

In an odd way he was heartened by Maurice's failure. It was as though, since their meeting at lunchtime, the two of them had been pursuing rival investigations. Maurice sounded as though he had run into a brick wall, which left Richard comfortably ahead.

Ten minutes later, Yvonne was back on the line. 'I've got that call for you, Mr Gillow. A lady asking for extension twenty-one.'

'Put her on.'

It was the gravel-voiced Julie again. 'Hello?'

'Hello, yes.'

'It's Julie from Star Escorts. You're the gentleman who was asking after Melissa . . .?'

'I am, yes.'

'And you still want to meet her tonight?'

There was a coyness about the way she said this that encouraged Richard to think she must have been successful in rousing Melissa. His spirits lifted.

'I do, yes.'

'Well, I've just spoken to Melissa and she'd like to meet you. So that's nice, isn't it?'

'It is.'

'Now, Melissa suggested eight o'clock,' said Julie, becoming more brisk, wanting to close the deal. 'Would that be all right?'

'Eight o'clock would be fine.'

'And, like I say, we do have to insist on hotel or restaurant premises —'

'I understand, yes.'

'There's somewhere I can suggest if that would be agreeable to you.'

'Please do.'

'Well, it's very pleasant and I'm sure you'll have no trouble finding it. Do you know the Queens Hotel? They've a very nice bar and you can meet Melissa in there — unless you've any objections?'

9

Richard raised no objections at all to meeting Melissa in the Queens Hotel. In fact, it was all he could do to stop himself giving a shout of triumph when Julie suggested it.

Wasn't this proof beyond question that this woman he was meeting was the Melissa? It would be too monstrous a coincidence otherwise. The Queens Hotel hadn't been his choice. It had been the choice of the agency or perhaps even of Melissa herself. It had to be significant that, out of all the possible meeting places in Manchester, this particular hotel had been chosen. It was here that, according to the letters, he was supposed to have met Melissa on at least four previous occasions.

And now he was going to meet her for real. The prospect of coming face to face with this mystery woman, this fiction that he was supposed to have been intimate with and been photographed with, excited and preoccupied him. He left his desk and prowled the room. He must prepare his game-plan, decide how he would approach her and what he would say.

He wondered whether he should let Claire know what was going on but decided against it. She would only dismiss the whole thing as another of his stunts.

Though he would let her know that he would be late home. They might not be eating together or sleeping together and their marriage might be on the brink, but they were still residing in the same house. It wouldn't hurt to show some basic consideration.

In fact, it was Diane who answered the phone. When he said hello and asked her how she was, she fell silent.

'What's the matter?' he said, alarm-bells sounding. 'Has something happened?'

'Has mum not called you?'

'No. Why? Should she have?'

'She's gone away. And, before you ask, I don't know where or for how long. She wouldn't tell me. She just said she can't stand being in the house anymore when you . . . ' Her voice gave way to silence, as though, whatever her mother's words had been, she couldn't bring herself to repeat them.

'It's all right, darling,' he said, desperately sorry for his daughter, that she should have been left to be the messenger between them like this. 'Don't worry. I can imagine the kind of things she must have said.'

'Well, you don't have to imagine them. You can read them. There's a letter she's left for you.'

A letter sounded serious. As though she were taking a considered step and not just acting on impulse. Did this mean that he should go home now? Should he drop everything and forget about meeting Melissa? Yet what could he do if Claire had already taken flight?

'She's actually gone?' he said, trying to get things clear in his mind.

'Yes. She went about an hour ago.'

'And how're you? I mean would you like me to come home?'

'No! Well, I mean don't come especially for my sake. I'm perfectly all right. I just hate having to be the one to tell you.'

She was beginning to sound more like her usual self, resenting his suggestion that she might need looking after. Perhaps he should stick to his original intention and stay in town to meet Melissa after all. Most persuasive was the thought that out of that meeting might come the information he needed to persuade Claire back again.

'Darling, I'm sorry you've had to be the one to tell me too. But don't distress yourself. You know what this is all about. It's about those letters, nothing else.'

'She said . . .'

'Yes?'

'She said she couldn't stand having to listen to you lying any longer.'

He could imagine Claire saying it and the bitterness her words would have contained. It hurt him that she should have had fled like this while his back was turned. They had always prided themselves on their ability to talk honestly, solving whatever problems had cropped up over the years across the dinner-table with the help of a glass or two of wine. It might have been that they had both placed too much faith in 'honest talk' and been caught off-guard when such talk had slid so abruptly into acrimony and mistrust. But to run away and leave him with a letter . . .?

He felt it as a sad betrayal after all those years and all the love that had been between them.

'I suppose it's my fault,' he said into the phone, his voice suddenly hoarse. 'I should never have shown your mother the letters. I should have just . . . I don't know, just thrown them away.'

'It's whoever wrote them, it's their fault,' said Diane, in a voice so low he had to strain to hear.

He pictured her alone in that large house, no longer the secure home in which she had grown up but a battle-ground contaminated by their exchanges. He wanted to take her in his arms and promise her, as he had when she'd been a child with a cut knee, that the pain would stop and everything would be all right again.

'I'll get home as soon as I can,' he said. 'I've got some business which is going to keep me in town this evening. But I won't be late.'

She brushed this aside, saying she would probably be out whatever time he returned and repeating that he mustn't rush back on her account.

He decided not to contest that, lest things should develop into an argument. He suspected it was for his sake she was being brave, wanting to avoid adding to his anxieties.

He applied himself to the tasks of the afternoon, seeking refuge in them. With every hour that went by he was learning more about how those people whose marriages were collapsing about their heads managed to keep smiling at the office. Whatever the complexities of business, they were child's play compared to the tortuous web that he and Claire and the anonymous blackmailer had woven between them. He even rode Lynne's continuing disapproval with a smile, dictating and signing his usual complement of letters.

Just once, when there was a gap in his schedule – somebody had gone and the next person due in hadn't arrived yet and so he had a minute or two alone – he felt the full force of Claire's departure. She had been his life, virtually the whole of his adult life. The thought that he might have to exist without her made him catch his breath. For a moment the room swirled and eddied about him.

He would do anything at all to save himself from that.

At half-past five his staff began to leave. He heard them calling out their goodbyes below him. Lynne stopped by to let him know she was leaving too. Either she had forgotten his strange behaviour of earlier or she had forgiven him for it. Anyway, she was all smiles when saying goodbye, making sure he didn't want her for anything else before she went. By six o'clock the building was sounding empty.

Richard had not moved since Lynne's departure. He sat at his desk, listening to the traffic outside. Where was Claire now, he wondered. Was she already regretting leaving, or had she found it a tremendous release?

He was tormented by the thought of the letter she had left him. As if their lives hadn't been plagued by letters, near enough destroyed by them! Still, he must be patient. He could do nothing about it until he got home. Then he might discover more of why she had gone away. Was it only for a short while to allow things to cool between them or did she intend it to be a final and irrevocable break?

It was seven twenty-five according to the clock above the reception desk of the Queens Hotel. He had planned to be early so that he might see Melissa before she saw him. That way he could approach her in his own good time and not have her come upon him suddenly, catching him off guard.

He glanced around but could see no-one who struck him as a potential Melissa. He left reception and went through into the bar.

Strange to think how, last time he was here, he had had Claire beside him, albeit unwillingly, and had been demonstrating to her how no-one recognized him and so he couldn't possibly have been here before. She, of course, had seen it as a demonstration not of his innocence but of his cunning. And so they had hit the downward path, which they'd been on ever since.

He was wiser now, and more cautious. He had relied on his

innocence for too long, believing it to be a life-raft that would keep him afloat. Only now did he realize how high were the seas and how fast he would have to bail.

He surveyed the bar as he entered it, looking for anyone who might fit, however remotely, the ringing endorsement that the agency had given Melissa.

But there were no single women that he could see. A few single men, yes, as you'd expect in any bar that time of the evening, hunched over their drinks. And a man and woman at the far end, absorbed in one another. But no woman on her own.

There was a line of tables parallel to the bar, each with its own tiny light and green shade. The place seemed quieter and less garish than it had on his first visit when he had stormed through with Claire in his wake.

He advanced to the bar and ordered a whisky and soda from the barman. Waiting for it to be served, he looked back to the door but no-one had followed him in. He looked at his watch. It was now seven twenty-eight. Still early. He took his drink and retreated to one of the tables, positioning himself so that he could see the door. He wanted to be able to appraise anyone coming in before they caught sight of him.

He found it difficult to picture the woman he was about to meet, or to anticipate her in any way. Oh, he had been given a full description by Julie over the phone: 'Melissa's very beautiful, like a model. She's five foot six, a brunette, with a nice, slim figure. In fact, one of our most beautiful girls. I'm sure you're going to have a very nice evening together.' But what did that add up to, other than an agency's blurb on one of the prostitutes they were pimping for?

There must be men who used prostitutes regularly. Face it. There had to be, otherwise how could there be such a multitude of them? There must be men who got to know them and felt at ease with them. Perhaps they felt more at ease than they ever did with a woman they *weren't* paying for. He couldn't imagine it, and had never done it.

Well, except . . . there had been one occasion, so long ago and so wreathed about with drink and shame that he could barely recall it. He had been a student at Oxford and he had spent the long vac holidaying with friends in Germany. They travelled on the *Deutsche Bundesbahn* and ended up in Munich, where they visited the Oktoberfest. Their first night there had found them putting back the foaming steins of beer at a rare pace. After a while, events became confused and were hazy five minutes after they'd happened so that Richard never understood how he came to lose his companions or to find his way to the *Bordellgegend*. Suddenly there was a young lady murmuring, '*Komm mit mir, Liebling.*' Their negotiations tested his German to destruction, then she set off briskly, instructing him to follow.

The only thing he could recall about her was that she had a streaming cold and laced up boots. And that she was a blonde probably, though he couldn't be too sure about that. They had gone to a hotel room. He recalled climbing the wooden stairs behind her and then going into a shabby room with a pink chenille eiderdown on the bed. He had begun to unbutton his shirt but she had objected, '*Du brauchst dich nicht auszuziehen*', gesturing that he need remove only his pants. Then she had hitched up her skirt and lowered her frilly knickers and arranged herself to receive him on the pink eiderdown.

Checking his money the following morning, he found much less than he had expected and wondered if she had robbed him. But then he couldn't remember what payment had been agreed and so he did nothing, never even admitting to his companions what had happened.

A single woman was approaching the bar but she was a blonde, coming not even close to the description he'd been given. She was now being joined by another blonde, which put her definitely out of the running. Whatever else Melissa might turn out to be, he was confident she would be alone.

The two women ordered drinks, attracting speculative glances from the men along the bar.

Early in their married life, when he had been heavily into the socially demanding world of rugby – as well as being a novice in the world of publishing, which had its own fair share of corporate piss-ups – he and Claire had been regular attenders of receptions and launches and dinners, coming almost nightly into just such a bar as he was now in to be greeted and handed drinks. There would be half-an-hour of jovial banter as others arrived and the bar would become overfull. The noise and the crush would become unbearable and then be suddenly relieved by a general exodus towards the dining-room or the ballroom or wherever the main event was taking place.

Looking back now, he could see how, in those first crucial years of their marriage, Claire had slowly but inexorably dissociated them from such goings-on.

She had never really enjoyed being one of a crowd and having to shout to be heard. She had conducted a low-level campaign to have him more to herself, leaving less of him for that public, hotel-bar world that he'd been used to knocking around in.

And, the truth could not be denied – she had succeeded.

Where were they now, his rugby pals, his drinking pals, his golfing pals? Not totally exiled – there had been a sprinkling of them at their Silver Wedding. But nor were they a major part of his life. Always cleverer than he was, Claire had manoeuvred him away from them. Having done that, she had then kept them away from him. In the process, she had turned him from a man who *happened* to be married to one who was married first and foremost.

All this she had done so slowly and so gently that he had barely noticed. Certainly he had never raised any substantial objections. He had been persuaded by her that that was the way he wanted his life to be.

A young woman had arrived at the bar. Lost in his own thoughts, Richard had failed to notice her. Now he saw her, and felt a rush of adrenalin.

He glanced at his watch and saw it was only a minute or two before the agreed hour of eight o'clock.

As far as he could judge, she seemed to be in her late twenties or early thirties. She was dark-haired, though how dark was difficult to tell under the half-lights of the bar. She was wearing high heels and what looked like some sort of lightweight suit in peach or perhaps primrose – the lighting was discreet to a fault.

Was this her? Was this *Melissa*?

Julie had said: 'Oh, and she'll have a red handbag with her. A bright red handbag. So that's something you can look out for if you're not sure.'

The problem was that this woman had her back to him. Any

handbag she might be carrying she would have placed on the bar where he couldn't see it.

There was only one way to resolve things. He stood up and, taking his drink, went to the bar and stood beside her. Coming up close, he saw that her hair was raven black and hung straight to her shoulders. She was fishing out coins from her handbag. He glimpsed a firm nose and a wide, lipsticked mouth. The handbag was a matching red, which encouraged him to speak.

'Excuse me,' he said. 'I'm looking for someone called Melissa.'

She turned towards him. He found himself looking into a pair of wary, blue eyes under dark eyebrows. She made no reply for a moment, as though she were assessing him, coming to a decision.

'And your name is . . .?' she said, in a voice that surprised him. It sounded educated, cultured even.

'Stephen,' he said.

He had been asked his name by Julie when they had been negotiating over the phone. 'Just your first name or any name, it doesn't matter,' she said. 'Just a name so that Melissa will know you.' He had borne in mind Maurice's warning and so shied away from using his real name. He had given his second name, which had been his father's, choosing it as the only other one it would be impossible for him to forget.

The woman gave a restrained smile of acknowledgement. 'Yes, I'm Melissa,' she said.

The barman had brought her a drink. 'One pound twenty-five,' he said, pushing a glass towards her.

'Oh, let me get that,' Richard said.

'That's very kind of you,' she said, dropping the coins back into her bag.

He saw it as a signal: from here on in he would pay for everything. Clearly she saw him as no different from any other punter, a sad man wanting company. She was anticipating an evening's work that would be little different from the last such evening or the one that might be to follow.

It removed one bizarre possibility that had plagued Richard: what would he have done had she appeared to recognize him? Even worse, if she had greeted him by his name and made reference to the four nights they were already supposed to have spent together in that very hotel?

He had been spared that surrealist nightmare. The one thing established so far was that he was as much a stranger to her as she to him.

'Keep the change,' he said to the barman, handing him two pounds.

'Thank you, sir.'

He was aware of the glances he was attracting from the other men along the bar. Were they impressed by his technique? Or were they men of a wide and sleazy world and recognized the situation for what it was? Either way, he felt conspicuous. He was about to suggest that they moved away to a table but she was ahead of him.

'I think we need somewhere more private, don't you?' she said. 'Let's go and sit down.'

Scarcely waiting for his agreement, she moved away from the bar and left him to follow.

'The agency explained about the payment, did they?'

'Oh, yes. Yes, ninety-five pounds.'

'Well, that's not all for me,' she said, in what sounded like a routine line. 'But that's what it comes to, yes.'

He reached for his wallet, then checked, conscious they were still in full view of anyone at the bar who cared to look in their direction.

'You want me to –'

'You can give it me now, of course you can,' she said briskly. 'Nobody's watching.'

She hadn't even looked towards the bar and so couldn't have known whether they were watching or not. She didn't care whether they were watching. She was hardened to this. He passed her the small wad of notes, which she counted before dropping them into her bag.

Yet, for all he could see that she had played this game before, he was pleasantly surprised by her composure and easy manner. He had been fearing, well, someone coarser. He could also admire the simple elegance of her appearance: a silk chemise beneath the suit with just the odd piece of jewellery. She as an attractive, elegant woman, distinctly superior to his *Strichmäd-chen* of distant memory.

'Right, well, that's that out of the way,' she said, snapping her handbag shut. 'So, Stephen . . . is that what you want me to call you?'

'If you wouldn't mind,' he said, treading carefully. 'You'll only confuse me with anything else.'

He couldn't understand why she should have asked such a question. She couldn't possibly know that Stephen wasn't his real name . . . could she?

She must have seen his puzzlement. 'It's just that clients sometimes like to use an alias when they make the booking,' she explained. 'But then once we meet . . . well, they sometimes prefer to switch back to their own names.'

'No, I'm not clever enough for that,' he said.

'So it is Stephen?'

'Yes.'

He had the odd feeling of being on the defensive. Why was he the one who was covering up and lying and pretending to be somebody he wasn't when he had come specifically to accuse her of these things?

She said: 'Before we talk about anything else, there's something I'd like to ask you, Stephen.'

'Please do.'

'The lady you must have spoken to on the phone, Julie . . .?'

'Yes.'

'She said that you'd asked for me specially.'

'I did, yes.'

'So why was that? Why me in particular? Because we haven't met before, have we?'

'No,' he said, wishing he had a record of that statement – *we haven't met before, have we*. Though he was also wondering how to answer her. What excuse could he give for having asked for her by name? 'Let's just say you came highly recommended,' he improvised desperately.

To his surprise, she seemed satisfied with this.

'Oh, I did? Well, thank you. I really shouldn't ask, should I. After all, we aren't here to talk about other people. We're here to talk about you.'

'Well, we can talk about you as well,' he countered.

'No, I'm not very interesting. Tell me about you. Where do you live? Surely you can tell me that?'

There was a glibness about this new line of questioning.

Where her initial quizzing of him had betrayed a genuine interest – *why was that? why me in particular?* – he sensed that she was now embarked upon her performance for the evening. Possibly it was one of several, scripted, rehearsed, and performed on many such nights as this.

'I live in Cheshire,' he said.

'And so what brings you here, into Manchester?'

'Well, I work in Manchester, so I was here anyway. But I'm here tonight to meet you.'

'Oh, isn't that nice,' she exclaimed, showing her even teeth. 'And I'm certainly here to meet you so – let's make a night of it, shall we?'

She had become coy and seductive, and was leaning across the table, smiling into his face. She has had enough of the chit-chat, he thought, and now wants to move things along.

Well, yes, let's do that – but not in the direction she wants. It was time he took control and let her know that this wasn't just another sad man she could smile at and flirt with so that she could tease even more money out of him. This was one night she was going to remember.

He sat forward himself so that their faces were almost touching.

'What's your *real* name?' he said.

He saw the wary, appraising look return to her eyes. Then she smiled and sat back in her chair. 'Melissa,' she said calmly.

'That's your *real* name?' he challenged.

'It is for tonight, yes.'

'Melissa what?'

'Just Melissa.'

'And you've done this sort of thing before, have you?'

She flinched slightly at that.

'Yes, I have,' she said, the seduction now gone completely from her voice. 'Why? Does that bother you?'

He sensed that his time was running out. Whatever he wanted to say had to be said quickly, before she gave up on him altogether.

'No, it doesn't bother me. In fact, it rather interests me.'

He had said the wrong thing, or anyway she took it the wrong way. She leaned forward again, the seduction switched back on like a light. 'Does it now? Well, we can talk about that. I don't mind. And you must tell me what else interests you so that we can decide just what it is you'd like us to do tonight.'

He shook his head. 'No –'

'No? Then I'll make some suggestions, shall I, and you tell me which –'

'No, no, I didn't mean that,' he said, stopping her again.

She sighed and folded her arms. It was a warning: she was not going to stand being messed about like this for much longer.

Richard said quietly, 'I am not looking for company in the sense that . . . well, in the sense that you normally provide it.'

'So what are you looking for?' She was watching him intently. No doubt she was trying to work out where this was leading, what kind of nutcase she'd got on her hands here.

'It's something I want to talk to you about,' said Richard. 'I mean *you* in particular.'

'And why me in particular?'

'Because I think you might be able to help me.'

'Go on.'

'I'm being blackmailed.'

She said nothing.

'I've received some letters. And what they say . . . what these letters say . . . is that I'm having an affair with somebody called Melissa.'

She frowned. 'Me?'

'I don't know. That's why I wanted to meet you.'

'You think this is some sort of set-up?'

'No,' he said quickly. 'Please don't think I'm accusing you of anything –'

'Just blackmail.'

'No, I'm not *accusing* you –'

'Then what?'

'I'm saying *somebody's* been blackmailing me –'

'Because of some woman called Melissa.'

'Yes –'

She shook her head, as though despairing of him. 'Look, I'm sorry, but I don't think I can help you –'

'The other thing these letters say is that I'm supposed to have met this woman in this hotel.'

She sighed. 'Do they really.'

'Yes. Four times I'm supposed to have stayed here with her.'

When she spoke again, she did do slowly and deliberately as though to a child. 'And did you?'

'Well, no –'

'No,' she said firmly, as though that concluded that.

For the first time since they had sat down together, she stopped looking directly at Richard and turned away to look across the room to where more people, a mixed group on some night out, had arrived at the bar and were engaged in friendly argument as they tried to put their order together. Perhaps she was reassuring herself that there were other people in the vicinity in case the lunatic she'd been landed with turned violent.

He needed to do something to unsettle her, to impress her with the seriousness of what he was saying.

'I'm afraid I lied to you a few moments ago.'

'You did?' she said.

'Yes. when I told you that Stephen was my real name. It's not.'

'That's all right,' she said flatly. 'You didn't want me to know your real name. You're not the first.'

'My real name is Richard Gillow.' He repeated it: 'Richard Gillow.'

She gave a sudden frown and her eyes narrowed. He saw that he had, at last, jolted her. She had been unable to disguise the fact that his name meant something to her. Now she was staring at him as though trying to assess what kind of threat he might pose.

'That's *your* name?'

'It is, yes. Look, I can prove it to you.'

He took out one of his business cards and held it for her to read. Despite Maurice's warnings, he was no longer concerned about what she might find out about him. In fact, he now *wanted* her to know who he was. It was not only that she had recognized his name, though she had certainly done that, but it had shocked her to hear it.

'You've heard that name before,' he challenged her.

'No, I can't say that I have,' she said, but it was a denial that carried little conviction.

'Oh, I think you have, yes,' he insisted. 'And I think you were very surprised when I told you it was my name. Now, why was that?'

She made no reply but, before he realized what she was planning, she had got to her feet and was hurrying away towards the door.

'No, wait . . .!' he called.

She paid him no attention but disappeared out of the bar. Richard cursed as he struggled to pull back his chair on the heavy carpet. Then he ran from the bar in pursuit.

10

Faces turned towards him as he sprinted through the hotel lobby. He leapt over a low table rather than have to slow down for a group of air crew arriving together. A distorted and fragmented glimpse of Melissa offered itself to him through the glass of the revolving door. As he attempted to follow her, an elderly woman entering from outside forced him to match his pace to hers so that he shuffled through the door with an agonizing slowness.

The street outside was quiet. He heard immediately the clacking of high-heels echoing from the surrounding buildings, and then he saw her. She was running, handbag tucked under her arm and hair streaming behind her.

'Wait!' he called, and started after her.

Suddenly she slowed and began to wave and shout. He saw she was trying to catch the attention of a taxi which was coming towards her. Now he was gaining upon her with every stride. He reached her about the same time that the taxi did and managed to grab her by the shoulder even as it was slowing to a halt.

'No!' he shouted to the cab driver, and waved frantically, indicating that he shouldn't stop but should continue down the road. He saw the cabbie's startled features. Melissa pulled forward, trying to grab the door handle but she was too late. The taxi accelerated away. Clearly its driver wanted no part of whatever might be going on.

Melissa was twisting and turning, trying to wriggle free. 'Let go of me!' she gasped.

'Listen to me, will you, just listen!' pleaded Richard.

'Help!' she cried, but she was too out of breath and there were too few people around for there to be much chance of help arriving.

'I'm not going to harm you,' he said, now grabbing her by

both arms and pulling her round to face him. 'I only want to talk to you.'

She was panting heavily. Her face, up close to his, was a mask of panic. Her heavy perfume engulfed both of them.

'Let me go!'

'No! Not until you've calmed down and we've been able to talk!'

'I don't want to talk to you!'

'So who would you rather talk to? You'd rather talk to the police?'

He saw a new, different fear come into her eyes and knew this was where she was vulnerable. Of the two of them, she had the most to hide.

'Yes, let's do that, shall we,' he said. 'Let's go to the police. You wanted help? I'm sure they'll give you all the help in the world.'

He attempted to pull her along the pavement, as though he really were intent on delivering her to the nearest police-station. She resisted fiercely. She clawed at his hands, raking the backs of them with her nails.

'Just let me go!' she said, 'You're hurting me!'

'What, you don't want to go to the police? You've changed your mind about that help you were asking for?'

'Get off,' she grunted and struck at him with her nails again, drawing blood from the back of his hand.

'I'll get off when you agree to talk to me.'

'Help!' she called again.

He knew he had to calm her down. It could only be a matter of time before somebody took notice of their struggle and her cries. 'Listen to me,' he said. 'Just *listen* for God's sake, and then I promise I'll let you go.'

She said nothing but at least she stopped struggling. She stood, breathing heavily, staring dully at him as he spoke.

'If you won't talk to me, well, all right, there isn't much I can do about that, not just now. So I'll let you go in a minute, just like you want me to. And then you can call a taxi and you can get it to take you home – wherever that is. And I bet it's a nice, respectable home, isn't it, yes? A nice, respectable home, where nobody knows anything about what you get up to in the Queens Hotel. Meanwhile I'll go to the police. 'Cause, you see, they've already seen the letters. They've already read your name in them. And now they'll know where to find you. All they have to do is go to the agency, go and talk to Julie, and she'll give them your address, won't she. Or at least your phone number, she must have that —'

Her terror at such a prospect gave her a new and desperate strength. She jerked away from him, breaking from his grip. For an instant she was free, but he was too quick for her and had hold of her again before she could run.

'No, wait —'

'Bastard!' she sobbed.

'Yes, I am, and you'd better remember that. I'm certainly enough of a bastard to make sure that your respectable little life will never be the same again. Because, after the police have finished with you, everybody is going to know what you do, aren't they. Everybody is going to know about *Melissa!*'

He was being a bastard and he knew it. He had never before bullied and threatened a woman like this, but what choice did he have? She was his only chance of salvation. After all that he had gone through to get to her, he couldn't simply let her go and watch as she disappeared back into the night.

He felt her body go slack, as if in surrender. He let his own grip on her relax. She was watching him through the strands of black hair that had flopped across her face during the chase and their struggle. From the elegant and poised young woman who had arrived at the bar of the hotel, she had become a cornered animal, weighing up where its best chances of survival might lie.

'I'm sorry,' he said, 'but it's as simple as that. Either you talk to me or you'll end up talking to the police.'

She swept her hair back and gazed up at him. 'How do I know you won't go to the police anyway?'

He sensed the beginnings of a negotiation and was encouraged.

'Well, for one thing, I give you my word —'

'I'm sure you do,' she said, scornful.

'All right, you don't have to take my word. Look at it this way — I need your help. I can embarrass you by going to the police, perhaps I can even ruin your life, but what good does that do me?' He looked into her fearful, calculating eyes and repeated slowly: 'I need your help.'

'What sort of help?'

'I just want you to talk to me. Answer some questions.'

'Suppose I can't answer them?'

He shrugged. 'Then we'll leave it at that. Let's just go some-where we can sit down and talk. Whenever you want to go, you can just stand up and walk out. That's all I'm asking. In return, I promise you won't ever have to see me again.'

Taking a chance, he let go of her arm and stepped back. She might bolt again or simply stand and scream for help now she had got her breath back. He could only hope and pray that her terror of the police and public exposure would be sufficient to stop her doing either.

There was a pub on the opposite side of the road – the Golden Ball. Its doors stood open in the evening heat, showing a near-empty interior, just a few young men leaning against the bar and watching the television-set that was high above it. It struck Richard as distinctly unappealing. However, Melissa insisted she preferred it to going back into the Queens Hotel and so they crossed the road and entered its warm haze of beer and tobacco smells. He left her sitting at a corner table, then kept a discreet eye on her while he bought their drinks.

'Cheers,' he said, placing a brandy and ginger before her.

'Thanks.'

She had tucked back her hair and tidied her make-up while he had been at the bar. 'Oh, look at your hand!' she said, seeing the scratches.

'Don't worry about that. And, listen, I'm sorry about all that. I didn't mean to frighten you.'

She shrugged. 'You're paying for the privilege. I just hope you're not going to ask for your money back.'

'Sorry?'

'The seventy pounds –'

'Oh . . . no.' He hadn't considered it. 'No, I'm paying for your company and, well, here you are.'

'Not much choice, have I?'

It dismayed him that she still seemed hostile and on the defensive. He needed her cooperation. What's more, he'd prom-ised her that, once she'd answered his questions, then he wouldn't try and stop her leaving. All she had to do was sit tight for ten minutes, then walk out, leaving him nowhere.

He noticed that she was tentatively exploring the top of her arms where he had gripped her.

'Did I hurt you? I'm sorry –'

'It's OK. So – what do you want to know?'

Well, everything. The problem was knowing how much she could tell him. He still didn't know whether she was an accomplice of the blackmailer or as innocent a dupe as he was himself.

He decided to ignore what he had already told her and go back to the beginning. 'I've received several blackmail letters, accusing me of staying at that hotel where we met with somebody called Melissa. The letters say there are photographs of me doing so. And – the real mystery – the hotel agree. They say yes, their records show I was there.'

She gave a wry smile. 'Well, you should know whether you were there or not.'

'I do know. I know that I wasn't.'

'And isn't that enough for you?'

'No, because I'm still being blackmailed. What about you? Have you ever stayed there?'

She said, 'Yes.'

'Have you ever stayed there with a man who called himself Richard Gillow?'

She hesitated, then said, 'I have, yes.'

'And it wasn't me?'

'It wasn't you, no.'

'And this was recently, earlier this summer?'

'Yes, it was.'

Richard gave a sigh of relief. 'Thank you,' he said. 'Thank you for telling me that.'

He was pleased and surprised at how quickly they'd got to the heart of the matter. It was as though the jury had returned sooner than expected and declared in his favour.

'And I'm sorry,' she said. 'It must have all been pretty unpleasant for you.' She reached for her bag and snapped open the clasp. 'Look, you must take the money back. I'm sorry, I didn't mean –'

She was pulling out the wad he had given her. Tenners spilled onto the sticky surface of the table top.

'No, no,' he said, putting his hands over hers, as though to scoop it all back into the bag. 'There's no reason why I shouldn't pay you for your time –'

'Like they all do, yes? Like they all pay me for my time . . .?' she said bitterly.

He realized with surprise that she was near to tears. Perhaps he had frightened her more than he had intended. Certainly the hostility she had been showing towards him seemed to have gone. He sensed that she might be rather less hard-boiled than she had been acting. Now she couldn't manage the act anymore, or perhaps didn't even want to.

He scooped up the money and pushed it back into the top of the bag. 'There, you keep that. And I'll go and get you another drink for when you've finished that one.'

She shook her head and managed a faint, tearful smile. 'Thanks but there's no need. I'll be all right.' Then she shook her head again and said, 'Oh, God,' as though despairing of something, which might have been herself or just the way things had turned out. She took out a tissue and blew her nose. She pushed back her hair and only when she was composed again, in her own good time, did she meet his gaze across the table.

'I'm sorry,' she said. 'I don't know why I didn't just tell you these things straight out, instead of trying to . . . to run away!' And she blew her nose again.

'No, I'm the one who's sorry –'

'No –'

'I frightened you. I can only say I didn't intend –'

'It's all right,' she said, stopping him. 'I've had worse. But we're here now so . . . what else is it that you want to know?'

He considered for a moment, then said, 'This man you stayed at the hotel with.'

'Yes.'

'Can you tell me about him? *Anything* about him?'

She nodded, as though acknowledging the fairness of the question: she could hardly expect him not to ask that. 'I met him through the agency,' she said. 'The same way that I met you tonight. In fact, it was exactly the same arrangement.'

'And he said his name was Richard Gillow?'

'Well, not at first. No, at first he called himself . . . Stephen I think it was.' She corrected herself quickly: 'I mean Graham. No, *you* were Stephen, weren't you. Sorry.'

The apology was for letting him see how they were all the same to her, these men sheltering behind aliases while they handed her rolls of money.

'He made the booking under the name of Graham?'

'Yes.'

'What did he look like?'

'Oh, well . . . ' she grimaced. 'I'm not very good at this. He was about your age, and average . . . you know, height . . . build. Not as tall as you. And he was fair. Had blue eyes. And he wore glasses for reading with because he had to put them on for the menu.'

It was an identikit picture that could have fitted half the male population of Manchester. It called no-one in particular to mind. Still, he was grateful to her, aware she was now trying her best to help him.

'Also,' she said, 'he was very well-spoken.'

'Yes?'

'I would say he was well-educated. And he knew about wine. And about food. I mean he was very self-assured when it came to ordering.'

It was beginning to sound as though his *doppelganger* had done him justice. No yobbo this but a gentleman fraudster of the old school.

'So when did he claim he was Richard Gillow?'

'Oh, well, we were in the middle of dinner and, to be honest, it was pretty hard going. I could hardly get a word out of him. Then suddenly he started talking and I couldn't stop him. And the first thing he told me was that his name wasn't . . . '

She hesitated.

'Graham,' he prompted.

'Wasn't Graham, but he was really called Richard. Then, later on, when he was talking about his publishing company, that was when he mentioned his second name – Gillow – because it was the name of the firm.'

He reeled, unprepared for the sucker-punch. 'He told you he was a publisher . . .?'

'Yes. Oh, I see. What, you mean you're . . . .?'

He nodded. 'A publisher, yes.'

'Oh, dear,' she said.

He sensed that she was as shaken by that as he was. The man

she had dined with had borrowed not only Richard's name but at least part of his identity. Perhaps now she would realize how finely spun was this web in which they were both held.

'He was very convincing,' she said.

'Convincing . . .?'

'What I mean – I've been out with men who've told me they've been airline pilots and film producers, and I haven't believed a word, but this man –'

'You believed him.'

'I did, yes. There was one meal when we talked about nothing else. He gave me a whole lecture on the importance of the title and cover design and how you had to maintain a balanced . . . *list*? Is that what it's called –'

'Yes.'

'I never doubted him for a minute.'

'I should employ him,' said Richard drily.

Or kill him, he thought.

But he didn't say that aloud. He didn't want to do or say anything that might revive her earlier fears of him. Her answers were immediate and without guile, so much so that he had become convinced of her innocence where the blackmail was concerned. She couldn't possibly have written the letters or been in cahoots with whoever had, not given the way she was now answering his questions.

'What else did he tell you about himself?'

'Oh, that he was something of a sportsman, went ski-ing and scuba-diving, that sort of thing. And he'd once played for England at . . . soccer, was it?'

He shook his head. 'Rugby.'

'Rugby, yes.' She put her hand to her mouth, as though realizing she had spoken out-of-turn. 'Oh, no, that wasn't you as well, was it?'

'It was, yes. Go on, what else did he tell you?'

'Well, he had a wife.'

'Called . . .?'

'No, I don't think he told me her name. But I do remember that she was in business herself. She was some sort of design-er . . .' He was about to prompt her but she remembered of her own accord and declared triumphantly: 'A textile designer!'

Nothing surprised him anymore. Or perhaps the only surprise

would have been if the impostor had made a mistake and got some detail wrong.

'Spot on,' he said.

'That's what your wife is?'

'Yes.'

'At least you know I'm not making this up.'

'I do. So go on.'

'You want to hear some more about yourself?'

'As much as there is.'

'Well, you have two children.'

'Go on.'

'Boy and a girl. Both very clever. One went to university and the other's still there, but I can't remember which is which.'

'My son went to Oxford, now lives in Wales and lectures in computer sciences.'

'Yes. Yes, I think —'

'Daughter's doing Russian Studies at Cambridge.'

'Right!' She clapped her hands together, as though pleased by their success in completing the jigsaw together. Then she pulled a little face. 'Though I suppose it must seem even more weird to you. I mean not only does he use your name but he knows all these things about you.'

It was a shrewd diagnosis; he had no option but to agree. 'It's weird all right. To begin with, I imagined this man must simply have taken my name at random from somewhere, say from the telephone directory. But obviously there's nothing random about it.'

'He knows you.'

'He knows me very well by the sound of it. Is there anything else you can remember about him? Or anything else that he might have said?'

She frowned, thinking back, then said, 'He told me about your house.'

'Yes?'

'It has a big garden, six bedrooms, and it has . . . what? Something that makes it easily noticed. A spire or a —'

'A turret,' he said, nodding.

She smiled. 'He made it sound very nice.'

He wondered if she were teasing him. He could hardly blame her. No doubt this business did have its funny side. Hadn't it all begun with the hilariously incomprehensible blackmailer's letter, a joke he had been happy to share with his wife?

'It is a very nice house. Or, anyway, it was. It hasn't been quite so nice since these letters started arriving.'

She interpreted: 'Because you and your wife have been worrying about them?'

'Because we've been *arguing* about them,' Richard corrected her. 'Because my wife believes them.'

'I'm sorry to hear that. Though actually it does remind me of something else. That is, something else that the other Richard Gillow said.'

'Yes?'

'He said that he didn't get on with his wife.'

Richard frowned. Though such a thing might well be said of his own marriage now, it couldn't have been said, not truthfully, at a time which pre-dated the letters. And yet this was what the alternative Richard Gillow had told Melissa. It suggested a man of extraordinary powers. Not only could he talk authoritatively about the real Richard Gillow's past and present but also about his future . . .!

'Didn't get on with her how?'

'He said she had no time for him. She was too wrapped up in her own life.' She hesitated, then asked: 'I mean does that apply to you too?'

'I suppose it does now, yes. But it didn't used to. We . . . my wife and I . . . we got on very well before this fiasco started.'

'Oh, I am sorry,' she said, with what struck him as a genuine sympathy.

He resisted the impulse to say more, to embark on an account of all that had happened between himself and Claire. No doubt this Melissa was a good listener – she was practised in the art – but it would be a betrayal of Claire for him to say anything more to her.

Instead, he said, 'I've also got to ask you about the letters, whether you know anything about who might have written them?'

'I've not the slightest idea, no.'

'Then that makes two of us.'

'And they're telling you you have to hand over a certain amount of money . . .?'

He nodded. 'Five thousand pounds. Only I'm not going to. That much I can promise you.'

'I'm sure you're not. I can't see that there'd be any point where you're concerned.'

'There wouldn't,' he said, grateful for her endorsement of his position on this, so different from Claire's perverse attempts to use it against him.

'So can I ask . . . why don't you just throw the letters away and forget about the whole thing?'

It was the one they all asked – Inspector Beresford, Maurice Townsend and now Melissa. He had the same answer for them all.

'If only I could. The trouble is I have to prove my innocence to my wife.'

'Oh, of course,' she said. She shook her head, as though exasperated by her own stupidity.

'Also it would be nice to understand just what's been going on. I mean this *other Richard Gillow*, the one you met – who is he? Why was he impersonating me? How does he know all these things about me and my family?'

She didn't reply for a moment. He sensed her thoughts were elsewhere. Then she winced as though coming to a difficult decision.

She said: 'You promised you won't go to the police.'

'I won't,' he said, surprised that she should raise that issue again. 'Certainly not in a way that would involve you, no.'

'It's just . . . well, you were right in what you were saying outside there. I do have another life.'

'I'm sure you do.'

He tried to guess where this might be leading but couldn't. She had become agitated and was tapping nervously with her long nails on the table top.

'I promise that I will never say anything to the police that will cause you to be involved in this,' he said, wondering if that was what was needed.

She sighed. 'OK, well . . . there is something I haven't told you.'

'Yes?'

'When I met the other Richard Gillow . . . you know that we took a room –'

'Yes.'

'And what I did, because it's something I've done before, with other men . . . ' She wasn't looking at him now but at a spot somewhere over his shoulder. 'As soon as I got the chance, I went through his pockets. Which I daresay you think was a pretty mean thing to do.'

Richard shook his head, not really knowing what he thought of it. He would be pleased at anything she might have done if there was a chance it would help in tracking down his *alter ego*.

She was still attempting to justify herself. 'It's just that when you meet a man like that . . . in a hotel . . . a man who's probably given you a false name . . . well, he could be *anybody* –'

'I understand,' said Richard impatiently. 'I don't blame you, not at all. So you went through his pockets . . . and what?'

'He had some business cards, and also credit cards with his name on –'

'His *real* name?'

'Yes. Oh, yes, I'm sure this was his real name.'

'And do you remember it?'

She nodded. 'Names I remember. Faces I'm not so hot on but –'

'What was it? Tell me his name.'

'Nevison,' she said. 'Lawrence Nevison.'

He made her repeat it, then asked was she sure. She said she was absolutely sure. Lawrence Nevison was the name on the cards she had found in the pocket of the other Richard Gillow's jacket.

Even then, Richard resisted the idea. He couldn't believe it – or, anyway, he couldn't easily believe it. Lawrence was someone he had long regarded as a friend and neighbour, and who he had rated highly as both. Besides, the man himself was eminently respectable, leading an unblemished life. He was a successful solicitor for Christ's sake. His wife was forever closeted with Claire while he and Lawrence . . . well, if they weren't quite bosom-buddies, they regularly met up at the local pub and had once been ski-ing together. Lawrence was one of the first people he would have turned to for help. In fact, he already had. It was Lawrence who had recommended Morris Townsend, which was

143

how Richard came to be sitting here in a pub in the middle of Manchester with Melissa and hearing her say Lawrence's name.

And yet.

For one thing, the description fitted. Lawrence was of a slimmer and lighter build than himself. He had fair hair and probably wore glasses for reading, though Richard couldn't now remember that for sure. Certainly he might well have impressed as 'educated' and 'self-assured'.

More important was that Lawrence knew enough about the whole Gillow family and its history for him to give a convincing performance of actually *being* Richard. All those facts about the children and the house ... none of them would have been a problem for him. He would even have known a fair amount about publishing after the innumerable conversations they had had over the years, Richard imparting to him his hopes and doubts when he had first gone solo.

To see Lawrence as the impostor made immediate, transparent sense of everything that had so far been an impenetrable mystery.

Though the question remained: *why had he done such a thing?* What terrible wrong could Richard have done him that it had transformed this man he had thought of as friend and confidant into an enemy who would so betray him?

'Do you know him?' asked Melissa.

He took a deep breath. 'Yes.'

'I thought you might.'

He looked at her in surprise.

'I mean I imagine that's how he knew so much about you.'

'He's my next-door neighbour. His wife is a close friend of my wife.' Baffled, he appealed to her, 'But why would he do it?'

'Sorry, I can't help you there.'

'No, of course.'

'Perhaps you can ask him that.'

He gave a grim smile. 'I shall certainly be asking him. I shall be asking him just as soon as I can.'

'I'd love to know what he says.'

He felt she would appreciate the irony of how he had managed to track her down. He explained how it had been Lawrence who had recommended a private detective and so had unwittingly

brought about his own downfall. She smiled and said, Well, it
served him right.

He again offered her another drink but she said no. It was
time she was going.

'Anyway,' she said, 'won't you want to be going after your
friend, Mr Nevison?'

He did, of course. Still, he'd have been happy to have remained there with her a little longer. Despite his chasing her
down the street and all but wrestling her to the ground, they
had ended up allies – and he hadn't met with many of those
over the past weeks. He insisted on walking with her back to the
hotel where there were taxis queuing outside.

'I hope things work out for you,' she said. 'I mean with your
wife. I know it might not look like it, but I'm not in the business
of breaking up marriages.'

'I'm sure you're not,' he said sincerely. 'And thank you. I
know that tonight must have come as a bit of a shock.'

'Just a bit, yes.'

'And I promise you won't be hearing anything from the
police.'

She nodded. 'I appreciate that.'

They shook hands and she climbed into a taxi. He noticed
that she didn't call out her destination to the driver until she
was safely inside with the door closed. This was presumably so
that he shouldn't hear and so be in a position to follow her
through the looking-glass to her other, respectable life beyond
it.

He hurried back to his own car. His intention was to drive
straight to the Nevisons' and confront Lawrence, even if he had
to drag him out of bed to do it. There was still Claire's letter
waiting for him at home. He hadn't forgotten that. But the letter
could wait, where this other business couldn't.

It occurred to him that he might ring first, to make sure that
Lawrence would be home. He rang the Nevison number on his
car-phone, then tensed as the ringing-tone stopped, but it was
Adele's voice.

'Nevison residence.'

'Adele, it's Richard. Can I speak to Lawrence please?'

'Oh, Richard, hello. No, I'm sorry, he's not here.'

He cursed silently. Then, striving to sound casual, he said, 'You don't happen to know where I can find him?'

'He's at some sort of dinner. He took his black tie and everything into work so he could get changed without having to come home.'

Richard knew that a wiser man might give up at this point and settle for confronting Lawrence tomorrow. But he couldn't do this, not while there remained even the slimmest chance of locating him tonight.

'Do you know where this dinner is?' he asked.

'Could you just hang on and I'll have a look at the calendar.'

There was a clatter as the receiver was put down, then a pause. He could hear a television set pumping out laughter. He pictured Adele as she would have been before he rang, alone and curled up for the evening. It made him recall what Melissa had said, when she had been reporting the other Richard Gillow's judgement on his wife: '*She has no time for him . . . too wrapped up in her own life.*'

The receiver was picked up. 'Hello? Richard?'

'Yes?'

'According to the calendar, he's at a Law Society dinner in Manchester.'

'You don't know just where —'

'The Midland Hotel.'

'Marvellous,' he said.

'Pardon?'

'I mean thank you.'

The Midland Hotel was no distance away. He could be there within minutes.

Though first he had to shake off Adele who was still on the line. She was asking about Claire. Apparently she had been round to the house and found her not there. Richard pleaded ignorance. He hadn't been home all day and so knew nothing of what might be going on. Then he wished her a quick goodnight and switched off the phone.

The dusk had thickened into darkness as he drove back across the city centre.

The Midland Hotel was a huge, solid building, encased in marble. Richard parked nearby in a restricted area, not caring, and hurried in beneath the great stone canopy. The lobby inside, with its raised terrace along one side, was a space for strutting and preening but he crossed it quickly, intent on his mission and indifferent to all else.

He was about to address one of the receptionists but then noticed a bulletin board to the side of the desk. The top line of gold lettering read: 'LAW SOCIETY DINNER – VICTORIA ROOM'.

'Can I help you, sir?' asked the receptionist.

'No, thank you.'

The bulletin board told him all he wanted to know. He came away from the desk and found a sign saying 'VICTORIA ROOM'. The arrow beside it directed him past the lifts and along a short corridor. At the end of the corridor he found himself entering a large, circular ante-room, which felt as though it might have been a well-kept secret. There were openings off, with signs identifying cloakrooms and toilets, and a pair of oak doors, one of which had the words 'VICTORIA ROOM' scrolled across it. He could hear coming from behind the doors the dull roar and clatter of the feasting.

He didn't hesitate but went forward. The door swung open at his touch and he was plunged into a vast room crammed with round tables. Each table had a dozen or so people around it, mainly men in dinner suits though he glimpsed the odd woman. The tables were loaded with glassware and food and bottles and white menu cards. Three brightly-lit chandeliers descended from the ceiling. The noise was deafening.

Richard gazed around him, his senses numbed. He was aware only of the general melee. He stepped up to the nearest table and stated loudly: 'Excuse me, I'm looking for Lawrence Nevison.'

A ring of faces turned towards him, displaying a variety of ages. Most were sweating with the heat and the clamour of the place.

'Lawrence Nevison,' he repeated.

There was a general shaking of heads, before they went back to the food, though one or two continued to eye him curiously. He went forward to the next table. The diners here seemed to have had a head start on the rest and were carousing drunkenly. Richard had to grab a bottle and bang it down on the table-top to get their attention. They turned their red faces towards him, surprised at the interruption.

'Lawrence Nevison. Does anybody know where I'll find him?'

There was another near-unanimous shaking of heads but, among it, a young man held up a hand to call Richard's attention. He had dark, wavy hair and a fat, schoolboy's face, which shone with perspiration.

'Nevison . . .?' he called.

'Yes.'

'I think you might find him over there,' he said, waving at the table behind Richard.

Richard mouthed a thank you at him, spun round and glanced around this new circle. And lo and behold, yes. There, third counting from the left, was Lawrence. He was absorbed in conversation with the man beside him and hadn't noticed Richard at all.

Richard stepped round till he was directly behind him, then placed a hand on his shoulder. Lawrence looked up and gave a start of surprise.

'Richard! What . . . ' – his expression changing to one of alarm – ' . . . what's the matter? Has something happened?'

'I want a word with you – now. Will you come outside please.'

Lawrence began to stutter another question but Richard didn't stay to hear it. He was already heading back towards the door, threading his way between tables. When he reached the door and looked back, Lawrence was following him. He looked puzzled and exasperated.

The two men stepped out into the carpeted foyer and Richard pulled the heavy doors closed behind them. The sudden calm was unnerving. Lawrence took out a handkerchief and mopped his brow.

'There's nothing happened, has there?' he enquired anxiously.

'Not the sort of thing you mean, no.'

His hostility must have betrayed itself: Lawrence stared at him and waited, running the handkerchief around his neck.

'I've just been talking to a young lady called Melissa,' said Richard, watching him carefully.

So far as he could see, Lawrence didn't react at all.

'Melissa . . .?' prompted Richard. 'Ring any bells?'

'No. No, I'm afraid −'

'Well, she certainly knows you. She says she met you several times, always at the Queens Hotel. At least you know the hotel, I take it . . .?'

'I do actually, yes.'

'That's where you met her. Which you might say is none of my business. Well, no, it wouldn't be, except for the fact that, when you met her − you pretended to be me.'

Lawrence frowned and shook his head. 'No,' he said. 'Sorry, old man, but I don't know what you're talking about.'

'Oh, yes, I think you do,' said Richard, determined to resist the tiny doubts that were beginning to grow.

Lawrence shook his head again. He thrust his hands into his pockets and looked down at the carpet. Then, looking up at Richard, he said, 'I'm supposed to have done what? *Impersonated* you, is that what you're saying?'

'Yes.'

'Well, I'm sorry, old man, but quite frankly that's the most ludicrous thing I've ever heard.'

'Is it. Well, let me tell you another ludicrous thing. I'm being blackmailed.'

'No!'

His surprise appeared genuine enough. Richard's doubts began to take a real hold. Still, he persevered.

'I'm being blackmailed because apparently somebody else believed your little performance. You convinced them that you were me, and so it's me they've been trying to blackmail.'

Lawrence was shaking his head. 'You've got the wrong man. I don't know how but −'

'No, I don't think so. You see, I tracked down this woman, the one I'm supposed to have been seeing. In fact, you helped me to do that.'

'I did?'

'I asked you if you could recommend a private detective –'

'Ah.' He evidently remembered.

'Maurice Townsend.'

'Yes.'

'He found her for me.'

'Well, I'm glad he did. But I'm damned if I can see what more it's got to do with me.'

'This woman named you as the person who'd been passing himself off as me! She'd gone through your pockets and she'd found your card or whatever and so she knew it was you!'

It shouldn't have been like this, with him virtually shouting and Lawrence coolly shaking his head in denial. Worse, he was looking at Richard in a concerned manner, as though he feared for his sanity.

'And what did you say this girl's name was?' he asked.

'Melissa.'

'Just . . . Melissa?'

'That's the name she uses when she's working, yes.'

'When she's working? What sort of work are we talking about?'

Richard hesitated then said, feeling his position weaken as he spoke: 'She works for an escort agency.'

Lawrence raised an eyebrow. 'Interesting work.'

'Never mind that. I've been talking to her tonight and she identified you as the person who's been impersonating me,' said Richard doggedly.

'And you believe her?'

Half an hour ago, yes, he had believed her every word. Now he felt obliged to hedge his bets.

'It's not a matter of whether I believe her. This is what she's said, so I've got to ask you, is it true?'

'I can see you have to ask me. But I'm afraid the answer is – no, it's not true, not a word of it.'

'You've never met this woman?'

'Never.'

'Lawrence, do you know *anything* about this? Anything at all that might help?'

'Nothing, old man. I only wish I did.'

Richard felt his earlier conviction being whittled away to nothing. He had come here determined to extract a confession from this man. If necessary, he would have grabbed him by the throat and squeezed it from him. Now he was beginning to wonder whether he hadn't been taken for a ride by the slippery Melissa. Was she a more accomplished actress than he had given her credit for? She hadn't been able to run fast enough to escape him and so had produced an Oscar-winning performance as that old favourite, the Whore With The Heart Of Gold. He had been the easy dupe, seduced into believing her.

And yet, if that were so, where had she got the name Lawrence Nevison from? Explain that and he would straightaway offer Lawrence a full apology.

The carpet on which they were standing was of a squared design. Lawrence had begun a slow dance, a kind of soft-shoe shuffle, that involved stepping on the blue-grey squares only.

'Are you really saying that you've never met her?' asked Richard, having to turn as the other man moved around him.

'Never.' He looked at his watch. 'Look, I don't want to be rude, old man –'

'Have you ever stayed at the Queens Hotel?'

'Er, I don't think I have, no. Listen, would you mind if we talked about this tomorrow –'

'And you've never gone to an escort agency and been put in touch with a woman called Melissa?'

Lawrence stopped his routine on the squares and looked at him sadly. 'I haven't, no. Look, old man, you sound like you're in a bit of a mess. If there's anything I can do to help, then I'd be delighted. But just now I should be getting back inside. Let's talk about this tomorrow, OK?'

Richard said nothing, stubbornly refusing to say yes to that and so release Lawrence to return to the jamboree continuing next-door.

Wasn't this the classical dilemma: having to choose between a liar and a truth-teller and not knowing which was which? He needed to find a test that would help him distinguish one from the other. And he needed it quickly. He couldn't detain Lawrence for much longer. In another moment or two he would be back behind the oak doors, safe among his own kind. Even if they were to meet up again tomorrow, Lawrence would have had time to prepare himself, and the truth would be even more difficult to distinguish.

He decided to gamble. 'Well, we can talk tomorrow, yes. But I've still got something else I have to do tonight.'

'What's that?' asked Lawrence, who had moved up to the doors and was about to go through them.

'I'm going to the police. Let them sort this out.'

Lawrence appeared to ponder that. He shrugged – as though to convey that he wasn't particularly interested but felt he should point something out. 'Just don't expect them to achieve too much, old man. And, if they do come to me, well, I can only tell them what I've already told you.'

'I don't intend they should come to you. I was thinking more of Melissa.'

'Oh, yes, this woman –'

'I'd like them to hear her story, the one she gave me.'

'Well, yes, if they can find her. I mean that type, they're notoriously –'

'Oh, they'll find her. All they have to do is what I did – go to the agency. Anyway, I hope I haven't spoiled your evening.'

He waited, but Lawrence seemed to have lost his inclination to return to the banquet. He remained where he was, one hand resting on the door. Yet his pose had shifted slightly. His head had bowed and his shoulders dropped, as though he were suddenly drunk or . . . defeated.

'No, please. I'd rather you didn't go to the police.'

He spoke so quietly that Richard couldn't be sure he had heard him properly.

'I beg your pardon?'

'It was me, yes. Richard, I'm sorry. I'm so terribly sorry.'

It was the confession he'd been after, but how long it had been in coming and how nearly had it eluded him! Now he was torn between going over and tearing the head off the other man's shoulders and going over to prop him up and stop him slumping to the floor. In the event he did neither but stood and stared while Lawrence extended his arms in a pathetic expression of helplessness, before finally pulling himself upright just as he seemed on the point of collapse.

'I'm sorry,' he said again. 'But you've got to believe . . . it wasn't deliberate.'

'It wasn't *what?*'

'I mean I didn't do it with the intention of harming you.'

'Oh, you didn't?'

'No. I swear. Not in any way. It was the last thing I wanted.'

'Well, shall I tell you what harm it has done to me?'

'I'm sorry —'

'I've been blackmailed by some nutter who wants five thousand pounds to keep quiet. As a result of that, my wife believes I've been seeing another woman and she has now left me. So do me a favour, yes? Just don't tell me that you didn't intend to do me any harm!'

He was shouting. He knew he was shouting but he couldn't stop himself. He wasn't even sure that he would be able to stop himself from seizing this fool in his fancy suit and throwing him to the floor. Lawrence had closed his eyes and bowed his head as though in submission, perhaps waiting for just such an assault.

The doors to the Victoria Room opened, letting out a wave of noise that made both of them turn. Two men — lawyers in monkey suits — emerged, one of them lighting a cigarette. They glanced without curiosity at Richard and Lawrence, crossed the ante-room and went into the gents.

Lawrence was speaking, though with his head down so that Richard had to step closer to make out the words.

'I'll do anything to make amends. Anything you want. I'm just so ashamed. I can't believe —'

'*Why?*'

His head came up. 'Why . . .?'

'Why did you do it? What have I done to you that you should —'

But Lawrence was already protesting, becoming animated again: 'No! No, it's like I said, it wasn't *deliberate*. It wasn't to harm you. It was just . . . well, to protect myself, I suppose.'

'Oh. To protect yourself . . .?'

'Which is something I am not proud of.'

'Jesus, you know what I should do to you . . .!'

He raised his clenched fist but then let it fall as the doors to the Victoria Room opened again. Along with the noise, a small procession of men emerged and trekked across the carpet towards the gents. One of them said, 'Lawrence, hi,' as he passed.

'Come over here,' said Richard, and led him out of the ante-room and into the corridor where he hoped there might be fewer interruptions. There was a chaise longue stuck there as a piece of decoration. 'Sit down,' he instructed Lawrence, then perched himself on the raised end of it. 'Now, will you please explain to me *why*.'

Lawrence nodded, then said, 'This is so humiliating.'

There was a note of self-pity in that that enraged Richard. 'Oh, for Christ's sake —'

'Yes, I'm sorry,' said Lawrence quickly. 'Why . . .? You want to know why I did it?'

'I do, yes.'

'Right, well, what happened, I went to this . . . you know, this escort agency. I went there because . . . oh, nothing original, just that my marriage isn't all that wonderful and I wanted . . .' He shook his head. 'God, I don't know why I went. I must have been mad.'

It was an explanation of a sort. He had been drawn to the agency by all those ancient and irresistible forces that kept such places in business. It didn't matter. The only part of what he was saying that registered with Richard was that he had not gone there as part of some master-plan to bring Richard's world crashing about him.

Lawrence said: 'I knew I was being stupid. Even when I picked up the phone and made the call, I knew it was a foolish, crazy thing to be doing. I mean for someone in my position . . .!'

The note of self-pity was creeping back in. Richard hurried him on.

'And they arranged for you to meet Melissa, did they?'

'Yes. Well, for me to meet one of their girls. I didn't ask for her in particular. She was just the one they came up with.'

'OK. And you met her at the Queens Hotel?'

'Yes.'

'But you weren't using my name then?'

'No. No, I'd just given some name off the top of my head. Graham I think it was.'

Richard nodded. The alias tied in with Melissa's account of things.

'Go on.'

'Er, well ... we met. And we decided we'd have dinner. Because, well, she was an attractive, intelligent sort of woman. Not at all what you might expect –'

'I've met her.'

'Oh. Right. Of course.'

He fell silent again and Richard had to prompt: 'So you had dinner . . .?'

'Yes, only you see what I hadn't anticipated was how difficult it would be having to carry on a conversation without giving away anything of who I was. And, if I wasn't supposed to be me, then who was I supposed to be? I'd told her I was Graham, but I didn't know who the hell Graham was. And I didn't want to tell her my real name or anything about my real self because, well . . . I suppose I was frightened of being blackmailed.' He winced, conscious of the irony.

'I'm sorry,' he said, as if gripped by a sudden despair. 'God, this is dreadful.'

'You were right to be worried about blackmail,' said Richard drily.

Lawrence took a deep breath, then plunged on: 'So I didn't know who *Graham* was, and I couldn't be myself, so I had to . . . well, I had to be somebody else. And the first person who came to mind was you. Call it a lack of imagination if you like, but I couldn't create a persona out of thin air. I had to borrow one from somebody I knew. So I thought – who would I like to be? And the answer . . . the answer was you.'

It was like hearing a lover confess an affection that had long been nursed in secret. Hearing it at the wrong time, when it was the last thing you wanted. If this bizarre notion of 'wanting to be him' was supposed to be a compliment, then it was one that had caused him untold misery and that he could well have done without.

Lawrence glanced at him, then continued: 'I wanted to be successful and to have a terrific wife and terrific children –'

This was too much. He had to be stopped and reminded of what had happened.

'Yes, well, I don't have a terrific wife anymore.'

'I know. I'm sorry. I'll do everything I can to put things right, I promise.'

155

'I hope you will.'

'Anyway, once I'd started talking as though I was you . . . well, I had to go on. I'd made myself you and I couldn't just switch off and stop being you. So when it came to signing the hotel register –'

'You used my name.'

'Yes. But I mean I wasn't intending any harm –'

'I don't care what you were intending. You've done harm. You've done me so much bloody harm that I don't know whether I've even got a marriage left anymore!'

There were fresh noises coming from the direction of the Victoria Room. The door seemed to be opening with more frequency, or even to have been wedged open to admit some air. People were tramping to and from the gents. One of them, straying further than most, appeared in the corridor, puffing at a cigarette. He pulled up, startled, when he saw the two of them already there. 'Sorry,' he muttered and withdrew.

'I don't suppose you'll ever understand,' said Lawrence. 'Life's easy for you. You get things right . . . instinctively, without even trying –'

'What?'

Lawrence gave a little laugh. 'You do. You've a beautiful home, beautiful garden. Yes, now there's a thing. You have this immaculate garden, yet I never see anybody *actually gardening*.'

Richard stared, wondering if Lawrence were drunk and he had failed to notice. Never mind the strange talk about the state of Richard's home and, more particularly, his garden, it was Lawrence's sudden switch of attitude that was so astonishing. From being the guilty man, issuing grovelling apologies, he had suddenly become the prosecutor, accusing Richard. Just what he was being accused of, Richard wasn't sure – of being successful or of having a happy family life? Whatever it was, he had become the guilty one, responsible for everything that had happened.

Lawrence was still talking. 'Whereas me and Adele, we work like crazy at our damn garden and never get half the effect you do. It's the same in the house – we spend a fortune, we take advice, but we never seem to get things quite right. Whereas you –'

'Yes, all right –'

'Everything is in such good taste.'

'Thank you. Only I don't think we're here to talk about *my life.*'

'No,' said Lawrence, seeming to accept the rebuke; then, a moment later, he was coming at him again: 'All the same, Richard, I've got to say – I don't think you know just how damned lucky you are.'

'We're talking about you impersonating me –'

'Yes.'

'And coming close to destroying my marriage!'

'Yes, I'm sorry.'

'So if I ever was happy, if I ever was lucky, like you say . . . then by God you've put an end to that, haven't you!'

Lawrence nodded, cowed again. Another dinner-suited man appeared, come to find out what the shouting was about. Richard glared at him and he retreated.

'What do you want me to do?' said Lawrence.

What did he want? Well, one thing above all else. 'I want you to tell Claire everything you've told me.'

'Yes.'

'*Everything.*'

For he knew Claire would be hard to persuade. She would see it as an old pals' act: Lawrence coming up with a ridiculous fabrication to get Richard off the hook.

'Yes, I will,' said Lawrence. 'Except didn't you say –'

'Oh, that she's gone, yes. Though I don't know where she's gone to, not yet. She's left me a letter.'

'But, as soon as she's back, then of course I'll be happy to speak to her.'

'Thank you.'

Lawrence stood up. 'Are you still thinking of going to the police?'

That's what he's really worried about, thought Richard. It's not a matter of remorse at the thought of the damage he's done. It's his own skin that's on the line here. He's scared that his cronies next-door might find out.

'No, I'm not,' said Richard abruptly.

'Thank you, old man,' said Lawrence, switching on a smile. 'I can't tell you how grateful I am.'

It's not for your sake, thought Richard. It's because I've already given my word to Melissa that I won't go to the police.

He saw no point in telling Lawrence that. The more Lawrence felt himself in his debt, the more effectively Richard could put the screws on when it came to the show-down with Claire. So now he, too, was turning to blackmail.

'And if there's anything else I can do . . .?' said Lawrence.

'Oh, I'll let you know.'

'Do you . . . do you want me to pay off this blackmailer?'

It was an offer that took Richard by surprise. This was not something he had even considered. Perhaps Lawrence hadn't really considered it either.

'I wouldn't think there's much point, would you?'

Lawrence shrugged. 'I just thought it might help get him off your back.'

'Would it though? Isn't the golden rule about blackmailers – once you pay them, they'll always come back asking for more?'

Lawrence nodded slowly. 'I suppose . . . well, yes, you're right. I just thought it might take the pressure off. Anyway, the offer's there if you change your mind.'

They had drifted back towards the doors to Victoria Room. There was a still a muffled hubbub coming from beyond them.

'Well, I'll leave you to your dinner,' said Richard.

'Can't say I've much of an appetite left. And listen, old man, I really am deeply sorry about all this. And deeply ashamed.'

Richard nodded. He felt that Lawrence was seeking a hand-shake and perhaps a few words of forgiveness to go with it, but he wasn't going to give him the benefit of that. He had been through too much, and hadn't yet come to the end of it, to grant so easy an absolution.

Instead, he said, 'I'll let you know as soon as Claire's back.' Then he turned and walked away.

If only he had got himself wired up with some kind of miniature recording-device, then he would have had everything he needed, on tape and instantly available to convince Claire of his innocence. But he hadn't, and so he was reaching the end of the long evening with nothing to show but Lawrence's promise that he would tell Claire everything.

And how much was that worth? He was beginning to realize

how ruthlessly his next-door neighbour would act to protect himself. There was a devious side to Lawrence that he hadn't appreciated before. Look how he had lied in his teeth, swearing he knew nothing of any Melissa till Richard had announced he was going to the police.

Even the offer to pay the blackmailer wasn't as magnanimous as it might have at first appeared. Assuming that the photographs which the blackmailer talked about in his letters actually existed – then they weren't photographs of Richard at all but photographs of Lawrence. Lawrence with Melissa. This had been his real reason for offering to pay. Not as a demonstration of his contrition but because he wanted to make sure that any such photographs were taken safely out of circulation.

Richard came out of the Midland Hotel into a night that was now studded with stars and distinctly cooler. He would now return home and read his wife's letter and discover whether she had left him for good.

He thought of Lawrence going home to resume his life with Adele. No doubt he would tell her nothing of this.

One surprise among the many that the night had provided had been the way Lawrence had turned on him and accused him of being over-privileged or having too many of life's blessings or whatever it was he had intended to say. There had been a real bitterness there, the hint of a long-held grievance. It had been a strange thing to discover.

Though no stranger than so much else he was learning about this topsy-turvy universe in which the whores spoke the truth and the lawyers would tell you anything to save their own skins.

12

'Do you want to read it?' he asked gently. he didn't want it to seem a challenge she would feel obliged to meet. He just wanted her know he was happy for her to read it if she so wished.

'No,' she said.

He nodded. 'Like I say, there's nothing in it that your mother didn't tell you before she went. Which is basically that she feels under pressure here and wants to be on her own for a while.'

He had found Claire's letter on arriving home after his epic struggle to get the truth out of Lawrence. The house was empty, which was a relief. He didn't want to think that Diane had been keeping a lonely vigil. The envelope was on the kitchen table with his name written on it in his wife's neat hand. He poured himself a scotch and opened it.

'Richard,' he read. 'I'm sorry but I feel to have been under constant bombardment from you and I have to get away for a while. I really care very little, a lot less than you probably think, about what might have happened in the past. It's what is happening now that I find intolerable. Please don't try and find me. I am perfectly all right, neither insane nor even particularly tearful, and will be in touch soon. Look after yourself, Claire.'

There was an assertive, plucky air to it that was typical of her. Though he also felt her sadness that they should have ever got into this mess.

Look on the bright side, he told himself. It could have been worse. She wasn't talking about separation or divorce. The letter read as though her going away was no more than a temporary device intended to enforce a cease-fire.

All the same, part of him felt betrayed by her: not so much in the fact of her going as in the manner of it. She had stolen away while he was out of the house and left a letter to say what she couldn't say to his face.

'Yes, and *why* did I steal away?' he could hear her challenging him. 'Just what would have happened if I hadn't gone like that? You would have tried to stop me going and then all hell would have been let loose!'

No doubt she was right. Probably he would have done everything possible to keep her there, leading to another almighty row. After which, she would have gone anyway, but then her departure would have been in an atmosphere of bitterness and recrimination that would have made it all the harder for her ever to return.

He sighed and took another sip of his whisky. So perhaps it was for the best that she'd gone this way. What really hurt was that she had gone only hours before he had met Melissa and uncovered the truth.

He was in bed before Diane had returned. It was at breakfast the following morning that they met up and he offered her the opportunity to read the letter. She was yawning and her face was full of sleep, but her refusal was considered and firm.

He respected it by folding up the letter and putting it in his pocket.

'Poor dad, this must be awful for you,' she said, and gave him a quick hug before going to the fridge in search of orange juice.

'You haven't to worry about me. Believe it or not, I've already sorted this whole thing out.'

She turned and stared in disbelief. 'What, the blackmail . . .?'

'The blackmail letters, yes. Oh, I don't know who's written them, not that. But I've tracked down this Melissa woman I'm supposed to have been seeing and I now understand what's happened.'

'You do?'

'Yes.'

'You know why the letters accused you of . . . of what they accused you?' she ended diplomatically.

'Of meeting this woman in a hotel? Yes. It's all because somebody else was passing himself off as me. And, what's more, I now know who the somebody else was.'

Of course he couldn't name Lawrence. It would have been malicious to have explained to Diane that this whole dreadful mess was down to their next-door neighbour and close friend. Husband of Adele, one of mum's cronies.

'Oh, but that's wonderful . . .!' she exclaimed.

'It certainly is.'

'So, if only mummy were here –'

'I could tell her. Which is why . . . listen.'

'Yes.'

'If she rings –'

'Yes.'

'I mean when I'm out, and if you speak to her, then it's vitally important you get her to give you her number or to agree to somewhere where I can go and meet her –'

'Yes.' She was nodding eagerly, eyes shining.

'Because I need to be able to tell her what's happened, and then she'll understand everything and then, believe me, darling, believe me all this will be over.' He could see she was struggling to make sense of this sudden reversal in their favour, and added: 'And I'm sorry I can't tell you any more. But there are some things I can tell only to your mother.'

'Of course. And, if she does ring, don't worry. I'll make sure –'

'I know you will.'

'In fact, I won't go out, not while you're at work. So that I'll be here if she does –'

'No, no . . . '

He held up a hand to stop her. She had been involved too much as it was. He didn't want her placing herself between them to be the carrier of further messages.

'You just do whatever you were going to do. Your mother will get in touch sooner or later. She makes that clear in her letter.'

'She didn't take very much with her.'

'No?'

'Just shirts and jeans, the sort of stuff she would take if she were going walking for a weekend.'

'Well, then –'

'And she can't stay away from her desk for more than a week without getting withdrawal symptoms!'

They laughed together at this. It was an old family joke and it now cheered Richard to hear his daughter resurrecting it. He knew she was looking for good news to give him. Not for the first time, he was struck by how fortunate he was in having her there, a delightful, loving daughter he could hardly have deserved.

The doorbell rang. He left Diane at the table and strode

through to the hallway, expecting it to be the postman delivering parcels or something to be signed for.

But it was Lawrence. Grim-faced and hollow-eyed. He wasted no time on the courtesies but blurted out, 'I've got to talk to you, old man. Sorry but – just got to.'

They collected coffees from the kitchen and passed on through into the garden. Diane was left gazing curiously after them. It was a bright, almost cloudless morning, with just enough dew to show a glint in the grass.

They paced side by side to the centre of the lawn which was already showing a good recovery after the ravages of the party. Richard waited patiently until Lawrence finally spoke.

'What I said last night. About telling Claire –'

'Yes?'

'Is there no other way?'

Richard was angered though hardly surprised. He might even have expected this. After Lawrence's evasions of last night, when he had denied everything until he had seen that there wasn't the remotest chance of his getting away with it, this attempt at back-sliding was the inevitable next step now that the morning had arrived and the sun arisen, bringing with it new hope for self-seeking bastards everywhere that they might yet manage to evade their responsibilities.

They had come to the far edge of the lawn and stepped into the shade of the apple trees.

'What other way?' demanded Richard, determined he wasn't going to give an inch. 'There is no other way.'

'Please, Richard. Try and see things from my point of view.'

'Your *what* . . .?'

'Yes, I know I've no right to ask you, but I am asking you. I *have* to ask you. If I tell Claire what I've done . . . '

'Yes.'

'Then Adele will learn of it.'

'No, there's no reason why that should happen.'

'Oh, come on! You know what those two are like. They tell one another everything! And something like this, Claire would have to tell her. Yes, she would. I know you'll say Claire isn't a gossip but something like this –'

Richard was shaking his head.

163

'Yes!' insisted Lawrence. He gripped Richard's arm and came close to him, his tone confiding and imploring: 'And all right, I know I said to you that my marriage wasn't up to much but, well, it's all I've got and I . . . I don't want to lose it.'

'There's no reason why you should. There's no reason why Adele should ever know anything about this.'

'But she will know. And now you're being unfair, because you know she will but you just won't admit it!'

Richard pulled away from him, resenting the inference he was somehow conniving at the destruction of Lawrence's marriage. He had no intention of telling Adele anything. And he was sure that Claire, once she knew the truth, would go out of her way to keep it private between the three of them.

'Lawrence,' he said, 'you are going to tell Claire what you told me last night.'

'Well, am I though?' he said, avoiding Richard's gaze.

Richard was quick to challenge him. 'And what's that sup-posed to mean? Just what are you saying?'

'I'm not saying anything. Not yet. All I'm doing is asking – *is there not any other way of doing this?*'

'You're asking that . . .?'

'I am, yes.'

'Well, then the answer is no – there isn't.'

They were now standing a couple of yards apart, facing one another, feet firmly planted. It might have been an early morning duel but for the absence of any obvious weapons.

'So it's my marriage that has to go then, is it?' said Lawrence.

'I'm not saying that. Who's saying that?' retaliated Richard.

'Well, yes, I think you are saying it. Oh, not in so many words, because you don't want to have to admit to it. But the truth is – if I tell Claire what you want me to tell her, then my marriage is going to be over.'

There were bees drumming among the apples above them. Even further above, a plane etched a thin line across the blue of the sky.

Richard was trying hard, so hard it amounted to a physical effort, to understand Lawrence's position and so not be spooked by it into grabbing him by the throat and threatening to beat a confession out of him. He understood that this man was out to protect his marriage and his reputation. On top of which he was no doubt desperate not to have to admit to Claire – and so run the risk of Adele finding out – tht he was a man who used prostitutes.

These were the fears that drove him and that made everything he did totally and utterly selfish. He was desperately casting around, trying every approach in the hope he might find one that would let him off the hook. Richard understood that.

'Lawrence,' he said, 'I don't want to harm your marriage but I'm sorry – you have got to tell Claire the truth about what happened.'

He believed he was speaking calmly, keeping his voice low. And so he was stunned by the defiant answer.

'No, I don't.'

'I beg your pardon?'

'I don't have to do what you say I have to do. I don't have to tell her.'

Richard stepped forward. Lawrence stepped back as far as the tree behind him allowed.

'And what do you mean by that? Are you telling me you're *not* going to talk to Claire?'

'Well, isn't that rather beside the point? I can hardly do that if she's not here, can I?'

It struck Richard as a mealy-mouthed, lawyer's answer, one that side-stepped the issue. He certainly was not going to let him get away with it.

'I'm talking about when she *is* here. Are you going to talk to her when she is here?'

Lawrence's face took on a pained expression as he considered that, then he said, 'Well, that's what I'm saying really. I don't know whether I can.'

'For Christ's sake . . .!' exploded Richard.

'I'm sorry,' said Lawrence, 'but you're asking me to sacrifice my own marriage. And I'm sorry but I just can't.'

Challenging Richard physically to stop him, he walked forward and past him. He even brushed against him as he did so. Richard went after him and caught him up, so they were walking together, side-by-side, heading back towards the house.

'As soon as she gets back, you are going to tell Claire everything that's happened. And I won't be responsible if you don't.'

'Oh, it's threats now, is it?' said Lawrence, his voice rising.

He was walking faster, veering away from the house itself and towards the gate beside it, which gave access onto the road.

Richard thought – you're lucky that threats are all it is; I ought to break your bloody neck.

What he said was: 'And so what was all that you were saying last night, about how ashamed you were of what you'd done? How you would do anything to help put things right?'

'And I will, yes – but not at any cost.'

'Do you not care what you might have done to my marriage?'

They had come to the gate. Lawrence tugged at it but it was regularly locked at night and resisted him.

He licked his lips and, without looking at Richard, said, 'Will you let me out of here please.'

'Did you hear me? I said don't you care what you might have done to my marriage?'

'Will you unlock this gate please? Or are you detaining me here, is that what you're doing?'

Richard didn't move for another moment, letting him sweat. Lawrence grabbed the handle to the gate again and rattled it harder but still it didn't budge.

'Never mind opening this,' said Richard. 'I ought to kick you right over the damn thing.'

He pulled his keys from his pocket and stepped forward to unlock the gate. Lawrence pulled back, keeping what distance he could. Then, once the gate was opened, he went through quickly, throwing a sharp 'Thank you' back over his shoulder.

Of course he could still tell Claire everything. Even if Lawrence did run for cover and refuse to confirm the truth of it, surely the story itself had its own compelling logic? Claire had remained sceptical before because she had found it too much to believe that he could have been mistakenly blackmailed on top of the fact that somebody had been taking hotel rooms in his name.

Now, once she returned, he could explain it all to her. He could tell her about his meeting with Melissa and then how he had confronted Lawrence and the whole truth had come tumbling out.

If Lawrence denied it then ... well, face it, anything could happen. Arguments, fist-fights, Claire leaving again, Adele leaving, both wives leaving together ...? The only certainty was that things looked a good deal less rosy than they had over breakfast when he had reassured Diane that the worst was over.

Richard went back into the house. Diane was still in the kitchen, glancing through the newspaper.

She looked up from it and asked, 'Is Lawrence helping you with this blackmail business?'

Richard hesitated. 'He's advised me on one or two legal points.'

'Right.' She smiled. 'It's useful having a solicitor living next door.'

He spent a slow morning going through the proofs for the new catalogue. He told himself that he must not even think about Lawrence Nevison or where Claire might be or when there might be another letter from the blackmailer; that side of his life was to be banished during office hours.

It was like trying to keep back an encroaching tide. The minute he stopped telling himself that these things must not even be thought of, they were there pushing to the forefront of his mind and the catalogue was forgotten. He could think only of Claire and what he would say to her and then what she would probably say in reply and where they might go from there.

Yesterday he had been optimistic, pinning his hopes on Melissa as the key to solving everything. As she had almost done. It was no fault of hers that the direction in which she pointed him proved a dead end, leading only to Lawrence Nevison, Moral Pigmy. And so the optimism that Richard had felt yesterday had today evaporated.

At a quarter to twelve Lynne rang through to say there was a Mr Nevison on the line wanting to speak to him and insisting it was urgent.

'*Nevison?*' echoed Richard, wondering if he had mis-heard. Why should he be making contact again so soon after their confrontation?

'Nevison, yes.'

'Put him on,' he instructed.

'Richard?' came the familiar voice on the other end of the line. It was less tremulous than it had been this morning. No doubt distance gave him confidence. Whatever he was going to say now, he wasn't risking a fist in the mouth.

'Yes?'

'First of all, I'm sorry about what happened earlier. I said things I didn't intend to say.'

Richard said nothing. If Lawrence thought a simple apology would be sufficient to erase the memory of his shifty twistings and turnings, he could have saved himself the trouble of making the call.

'I've been thinking about things since,' went on Lawrence. 'And I've got an idea – something that I think might help both of us clear this whole thing up.'

'I didn't know we needed any *ideas*,' said Richard, antagonized. 'As far as I'm concerned, all we need is for you to stand up and tell the truth.'

'Well, yes. And I will. I mean forget all that that I said about not speaking to Claire. I will speak to Claire, you have my word on that.'

His word. Well, that hadn't proved worth much up to now.

'I'm glad to hear it,' he said guardedly.

'I will talk to Claire, and I will explain to her how everything was my doing. Even so, there's still another aspect of all this that I'd like to talk to you about.'

'Go on.'

'No, I mean meet you to talk about it. Anywhere you like. Lunchtime if possible. Just tell me what's convenient.'

'Lawrence, I am not in the mood for a social drink.'

'I'm sure you're not. Especially not with me.'

Richard said nothing.

'But this wouldn't be just a social drink, I promise you that,' said Lawrence. 'This would be to discuss something quite different and quite new.'

Richard felt his resistance being chipped away. Perhaps Lawrence might have something useful to contribute after all. At least his change of heart on what he would and wouldn't say to Claire was to be applauded.

He still felt he must remain on guard. Lawrence, as he now understood him, did nothing for other people that didn't also benefit himself.

'Yes, all right,' he said.

'Thank you. Richard, I appreciate this.'

'Never mind appreciating it. Just understand one thing.

Whatever it is you want to talk to me about, it's not going to get you off having to talk to Claire.'

'No. I wouldn't expect it to.'

'Good. Where are you? In Manchester?'

'Yes, but I can get myself to anywhere that —'

'Do you know a pub in the centre called the Fat Scot?' It was where he had met Maurice barely twenty-four hours earlier.

'No, but I'm sure that I can find —'

'I'll meet you there at one o'clock.'

Lawrence not only found it but had arrived first. He had secured a table and had a scotch-and-soda standing on it waiting for Richard.

'Richard . . .!' he greeted him warmly. 'Thank you again for coming.'

He put out a hand, which Richard had little option but to take. On the way there, he had vowed that he would say as little as possible and leave it to Lawrence to make the running.

'Once again can I apologize for what I said this morning. I was . . . well, panicking.'

He paused a moment for Richard's response, then continued when no response was forthcoming.

'See, it's not just my marriage that I stand to lose here. It's also my career.'

This at least Richard felt he had to challenge. 'What, because of what Claire might say to other people?'

'No. No, I don't mean that. I respect Claire. I know that she isn't a gossip. Please, let me make that clear.'

'You have.'

Lawrence lent forward as though what he was about to communicate was confidential. Or perhaps it was to show that he felt the breach between them had been repaired and that they were buddies again.

'What you must realize, old man, is that I'm something of a public figure in this city. I'm known. I'm known in the courts, I'm known to the police . . . and to other people, journalists for example.'

'You think that should buy you special privileges?'

'On the contrary. I think it presents me with special dangers.'

'Like what?'

'Well, I'm thinking for instance of those photographs the blackmailer has taken.'

'What about them?'

'To start with, they're of me. I mean you must have realized that already. If there are any photographs, then they're of me and . . . and this Melissa woman.'

Richard couldn't quarrel with that and nodded his agreement. He had initially assumed that there couldn't be any photographs since they couldn't be of him. Now, knowing that Melissa existed and that the other Richard Gillow existed, it was likely that the photographs also existed. In which case they had to be of Lawrence with Melissa.

'And so you see the threat is to me,' went on Lawrence. 'With all respect, old man, the threat is to me, not you.'

'Yes.'

'What worries me is that those pictures will sooner or later surface. Whether we pay him or not – I doubt that would make any difference one way or another. For one thing, this black-mailer might well be blackmailing other people. In fact he probably is. There's no reason why we should be monopolizing his talents. So let's say that these other people go to the police and let's say that the blackmailer is arrested. Then what hap-pens? The police search wherever it is he lives . . . and, along with whatever else they find, they're going to find photographs of me.'

However unsympathetic Richard was, it was hard to deny the man had a valid point.

'I suppose they might.'

'I dread to think what would then happen if the press got their hands on such photographs. Or even if colleagues of mine should chance to see them.'

Richard found he was nodding in agreement. Be careful, he warned himself. You don't know where all this is leading.

'I can see all that,' he said. 'What I don't see is what you think I can do about it.'

Lawrence raised a finger, as though to say yes indeed, now this is the point.

'It's not what *you* can do, but what *we* can do together.'

'And what's that?'

Lawrence lent forward again and, with the air of a man

playing his trump card, said slowly, 'We can try and find the blackmailer before the police do.'

As a Great Idea it was something of a disappointment. Even as a relatively modest idea, it hardly justified dragging him from the office so that he might be present at its unveiling.

He tried to hide his exasperation. 'Lawrence, you seem to be forgetting that I've been to the police. And I've talked to Maurice about this. And there's no way you can just *find a blackmailer* without ... well, I don't know but some kind of major police effort.'

Lawrence's confidence seemed strangely undimmed. 'In most cases, yes. But not in this one. In this case I think we can find this blackmailer relatively easily.'

'We can?'

'Yes.'

'And how do we do that?'

'Well, firstly, we employ Maurice Townsend again.'

Richard was disappointed for a second time. He had been expecting something more imaginative.

'And what's he going to do?'

'Well, I'll come to that in a minute. But first let me say – I am going to pick up the bill for this. All Maurice's charges, up to now and anymore that we incur, I'll be paying them.'

Good manners prompted Richard to argue but he restrained himself, just saying: 'Let's not argue about that now. What I want to know is how Maurice . . . for whom, by the way, I have the highest regard . . . he did wonderful things in finding Melissa, but at least then he knew where to look . . . how is he to find the blackmailer?'

Lawrence gave an unexpected smile. 'That's what I've been thinking about. That's why I rung you this morning.'

'Go on.'

'There's only one place the blackmailer can be.'

Richard was bemused. He was also running out of patience and didn't appreciate being teased along like this. He shook his head, which made Lawrence smile again and which, in turn, made Richard even more impatient.

'Lawrence, can we please stop playing games –'

'Where did I meet Melissa?'

'Where?'

'Where did I meet her? Not just once but on all four occasions. And then where did you –'

Understanding flooded in.

'The hotel,' said Richard.

'Well, doesn't it have to be? I've only ever met this woman there. And it was at the hotel that I used your name. It was at the hotel that I used your address. Whoever saw me was at that hotel.'

'Well, yes, but it doesn't mean they were working there. They might have been just staying there,' said Richard, trying to pick holes.

Lawrence became animated. 'No, no! Don't you see? That's the beauty of it. They could only have got the wrong name and wrong address if they had access to the hotel records.'

It made sense. Richard began to share something of Lawrence's excitement. 'So it has to be someone working there.'

'If this blackmailer had actually recognized me then he would never have sent the letters to you by mistake. He only did that because he was relying on the information I'd given when I'd registered.'

It was an argument Richard couldn't fault. Nor did he any longer wish to. 'The blackmailer is somebody who works at the Queens Hotel,' he said slowly, relishing this new discovery, and not even resenting the fact it was Lawrence who had made it.

'Well, don't you think it has to be?'

'I do, yes.'

Lawrence sat back, wreathed in smiles, the conjuror whose latest trick has brought the house down.

But Richard was already foreseeing complications. 'But how is Maurice to identify him among a staff that might run to hundreds?'

'All I'm saying is – let's give him the chance. He found Melissa. Let's see if he can't find the blackmailer as well.'

13

Richard insisted he would be the one to go and see Maurice and put the proposition to him. He didn't trust Lawrence, whose only interest was getting himself off the hook. He would surely destroy the incriminating photographs if he ever got his hands on them. After that, he would be able to deny everything, leaving Richard without a leg to stand on.

He would see Maurice himself and that way remain in the driving-seat.

Lawrence didn't argue. In fact, he agreed that it would perhaps be better if Richard did go alone. It would, he said, help to keep things nice and simple.

'Fine, then let's do that,' said Richard, privately observing that it would also help keep Lawrence out of the limelight. The last thing Lawrence would want would be for Maurice Townsend to become aware of his role in all this.

Lawrence had more to say: 'And, if I were you, old man, I'd make it clear to Maurice that this is absolutely urgent. Top priority.'

'Would you,' said Richard, resenting the instructions. Wasn't it enough that he was offering to do the dirty work instead of forcing Lawrence to break cover?

'I'm only thinking – the blackmailer's waiting for his money. If he has to wait for too long and gets the idea he's never going to be paid . . . well, you never know what he might do. He might send those pictures to anybody.'

'Like Claire you mean.'

'Pardon?'

Richard spelled it out. 'If he starts sending out pictures, then Claire is going to be top of his list. My wife. The wife of the man he thinks is in those pictures.'

He took a certain amount of pleasure in watching Lawrence turn that thought over. Clearly it had only just occurred to him that such an outcome would do Richard no harm at all. It would deliver incontestable proof of his own innocence straight into Claire's hands. Lawrence had unwittingly pointed to the strongest card in Richard's hand. All he had to do was refuse to pay the blackmailer, sit back and wait for the photographs to arrive.

'Don't worry, I'll tell him it's urgent,' he said, putting Lawrence out of his misery. 'I assume you won't want me to mention your name . . .?'

'Ah, well, no. That is, if it's at all possible not to.'

'I daresay it will be.'

'I am very, very grateful. Believe me, Richard –'

'Save it,' said Richard, not sure he could stomach a dollop of gratitude coming on top of everything else – evasions, deceit, defiance, cowardice – that he had had from Lawrence during the last twenty-four hours. 'I'll let you know what happens.'

He stood up, not bothering to wait for Lawrence's reaction, and shouldered his way out of the crowded pub. Once outside, he was surprised by a light shower of rain and had to jog back to where he had parked his car in the multi-storey behind Kendals.

He rang Maurice to arrange a meeting. True to form, Maurice was able to fit him in later that same afternoon. He was curious to know how the date with Melissa had gone.

'It couldn't have been better,' Richard reassured him. 'She was certainly the lady referred to in the letters.'

'She admitted that?'

'Eventually she did, yes. She was even able to tell me the real name of the man who'd be passing himself off as me.'

'Was it somebody you knew?'

Richard hesitated, then said, 'Vaguely. It was certainly somebody who knew me.' That was an avenue best avoided. 'No, I think we're well on the way to clearing up that side of things. It's just that there's something else – another aspect of this – that I'd like to talk to you about.'

And so at six o'clock that evening Richard found himself once again parking outside the bookies' and ringing the bell on the reinforced brown door beside it. He felt the chill of an evening breeze as he waited for the ancient intercom to crackle into life.

Above him was a solid mass of cloud, threatening more rain. So the summer was over then, was it? It was one he would be glad to put behind him.

The intercom invited him to open the door. He took the steps two at a time and went through the small room at the top into the main office. Maurice rose from behind his desk to greet him. He was wearing his battered brown suit but this time there was a blue turtle-neck sweater beneath it.

'I'm very pleased things worked out with this Melissa woman,' he said solemnly.

'I'm very grateful. You did a wonderful job finding her.'

'So is your wife happier now?'

Richard made the split-second decision to lie rather than attempt to explain the complexities of his relationship with Claire or the reasons for her absence.

'Yes,' he said. 'Much happier.'

'I don't often have the chance to make people happy,' said Maurice. 'Unhappy, yes. I do that all the time.' He made a gesture of helplessness, as if to say: but this is what people insist of me so how can I stop them?

Then he said, 'And this Melissa.'

'Yes?'

'From the way you spoke about her on the phone, I gather you don't think she's been doing the blackmailing?'

'No, I don't.' His conviction on this surprised himself. He had to pause to find the reasons behind it. 'For one thing, she knew the real identity of the man she was with, so she would never have made the mistake of sending the letters to me. For another . . . well, she just didn't strike me as the type to be involved in something like that.'

'No? Well, I'm sure you're right.'

'But Melissa was only part of the problem. I'd still like us to try and find this blackmailer.'

Maurice frowned. 'That's not so easy.'

'I know. And I know you're going to tell me it should be a police matter –'

Maurice nodded.

'But there are reasons why I don't wish to put this into the hands of the police. Forgive me if I don't go into them.'

'Mr Gillow, sir, I'm just paid to do a job. You don't have to

explain anything. Though what I can't help wondering . . .
Sorry. Do you mind if I say this?'

'Go ahead.'

'Why does the blackmailer matter anymore? Why can't you
just ignore the letters now that your wife no longer feels threatened by them?'

Richard was trapped by his own lie. It was a fair question.
What was he doing here at all if Claire was at home happily
getting the dinner on?

Rather than risk becoming entangled in yet more lies, he
smiled and said, 'It's just the kind of person I am. I don't like to
leave things unfinished.'

Maurice raised his hands in apology for ever having asked. 'I
can understand that. But I have to say to you, Mr Gillow, that
when it comes to finding whoever has been writing these letters,
I'm not sure I'd even know where to start.'

'I think I might be able to help you there,' said Richard. 'I've
been thinking about this and I have an idea where you might
find him.'

Maurice looked surprised but said nothing. He listened with
his customary attentiveness to what Richard had to say: which
was basically a re-hash of Lawrence's idea that, because everything had happened in and around the one hotel, then it was
probable that the blackmailer worked there. His mistake in
sending the letters to Richard virtually confirmed the fact, since
only someone with access to the hotel records could have mis-
identified Lawrence Nevison as Richard Gillow in that way.

Maurice nodded. 'Makes sense,' he said. He thought some
more, then said, 'Makes a lot of sense.'

'It also occurred to me,' went on Richard, 'that anyone doing
this now might have done it before. I mean, why should I be his
first victim? Odds are he's been doing this for years.'

This was now, genuinely, an idea of his own, one he had
developed since leaving Lawrence and returning to his office. If
the blackmailer were indeed a hotel employee, then he would be
permanently in a position to blackmail the hotel's guests. Richard had no reason to believe himself the first or last to suffer like
this.

'It's certainly possible,' agreed Maurice.

'And if he has done this before – perhaps in other hotels, I don't know – but if he has, then he might have come unstuck. Which means he'll have a police record.'

'That's possible too.'

'Can you find out for me?'

Maurice grimaced. Clearly he was reluctant to commit himself on this.

Richard tried to think of something more to say, sensing that a little bit of encouragement might tip the balance. 'I don't know what you think might be the best way to set about this. Whether you can get access to information that the courts have or the police? Or should we be approaching the hotel and talking to them?'

Maurice contemplated a moment or two longer, then he said: 'I can't guarantee anything.'

'No, I understand –'

'And I have to emphasise again – this is a criminal matter. It's not something I would normally touch with a bargepole.'

Richard waited, placing his faith in that word 'normally'. So did that mean he was willing to make an exception in this case?

There was another pause then Maurice said, 'It might cost a couple of hundred. I mean on top of my fees. Or even more – three, four hundred even.'

'That's all right.'

'And another thing . . .'

He glanced round, as though to check they were alone and couldn't be overheard.

'Anything I tell you I won't be telling you.'

It took Richard a moment to decipher this but, once he had, he was happy to endorse it.

'Of course. Whatever happened, I would never mention your name in connection with any of this.'

'We haven't even had this conversation,' said Maurice solemnly.

'No.'

'And when I've anything to report, which might not be for a few days, well, then that will be another conversation that we won't be having.'

Richard was barely home, with time only to check with Diane

that there had been no word from Claire, before Lawrence was at the door. He must have seen his car arrive and was calling to ask what had happened.

They went into the lounge and Richard closed the door. It was useful that Diane had assumed that Lawrence was weighing in on their side with legal advice. It meant she wouldn't question these sessions they were suddenly having together.

'Will he do it?' demanded Lawrence.

Richard explained how Maurice had been initially reluctant to involve himself, since this was a criminal matter and so outside his usual jurisdiction. Lawrence scowled, displeased. His expression only cleared when Richard went on to explain how Maurice had changed his mind once he had heard their idea that the blackmailer was probably working at the hotel.

'That's wonderful. Congratulations, Richard, it sounds like you did a marvellous job.'

'Thank you,' said Richard, wondering how he could have ever thought this man trustworthy and on the level.

'And you told him it was urgent?'

'I'm sure he understands that it is.'

'And you didn't have to use my name?'

'I didn't, no. Maurice hasn't the slightest idea you're involved.'

Lawrence began an elaborate litany of thanks but Richard cut him short.

'There is one thing I ought to make clear,' he said.

'What?'

'If Claire gets back before Maurice comes up with the goods . . . ' He paused to give Lawrence a chance to appreciate the implications of that particular scenario. Then he went on, 'I shall have to tell her what's happened. I mean including the part that you've played in everything. I can't afford not to.'

Lawrence gave a tight, little smile. 'I understand.'

'Well, good. And I hope you'll also understand that I'll be expecting you to talk to Claire as well and to confirm everything I'll be telling her.'

This time Lawrence gave a sigh and shook his head. Richard thought he was going to protest again or plead to be granted a stay of execution, but no.

'I'll tell her,' he said, in a quiet, strained sort of voice that

Richard assumed was intended to convey something of the agony he was going through.

In fact, the question of who would say what to Claire remained academic while she was still absent and incommunicado. After the second day ended and then a third passed without anything from her, Richard began to wonder what he might do to track her down. Who might she have spoken to before leaving? Or perhaps she had rung someone once she'd made her escape and felt secure in her bolthole? He could think only of Moira. Claire wasn't one of those women who needed a whole team of confidantes around them. Moira was the only one she might have spoken to about something like this. He decided to ring her, and never mind what she might make of his enquiries.

'Moira, hello. It's Richard here.'

'Oh, hello.'

'Look, why I'm ringing – you don't happen to know where Claire is, do you?'

'I'm sorry. I don't, no.'

He might have left it at that. But then, when she failed to follow that up with the kind of questioning he would have expected – *why? has something happened? was she all right? when had Richard last seen her?* – he realized she must know more than she was admitting to.

'You know she's gone away . . .?' he said.

'I . . . I thought she must have, yes.'

'So do you know where?'

'No. No, really I don't, Richard. I'd tell you if I did.'

'OK, sorry to have bothered you,' he said, prepared to leave it at that.

Moira said quickly, 'I know she was thinking of going away. I mean just for a while. We talked after your party.'

'She told you what's been going on?'

'Well . . . you mean about the letters?'

'Yes.'

'She told me something about them, yes.'

'So have you got the slightest idea where she might have gone?' he appealed.

'None. Honestly and truly.'

'OK. But can I ask you one thing, one favour?'

'Of course, yes.'

'If Claire does ring you, can you tell her that I've sorted this whole thing out and it's vital I speak to her.'

'Yes. Oh, have you really? What, you mean sorted out the letters?'

But he wasn't going to be drawn into further explanation. By the sound of it, Moira knew too much already. And, if she knew, then how long before the collapse of the Gillow marriage would be dinner-table gossip over a ten-mile radius? There would be those who would claim to have always believed such a collapse inevitable – well, with him away so much, and staying in London . . .! There would even be those who would claim to have detected early signs of such a split way back, years ago even, citing as evidence disagreements witnessed at parties or the excessive number of empties delivered by Claire every Monday morning to the village bottle-bank.

And there would certainly be those who would cling more tightly to their own spouses for a night or two, thinking *there but for the grace of God.*

There was only one other person he could imagine Claire having contacted. Making sure Diane was out of earshot, he looked up David's number in their leather-backed address book on the hall table, then dialled it.

'Oh, dad, hi,' responded David, sounding comfortable enough. Not on his guard or hostile.

'You haven't heard from your mother over the past day or two, have you?'

'No. Why?'

'No, it doesn't matter –'

'Dad, what's happened? Is this to do with that business you told us about after the party?'

Richard knew immediately that it had been a mistake to ring. He had stirred up a hornets' nest where all had been peaceful. Still, having come this far, he had no choice but to bring David up to date on developments, explaining how he'd gone to the private detective and so located the woman in the case and, through her, had been able to identify his impostor.

'Who? Who was it?' demanded David.

Richard sighed. 'I'm sorry. I can't tell you that.'

'Why not?' Meaning – *I'm not going to believe you if you don't.*

'Because I promised I wouldn't,' said Richard, knowing how feeble David must find this answer.

He had been sceptical from the outset. The news that his mother had walked out and that his father was refusing to name the villain of the piece could only confirm him in his opposition.

'You promised . . .? Dad, am I really hearing this? You've found you who this guy is but you've promised you'll keep his name a secret?'

'There are reasons.'

'What sort of reasons?'

'I'm sorry, David. I can't tell you that.'

This was sounding even more feeble. He wished he had never gone near the phone. He struggled now to find a way of putting it down, but David had the bit between his teeth and was wanting answers.

'Dad, what is going on? I demand to know. For Christ's sake, I have a right to know!'

'And I've told you as much as I can –'

'Well, no, I don't think you have. I don't think you've told me fuck-all!'

'David –'

'Dad, why don't you just come clean and tell the truth?'

Richard felt the first stirrings of anger. Yes, he could understand David's point of view but that hardly gave him *carte blanche* to revile him like this. He was a hundred and fifty miles away, in the middle of the Welsh hills, knowing, as he put it, fuck-all. He had no right to behave like a bad-tempered barrister.

'I am telling the truth.'

'Really? Well, I've got to say it doesn't sound like it to me.'

'Oh, you can recognize the truth when you hear it, can you?'

'Dad, the truth as I see it . . . I mean if you really want me to say this –'

'No –'

'The truth is that you've been having an affair. Now you might not want to call it that. You might want to call it a *relationship*. Doesn't matter, call it whatever you like . . . you've been found out.'

'David, that is not the truth. That has never been the truth.'

'Oh –'

'No, you listen to me a minute please. Those letters were only sent to me because somebody else had been using my name –'

'Who?'

It was that direct challenge again, which stopped him in his tracks and had him floundering for an answer.

'I can't tell you his name.'

'OK, dad,' said David flatly, not bothering to hide his disbelief. 'Well, when you can, maybe we can talk then.'

'I certainly hope so.'

'Bye.'

And the phone was replaced at the other end.

So now I've lost my son too, he thought. First my wife walks out, then my son puts the phone down on me. And why? Because of my friend and neighbour Lawrence Nevison – *whose good name I am seeking to protect!*

He was sorely tempted to ring David back and tell him yes, I will tell you the name of the man who was impersonating me. Why not? When the man was shifty and evasive and selfish and deserved nothing but exposure and general contempt?

Yet, even as he teased himself with the thought, he knew that he wouldn't do it. He had promised Lawrence that only Claire would ever know the truth and he would abide by that.

When the doorbell went next morning as he was having breakfast, Richard's first thought was that it must be Lawrence come to ask if there were any news yet. He must have asked a dozen times over the past few days. What he wanted to know was whether there had been any communication from Maurice – which might be good news – or from Claire – which would not be.

Up to now, Richard's reply had been a flat no. Lawrence would nod resignedly. 'You'll let me know as soon as there is, won't you,' had become his parting-shot.

In fact, this time it wasn't Lawrence at all: it was Adele. She was wearing a white smock and open sandals and smiling up at him in that nervous fashion of hers.

'Oh, I'm sorry for disturbing you at this time. What will you think of me,' she exclaimed.

'No, come in,' he urged, unable to do otherwise.

His first thought was to wonder whether Lawrence had told her the full story after all. Perhaps she had found it incredible and was round here in search of corroboration. Though it seemed unlikely. She didn't seem particularly upset, as she congratulated him on the impressive display of their front garden, still full of blooms though they were now in September.

Diane had appeared, with heavy eyes and straggly hair, looking as though she had leapt out of bed and pulled on her long Greenpeace T-shirt. Richard guessed that the sound of voices had made her curious. Perhaps she had thought it was Claire returning.

''Morning, Adele,' said Diane, hiding any disappointment she might have felt.

''Morning, dear. Now look, I'm disturbing everybody, aren't I. And I only came over for a quick word with Claire, if she's around.'

The innocent, wide-eyed way in which she asked this struck Richard as contrived. A not wholly convincing performance. You actually don't expect Claire to be around, he thought. So that was the reason for the visit: she was fishing for information on where Claire might have disappeared to.

He saw that Diane was looking at him, waiting for her cue.

'No, she's not,' he said. 'In fact, she's away for a few days.'

Adele didn't seem too surprised. 'Anywhere nice?'

'Not really. Just business. Meetings here and there, you know how it is.'

'I think she hates it really,' Diane chimed in, playing the supporting role. 'Always moans before she goes.'

'I see. Only she was booked to come and talk to my luncheon club tomorrow. You know the club that I . . . well, no, you might not. There's really no reason why you should know anything about it. But Claire was due to come and talk to us and, well, I'd noticed she hadn't been around and so I wondered –'

'Whether she'll be here tomorrow? I rather doubt it.'

Diane nodded her agreement. 'I think she said something about being away till the end of the week at least.'

'Oh, dear,' said Adele, looking genuinely crestfallen.

Richard felt a pang of sympathy. 'And I apologize on her behalf. Obviously she's forgotten. All I can say is that she's been very busy.'

'Run off her feet,' said Diane.

Adele managed a brave smile and said they would manage somehow and now she mustn't keep them any longer. Richard escorted her back through the hallway.

As he opened the front door, she said, 'Can I ask you something?'

Richard held his breath. Did her visit have an ulterior motive after all? 'Of course.'

'Has Lawrence shown you his novel he's been writing?'

He breathed again. 'His novel, no. Is he writing one?' He knew that Claire had told him this but he couldn't for the life in him remember whether it had been told in confidence.

'Yes,' said Adele. 'In fact, I think he's finished it.'

'Well, I'll be happy to read it. You must tell him.'

Even after that, she seemed reluctant to leave, hovering on the doorstep. 'It's just that I know he's been round here to see you a couple of times –'

'I suppose he has, yes.'

'And I wondered if he'd shown it to you and you'd said you didn't like it?'

'No,' said Richard. For once he could tell the truth. 'I've never even seen his novel. He's never mentioned it.'

Adele continued as though he hadn't spoken. 'Because he seems upset about something. And, well, angry about it too. As though he's had some sort of . . . set-back. Something that he wasn't expecting.'

He realized suddenly that she was wanting his advice. Perhaps this was the true reason she had come round, calling early to catch him before he left for work.

He thought of what Melissa had told him. Lawrence had complained to her about his wife – '*He said she has no time for him. She's too wrapped up in her own life.*'

'Well, I don't know what that can be,' he said. 'So I'm afraid I can't be much help.'

'I just thought he might have said something to you.'

''Fraid not. All we've been talking about is some legal business that Lawrence has been helping me with.'

'I see. Of course, I should have expected that. I'm sorry, Richard, you must think I'm such a nuisance.'

He saw the tears spring into her eyes and was drawn forward, seeking to reassure: 'No, I don't, really – ' But she had already turned and was hurrying away towards her own house.

He returned to the kitchen, where Diane was waiting.

'So I wonder who's going to speak at Adele's luncheon club,' said Diane.

He knew she was inviting him to make light of it, but he couldn't. The sight of her hurrying away, trying to conceal her tears, had touched him.

'I'm just sorry we've had to deceive her,' he said.

'Oh, but we'd no choice . . .!'

'Exactly. That's what I'm saying.'

'Anyway, Adele would never understand.'

Wouldn't she? he thought. Perhaps Adele would understand a great deal more than they had ever given her credit for.

He marvelled at the way they had all lived for so long in what now, looking back on it, seemed to have been a state of innocence. Or perhaps the innocence had been his alone. He had viewed the people around them as generally content and successful, with only the odd spillage to interrupt life's pleasant routines. Lawrence and Adele would have been a case in point, happy and settled with little to worry them.

It had probably never been like that at all. First Lawrence had surprised him, turning out to be ruthless where his own survival was concerned. And now here was Adele, in tears on his doorstep.

He felt a deep sympathy for her. After all, she had had to deal with Lawrence too, and no doubt knew better than he did the kind of spineless bastard she had married. He wondered whether she had considered the various possibilities – divorce, playing him at his own game – but had rejected them as dishonourable and had buckled down to support him, come what may.

For her sake, he would do what he could to protect Lawrence. He would name him neither to David nor to anyone else. He would even try ringing Maurice and stressing the urgency of finding who among the staff of the Queens Hotel might be the blackmailer.

14

Maurice Townsend rang that same morning even before Richard could ring to impress him with the urgency of the case. The call was taken by Yvonne and put straight through to Richard, who had instructed her on this, stressing the priority that had to be given to any calls from Townsend Investigations.

Maurice was at his most enigmatic: 'Regarding those enquiries you asked me to make.'

'Yes?'

'I have something that I think might interest you. Could we meet as soon as possible?'

Just tell me now, thought Richard, desperate to know what Maurice had turned up. But he knew Maurice's policy where phones were concerned and so kept his thoughts to himself.

'Let me see,' he said, and glanced over the sheet that Lynne had made out, listing his commitments for the day. There were no gaps anywhere. He was booked solid through to six this evening. 'Yes,' he said. 'Anytime. Today if possible.'

'Today, yes. What time would suit?'

'The sooner the better.'

The outcome was that they were to meet at eleven-thirty in the buffet on Victoria Station. The venue was Maurice's choice, whether for convenience or security or because he liked trains Richard had no idea. He reminded himself that Maurice must have discovered something to be putting them both to this much trouble.

He delegated a couple of his planned meetings to Simon, told Lynne that he had been called away on personal business and then left quickly before she could show her displeasure.

The station clock showed eleven-twenty then jerked forward one whole minute as he came along the concourse heading for the buffet. It had an ornate, rather grand exterior, on which was displayed a map showing routes served by the station, north into the Lake District and south into Wales.

Inside, the buffet had a high ceiling and displayed sepia photographs of its former glory, when waitresses dispensed tea and cakes to travellers seated at tables which were covered in white table-clothes. Now it was chrome and potted plants and serve-yourself. A pigeon, caught under the high ceiling, fluttered overhead.

Richard looked around but could see no sign of Maurice. In fact, there was hardly a sign of anyone. The place seemed becalmed in a late morning doldrums. Richard bought a coffee and took it to an empty table.

He had barely sat down before he spotted Maurice coming in through the swing-doors. He raised a hand in greeting and Maurice came striding over.

'Sorry about this place,' he said as he took the chair across from Richard. 'But at least you know you're not going to be overheard.'

'I wondered if you might be a train-spotter.'

'No,' said Maurice, without the slightest twitch of a smile.

'I mean,' said Richard, forced into an explanation, 'I wondered if that was the reason for having us meet here.'

'I see,' said Maurice, though he remained unsmiling. 'No, I chose it mainly because I'm engaged on surveillance work which means I have to be here for the twelve-oh-five from Blackburn.'

So there were other souls in torment, engaging Maurice to find them absolution or, no doubt in many cases, to confirm their worst fears. It was small wonder the man wasn't given to outbursts of gaiety. His daily routine of turning over stones and noting what moved beneath them made the business of book-publishing seem suddenly frivolous.

Richard offered him a coffee, or a drink perhaps . . .? But he declined. He seemed a shade nervous, less composed than on the other occasions when they had met. Either he was pressed for time, frightened of missing the twelve-oh-five from Blackburn, or he was eager to get this blackmail business over and done with.

'Now, Mr Gillow,' he said, getting down to business, 'we were investigating the possibility that the blackmailer might work at the hotel.'

'Yes.'

187

'What I did, I got a list of the hotel employees. It's possible the management got the wrong impression and believed they were dealing with the Inland Revenue.'

Richard gave the appreciative smile this called for.

'Of course, if I were asked, then I would have to deny all this. As I would have to deny that this conversation we're having has ever taken place.'

'I understand that, yes.'

Maurice nodded. 'Anyway, what I did then, I took this list of hotel employees to a friend of mine who's still on the force. And he ran it through the police computer to see if it could tell us anything.'

'And did it?'

'It did, yes. It produced quite a crop of minor convictions, nothing of importance. With one exception, which I think you will be interested in.' He took a folded sheet of paper from the inside pocket of his jacket and placed in on the table between them.

'Someone with a record for blackmail . . .?' ventured Richard.

'Exactly. Just as you suspected.'

'Ha!' said Richard, triumphant.

Maurice unfolded the paper and read: 'Philip Conway Thornton.'

'That's our man?'

'That, I believe, is our man. Unless there should turn out to be two blackmailers operating from the same premises.'

'He works at the hotel?'

'He does, yes. He's a barman.'

'Barman . . .?'

'Bar supervisor is how they've dressed it up. But barman is what it comes down to.'

It was like completing a jigsaw and seeing the whole picture, simple and clear, for the first time. A barman. Well, yes, of course. Who could be better placed? A barman was in the ideal situation to witness the comings and goings and to notice the couples who had that tell-tale self-consciousness about them. What's more, if the girls from the Star Escort Agency were in the habit of nominating the Queens bar as the place where they regularly met their clients, then wouldn't he come to recognize them after a time and so know that these men smiling and buying drinks were most of them shaking in their shoes lest they be recognized?

It would be like lambs to the slaughter.

The ones who had taken a room for the night or who were resident there anyway would no doubt charge their drinks to their room number. This would leave Philip Conway Thornton with the laughably simple task of looking up that number in the hotel records and extracting a corresponding name and address. Maybe he even had a computer link-up in the bar that would do it for him and so save him the fifty-yard trip to reception.

A barman. And one with a record for the identical offence. It had to be him.

Richard even wondered whether it might be the same barman who had served him on that terrible night when he had tried proving to Claire that he couldn't have been there before because no-one recognized him. He tried to picture the man but couldn't. Who could ever picture a barman? They were invisible, as servants had once been.

Maurice was handing him the sheet of paper. 'I've jotted down a sort of CV of this man for you.'

'Thank you.'

'The important thing is that in 1982 he was charged with blackmail, found guilty and got three years. That was while he was working in a hotel in Brighton. According to the notes on the case, it looks like he was running a similar racket there. Working out which guests wouldn't want it broadcast who they were sharing a room with and then putting the screws on.'

It was all summarized on the paper Maurice had given him. 'GUILDFORD CROWN COURT, 17.9.1982. DEMANDING MONEY WITH MENACES. VERDICT: GUILTY. SENTENCE: THREE YEARS.'

'Has to be him,' muttered Richard. 'It's just too much of a coincidence otherwise.'

'I'd put money on it.'

'How does he take the photographs though?' said Richard, thinking aloud. 'According to the letters, he has photographs of these people together.'

'Couldn't be easier,' said Maurice. 'I have a camera myself that's no bigger than . . . than the bowl of your coffee spoon. You can hold it in the palm of one hand and you can take photographs and no-one would ever spot it. Believe me, I've done it.'

Richard nodded. Put like that, he could imagine it wouldn't be too difficult a feat. The barman would be helped by the fact that his subjects would have been preoccupied with one another. The man in particular would be anxious to conclude the business of handing over the fee, trying to do it discreetly so that no-one else would notice.

Hadn't he been just the same when he'd met Melissa? He would hardly have noticed had a gang of *paparazzi* come swarming around them, never mind a miniature camera taking snaps from behind the canapés.

'So he'll be what, fifty-three,' mused Richard, seeing the date of birth.

'Can I ask you one thing, Mr Gillow?'

'Yes?'

'Are you intending taking this information to the police?'

'No, I'm not.' Of that at least he was certain.

It came as a relief to Maurice. 'Then I need say no more.'

'Don't worry,' Richard reassured him. 'I'm not quite sure what I will do yet. But the one thing I can promise you is that it won't involve the police.'

Maurice glanced at his watch and said, 'I'm glad to hear that. And now, Mr Gillow, I'd better be on my way if you don't mind.'

They shook hands. Richard said that he would look forward to receiving his bill, and then Maurice was departing, a gaunt figure stalking away across the tea-room.

Richard remained where he was, feeling there was some obscure code involved here, one that forbade their leaving together. Besides, he wanted time to consider all he had just been told. He re-read the details on the sheet that Maurice had given him. 'PHILIP CONWAY THORNTON, BORN 1941. PRESENT ADDRESS ... ' There followed a history of his employment, which was mostly in hotels, and then a stark outline of the Demanding Money With Menaces charge, on which he'd been found guilty.

Richard was gripped by a sudden urge. He wouldn't go back to the office, not yet. First, he would go to the Queens Hotel where he would have a look at this Philip Thornton, this man who had come so close to bringing down his marriage. He wouldn't do anything or say anything to him; the time for that would be later. But the urge simply to go and look at him was overwhelming.

He walked past the Cathedral and into the city centre. Lunchtime was getting underway, with people casting wary eyes at the swollen clouds overhead.

The Queens Hotel in the middle of the day wore a markedly different face to the one it presented in the evening. It had a sombre, almost gloomy air, as though caught dozing without its make-up on. There was no pianist and little activity, only the whirring of the lifts to break the general hush.

Richard crossed the foyer and headed for the bar. He felt a righteous anger but also a distinct sense of anticipation. For the first time since the beginning of this fiasco, he held the upper hand. He had discovered the identity of his blackmailer while the blackmailer was no nearer understanding that he had all along been sending letters to the wrong man.

The bar had a few people at its tables but nothing like the numbers that might congregate there in the evenings. It had already occurred to Richard that Philip Thornton might not be working. There must be several barmen employed in an establishment of this size. Philip Thornton was just one among them and might be having a day off.

There was only one man behind the bar at the moment. Approaching, Richard saw it was the same man who had served him when he had been with Claire. He was probably somewhere in his fifties. Short and balding; what hair he had was brylcreemed back. A candidate then.

But why speculate? What Richard hadn't noticed on his earlier visits, probably because it had been of no significance, was that the staff wore small, blue plastic name-badges pinned to their lapels.

And this man's said 'PHILIP THORNTON'. No more, no less. It was what might have been regarded as a full confession.

'Yes, sir?'

'Scotch and soda please.'

'Certainly, sir. Ice?'

'No, thank you.'

Richard watched him as he moved around the bar, going to the optics and then back to the refrigerated shelf of mixers. So this was his enemy. This was the invisible aggressor, the sniper firing from the roof-tops.

He didn't look particularly lethal. Five foot six or seven, no more than that. And with Geordie origins if Richard's ears weren't misleading him.

He placed Richard's drink on the bar in front of him. 'Shall I charge it to your room, sir?'

'No, I'll pay you for it.'

'Thank you, sir. That will be two pound thirty.'

Richard found it difficult to take his eyes off the man. So this was their blackmailer, the cause of all their suffering. It was amazing to realize that Claire had also stood here before him. They had both been served by him when neither he nor they had been aware of the link between them.

He watched him go to the till and throw money into its various drawers. Viewed from behind, he had a considerable bald spot on the crown of his head and the backside of his trousers was shiny from use. He had also, Richard now saw, a slight limp, just the smallest, almost imperceptible, list to starboard as he came away from the till.

He presented Richard with his change. 'There we are, sir.'

'Thank you.'

'Thank you, sir.'

Richard watched him move away down the bar and thought – we will have our hour of reckoning, you and I. And it will be soon.

He must choose his moment carefully. This was not about simple, straightforward vengeance, though a certain amount of that would be pleasant. It was first-and-foremost about how to get the photographs from him, the ones that were so terrifying Lawrence and which would be so extremely useful in proving his own innocence before Claire.

He remained at the bar for a further ten minutes, watching Philip Conway Thornton as he served other customers. He looked like a man at ease in a world he regarded as his own. A man who believed he could assess his customers and pick out the ones whom lust had made vulnerable.

'Anything else, sir?' he asked Richard, seeing his empty glass.

'No, thank you. Are you on tonight?'

Philip Thornton looked surprised at the question. 'I am as a matter-of-fact, sir, yes.'

'Might see you again then,' said Richard. 'Good-bye.'

'Good-bye, sir.'

On the way back to the office, he bought a midday newspaper. Turning to the inside pages, he found the Personal Column. In it, sure enough, was a two-line advertisement for Star Escorts: '*A wide choice of intelligent and lovely girls for evening engagements*'. It gave the phone number which he had once been given by Maurice but which he had disposed of once the original date with Melissa had been set up.

Now, back at his desk, he dialled the number again.

'Star Escorts. Julie speaking.' It was old gravel-voice herself.

'Hello. I wonder if I could arrange to meet one of your young ladies, this evening if possible.'

'Certainly, dear. Are you ringing from a hotel?'

'No, but I could arrange to meet her in one. Look, it has to be one young lady in particular. The one called Melissa.'

He had expected that she might try to tempt him with somebody else. He was certainly expecting her to say, as she had last time, that she would have to check with Melissa then ring him back. In fact, what she did say was the one thing he wasn't expecting at all.

'I'm sorry,' she said, 'but I'm afraid Melissa's not with us anymore.'

'She's not?' he exclaimed.

'No, but don't let that worry you. We do have lots of other girls who I'm sure you'd find just as attractive.'

She launched into a description of several of them, who had names like Tina and Cindy. Richard let her go on, barely hearing a word, as he cast around for a way around this surprise obstacle. '*I'm afraid Melissa's not with us anymore.*' Did that mean she was with someone else? Or that she had disappeared forever and was beyond recall?

'No, I'm sorry but I really don't want anybody else,' he said, stopping her. 'It has to be Melissa.'

'Well, then I'm sorry, dear, I'm afraid we can't help you.'

'You must still have her number or know how she can be contacted?'

'I'm sorry but it is strict policy that we don't give out any numbers –'

'I know, yes. I wouldn't expect you to. No, what I'm asking is – would you give her a message from me?' Then he added, 'Please. This is important.' He found the woman exasperating, with her mixture of coyness and mendacity, but just at the moment he needed her cooperation; without her, Melissa might as well have been on the far side of the moon.

He said, 'I'd of course be happy to pay you the usual fee.'

There was a pause. He was beginning to lose hope, then she said, 'Well, all right, dear. I'll try my best for you. But I can't promise anything.'

'Thank you. I appreciate it. Could you tell her that I'd like to meet her tonight. At the Queens Hotel. Anytime after nine.'

'After nine, yes.'

'And tell her it's Richard Gillow. The man she met last week.'

'Oh, yes, I thought I recognized the voice.'

'Well, yes, it's me again. Richard Gillow.'

'Richard Gillow, yes, I've got that.'

'And if you could tell her one more thing. And that is that I need to speak to her regarding the letters.'

The afternoon slowly passed away without Julie ringing back. Never mind, he told himself. Even without Melissa, he would go to the hotel that night and confront Philip Thornton. He would put the fear of death into him and force him to hand over the photographs. It would be best attempted after dark, perhaps when Thornton had finished work.

Melissa's presence would have been useful because Thornton would have seen them together and been reminded of the letters. He might even have seen Richard as another potential victim. It would have been an effective piece of stage-setting for the moment that would come later when Richard would grab him and tell him what he knew.

There was another reason that he had attempted to contact Melissa via Star Escorts and that – why not admit it? – was that she would have been pleasant company, helping to while away what might turn out to be a very long evening.

Later in the afternoon it began to rain. Richard adjusted the skylight windows to keep the drops out. His pretence of a man concentrating on his business had been tolerably successful. Lynne had glanced at him a time or two as though doubtful whether he was fully compos mentis but she had largely refrained from comment. About four-thirty she brought his correspondence through to be signed.

'And will you be going to London this week?' she asked.

He felt suddenly cornered, not knowing the answer. His planned confrontation with Philip Thornton had dominated all else. He hadn't been able to think beyond it.

His phone rang. 'Excuse me,' he said, and picked it up.

And there she was – instantly recognizable, *basso profondo* Julie saying, 'Hello, dear. Sorry it took so long.'

'That's all right. One minute.' He placed a hand over the receiver and said to Lynne, 'I'll talk to you later about London. I have to take this call.'

'Of course,' she said, with a smile that seemed designed to conceal a bitter wound. She retreated across the room and closed his door carefully.

Richard spoke into the telephone. 'Did you manage to speak to Melissa?'

'Yes, I did. And you know what?'

'What?'

'She says all right. She says she'll see you tonight. At the Queens Hotel, nine o'clock.'

Richard could have cheered. This was a sign from the gods, telling him they were on his side. He would meet Melissa this very evening at the Queens Hotel, as he had supposedly done so many times in the past. Philip Thornton would witness that meeting.

After which, when he had tidied up his bar and seen the last of the guests stagger off to their beds, he would receive the shock of his sad, criminally-inclined life.

Richard returned home, preferring to make the journey out to Cheshire and back again rather than to be killing time in Manchester. Diane was in the kitchen and came to greet him, as Claire might once had done.

He asked what had become the routine question: 'No word from your mother I suppose?'

'No.'

At what point, he wondered, should they begin to fear for Claire's safety? Whatever she might think of him, or believe he had done, he surely didn't deserve this kind of treatment. There had been neither card nor phone-call to reassure them that she was safe and well, which surely was the minimum any family had a right to expect.

'I'm sure she's fine,' said Diane, reading his mind.

'Of course,' he said, sorry that he should have betrayed his worries to her. He should have been the one supporting his daughter; not vice-versa. 'She's probably having a terrific holiday. I hope she is.'

'I thought I'd do us an omelette,' said Diane. 'What do you want – Spanish, ham or what?'

He said he didn't mind, then sat and watched her as she bustled about. She had made heroic efforts to fill the gaps left by Claire. She had not only run the home, organizing the cleaner, shopping, laundry and the rest, but had had to deal with the various social commitments that Claire had left trailing in her wake. There had been a stream of enquiries, asking where she was or why she hadn't been where she should have been. Diane had handled them with patience and good humour, lying only when necessary.

What neither she nor Richard had done anything about was the growing pile of correspondence awaiting Claire. To judge by the envelopes, most of it was business correspondence of one sort of another. It had been left to accumulate on the mantelpiece in the time-honoured manner.

So there was that, too, to draw her back. Only when for God's sake? For how much longer did she intend to torment them like this?

He explained to Diane that he would be going out later that evening and would probably be late home. Then, after they had eaten and he had cleared away, he shut himself in his study and rang Lawrence next-door.

Lawrence asked him to wait as he switched phones, which meant he was getting out of earshot of Adele. He came on the line again, sounding fearful: 'Yes? Has something happened?'

'Maurice has come up with the goods.'

'You mean he's . . . what, he's identified the blackmailer?'

'He has, yes. It's one of the barmen at the hotel.'

There was a pause as Lawrence considered the implications of this. 'A barman . . .?'

'Yes. I called in this lunchtime to have a look at him.'

'Does he know that you know?'

'No. Not yet anyway.'

'So what are you going to do?'

'I'm going to do what you wanted. Get those photographs off him.'

'Yes. I mean you're not thinking of going to the police or –'

'No.' How many times did he need reassuring? The longer he had had to consider these photographs, the more they seemed to terrify him. Was it because, unlike the letters, they could not be denied?

'No police,' said Richard.

'Good,' said Lawrence, with undisguised relief. 'Look, is there . . . I mean if you're going to tackle this chappie . . . well, is there anything I can do to help?'

Richard had considered this. 'No. Nothing.'

'You don't want me along just to sort of make up the numbers?'

'No. Leave it with me. I'll see him. And, as soon as I have, I'll let you know what happens.'

Richard wanted those photographs to end up in his own hands. He would then be able to show them to Claire, after which he would probably destroy them. He didn't know. What he must guard against was the risk that Lawrence might yet do some smart deal with Philip Thornton which would protect the two of them but leave him nowhere.

Besides, he wanted this Philip Thornton. He wanted to see his face when he told him who he was and what he knew and how his sordid, nasty little scheme had gone badly wrong. He was looking forward to that.

He showered and changed into a sports jacket and flannels. Diane had gone out with Will. Richard went round the house locking up. Closing the front door, he stood under the cover of the porch for a moment, looking out at the lightly falling rain and the houses of their neighbours, their lights glowing in the dusk.

It was a scene of suburban tranquillity, no doubt envied by many who passed this way. And why shouldn't it be? It was a comfortable enough life most of the time, certainly not an obvious breeding-ground for deceit and sexual intrigue.

He made a short dash to his car, keeping his head down against the rain. Seen through the rain-studded car windows, his own house was in darkness and had, he fancied, a gloomy and deserted air to it. It was a relief to drive off and leave it behind him. He was, if the truth be told, quite looking forward to his date with Melissa in the bar of the Queens Hotel.

15

He parked his car behind a whole line of others that were on double yellow lines. The rain had stopped, or perhaps it hadn't reached here yet. He looked at his watch and saw it was still only a quarter to nine. Of course, she might be there early but he suspected not. More likely she would arrive spot on the time agreed, as she had before. He strolled along the quiet pavements, past the closed bookshops and gents outfitters.

It occurred to him that he might invite Melissa to have dinner. Of course he'd already eaten Diane's omelette but the evening ahead stretched interminably. He would see how things went.

The hotel had thrown off its slothful, lunchtime appearance and was an explosion of light. Richard went in through the revolving doors and found himself deposited into that now familiar world of chandeliers and ormolu furnishings. The pianist was playing 'What Kind Of Fool Am I?', but was barely audible in a foyer crowded with people in evening-dress who were talking loudly and embracing one another.

Richard picked his way through the gathering, breathing in a heady mixture of perfume and cigar smoke. He became hemmed in as a group in front of him came to a standstill. Never mind, he thought, and waited patiently till a way through appeared. At eight fifty-two, the night was still relatively young. It wasn't too distressing to have to spend a small portion of it trapped in the middle of so many happy and carefree people.

His only worry, which now surfaced as he eased his way out of the crowd and came into the bar, was that Philip Conway Thornton might not be there to greet him. Oh, he had said yes when Richard had asked him was he working that night. But since then anything could have happened: shifts might change, somebody fall ill . . . anything.

He need not have worried. Philip Conway Thornton was

there behind the bar, as he had been at lunchtime. The only difference was that he was no longer on his own. Tonight there were three bar-staff on duty.

He gave Richard a welcoming smile as he approached.

'Evening, sir. Scotch-and-soda is it?'

'Yes please.'

'Right, sir.'

Richard watched him as he moved from the optics to the cold shelf where the mixers were kept, tossing glass and drinks and ice together with a practised skill. There was no question that this man was an experienced barman; but was he a blackmailer? All the evidence pointed that way but there remained at least the theoretical possibility that all the evidence was misleading.

Suppose, for instance, that Philip Thornton had a pal working here, a fellow barman or waiter, whom he'd entertained with tales of his criminal past, and suppose that it was the pal who had decided to imitate Thornton's earlier *modus operandi* and who was doing the blackmailing while Thornton was guilty of nothing more than having supplied him with the idea?

Unlikely, yes, but then so was being blackmailed for something you hadn't done.

'Two-thirty, sir.'

Richard paid, then remained standing at the bar where he could most easily be seen by Melissa when she arrived. He also wanted Thornton to see her arrive. It would be interesting to observe Thornton's reaction on seeing them together.

What he needed was a copy of the man's handwriting. Ideally, to have him *print* something, in the style of the letters. That would surely settle things one way or the other.

These and other thoughts had begun to crystallize into a rough-and-ready plan of campaign. He wouldn't attempt to tackle Thornton inside the hotel, or even outside it as he was leaving. What he would do was wait until Thornton had finished his shift and gone home. The information Maurice had provided on him included his present address, which was in Salford, cheek-by-jowl with Manchester. Richard would follow him and tackle him there, in his own home – since it was there that the photographs and samples of his handwriting were most likely to be found.

'Well, hello.'

He turned and saw that Melissa had arrived beside him.

'Hello,' he said, and shook her hand. 'And listen, thank you for coming. I appreciate it.'

'Not at all. Thank you for the invitation.'

'I've got a great deal to tell you. But first of all let me get you a drink, then we'll go and sit down.'

He turned back towards the bar and saw Philip Thornton coming to serve them.

This was how he would have planned it. For Thornton to see Melissa arrive and join him. Assuming that this was their black-mailer, then they must already have his undivided attention.

'What would you like?' Richard asked her.

'A dry martini please.'

'A dry martini, barman please.'

'Certainly, sir,' said Thornton. 'With ice, madam?'

'Yes, please.'

If he had recognized Melissa, then he betrayed no sign of it. His performance was that of the perfect hotel barman, swift and courteous, allowing not even a split-second glance to betray him.

'And how are you?' said Melissa, making conversation as they waited for her drink to arrive.

'I'll be better when all this is over and done with. And you?'

'I think I'll be glad when it is too.'

She was dressed in a different style from last time. Then she had been in what was decidedly evening-wear, sophisticated, seductive, and difficult to run away in. Now she was wearing a loose, khaki-coloured jacket and trousers, with bronze bangles dangling around her slim wrists and a necklace to match. It gave an overall more casual air than before and made him think that for her too this evening must be a happier prospect than their first meeting, when he'd been just another, anonymous client to be wooed and feared in equal measures.

'First things first,' said Richard. 'Let me pay you.'

'No! I mean thank you but that's not necessary. It really isn't.'

They had retreated to one of the tables in the area of the bar. It was still Richard's intention to offer her dinner but that could wait. He wanted them here, within sight of Philip Thornton, when he told her about the latest developments. He wanted to observe her reactions. In particular, he wanted to know whether she'd had any past dealings with Philip Thornton that would help substantiate Maurice's findings.

He would even have been happy had Thornton witnessed him paying her the twenty-five pound agency fee, plus the seventy for herself. Let him get the idea that there was another potential victim here. Let him get out his midget camera and start snapping.

But Melissa was refusing the money, and sounding like she meant it.

'I asked you to come here,' he urged. 'I'm taking up your time and so I should be paying you for that.'

But she was adamant and pushed the money back at him. 'You paid me last time and didn't get much for it. Besides, I'm not . . . I'm not doing that anymore.'

For a moment he didn't follow. 'Not doing what?'

She raised her arms as though in response to a silent fanfare and announced: 'I have retired from the escort business.'

'Oh, you have!' he exclaimed.

'And not before time,' she said, letting her arms fall.

It suddenly became clear to him why Julie at Star Escorts had needed so much persuasion to arrange this meeting. Melissa was no longer on their books. Or on anybody else's books. She had left the sisterhood, returning to the normal world.

'Congratulations,' he said.

'Thank you.' Then she added, 'Actually I really do have to thank you. If it hadn't been for you, I probably would never have got out.'

'If it hadn't been for me . . .?'

'Yes.'

He was genuinely perplexed. 'What did I do?'

She smiled. 'What you did was scare me to death. I mean everything that happened when we last met, you talking about blackmail and going to the police –'

'Well, yes, but I can assure you –'

'Oh, I'm not saying you have.'

'Well, I haven't. And I've no intention of doing.'

'No, I know.'

She seemed amused that he should be going to such lengths to reassure her. As though all this was beside the real point.

'But you might have gone to the police,' she said. 'I couldn't have blamed you if you had.' She took a sip of her drink. 'I always knew that I was running a risk. Well, not just a risk – any number of risks. You take your life in your hands with every man you meet in that business. I just kept telling myself that I was going to be the exception. Nothing would ever happen to me . . . till all of a sudden it nearly did.'

'So you're getting out while the going's good.'

'I'm getting out while I'm still alive,' she said.

He nodded. 'Yes, of course.'

He slipped the money back into his pocket. It was an odd turn of events, to find he had affected this woman's life in such a way. Perhaps he might even have saved it, as she seemed to think. Though it hadn't been his intention so he could hardly take any credit.

'What happened with Lawrence Nevison?' she asked.

'Oh, yes, well . . . quite a lot.'

Of course, he had all that yet to tell her. He would have done so immediately had she not surprised him with her announcement that she was retiring. Now he explained to her what had happened after their last meeting. How he had tracked down Lawrence to the Midland and dragged him out of his Law Society dinner.

She gasped at the thought. 'He must have been furious.'

'He wasn't very pleased.'

'And did he admit . . . you know, that he'd been with me?'

'Not at first. But then finally, yes, he admitted everything.'

'Ah,' she smiled.

'Then later on he changed his mind and denied everything.'

'Oh, no . . .!' she cried.

'Don't worry,' he said quickly. 'He then changed his mind again and agreed that what you'd told me was true.'

'Thank God for that.'

'Apparently he'd pretended to be me because he was frightened to tell you who he really was and . . . well, I think I was just the first person who sprang to mind.'

'And I think you're just being modest,' she said, looking him in the eye.

'I am?'

'I've been thinking about this. I mean why he acted that way, pretending to be you. And I think the only reason he could have done that was because he admired you. Even that he wanted to be you. So, when he was with me, he pretended that he was you.'

Richard couldn't help but award her full marks for perspicacity. But he wasn't going to let her know how accurate was her diagnosis, not yet anyway.

'I'm not sure about that,' he said.

She smiled. 'Well, OK. Never mind *why*. Just so long as he didn't deny ever having heard of me or ever having been to this place.'

'He didn't deny either of those.'

'Great.'

He saw her relief and realized that she must have been in some suspense waiting to hear what had happened. Until now, she couldn't have known that Lawrence had come clean and confessed. After all, he might have denied everything. In which case Richard's wish to meet her tonight would have been in order to accuse her of lying to save her own skin.

It made him all the more grateful to her for having come at all.

'So you've told all this to your wife?' she asked.

'I'm afraid I haven't had the chance. I don't know whether I told you when we last met, but on that very same day, while I was talking to you, she was packing her bags. So, when I got home, I was greeted with a letter, telling me she'd gone away for a while.'

'And you haven't heard anything from her since?'

'I'm afraid I haven't, no. So what you were able to tell me – I'd afraid I haven't had the chance to pass any of it onto her.'

'That's a pity.'

'It certainly is. But, beside bringing you up to date on developments, I did have another reason for asking you here tonight.'

She seemed startled by that and drew back. She didn't want to know about what other reasons he might have, he interpreted, or to be involved further. She had come to find out what had happened with Lawrence Nevison and also, possibly, to lay the ghost of her own, injudicious past.

'It's all right,' he went on quickly. 'It's nothing to worry about. In fact, you might find it reassuring.'

'Yes?' she said, still nervous.

'As I say, Lawrence Nevison has admitted everything. But now he's worried sick about these photographs that the black-mailer claims to have taken. Because, of course, they're not photographs of me —'

'They're photographs of him,' she anticipated.

'Exactly.'

'With me.'

'With you. Anyway, Lawrence was desperate that we should try and track down this blackmailer and get hold of these photographs before anybody else does.'

'That would be nice,' agreed Melissa, nodding eagerly.

Richard got the impression it would be a lot more than just nice: it would be a load off her mind too.

He explained: 'So I went back to this private detective, the one who helped put me in touch with you. And we talked about it and came up with one or two ideas as to where he might start looking and . . . well, that's what he did. He started looking.'

'And did he find anything?'

Richard smiled, enjoying the moment. If Claire chose not to be around to be told these things, Melissa was a very good substitute.

'He did, yes. He's come up with a name, and I'm ninety-nine percent certain it's the right one.'

'That's wonderful,' she said.

She was genuinely pleased. All the same, he could see the calculations going on behind her eyes, as she tried to stay a jump ahead of him and work out what the implications of this might be for herself. If the blackmailer had been found, did that make going to the police inevitable? After which, as surely as night follows day, there would come the court case and the newspaper headlines and the public exposure she feared.

'Is it someone you know?' she asked.

'No. But you might.'

'Me?'

The notion alarmed her. She drew back, suddenly suspicious of where this was leading. 'You're saying I'm involved in this?'

'No! No, please don't think that.'

205

'Then how can it be someone I know?'

'It's someone who works here.'

Her eyes grew wide with astonishment. 'Here? In this hotel?' she said, leaning forward again and whispering.

'Not just this hotel. This bar.'

This time she simply gasped and remained staring at him, as thought frightened to turn her head.

'Don't worry,' he said, wanting to reassure. 'He has no idea that I know. Don't forget, he doesn't even recognize me as the person he sent the letters to.'

'Is he here now?' She spoke without moving her head.

'Yes, he's behind the bar. He's one of the barmen.'

She caught her breath, looked over quickly at the bar, then looked back again at Richard. 'Which one?'

'The small, middle-aged one.' He risked a look himself, then told her, 'He's down this end of the bar now, nearest to us. It's all right – you can look. He's serving somebody.'

This time she was in no hurry and took a good long look towards where Philip Thornton was serving. Then she nodded and said, 'Yes.'

'Yes? What, you mean you do know him?'

'Only by sight. I mean he's always here, or nearly always. And I'll tell you something else – he knows what I do.' Then she added, correcting herself, 'Or what I did.'

'How do you know that?' said Richard, wanting more. This could be important when it came to weighing the evidence. It might even be the final proof he had been seeking.

'Oh, from his, you know . . . his *attitude*. The way that he'll be a little off-hand when he's serving you, or just give a little smirk.'

'I didn't notice anything.'

'You wouldn't. He doesn't do it when you're there. Oh, no, he'll be as nice as pie once the man's arrived. Then it's yes sir, yes madam . . . all that. But if I ever get here before the man and so have to sit up there on my own . . . that's when he'll let me know, just by the way he acts, that he isn't fooled. He'll take his time serving and he'll look me up and down, as though to say well, you might look like a lady but we both know what you really are, don't we.'

It was close to being conclusive, as close as anything could be.

So this Philip Thornton not only had a history of blackmailing hotel guests; he also had the information that would allow him to do it again and an attitude to go with it.

'And when you used to meet Lawrence, you'd meet him in this bar?'

'Yes. Lawrence, or anybody else for that matter. We most of us use this place. Mainly because they don't seem to mind. Some of the other hotels throw you out once they realize what's going on.'

'So Thornton could have taken those photographs of you and Lawrence in here? Did you ever sit at these tables?'

'Yes. Not this particular one I don't think, but we used to sit down for a while before we'd go off and have dinner or whatever.'

'Well, then it looks like that's how it happened.'

Melissa frowned. 'But why him? How d'you know it's not one of the others?'

Of course, he hadn't told her this. 'Oh, because he's the one with the record. He's pulled the same stunt in other hotels and served time in prison for it.'

'Well, the little creep,' she said.

'Yes,' he agreed, and gave a small laugh, amused by the way she had set her jaw and was staring defiantly across at the bar. A kitten ready to spring.

Then she turned back to him. 'Does this mean you'll now have to inform the police?'

'No. No, you mustn't worry about that.'

'Really?'

'Oh, yes. Look at it this way. Now that I know who the blackmailer is, I've even less reason for going to the police than I had before. I don't need them. I can sort this out myself.'

'That's great,' she said, highly relieved. 'Thank you.'

'I should be thanking you. You've helped me get this far.'

'Only because I couldn't run fast enough.' They laughed about that, then she asked, 'So what are you going to do?'

'Well, nothing right now. I'm going to wait till he goes home tonight. Then I'm going to follow him. And I'm going to tell him who I am and what I know, and I'm going to make him hand over the photographs. Oh, and then, of course, I'll destroy them.'

She smiled. 'That would be wonderful. Then I would really feel that there weren't any loose ends.'

'There won't be. I promise you that.'

She gave him another smile, trusting him again now. 'I'll tell you what,' she said. 'Let me buy us another drink. I want to get a close look at this creep.'

'Whenever I was coming here to meet some man –'

'Yes?'

'I'd always leave a letter on my kitchen table at home, lying where anybody coming into the house couldn't miss it. And I'd put on the envelope – Please open if I have not returned by – and then a date and time that would probably be about, oh, twelve or fifteen hours after I'd started out. In case anything happened to me.'

'And what was in the letter?'

'An account of where I'd gone and the name and phone number of the escort agency. Then, when I came home in one piece, I'd tear it up. Usually I'd be very down after I'd, you know, been with somebody, and I'd tell myself right, that's it, never again. And so tearing up the letter would feel like I was tearing up that side of my life.'

'But then what would happen? The agency would contact you again?'

'Exactly. Julie would ring and I'd think, well, there's a gas-bill needs paying or it'd be nice to get some new shoes. Anyway, the after-effects of last time would have worn off, so I'd say yes. Then I'd have to write another letter explaining where I'd gone in case this was going to turn out to be the one who killed me.'

They were having dinner in the restaurant. She had ordered lamb while he, mindful of the omelette he had put away earlier, had gone for the salmon. With a bottle of Chardonnay to wash it down.

It had been an uphill struggle to persuade her to join him. When he had first suggested they moved to the restaurant for some dinner, she had politely refused. When he had repeated his invitation, she became flustered. For a minute or two he feared she was about to walk out on him. He understood, of course, that she was desperate not to go down the route from bar to restaurant to bedroom which she must have followed on so many nights in that same hotel with different men.

In the end he took out the money with which he'd intended to pay her and said, 'Look, let's pretend I gave you this and now you're going to use it to buy me dinner.'

It helped ease the tension which had sprung up between them. Well, all right, she said finally, thank you. Even so, she didn't really relax until the meal was underway. It was then that he realized how little he knew about her. Nothing really, not even her real name. The one thing he did know was that she had led this secret, other life, working as a call-girl but he had shied away from raising that as a topic of conversation.

However, she didn't seem to mind talking about it; in fact, she raised it as a topic herself. Perhaps it was a rare opportunity for her. It was not something she could ever talk about to anybody else. And so here she was, pouring out to him this account of her life after dark, an account he felt himself privileged to be hearing.

'I know I'm making it sound incredibly dangerous,' she said. 'That was how I saw it afterwards. When I was away from here and could think about it in cold blood.'

'I'm sure it was dangerous.'

'Once I'd got here and met the man, it was usually all right. In fact, most of them were extremely considerate and, you know, attentive.'

He risked a small joke. 'Probably far more attentive towards you than they ever were towards their own wives.'

'Oh, yes. Oh, I'm sure.'

Like me, he thought. Here he was, wining and dining this attractive young woman and not giving a thought to his own wife's whereabouts. Was it an adequate defence to claim that, if he were treating Melissa better than he had his wife, that was largely because his wife had chosen to remove herself from his life?

'The best ones were the kinky ones.'

'Sorry?'

'The men that I used to entertain –'

'Yes?'

'The kinky ones were the ones I preferred.'

'Really?'

209

She laughed at his startled expression. 'Oh, I just mean they were the easiest.'

He wasn't sure whether he should ask for details. But then, without his asking, she gave them anyway.

'When I say kinky, I mean the ones who liked dressing up and who wanted to act out their fantasies. Sometimes with some kind of sex as well but, honestly, with most of them, I'm sure it was the fantasy that was the most important.'

'What kind of, er . . . fantasy?'

'Usually it was dressing up in women's clothes. Sometimes just underclothes, sometimes whole outfits. They'd bring them along with them, all packed up alongside their own, normal clothes. Sometimes they'd bring make-up as well. And they'd put these things on . . . get themselves made up . . . then sometimes they'd just want us to sit and talk, like two ladies together.'

'Yes, I can see that must have been . . . easier.'

'Oh, much. It just to puzzle me at first. Then I thought it must be that it's not enough for them simply to get dressed up. They have to have somebody else there, somebody who's going to relate to them as a woman. And that's what they were paying me for.'

Poor sods, he thought. As if life weren't complicated enough without having being driven by such ludicrous obsessions. Imagine the time and energy expended by these men with their exotic tastes simply to create the opportunity to indulge them. No, that he could do without and, if others couldn't, then they had his deepest sympathy.

He wondered if she had had a similar view. 'And how did you feel towards these men that you had to deal with?'

'The kinky ones?'

'Or any of them?'

She considered and slowly shook her head. 'I suppose I tried not to feel anything. I used to tell myself I was an actress and this was my stage and it was just a role I was playing.'

'You didn't despise them?'

'No.' Then she added, 'The only ones I ever despised were those who spent the whole night running down their wives and the women they worked with and who then wanted you to tell them they were the greatest lovers you'd ever met. One or two of them frightened me a little.'

He proposed a toast – 'To your retirement!'

'And this time it's for real,' she said. 'I've told myself before that I wasn't going to do it again but Julie's always talked me back into it. This time nobody's talking me back.'

After this, she fell silent and he was hard-pressed to get a word out of her. They finished eating and ordered coffee. He wondered whether she might be regretting confiding in him to the extent that she had. It wasn't the alcohol that had made her talkative: he had consumed the lion's share of that. Probably it was simply being there, in that hotel where she had acted out this secret life of hers. She had needed to confide it all to somebody, and who better than somebody she would never see again.

'You see, all this is a bit unfair,' he said, as they waited for coffee.

'Unfair . . .?'

'Thanks to Lawrence, you know all about me . . .'

'I suppose . . . quite a lot anyway.'

'Whereas I don't know the first thing about you, not even your name.'

She grimaced. 'Do I have to tell you?'

'Of course not.'

'Well, then I think I'd rather stick at Melissa. At least while I'm still in this place.'

'I understand,' he said.

'And what else? Well, I was married for three years, just over, but now I'm divorced and I live by myself. No family. I have two cats and I work in a hospital as a radiographer.'

The small torrent of information took him by surprise. First a drought, then a deluge.

'And so now what?' he said. 'You're going to go back to being a full-time radiographer?'

'I am,' she said, with a wry smile. 'And at night I'm going to stay at home and watch telly like everybody else.'

It was gone midnight when they emerged from the hotel and stood on the pavement, looking about them for a taxi.

Before coming out, they had gone together and peeked in at the bar. It was still open, though there weren't more than half-a-dozen customers remaining. What mattered was that Philip Thornton was still there serving them.

'Why do you think he does it?' asked Melissa.

A thin drizzle had driven them back under the hotel awning.

'Why do I think –'

'The barman, whatever he's called –'

'Philip Thornton.'

'Yes. Why has he risked so much in trying to blackmail you? All right, he's doing it for money, I'm not denying that.'

Richard frowned. 'You think there might be another reason?'

'I just wonder . . . I mean trying to see things from his point-of-view. He's there every night, watching people enjoying themselves. Could it not be some sort of jealousy? Could he not be out to spoil things for other people because he can't be part of that world?'

'Maybe. Quite honestly, I don't give a damn what his motive is. It's what he's done. That's why I'm going after him.'

She looked at him intently. 'Be careful.'

'I shall be.'

There was a taxi approaching, with its light on, and he stepped out to hail it. When he rejoined Melissa, she surprised him by reaching up and planting a kiss on his cheek.

'You're very nice,' she said. 'And I'm sorry for all this trouble I helped get you into.'

'No,' he protested, 'you've helped get me *out* of it.'

But now she was climbing into the taxi, calling over her shoulder as she did so: 'And the best of luck with you-know-who.'

'Thanks.'

She closed the door on him, as she had at the end of that first night when they had met, so that he shouldn't hear her directions to the driver. He saw her black hair swing as she turned to look through the rear window. He waved as the taxi went away but there was no response.

He prowled around the block, not wanting to return to the hotel bar. He'd already had more to drink than he'd intended and needed to clear his head. Besides, to march back in there at this late hour would be to draw unnecessary attention to himself. So he set himself to do a circuit of the hotel, at the end of which he peered in through the one window which gave a partial view of the bar. Not much but enough to tell whether it was open or closed.

The rain was thin but persistent. He put up a tentative hand and found his hair was plastered to his skull.

There should have been a better way of planning this, he thought. Another ten minutes and I'm going to be drenched. A woman sauntered down the other side of the street, secure beneath a golf umbrella. He was looking enviously at the umbrella when she startled him by calling out, 'Hello? Are you looking for company?'

He laughed aloud and called back, 'No, thanks.'

'So what're you doing out in the bleeding rain?' she retorted. Without waiting for an answer, she went clacking away down the street.

Yes, what am I? he thought, gazing around him at the shining street-lights and the office-blocks empty as mausoleums.

He completed another circuit and came past the front entrance of the hotel and to the window which allowed him a view of the bar. Even as he looked, the final lights went out, leaving everything in darkness. The bar had closed at last.

16

Earlier that day, when the evening was in its planning stages, Richard had taken ten minutes to consult the dog-eared 'A-to-Z' that Yvonne kept on her desk. The address he was looking for was number 22, Meredith House, Willow Tree Road, Salford. It was here, according to the information gleaned from the police computer and passed on to him by Maurice, that Philip Thornton currently resided.

He finally located Willow Tree Road in the middle of a spider's web of tiny arteries that sprouted from both sides of the A57 Liverpool Road. It was not an area he knew. He had stared hard at the map, attempting to commit it to memory. Now, without the book, he tried to recall the awkward little maze it had presented and the key points of roundabouts and junctions.

He was in no hurry, driving lazily north-west out of Manchester and into Salford. He must allow Philip Thornton time to get home before he arrived or the surprise he was counting on would be lost.

He lowered the side window, letting the thin mist drift in. He needed to be alert for this encounter. The man he was about to call on had a track-record for being devious and cowardly. Show him the half-chance of a way out and he'd jump at it.

Psyching himself up for the encounter, Richard reminded himself that this was the man who had brought misery and conflict to a family that had never known these things but who had lived happily until he had contaminated them with his poison. They had been the victim of a lazy and unscrupulous man whose only concern was to get his hands on other people's money. There had been no spur-of-the-moment anger or abiding passion at play here but cold-blooded evil.

He was pleased to feel himself growing angry, even as he slowed down and peered through the sweeping windscreen-wipers to read the names and numbers beneath the street lights.

*

Had he been looking for it in day-time, with the streets busy and clogged with traffic, Willow Tree Road might well have eluded him. Now, with only the odd car or the distant shriek of a siren to distract, he drove confidently along the glistening roads, re-running the 'A-to-Z' map in his head, and found Willow Tree Road without a hitch.

It was part of a small estate. There were a dozen or so separate blocks of flats, surrounded by grassy areas and num-bered parking spaces. None of the blocks rose to more than four or five storeys. Meredith House was the second he came to. It was bigger than its neighbours but in matching yellow brick, with light spilling out through the glass door of the entrance.

He parked on the roadway and took shelter beneath one of the thin trees that formed a line along the roadside. From here he could see that the entrance door had a row of bells beside it. He cursed quietly. How was he to get past this barrier without letting Thornton know he had an unwelcome visitor on his way?

He saw a flash of movement from inside and deciphered it as meaning that there were people approaching the door. Almost certainly they were about to come out. He had to take the chance while it was offered. He sprinted forward and positioned himself to the side of the door. The outline of two people loomed behind the frosted surface of the glass. There was a heavy click as the door was pulled open.

A white woman, all bare arms and legs, hugging herself against the night air, came out first. 'Well, get that brolly up then,' she said complainingly. A much taller, black man stepped out quickly after her. 'Ah, you're OK,' he laughed. 'Just a little rain.' 'Not so fucking little,' she moaned, keeping her head down. He laughed again and opened a small, red umbrella, then had to chase after her with it.

Neither had seemed to notice Richard at all. Now, as the door swung back closed, he put out a hand to catch it and hold it open. Then he stepped inside.

The hallway smelt stale and warm. There was a single lift and a staircase rising beside it. A notice indicated which flats were on which floors: number 22 was on the second. Other notices warned against committing damage or allowing dogs to roam.

Richard went up the stairs slowly, aware that he was now on enemy territory. He had no way of knowing whether Thornton had got back here ahead of him. He didn't want to bump into him out here on the stairs or on one of the landings. It was vital to get inside his flat since it was there that the photographs were most probably hidden.

Number 22 was a door at one end of a corridor on which there were about eight similar doors. There was an empty milk-bottle standing outside it and a section of unpainted wood around the handle, perhaps where the lock had once been changed.

Richard put his ear to the door and listened. He could hear faint pop music and raised voices that might have been coming from a television-set. However, they were both too distant and indistinct for him to be sure whether they came from inside this particular flat or from the ones on either side. He dropped to his haunches so that he could peer through the keyhole. It showed him a segment of a dimly-lit, narrow hallway but he could see nothing that confirmed whether his prey was there or not.

He knocked sharply on the door and brought his ear close, listening for movement. When there was none, he knocked again, this time more loudly, hammering on the thin wood.

Now there was someone coming, shouting something. Richard's heart leapt. There was the sound of bolts being withdrawn, then the door was half-opened and Philip Thornton peered out, belligerent and puzzled.

It was the same man who had served Richard across the bar of the Queens Hotel, though now he appeared older and more unkempt. His wispy, brylcreemed hair was beginning to stray and his barman's white shirt had been pulled open at the neck.

'Yes? What?' He blinked and stared, then said, 'I know you. Weren't you in the hotel? Wasn't I serving you this evening?'

'You were.'

He straightened up and brushed his fingers over his hair. 'Well, and so what can I do for you?' he said in a more deferential, accommodating tone.

Though he was still puzzled. You could see that. He didn't know how to react to this intrusion from his other world.

'You can talk to me about some letters,' said Richard.

'What letters? Sorry, but I still don't understand.'

'Blackmail letters. And let's talk inside, shall we.'

Richard moved forward, so that Thornton had no option but

to step back into his own tiny hallway. He kept a hand on the door but now was unable to close it with Richard in the way.

'No, I'm sorry, I can't allow that,' he blustered. 'Not until you tell me what this is about.'

'Let me come in and then I'll tell you,' said Richard. 'I'm sure you don't want us to talk out here where all your neighbours can listen in.'

'Look, whatever it is you want, you come and see me at the hotel, OK? This is my private time, and where you're standing now is my private property.'

'You sent me some letters, Mr Thornton. Four letters.'

'You keep going on about letters. I don't know what you're bloody well on about!'

'Oh, I think you do.'

'All right, last chance. If you don't go now, then I'll call the police.'

'Why don't you. Then they can be in on this as well.'

If Thornton had realized what this was about, he was a clever enough actor not to show it. He shook his head in apparent bewilderment.

'Look, I can have you thrown out of here, you know,' he said. 'I only have to shout, there'll be people come pouring out of all these doors.'

'My name's Richard Gillow. You sent me some letters. Remember? Yes?'

Thornton flinched at the name. It was a barely perceptible jerk of the head. All the same it was sufficient to betray that yes, he did remember.

'Richard Gillow,' repeated Richard.

'Sorry, no. I've even never heard that name before.'

It was a spirited attempt but he had already given himself away. The air of bafflement and outrage at being disturbed like this was no longer convincing. Richard took another step forward.

'Yes, you have. You've written letters to someone of that name. And those letters came to me.'

'What are you, some sort of maniac? I don't know anything about any letters. I don't know anything about any of this!' he said, his voice rising.

'Close the door.'

'No –'

Richard took hold of the door, so that for a moment they were both tugging at it, but it was an unequal contest. In a moment he had brushed off Thornton's feeble grip and sent the door slamming closed behind him. Thornton gave a small cry of fear and pulled back.

'We're going to go somewhere we can talk now?' said Richard.

'No. You get out. I don't know who the hell you think you are –'

'I've told you who I am. Richard Gillow.'

'Sorry. Don't know you. Well, I mean I've seen you, yes. At the hotel. But I don't know what you're doing here and I want you out. Now go on!'

He might have been physically intimidated but Thornton wasn't cowed. Give him that. He stood facing Richard, making little shuffling steps from side-to-side, a boxer waiting for the imminent assault.

'I'm not going anywhere without the photographs,' said Richard.

'What bloody photographs? I haven't got any bloody photographs, not of you!'

'Not me, no –'

'So what photographs?'

Rather than allowed himself to be pushed in that direction of ever more elaborate explanations and denials, Richard reached into his jacket pocket and produced the letters. 'You see these?' he said, holding them before Thornton's face. 'These are the letters. You wrote these.'

'No, I didn't. Look, I don't know what this is all about –'

'Yes, you do. You wrote these letters. Look at them!'

'So who're they to? Who is it I'm supposed to have written them to?'

'That doesn't matter,' said Richard, seeing where Thornton was being crafty and attempting to shift the argument. He had had time to work out what his mistake had been, the fact the letters had gone to the wrong man, and was now trying to take advantage of it.

But Thornton persisted: 'To you, are they? 'Cause why would I ever be writing letters to you when I've never seen you before?

I don't know you from Adam, except for what I've seen of you today!'

'That's your handwriting.'

'No.'

'Yes, I think it is.'

'For Christ's sake, shouldn't I know my own handwriting? And how many times do I have to tell you – this is my private property. Will you get out of here!'

'I'll go the minute you can prove to me that you did not write these letters.'

'What?'

'You say this isn't your handwriting –'

'It's not!'

'So prove it. Show me something that is in your handwriting.'

'I haven't got anything'

'You must have something –'

'No. Now just get out –'

'Somewhere in this flat –'

'I'm not telling you again!'

'A sample of your writing –'

Suddenly Thornton lunged forward, pushing Richard on the chest. Up close, he stank of stale alcohol and tobacco. Richard knocked aside his hands, grabbed the front of his shirt and threw him back into the wall behind him.

Thornton gave a loud gasp as the air was forced from his lungs, then his hands were up across his face and he was pleading, 'No, don't. Don't hit me.'

'Then you keep your hands to yourself.'

'Just get off me, will you! Leave me alone!'

'I'll leave you alone.' He stepped back, happy to be out of range of the stink Thornton gave off when you got too close.

'That's assault,' said Thornton, still gasping. 'What you just did – that's assault!'

'Is it.'

'Yes. You touch me again and I swear I'll call the police.'

'You will?'

'Yeah.'

'Then they can arrest you again? Then they can put you in jail again? Like they did before? Like they did when you were working in Brighton?'

Thornton stayed leaning against the wall where Richard had thrown him. He said nothing. Then he pulled himself upright and stuffed his shirt back into his trousers where the struggle had pulled it free.

'So all right,' he said. 'Just what have you come here for?'

'I told you –'

'The photographs.'

'Yes!'

Thornton said, 'Yes, well . . .OK.'

It was a surrender so sudden and complete it took Richard by surprise. 'You're going to give me them?'

'Look, I need a drink. I wasn't expecting any of this. Come in.'

He turned and pushed open the door to the interior of the flat, leaving Richard to follow.

The room they entered was small and crowded with furniture. There was a television-set to the side of a gas-fire and a low, leather sofa facing both. On the wall behind the sofa were three framed pictures of galleons at sail; above the gas-fire was another picture of a warship, its guns spouting fire. There was a bookcase holding an assortment of paperbacks, with the bottom shelf given over to bottles of spirits.

It wasn't so much a living-room as a den. Richard wondered how long it was since the last visitor, welcome or otherwise, had crossed its threshold.

'Sit down,' said Thornton, with a wave towards the sofa.

Richard shook his head, suspicious of this sudden change in manner. He perched on one of two upright wooden chairs that were lined up against what little wall space there was.

'You want a drink?'

'No, thank you.'

Thornton sat down on the sofa. There was a bottle of whisky and a glass on the tile-topped table beside it. Also an ashtray in which the remains of a cigarette were smouldering.

'Well, I will if you don't mind. Enough to scare a man to death, having you arrive at this time of night.'

He set about topping up his whisky and lighting another cigarette. It was as though he regarded his surrender in the hallway as somehow settling things, with only the small print left to be decided upon.

The Allegation

'I'm still waiting for those photographs,' said Richard, determined to move things along.

Thornton sighed. The leather sofa creaked as he lay back.

'Mr Gillow. If that's your name.'

'It is.'

'Right. Well, then listen, I think there's been some mistake here.'

His tone of voice had moved back towards that of the clubbable fellow, the barman who understood and accepted the little foibles and weaknesses of his regular customers and expected a reciprocal understanding on the odd occasion – like now – when he might himself need it.

'I think there has,' said Richard evenly.

'If I wrote any letters – which I'm not admitting that I have, understand – but, if I have, then they weren't intended to go to you.'

'I know they weren't.'

'Oh, you do.' He considered this, sipping at his whisky, then said: 'Well, then, what you might also know is that any photographs I might have – and, again, I'm not admitting –'

'No.'

'But any I might have – they're not any of them photographs of you.'

'I know that too.'

'I see.'

'They're not photographs of me. They're photographs of somebody you *thought* was me.'

Thornton took a moment to consider. Richard was expecting further denials and a return to the squabbling in the hallway. But Thornton, after a sip of his whisky, remained equable.

'Then forgive me if I'm being stupid, Mr Gillow,' he said, 'but, if you know they're not of you, then why are you taking all this interest in them?'

'That's none of your business.'

'Ah, well, be fair. If they're my photographs, then it's bound to be my business, wouldn't you think?'

The gall of the man astonished Richard. Here he was, a blackmailer, and as good as admitting the fact. Yet, far from being contrite or even scared, he had adopted the calm, reasonable approach of a man who might be willing to negotiate once he understood what was on offer.

Richard had to fight an impulse to grab him by his scrawny neck and squeeze some contrition out of him. And squeeze some fear into him at the same time. But he knew he mustn't allow such thoughts to cloud his judgement. He was here for the photographs, not vengeance, delicious though that would be.

He decided to try a different tack. 'That lady I was with tonight.'

'What about her?'

'Melissa.'

Thornton hesitated, then said, 'That's her name, is it?'

'I think you know it is.'

'How should I?'

'I don't know how, but you certainly do. You named her in the letters. You said you wanted five thousand pounds or you'd tell my wife about my relationship with Melissa.'

Richard felt his anger re-kindling. Why not just shake the truth out of him after all? Remember what this man has done for Christsake. He doesn't deserve the courtesy of this kind of nit-picking argument.

Yet still he went on, like a lawyer conducting his own defence and rather enjoying it. 'That's only if I wrote the letters. Which I'm not admitting to.'

'You don't have to. I *know* you wrote them.'

Thornton looked puzzled again. 'But you also know that you aren't on the photographs . . .?'

'Yes.'

'So why are you after them? What's in this for you is what I want to know.'

It took all of Richard's self-restraint not to grab him there and then.

'Well, you're not going to know. It doesn't matter what's in it for me. All you have to know is that *I want those photographs*, and I'm not leaving here without them.'

Thornton eyed him, saying nothing. Evidently he was still not satisfied.

Was this possible? A blackmailer, trailing previous convictions, caught virtually red-handed, sitting back and demanding explanations, demanding that Richard should explain *his* motives!

He began again: 'But if they're not of you –'

'It doesn't matter *why* I want them. I'm giving you a chance to get out of this while saving your own worthless neck!' He knew he was beginning to shout. 'Where are they? They're here, yes?'

'I'm not saying where they are. I'm not saying they even exist.'

Richard stood up. He didn't know what he was going to do; all he knew was that he could take no more of this smart-arsed performance. He'd put up with too much already in allowing himself to be toyed with like this.

'Get those photographs. Now,' he instructed.

'All right,' said Thornton, raising his hands. 'There's no need to get excited –'

'Oh, I think there's every need.'

'Just sit down a minute. Sit down –'

'You're not going to give me them?'

'I'm not saying –'

'OK, I'll find them for myself.'

He took a step towards the bookcase, suddenly bent on ransacking it. He would ransack the entire dirty, little flat if necessary. But Thornton jumped to his feet, sending the whisky flying out of his glass, and put out an arm to block him.

'No, no, let's have none of that. That's not necessary!'

'And if you don't get out of my way –'

'Make me an offer. That's all you have to do – make me an offer.'

Richard stared. He couldn't believe what he was hearing. Yet Thornton was nodding and smiling to reassure him that this was no joke.

'These pictures are valuable to you, aren't they. I mean they must be, else you wouldn't be here like this. All right, give me a fair price and I daresay I'll be able to find 'em.'

The audacity of the offer took his breath away.

'You expect me . . . to *pay* you?'

'Well, fair's fair. I've got something you want. You make me an offer for it.'

He was being blackmailed again. This man, having made his demands by letter, was now continuing to make them face-to-face.

'You little bastard.'

'You can call me what you like –'

223

'Are you going to give me those photographs?'

He could feel his rage building and about to take over, as it had been near to doing since he stepped into the flat. The difference now was that he would allow it to.

'Well, make me an offer –'

Richard lashed out with his balled fist and caught Thornton on the side of his head. He lurched sideways, colliding with the bookcase.

Richard hit him again, landing another blow with the same hand, this time to the chin. Then again, and again. The blows sent his head snapping back, then his knees buckled and he slid to the floor.

Gradually the surging inside his own head diminished and he was able to hear the night sounds again coming through the walls and from outside. With them came the realization of where he was and what he had done. He looked down and saw Thornton lying at his feet, his arms thrown wide. Richard stepped back.

'Get up,' he said.

How many years had it been since he had stuck out in anger? He wasn't proud of doing so now, though he believed he could well claim to have been provoked beyond endurance. He had come to see this creep, intending to deal leniently with him. He had not come to deprive him of his freedom. All he had demanded of him was that he hand over the photographs. Photographs that were valueless since they weren't even of the right person.

But it hadn't been enough. Or perhaps it had been too much, allowing Thornton to see him as a soft touch who could be pushed further and further, even as far as paying for photographs on which he didn't appear.

Richard went down on one knee and peered into the face which was pressed against the carpet. One eye had been pulled closed; the other was open and staring. He was either unconscious or feigning. 'Come on,' Richard said. He put a hand on his shoulder and shook him. Then he saw there was blood coming from the man's mouth, a thin trickle that had already gathered and made a sticky pool beneath his head.

In an instant he glimpsed a whole range of possibilities, each more horrifying than the next. That he had done Thornton serious damage . . . perhaps he would be left crippled for life . . . or would never even regain consciousness. He would die and so leave Richard facing a charge of murder.

'No, no . . . come on . . . ' he said. He placed a finger against the thin, white neck, feeling for a pulse. Well, yes, it was there, thank God, but hardly strong. He must do something, but what?

He took a small, round cushion from the sofa, lifted Thornton's head with his other hand, then stuffed the cushion beneath it. The hand that had been beneath the head came away smeared with blood. He pulled his handkerchief from his pocket and wiped it away.

Thornton was still unconscious and not moving, but at least changing the angle of his head seemed to have cause the bleeding to stop. Though that in itself might not be a good sign. He felt again for a pulse.

Was that weaker than before? He had no way of telling.

He must get assistance. Yet he couldn't afford to be found there. He thought of Diane, at home and expecting his return. And of Claire, whom he must find and who must hear the truth. He must get out, flee that dreadful hovel while he had the chance.

Hadn't there been a telephone . . .? He looked round and spotted it on the low table beside the whisky bottle. 'Yes,' he said, encouraging himself. He spoke to the unconscious body beside him on the floor: 'I'm going to get some help.' Then he picked up the receiver and jabbed at the nine button.

'Emergency. Which service?' said a brisk, female voice that seemed to come from another world, a world he now feared.

'Ambulance,' he said.

Almost immediately another voice, a woman again, was saying, 'Ambulance.'

This, he knew, was his cue, but he was barely able to coordinate his thoughts. 'Yes, there's, er, there's a man here . . . unconscious. He's, er, he's collapsed.'

'What's the address?'

Address, yes. What was it? 'It's in Salford,' he said, struggling to recall. 'It's, er, twenty-two . . . twenty-two, Meredith something . . . House. Meredith House.'

'Is that the full address?'

No, it wasn't. 'Er, Willow Road. Willow Tree Road.' He had surprised himself by managing the full address and repeated it, as though it were a small triumph to be set against the horrendous disaster about to overtake him: 'Twenty-two, Meredith House, Willow Tree Road, Salford.'

'And your name please.'

He almost answered, checking himself in the nick of time. 'Ah, no, that doesn't matter. But it is urgent –'

'I do require your name, caller –'

'*Very* urgent. Thank you.' And he set down the receiver.

With the ambulance on its way, he knew he must leave as quickly as possible. He went back to the fallen body. 'There's help coming,' he said. 'I've sent for an ambulance.' He spoke for his own benefit as much as anything. He needed to reassure himself that he was doing all he could – or, anyway, all he could without jeopardizing his own freedom.

Thornton was still breathing and help was on its way. Keeping that thought in the forefront of his mind and refusing to countenance the other, unhappier thoughts crowding in behind it, Richard went out into the hallway and opened the front door. The corridor was mercifully empty. He stepped out, leaving the door open so that the ambulancemen shouldn't be delayed by having to break in. Then he hurried to the top of the stairs.

So far as he could judge, there was no-one coming up. He started down, wincing as the rasp of his shoes on the stone went echoing up and down the stairwell. He heard a clash of lift doors from below and froze. There was the drumming of the lift motor, then a faint rumble close-by as the lift rose past him. The calculating part of his brain told him that this was to his advantage: whoever had been waiting below had now been spirited upwards, out of his path. He started to go down again, now moving more quickly, wanting to be out before the lift had a chance to return.

There was no-one in the hallway. The lift indicator showed that it had gone to the third floor and stopped.

Richard fumbled with the locking mechanism on the inside of the entrance doors, then found it was a simple matter of depressing a handle. And at last he was out, escaping into the night air.

He was in his car and pulling away when the ambulance arrived, its lights flashing. The sight of it brought back a spark of hope. Thornton had been unconscious for what? It couldn't be more than five minutes or so. Another five minutes and he would be on his way to hospital.

Surely the odds had to be on a quick recovery? Come the morning, he would be sitting up in his bed, suffering from no more than a few cuts and bruises.

17

It was one thirty-five as Richard came off the main road and into the village. There were few lights showing and no-one to be seen. He passed the cenotaph, then came to the pub, with its windows shuttered and its carpark empty save for the landlord's ageing Lotus. He might have been arriving in another country, a safe haven after the horrors of Meredith House.

It was a relief to find his own home in darkness. The last thing he wanted was a late-night chat to his daughter. He wasn't sure he was capable of the effort needed to lie to her.

He moved quietly around the kitchen, not ready for sleep. When would he ever be? He was tormented by thoughts of what must be happening at the hospital to which Thornton would have been taken. The police would have been called: that went without saying. They would wait on Thornton recovering consciousness, eager to question him and find out did he know his assailant.

It might have already happened. In which case the police would be on their way, only minutes behind him.

Perhaps he shouldn't even consider going to bed but should remain downstairs so that he could admit them when they arrived and talk to them without Diane being disturbed. And no more alcohol: he was going to need his wits about him.

And if Thornton hadn't regained consciousness?

Well, then they were in Limbo, weren't they, both he and the police, waiting in a sort of suspended animation. One branch of his family had been Catholic. It had been an aunt of his, a devout spinster given to Novenas and trips to Lourdes, who had explained to him the distinctions between Heaven and Hell, Purgatory and Limbo. This without a doubt was Limbo, the ante-chamber to Heaven or Hell where souls lingered till their number was called and their fate announced.

His imagination would not be stopped, not tonight. What if

Thornton *never* regained consciousness, it asked. What if Philip Conway Thornton died?

He shook his head, refusing to contemplate the possibility, frightened of what it might reveal about himself. Would he even welcome such an outcome? Wasn't what he was now praying for, in prayers so secret that they were cloaked even from his own consciousness?

He told himself that he must think instead of how the ambulance had arrived so promptly. He must remind himself that Thornton had been struck not with an iron bar or baseball bat but with a fist.

There was every reason to expect a full recovery. It was senseless and even masochistic to speculate about any other outcome.

He sat in the kitchen as two o'clock and then two-thirty came and went. Still the police did not arrive and the phone remained silent. He felt a growing conviction that whatever was to happen would not do so that night but would wait till the morning.

It allowed him to see with a little more clarity just where he had gone wrong. Whatever was yet to happen, even if he got off scot-free, his mission was already a failure. He had not got the photographs. It was as simple as that. He had gone to Meredith House to force Thornton to hand them over and he had come away without them.

He should have done a deal. It was what Thornton had wanted and he should have played along. He should have even paid the man if necessary. What would it have mattered? But no, he had worked himself into a fury and lashed out blindly. In that single instant he might well have thrown away everything, not only the prospect of getting his hands on the photographs but perhaps even his own future and the chance of living happily with his wife ever again.

Cursing softly, and with tears of self-pity and self-loathing pricking his eyes, he went into the lounge and threw himself upon the sofa.

He awoke early and instantly recalled everything. There wasn't even a moment's remission when, half-awake, he might have imagined that life was as it had once been and his only problems today would be to do with agents and printers. No, he knew immediately; and immediately he wanted to lose himself in sleep again but couldn't.

So the night had passed and the police had not arrived. He couldn't even guess what might be happening and yet had a desperate need to know. That, before food or drink or emptying his aching bladder, was his first priority.

He pushed himself to his feet and went upstairs to his study, noting Diane's door firmly closed. May God spare her having to learn about all this, he prayed. And David too. It was enough that both children had been forced to witness as much as they had without now having to live through their father's arrest and trial for a crime of violence. Unlike the accusations of adultery in the letters, these would be allegations he would be unable to deny.

He carefully closed the study door, then went and sat at his desk. There were bright bars of light across it where the sun slanted in through the window blinds. Just the act of sitting there, with the familiar photographs of Claire and the children lining the window-sill before him, brought tears to his eyes. Did he really have to lose all this?

He had already calculated that Manchester Royal Infirmary was the nearest hospital to Meredith House and so the one to which the ambulance would probably have gone. He got the hospital number from Directory Enquiries, then dialled it.

'Manchester Royal,' said a man's voice.

'I'd like to make an enquiry about a patient.'

His brain was on alert, warning him that he mustn't give his own name, or his number so that they might ring him back, or anything that might later help identify him.

'Which ward is the patient on?' asked the hospital telephonist.

'Sorry, I don't know. He was taken in by ambulance early this morning.'

'Can you tell me the patient's name please?'

'Yes, it's Thornton, Philip Thornton.'

'If you could just hold a moment, I'll see if Accident and Emergency can tell us anything.'

'Thank you.'

There was always the remote possibility that Thornton had

made a dramatic recovery, sitting up and talking within minutes of help arriving. He might even have refused to be taken to this or to any other hospital. An outcome devoutly to be wished, though one difficult to believe.

'Hello, caller?' The hospital telephonist returned.

'Hello, yes?'

'The patient you're asking about, Philip Thornton, has been transferred to Intensive Care. Would you like me to put you through, see what they can tell you?'

'Please, yes.'

So he had been taken there and he had been admitted. Well, that was hardly a surprise, but the fact he had then been transferred to Intensive Care . . .? What could that mean except that his life was in danger? Perhaps he had slipped from unconsciousness into a coma? Whatever had happened, those words Intensive Care had a threatening and unpleasant ring to them, suggesting that everything – all their lives – were hanging by a thread.

'Intensive Care. Sister Yeats speaking.' This time it was a woman's voice, light and with an Irish accent.

'Good morning, Sister. I'd like to enquire about one of your patients. It's a Mr Philip Thornton.'

'Are you a relative of Mr Thornton's?'

'No. No, I'm a . . . friend.'

'Well, Mr Thornton is still unconscious but otherwise his condition is stable.'

That word 'stable' was encouraging, though doubtless it was an anodyne part of most bulletins and meant little. He needed to know more, a hint as to how things might develop.

'So I mean . . . is he going to be all right?'

'We really can't say at this stage. Perhaps if you could make an appointment to speak to doctor later on, he'll be able to tell you more than I can.'

There was a finality about that that told him she had said as much as she was ever going to. He thanked her and rang off.

So the jury was still out. Thornton hadn't made the quick recovery that would have got Richard off the hook; but nor had he died. He was still unconscious, as Richard had left him. It was to be more long hours of Limbo, the haunt of the unbaptised and the pagan, those tormented souls whose eternal fate hung in the balance.

He went from his study to the bedroom, the one that had been his and Claire's, where he showered and shaved and changed into fresh clothes. He completed these preparations for facing the long day ahead without coming to any decision on what kind of day it was to be. Should he go into the office and try and conduct himself as though everything were normal? Or would he be better staying at home and waiting for events to resolve themselves?

He went downstairs and collected the post from the hallway. At least there was no longer the need to sift through in search of further blackmail letters. They had been stopped, if nothing else had been achieved. His reason for going through the mail now was in the hope that Claire might have written.

But there was nothing from her, not even a card to say she was well and that they were not to worry.

He heard Diane singing out good morning and looked round to see her coming downstairs in her long T-shirt, her face rosy from sleep. He forced himself to smile and respond, hoping he didn't look too haggard.

'So what time did you get in?' she asked as they went into the kitchen together.

'Oh, some time after midnight, I'm not sure.'

He realized as he spoke and committed himself to the half-lie, that she might one day soon be questioned on this. Some policeman and then perhaps later a barrister in court would want to know the precise time at which he had returned. It would be unforgivable if he were to use her as an alibi.

'Or it might have been even later,' he added. 'To be honest, I think it was well after one.' And then quickly on, to change the subject: 'There hasn't been any word from your mother, has there?'

She grimaced. 'No.'

'Well, it's time there was.'

He felt suddenly the extent of his wife's desertion, the way she had so abruptly taken herself out of his life – out of all their lives – and left them to sink or swim. Attempting to explain it, he had told himself that she had needed to get away. He had tried even to sympathize: the shock of the letters must have been much greater for her than for him since he had always had the consolation of knowing his own innocence.

He was no longer convinced. Granted it was the tension surrounding their anniversary celebrations and then the dreadful rows that followed that had driven her away. He was willing to shoulder the responsibility for that. But for her to remain not only absent but incommunicado like this tested his sympathy to its limits.

'She's no right to do this,' he said, unable to contain his bitterness.

'It's only been a few days,' said Diane gently.

'I know. It's just . . . just the wrong bloody days.' He tried to laugh. 'Don't worry. Ignore me. I'm just tired, that's all.'

'You look a bit worn out.'

He had to leave. Being with her was a strain. He feared what he might find himself saying next.

'I'm going to get off to work,' he said. 'Make an early start.'

The decision had been made for him. He would spent the day in the office. Perhaps it would be there that the police would come for him.

He wondered if he should warn Diane. But what could he say, other than that he might at any minute be arrested and taken away, after which their lives would never be the same again? So he said nothing. He gave her a kiss, took his briefcase and went out to the car, as though this were just another day and not the day on which judgement would be passed on all of them.

He did not immediately embark on his journey into Manchester. First he had a visit to make, one he could put off no longer. He dumped his briefcase in the car, then walked down his own short driveway, turned left and came to the stretch of hawthorn hedging that fronted the Nevisons' property. Fifty yards along he turned into their driveway, which was a little longer than his own, their house being set further back. He came to the front porch, which was filled with geraniums in pots, and rang the bell.

It was Adele who appeared. Richard gave an inward groan on seeing her. He had been hoping for Lawrence, then he could have skipped the social chit-chat and got straight to the point.

Adele was dressed in a striped smock, her hair pinned back in a barrette. She smiled when she saw who it was and waved through the glass as she unlocked the door.

'Richard, hello . . .!'

'Sorry to call so early –'

'No, no, come in.'

'Thank you,' he said, and followed her into the hallway. 'It's actually Lawrence I was looking for.'

'He's in the kitchen. You've just caught him. It's about his time for leaving.' Then she turned quickly. Had Richard kept going, they would have embraced. 'You haven't any idea when Claire will be back, have you? I'm quite missing her.'

'No, I haven't,' he had to confess. 'Any day now I should think.'

She shot him a look of pure disbelief. Clearly her suspicions were growing. Perhaps she had heard something of the confrontations they had had and had put two and two together. He wondered what local gossip was making of Claire's abrupt disappearance, what stories were circulating.

Lawrence came out from the kitchen, drawn by their voices. He had a newspaper in his hand and his reading-glasses were pushed low on his nose. He looked anxious. The little performance of surprise he gave on seeing Richard and then the hearty 'Well, and what can we do for you?' struck Richard as horribly unconvincing, though Adele, the audience for whom it was intended, seemed to notice nothing. She offered coffee which Richard declined.

'I just wondered if we could have a quiet word,' he said, turning to Lawrence. 'Regarding that business I was telling you about the other day.'

'Let's go in here, shall we,' said Lawrence, and directed him into the lounge.

'Oh, but I haven't had chance to tidy up in there –' protested Adele.

'Doesn't matter,' said Lawrence abruptly.

Richard followed Lawrence through into the room. He caught a last glimpse of Adele's pained expression as Lawrence closed the door, excluding her.

The lounge was a long room, with french windows onto the garden. There was a fireplace of rough-hewn stone with pine cones filling its empty grate. Lawrence threw his newspaper onto a chair and pulled off his glasses. His expression when he turned to Richard was one of desperation and hope.

'What's happened?' he asked. 'You've seen him, have you – this blackmailer?' It was an appeal for good news, for something that would rescue him from whatever torments he had been silently enduring beneath Adele's watchful eye.

Knowing that the only news he could deliver was of the desperately bad variety, Richard set himself to get through it as quickly as possible. 'I've seen him, yes, last night –'

'And he admitted it?'

'Wait. Let me tell you –'

'What?'

Richard said: 'I assaulted him. He's in hospital.' Then braced himself for the response.

Lawrence stared. '*What?*'

'I said I –'

'*Assaulted* him! But why? What . . . what happened?' Then, before Richard could answer, he went on: 'And when you say he's in hospital . . . what, he's injured, is he? *Badly* injured . . .?'

'I don't know. I rang this morning –'

'And they know you assaulted him? Do the police know it was you? Because for Christsake –'

'No!' said Richard, raising his hands in an attempt to silence him. The man was becoming hysterical. 'Nobody knows anything. He was taken in unconscious and, so far as I know, he's still unconscious.'

'But you did –'

'I assaulted him, yes.'

Lawrence groaned and shook his head. No doubt he had been counting on Richard arriving with pockets bulging with photographs. They could have had a high old time burning them in the empty fire-grate. Instead, there were no photographs. Just the prospect of things getting immeasurably worse.

For a moment, at least, he had been shocked into silence. Richard took the opportunity to give him a summary of last night's events: how he had gone to the Queens Hotel, and then followed Philip Thornton home before tackling him inside his own flat.

'The stupid, bloody man just wouldn't accept that the game

was up. He still wanted to make a deal. Never mind that I wasn't going to go to the police. That wasn't enough. The man wanted money!'

'So you could have given him –'

'No! No, I couldn't, not after everything he'd done to my marriage. Remember that, Lawrence, please. This was the man who had virtually destroyed my marriage!'

It was a defence for his own behaviour that he needed, whether he believed it himself or not. He felt himself to be rehearsing it, in preparation for the appearance in court which must surely lie ahead.

Lawrence nodded, accepting rather than understanding. And, by the look of him, still savagely resentful that Richard should have dragged them both further into the mire.

'And, anyway, he was enjoying it,' Richard went on. 'The bloody man was standing facing me – and he was enjoying it!'

This was closer to the truth. More than anything else, it had been Thornton's attitude, provoking and taunting him, that had led to the violence. If only the man had shown the slightest sign of contrition. If only he had once apologized or pleaded for mercy.

Instead of which, he had strutted like a bantam cock, virtually inviting Richard to take a swing at him.

Lawrence had remained silent throughout Richard's explanation. He asked quietly, 'So you didn't get the photographs?'

Richard sighed. 'No.'

'Christ.'

'I'm sorry.'

'*Christ!*'

'Once I'd hit him, and he'd collapsed . . . I didn't even think about them.'

Having absorbed the shocks, Lawrence was now getting back into his stride. 'So not only have we not got the photographs – the fucking man is as we speak lying in hospital, with a policeman next to his fucking bed! Because, no question, the hospital will have informed the police. It's routine. They'll have rung the police the minute he was brought –'

The door opened, startling both of them. Stopped in mid-flow, Lawrence gave a choking sound, then coughed to clear his throat.

It was Adele who entered, carrying two cups from which the steam was rising.

'I brought you some coffee anyway, just in case. If you don't want it, then you don't have to have it.'

She smiled at Richard, who said, 'Thank you.'

'You're welcome.'

Lawrence's expression was impassive as he followed her to the door and closed it after her.

'I know,' said Richard. 'I've made things worse, much worse.'

'I think you have.'

'But that's *my* doing and *my* responsibility.'

'It might be your doing but it's going to drag me in, isn't it.'

'I don't see that –'

'Oh, come on, Richard, of course you can see!' accused Lawrence, his voice rising again. 'They're going to want to know why, aren't they! Why you were at that man's flat in the first place. Why you attacked him. And you're going to have to tell them about the letters. And then it'll all come out, all about those fucking photographs and . . . everything.' He repeated with a desperate emphasis: '*Everything*. I might as well pick up the fucking phone and ring the fucking newspapers now!'

'You don't know. It might not happen like that.'

'Jesus, Richard, what have you done to me?'

Richard resisted the urge to point out just who it was who had done what to whom. By a supreme effort of will, he said nothing at all but waited in the hope Lawrence would calm down as he had before.

Lawrence strode up and down the narrow lounge, shaking his head and muttering ferociously to himself. Then he stopped and gave a little laugh, as though the whole thing were too much, a wild and unstoppable farce.

'You want some of her fucking coffee?' he said, gesturing at the cups which Adele had brought.

Richard shook his head.

'Neither do I.'

Richard took the opportunity to speak. 'Look, I've been thinking about this. All right, I assaulted him. I'll admit to that. In fact, I'd have probably admitted it already but I was just hoping Claire might have turned up and then I could have talked to her first.'

'You don't admit to anything, not yet,' said Lawrence, shaking his head. He absently picked up one of the coffee cups and began to drink from it.

'OK, but when it comes to it. The point I'm making is that I don't have to mention you or even say that it was photographs that I was after. I'll show them the letters. I can explain how I had this man traced and then went to confront him because of the letters.'

'But the letters talk about photographs,' objected Lawrence.

'Well, all right. But nobody's ever seen them. So far as the police know, they're photographs of me.' He paused to let that sink in, then repeated: 'They'll take it for granted they're photographs of me. There's no need for your name even to be mentioned.'

Lawrence gave a tired smile, as though to say Thanks for the effort even if it was feeble. 'And then you know what they'll do?' he said sadly.

'What?'

'They'll search the flat.'

'Well –'

'Oh, yes, they'll search the flat. And that's when they'll find the photographs. One look and they'll recognize me. So it won't matter what you've said or what you haven't said.'

It had all the force of the incontestable truth. Of course the police would search the flat – just as he should have done but didn't.

He tried desperately to find some flaw in Lawrence's depressing scenario. 'Even if they do search, and even if they find the photographs, they don't have to publicize the fact. They can make out a case against me without even mentioning any photographs.'

This time Lawrence's look was of undisguised contempt. 'Oh, and they'll do that for me because they're my bosom buddies? These policemen whose evidence I've been tearing to pieces for the past twenty years, they're going to keep quiet about this for my sake?'

'I still don't see that –'

'Christ, Richard, they're going to love it! They're going to use those pictures to crucify me!'

He turned and strode away towards the French windows. For

a moment Richard thought he was going to plunge straight through the glass and out into the garden. But he stopped up against the windows and remained there, staring out. Then he lent forward and, slowly and gently, bumped his forehead – once, twice, three times – on the glass.

Whatever Lawrence had done to bring this on himself and to ruin Richard's own happiness, it was difficult not to feel some sympathy for a man who beat his head against his own French windows. No doubt he was right in thinking that the press would be rough on him once all this came out. It was a tale that had all the ingredients to bring them running. Seeing Lawrence's anguish, it was almost possible for Richard to forget for a moment how much more serious was his own predicament, with not just his reputation or career but his marriage and liberty at stake.

'All right,' Lawrence said, sighing. He turned and came back into the middle of the room. 'All right, let's think about this. The bastard who's responsible for all this, he's in hospital and he's unconscious. What did you do, just hit him or – ?'

'Just hit him, yes,' said Richard, glad to get back to what few facts there were to cling to. 'Four or five times, I don't know.'

'And he went down –'

'Like a felled tree. I thought he was faking it. It was too . . . too neat. Just down and out.'

'And then you . . . what, you left him . . .?'

'Not straightaway, no. First, I rang for an ambulance –'

'*You* rang?'

'*I* rang. Then I left him. I mean I was out before the ambulance got there.'

'OK, right,' muttered Lawrence. He was pacing the room, back to being a lawyer again, facing up to things with a lawyer's determination to make the best out of a bad job. 'When did you ring the hospital?'

'Oh, about seven o'clock this morning.'

'You want to ring them again? See if anything's happened?'

'Now?'

'Why not? Everything depends on what's happening in that hospital. We have to know what it is.'

So there and then, with Lawrence standing close, trying to catch what was being said on the other end of the line, Richard rang the Manchester Royal Infirmary once again and asked to be put through to Intensive Care. It was no longer Sister Yeats on duty but a Sister Georgeson, who briskly announced that there had been no change: Mr Thornton remained unconscious but stable. Richard thanked her and rang off.

'Unconscious but stable,' he repeated in case Lawrence hadn't heard.

'And what the hell does that mean? Is he dying? Is he going to live?'

'I don't know. At least it means he can't have said anything yet.'

Lawrence nodded. 'True, yeah. Look, will you just promise me one thing.'

'What?'

Richard found himself on the receiving end of a gaze that was earnest and sincere. He couldn't help but see it as one perfected over the years before various juries and judges and panels of magistrates. This was Lawrence summing up for the Defence.

'Richard, I'm not trying to off-load all the responsibility for this onto you. How could I? It was my foolishness that got us into this mess in the first place, of course it was. However, once you'd identified this barman as the man behind the blackmail letters, well, then I have to point out that I did offer to go with you to see him –'

'Yes –'

'But you said no. You insisted you'd do it on your own –'

'Look, I'm not denying this is all my fault,' said Richard. 'I'm the one who hit him. I'm responsible for whatever happens. So what is it you're asking?'

'Just that you don't go confessing to anybody, the police or anybody. Not yet.'

Richard hesitated, surprised this was all he was being asked to do. He had no intention of going to his nearest police-station and making an immediate confession. Not until he at least knew what the charge might be. He could understand if Lawrence had been attempting to persuade him from confessing at all; or to urge him to leave the country at the earliest opportunity. But what gain there might be in delaying a confession . . . no, that he couldn't see.

'Why?'

'Well, suppose that this man . . . what's his name?'

'Philip Thornton.'

'Suppose he comes round?'

'I hope he does,' said Richard.

'And so do I, of course. What I'm thinking is – he sounds like a pretty cool character.'

'Too cool for his own good.'

'So he might,' said Lawrence, seizing on that, 'he might decide to keep quiet . . .?'

Richard was unimpressed. 'Why should he?'

'For his own benefit. To keep himself out of jail. Don't forget that, the minute he accuses you, he's as good as putting the noose around his own neck. If he says that you assaulted him, then the police are going to ask *why* did you assault him? And, once that question is answered, then he's up on a charge of demanding with menaces – and not his first either, from what you've told me.'

Richard nodded. It was a persuasive argument. Perhaps Thornton did have as much to lose as any of them if this were to come out into the open.

'I suppose it's possible.'

'You're the one who's been telling me what a cool and calculating customer he is.'

'I know –'

'So let's just hope he's cool enough to see that it's in his best interests to say nothing.'

How wonderful if things could be resolved so easily. Even better if Thornton should destroy the photographs himself. It was possible. He might realize how vulnerable he would be if the police started asking around. He might also be frightened that Richard would return to give him another sock on the jaw. Either way, he might judge himself better off if he put a match to the damned things first chance he got.

'Suppose he doesn't recover?' said Lawrence. 'Suppose he dies?'

Richard flinched away from the brutal question. Of course, he had asked it of himself a hundred times but then he had refused to answer, glimpsing the awful dilemmas that lay beyond. In fact, Lawrence answered the question for him. As he did so,

Richard realized that he was obsessed only with the consequences for himself.

'Well, they'll search the flat, won't they,' he said. 'They're bound to. And then they'll find the photographs. Photographs of me!' His voice began to rise again as his calm deserted him. 'So it doesn't take them long to work out what's happened. He's been blackmailing me, and *I've* killed him.'

'No –'

'Yes! I'm there, aren't I. I'm the one in the fucking pictures!'

It was an inference that roused Richard to anger. 'So what are you saying? You think I'd stand by and see you charged with this man's murder?'

'I'm saying . . . ' He hesitated but only for a second. 'I'm saying we none of us know what we'd do under those circumstances.'

Richard felt the anger that had been given its head with Philip Thornton flaring within him again.

'I'm going,' he said. 'I've told you everything I came to tell you –'

'You'll be ringing the hospital again?' said Lawrence quickly.

'Well . . . I suppose I'll have to, yes.' Otherwise, how would he ever know whether the man lived or died?

'OK. So let's keep in touch.' Lawrence had suddenly returned to his role of ally and supporter. He placed a reassuring hand on Richard's arm. 'And, like I said, don't say anything to anybody, not yet.'

'I wasn't planning on doing,' said Richard, a touch stiffly. The suggestion that he might keep quiet and let Lawrence take the rap should Thornton die still rankled with him.

'Hey, look,' said Lawrence, noticing. 'I'm sorry if I said . . . well, whatever it was. I know this is just as tough on you. Worse even.'

Richard nodded. He believed it was. Much worse.

Lawrence kept his hand on his arm and came close, as if he was about to share a joke. 'All that I'm saying – if I were your lawyer, then my professional advice would be that you say nothing. So what if the man dies? There were no witnesses. You say nothing and you'll walk out of any court in the land a free man.'

*

It was gone eleven o'clock and Richard had been in his office for more than an hour. He had managed a passable performance of a small publisher absorbed in his work. Simon presented him with an analysis of current sales figures. He felt he was reading them in a dream. Even so, he was forced into a whole series of minor decisions, none of which was individually of great importance but which together, along with other, similar decisions, taken on what had seemed like similar days, would determine the future of the company, its survival or its gradual decay.

It was then that the phone rang and he answered it. Yvonne asked if he could speak to a Mr Nevison.

'Yes, put him on.'

There was a pause then: 'Richard?'

'Yes?'

'Do you have anybody with you?'

His heart began to race. 'No. Why?'

'You haven't heard the news?'

'What news?'

'It's just been on radio. Local radio.'

It was like coming up over the hill of the roller-coaster, that moment when the car is almost at a stand-still, about to swoop down. When you know what is to come and experience a feeling that is a mixture of delight and fear because there is nothing you can do to prevent it.

'What?' whispered Richard.

'He's died,' said Lawrence. 'Philip Thornton. They said he died without regaining consciousness and so it's now a murder investigation.'

18

Claire came down into the empty hotel lounge and placed her canvas hold-all on one of the low, oak tables. There was a smell of polish mixed with the fresh air blowing in from where the outer door had been propped open.

Sounds of activity came from the bar, bottles being tossed into a skip, but no-one appeared. She was in no hurry. Rather than call for attention, she flopped down onto one of the well-worn leather sofas and waited for them to come and find her.

In her flight from her husband, she had headed north to the Lake District. She might have gone anywhere: it was getting away that mattered. Perhaps she had settled on the Lakes because they had always been *her* holidaying domain, never *theirs*. It was an area she had tramped and climbed as a student and returned to regularly since. Sometimes she had been alone. Twice she had taken Diane along, hoping to infect her too with a passion for its wild beauty.

Having no real plan, she had come to Windermere, then struck off west till she reached the quieter, faintly bleak waters of Coniston. Here she had stayed for two days and nights, strolling around the town and the northern edges of the lake or sitting in little tea-shops. She tried not to think of what she had left behind and when, if ever, she might return to it.

She remained uneasy, fearing pursuit if only by telephone or letter. Of course Richard couldn't know where she was. But she knew him to be resourceful and determined once he set his mind to something. She was haunted by the thought that he would find some means of tracing her.

Her fears propelled her forward. She left Coniston and travelled further north, till she arrived at Buttermere. There were fewer tourists here, fewer people altogether. She took a room in the Salutation Arms, which was more pub than hotel, with the bar doubling as its dining-room and the locals drifting in through the evening.

Here she felt oddly safe. Nobody bothered her or made polite enquiries about how she had spent her day or where she was heading, as they had in the larger hotel at Coniston. She began to relax, finding some enjoyment in her exile. She developed a small routine: eating a hearty and leisurely breakfast, then pottering about the town, looking through junk shops and charity shops for any interesting bits of fabric. In the afternoon she embarked on a two- or three-hour walk, her favourite being the round circuit of Buttermere itself. She would scour the shore for pieces of driftwood or bleached bones. After which she returned to base for the evening, dining alone in a corner of the bar.

The landlord, a small, red-faced man who went by the name of Davy Norman, came in from outside and stopped in surprise on seeing Claire.

'Mrs Gillow, is no-one attending to you?'

'That's all right, I've only just come down. I'm just waiting for my bill.'

'Your bill – of course. I'll be with you in a jiffy.'

And he hurried through to the bar, leaving her alone once more.

There had been no single moment when she'd been conscious of reaching a decision regarding their marriage. What had happened was that, during the long walks and the slow meals taken alone, the whirl of competing thoughts that had filled her mind and left her unable to rest or to be still for long had gradually subsided. As she had walked the lake shore and observed how the reflection of the mountains opposite moved with her across the water's glassy surface, the din inside her head had fallen silent. She saw that what she was faced with was not a complex problem at all but a very simple choice. It was the choice of whether she wanted her marriage to continue or not.

Her answer was equally simple. It was that yes, she did wish it to continue. What life could she imagine for herself otherwise?

After that, secure in the knowledge that she knew how she wanted all this to turn out, she could afford to review what had happened without letting it distress or alarm her.

So what about those letters and their claim that her husband had been conducting an affair with a woman called Melissa?

Was this one enormous lie, as Richard would have her believe? Or was it the truth?

The more she considered the matter, the more certain she became that it was the truth. It had to be. If nothing else, the letters constituted a serious attempt at blackmail. And it was not possible to blackmail anyone on the basis of a lie. Ergo, the letters spoke the truth.

Looking back, she could see what had happened. Richard had been panicked by the first letter and, without considering the consequences, had leapt in with an immediate denial. Then, when more letters arrived, he had no option but to elaborate upon that initial lie till he had ended up cocooned in lies, with no way of ever escaping.

A consoling thought was that only a man who was deeply ashamed of his affair would afterwards deny it with such vehemence. Poor Melissa, whoever she had been, was clearly part of history, and a part he would sooner forget.

Claire reminded herself that she always known this was going to happen. Well, hadn't she? She had said as much to Richard, when she had been trying to persuade him to confess. Sooner or later there had had to be The Other Woman elbowing her way into their lives. Well, now she'd been and gone. It had all been so predictable. In fact, she had predicted it. The only strange thing, the thing to be wondered at, was that Claire, who had believed herself prepared for this to happen, should have fallen apart as she had.

Davy Norman returned with a plate on which lay a hand-written bill.

'I trust everything has been to your satisfaction?'

'Yes, thank you.'

He waited while she took out her cheque-book and fountain-pen and wrote out a cheque.

'Thank you very much indeed,' he said, when she handed it to him. 'Do you have a long journey?'

'Oh, about three hours. Perhaps a little more.'

'You never know what the traffic's going to be these days.'

They agreed on that and he again thanked her for her custom. She took up her trusty, old bag, now heavy with the bric-a-brac it held along with her clothes, and went out to her car. The brightness outside took her by surprise after the low-ceilinged gloom of the inn.

Her stomach was full of butterflies at the thought of coming face to face with Richard again. She was still unsure of what she should say to him. She must make it clear that Melissa did not matter. The letters did not matter. She was returning to make a new start in which they would put the whole wretched business behind them.

'He's died without regaining consciousness,' Lawrence repeated.

'Yes,' said Richard. 'Yes, I understand.'

He knew that this was terrible news, changing everything. Yet his first and clearest reaction was the odd feeling that he wasn't at all surprised.

Of course Thornton had died. What else could happen to deepen the tragedy that his life had become? From the opening of that first letter – which, like foolish children, he and Claire had laughed at and treated as a joke – he had been in free fall, without a hope of salvation.

'Richard?'

'Yes.'

'You all right?'

'Yes, just, er . . . just trying to come to terms –'

'OK, well, listen. Whatever you do, don't say anything about this to anybody,' said Lawrence, sounding as if he were ahead of him. He had already come to terms with Thornton's death and had a strategy to handle it. 'Just say nothing, OK?'

Richard still couldn't think clearly enough to discern whether this was good advice or bad. 'But supposing that the police –'

'If the police get in touch with you, then tell them about the letters but *nothing else!*'

He sounded scared. Richard could hear that now, the fear in his voice.

'Then let me know. Remember you can always say I'm your solicitor, right? They'll always let you speak to me. They have to.'

'I suppose they do.'

'So promise me.'

'What?'

247

'Well, to start with, you won't go to the police or anything stupid like that . . .?'

'I don't know what I'll do,' said Richard, resenting being hustled like this. 'God, I've only just heard –'

'I know, I know. Only, believe me, the best thing is if you don't say anything to anybody, not yet. Not till we see just how the police are thinking.'

He couldn't see how it mattered what the police were thinking. The reality was that Thornton had died and it was he, Richard Gillow, who had killed him.

'I think I'm going to go home,' he said, wanting to get Lawrence off the line. He needed time to absorb the enormity of what he had just been told. He could do nothing, not even think, with Lawrence heckling him like this.

'OK, well, fine. That's probably best. But please remember what I said –'

'That I should say nothing,' he said. 'Yes, I'll remember.' And he put down the phone.

He left the office, instructing Lynne to cancel all his appointments, not only for today but for tomorrow too. Her lips began to purse in disapproval but then she must have read in his face something of the bleak despair he was feeling.

'Is something the matter?' she asked, concerned. 'Is there anything I can do?'

'There's nothing you can do, thank you,' he said. 'Something has happened, yes, but I can't talk about it now.'

He all but fled the building, fearful of meeting anyone else or having to face further questions. Manoeuvring out of his parking space, he was tempted by the notion of driving to the nearest police-station and insisting they took down a statement in which he would tell them everything. That way, he would be placing himself in their hands and shedding all responsibility.

But he knew such temptation must be resisted. It wasn't only because he had promised Lawrence. He still had a faint but abiding hope that Claire might have made contact with Diane during his absence. Or even that she might have returned, in which case any statements to be made must first be made to her.

The house was unexpectedly busy with people. Even before he

could enter it, Richard had to exchange a greeting with their gardener who was trudging behind the mower up and down the front lawn. Inside, the woman who came in to clean three days a week was vacuuming the hallway. Richard moved swiftly past her and on into the kitchen. Here he found that Diane and boyfriend Will were already in residence. Will had placed his crash-helmet on the kitchen table but lifted it off when Richard appeared.

'Daddy, what's the matter?' asked Diane. 'Why are you back at this time?'

He muttered something about taking time off while he could. Normal conversation was beyond him. He excused himself and made his way upstairs towards his study. Diane came after him, asking if he wanted coffee, and had he had any lunch? Rather than argue, he agreed that she might bring him a sandwich and cup of coffee. He reached the sanctuary of the study, threw off his jacket and tie and sank into the old armchair that had landed up in there with him because Claire had considered it too much of an eye-sore for the rest of the house.

He sat for some time without moving, giving way to a belated state of shock. He roused himself only when Diane arrived to deliver the promised refreshments. He knew there was something he must ask her.

'You haven't heard anything from your mother?'

'Not a thing.' And now she was staring at him. 'Dad, you look terrible. Has something happened? I mean something new?'

He wanted to alert her to the dark night that was about to descend on them all but he didn't know that he could, not without running the risk of breaking down in front of her. He needed more time to grieve for himself before he could involve others and so gave her only a partial answer.

'Something has happened, yes. It's all to do with those letters. You know, the ones that –'

'Yes.'

'Well, I've . . . I've found out who's been sending them.'

'You have . . .?'

She seemed delighted. Oh, you poor girl, he thought. Will you ever forgive me for misleading you like this?

'I have, yes. But . . . well, things have got a bit tricky.'

'But surely, if you've found out who's sending them, can't you just go to the police and leave it to them to sort it out?'

'I suppose I could,' he said, 'yes.'

'Well, that's what I'd do. Anyway, I can see you want me to leave you alone. Give me a shout if you want anything else.'

She planted a kiss on his forehead and left him to his thoughts.

He heard the doorbell and gave a start of alarm. So they were here already, were they, and he had done nothing. He had come to no decisions, made no plans.

He looked at his watch and saw that the best part of an hour had passed. It was time he had wasted, sitting there in his chair, mesmerised by thoughts of Thornton's death and the horrors that were soon to come crowding in upon his own life.

He got to his feet and made for the door. He must be the one to speak to the police. Such a task must not be left to his daughter.

He hurried down the stairs but he could hear that Diane was already at the open front door. She was inviting somebody to step inside. As he came into view, Richard saw that it wasn't the police at all but Lawrence.

'Oh, here he is,' said Diane brightly. 'Daddy, it's Lawrence for you.'

'I thought we should talk,' said Lawrence.

'Yes, of course. Come on up.'

He led him back upstairs and into his study. It was a heart-stopping relief to find it wasn't the police. Even so, he could have done without another punishing confrontation with Lawrence, which he feared this might well turn out to be. He had urgent matters to attend to. He must rearrange his affairs, both personal and business, as best he could before the doorbell should ring again and begin a process that would place him out of reach.

'You haven't done anything?' demanded Lawrence the moment the door was closed.

'If you mean have I told anybody . . .?'

'Yes.'

'I haven't, no.'

Lawrence let out a long sigh of relief. 'Good. Wonderful. Because listen, I've been thinking.'

'What?'

'When you were at this man Thornton's flat . . . did anybody see you?'

Why? Richard wanted to ask. What would it matter if a passing coachload had seen him? But he knew that any such challenge would only lead them into a protracted argument. It would be simpler just to answer the question.

He thought back to when the man and woman had been coming out of the flat and he had sprung forward to catch the door. They had both been preoccupied, running to their car to escape the rain. Leaving, he had seen no-one.

'I don't think anybody saw me, no.'

'And you didn't leave anything there?'

'Leave anything . . .?'

'In the flat,' said Lawrence impatiently. 'You didn't leave anything lying around that might prove you were there?'

'No, I don't think . . .' Nothing he could think of anyway. 'No.'

Lawrence was further relieved. 'OK. Well, listen then. Whatever happens, you must *say nothing*.'

Richard sighed. 'We talked about this on the phone.'

'I know but −'

'And what I don't understand. Even if I don't say anything, they'll find the photographs, which are photographs of you −'

'I know −'

'We'd talked about this while Thornton was still alive, and you were the one who said −'

'I know what I said then, but now things have changed.'

'You said they're bound to search the flat and then they'll find the photographs and that will lead them straight to you.'

It reminded him how Lawrence had hinted that Richard might keep quiet and let him take the rap. Was that what this was all about?

'I know they'll find the photographs,' said Lawrence. 'But listen −'

'So then what does it matter whether anyone −'

Lawrence gave a groan of exasperation, then said loudly: 'What does it matter? I'll tell you what it matters. It matters because *they'll probably find other photographs too*!'

'Could you stop shouting please,' said Richard.

'I'm sorry but −'

'There's no need for it.'

'OK. I'm sorry. But don't you see what I'm saying? It's not just going to be photographs of me they'll find. Odds are there are going to be photographs of lots of other people besides.'

'I suppose that's possible,' granted Richard. Still, he couldn't see why Lawrence should feel it was a fact of such significance.

'It's more than just possible. Think about it. You were the one who said this man had form. He's done this kind of thing before.'

'Yes.'

'So it's unlikely that this is the one and only time he's bothered to try it on again. I mean if he's gone to the expense of buying himself some sort of miniature camera . . . he hasn't just done that for my benefit. He's most probably been doing it for years, blackmailing hundreds of people!'

The logic was undeniable, though Richard still failed to see where it was leading. 'That's true, but even so –'

'So the police won't just find photographs of me. Right? They're going to find other photographs of other people as well. And perhaps there'll be lists of name and addresses to go with them. Yes?'

'Yes, all right –'

'Well, what I'm saying is that every one of those names has a motive for killing this man. Every single one of them!'

'I suppose they do,' said Richard quietly.

He now understood the point that Lawrence was hammering home. He also saw the proposition towards which Lawrence was leading him, the deal he was offering.

It was that Richard should say nothing. Let the police uncover the photographs. Lawrence would manfully take whatever fall-out there was from them on his own head. While, with neither witnesses nor evidence to connect him to the case, Richard would be spared the capital charge of murder.

Lawrence was watching his face, waiting for his response. There was a desperate eagerness about him which Richard knew he could only disappoint.

'It's the fact that the man's dead,' urged Lawrence. 'It changes everything. He can't testify against you. And, if he can't, then who else is there? You've said it yourself – *nobody*. No witnesses, no evidence. There's no case. Can't be.'

'But the police will still come to you.'

'Yes.' Lawrence seemed happy enough to accept this. 'Of course they will! And then all I'll have to do is tell them about the blackmail threats, the ones that were mistakenly directed at you. And, all right, that'll probably mean that the police will want to talk to you but only to check that you received those letters, nothing else. And you can handle that . . .?'

Richard said, 'I could handle that, yes, but that's not the point –'

'But that's all they're going to ask you about,' Lawrence hurried on, seeking to reassure. 'From then on you'll be . . . incidental. They're not going to suspect you of anything. They'll just talk to you about the letters and then they won't ever come near you again.' He was growing excited as he believed himself to be making his case. 'And my only involvement will be as one among any number of blackmail victims. How many we don't know – could be dozens or even hundreds. So they'll investigate me, along with the others. But, of course, they'll find nothing else to link me with this man. How can they? There isn't anything. Face it, I didn't even get the letters – they went to the wrong house!' He couldn't restrain himself and chortled at this.

'Yes, I can see all that –'

'And because . . . wait. You see the beauty of it? Because I'm a blackmail *victim* – victim, yes? – that means they have to keep it all confidential. I mean it might amuse them privately to have these pictures of me, but they can't let the press see them, they can't even let Adele see them . . .! Because they have to respect my confidentiality.'

He stopped and looked at Richard, waiting not just for his agreement but for his acclaim. Here he was the hot-shot lawyer pulling the cleverest stroke of his career, one that would mean the defendants wouldn't even have to go to court, all charges would be dropped and they'd all live more or less happily ever after.

Richard sighed and shook his head.

'What?' demanded Lawrence. 'You want me to explain it to you again?'

'No. No, I think I understand –'

'Well, then what's the problem?'

'The problem is that I can't do it,' he spoke firmly, wanting this to be over. 'I can't live with a secret like that for the rest of my life.'

Lawrence stared, horrified. 'For Christsake –'

'I'm sorry –'

'You can't be serious!'

'I know that it'll implicate you, and I'm sorry about that –'

'Do you know what you'll be facing?' Lawrence, who hadn't sat down since entering the room, was now bending to bring his face level with Richard's, trying to fix him with his gaze, while banging softly on the desk top to emphasise his word. 'Do you know what you'll be facing?'

'I imagine it might well be a charge of murder –'

'Yes, which carries life imprisonment. You understand that? Mandatory *life imprisonment*!'

'I know.'

Lawrence shook his head in disbelief. 'You're telling me that you'll be happy to be locked away –'

'Not happy, no –'

'To be locked away from your wife and family for the rest of your life?'

'It seems to me it needn't necessarily be a charge of murder,' said Richard. 'Might it not be manslaughter?'

Immediately he had spoken, he regretted his words. He knew Lawrence would take them as an invitation to debate, which was the last thing he wanted. He intended to confess, no matter what the resulting charge might be. The only alternative was to pile more lies and deceit on top of what had already gone before and he wasn't willing to be a party to that.

'Look at it this way,' said Lawrence, not giving up. 'Think about this man who's died. This Philip Thornton.'

'Yes?'

'What sort of a man are we talking about? This man's a shit. A blackmailer, a nasty, evil, conniving shit! Jesus, you said that yourself. Wasn't that why you beat him up – because he was still demanding money from you even when you had him bang to rights?'

Richard shook his head. Here they were sliding into the kind of point-scoring debate he had been determined to avoid. It was one that could go on forever or at least until the police were at the door. It was, anyway, beside the point since he had no intention of letting it shake his resolve. Lawrence was desperate and frightened, he could see that. Nevertheless, he would have to accept that the decision was Richard's and not his.

'I don't think it matters who the man was –'

'He was scum! A piece of shit, and you're going to let yourself be locked away –'

'No, I'm not,' protested Richard. 'I'm going to protect myself in court. I'm going to explain how this happened. But what I'm not going to do is to go on lying about it –'

'But that's what I'm telling you! You won't have to lie –'

'To the police I will, yes. And to Claire. What do I say to her?'

Lawrence was stuck for a moment, then came back with: 'You say to her just what we were always going to say to her. How the letters were a mistake. *But no more than that!*'

They had reached stalemate. Richard felt that, even if they remained in that room shouting at one another forever, there would remain a chasm between them that would never be bridged. He stood up.

'Lawrence, I'm going to have to ask you to leave.'

He was alarmed. 'Why? What're you going to do?'

'I'm going to do various things, but one of them will be to telephone the police and tell them what has happened.'

Lawrence gave a howl of despair and brought a hand crashing down on the desk so that the lamp and the selection of pens beside it jumped into the air. 'No, no, for the love of God, Richard, *no!*'

'I have to.'

'Of course you don't have to! I've just been telling you precisely why it is you don't have to!'

'I can't go through the rest of my life with this on my conscience.'

Lawrence turned like a cornered animal, a finger pointing in accusation. 'You bastard. I know why you're doing this.'

'I've already said –'

'To get back at me. To have your revenge on me!'

It was such a ludicrous notion Richard couldn't at first believe he was serious. Though he certainly was. His face contorted with rage, he went on: 'Because you think I got you into this, so you'll do anything to make me pay, won't you, you fucking bastard!'

For a moment Richard thought the other man was about to assault him. It would be a grotesque finale, should it come to that. But Lawrence evidently thought better off it. He stepped back.

Richard indicated the door. 'OK, that's it. Out of here please.'

Lawrence performed an instantaneous transformation from threatening madman back to solicitous friend. He held out his arms imploringly. 'Why? What have I said?'

'It doesn't matter. Just go.'

'Richard, I'm begging you –'

'Go!'

'Don't go to the police. That way we're both in the shit, both of us!'

He looked on the verge of tears, or about to fall to his knees. Not relishing either of these possibilities, Richard stepped past him and opened the door.

'And can you please keep your voice down,' he said. 'There are other people in the house.'

Lawrence gave a low, mirthless laugh. 'So you're going to do the right thing. Well, yes. Why not,' he said bitterly.

Richard waited, still holding the door, demanding that the other man to depart. Lawrence gulped, as though fighting back a tear, then surprised Richard by offering his hand.

'I'm sorry about all this,' he said. 'It was my stupidity that got us into this, don't think I don't know that.'

'I shall do all I can to keep your name out of it,' said Richard, feeling obliged to offer something in return.

Lawrence smiled. 'Thanks. Though I don't think it'll do an awful lot of good.'

They shook hands, then Lawrence walked away along the landing and disappeared down the stairs.

He understood Lawrence's terror, of course he did. It was a terror he shared. He was dreading the moment when the police would arrive and his awful secret, which up to now had been shared only with Lawrence, would pass into the public domain.

If only he could confess privately. He thought once again of his Catholic aunt who used to visit her priest in his confessional-box every Saturday evening. It was the kind of one to one repentance he could have welcomed. But no, what lay ahead for him would be mercilessly public. Floodlit even. He was about to bring a sudden, nationwide infamy upon himself and those he loved. His family would be devastated, the village awash with rumour and gossip; and finally would come his big day in court with the press gaily turning all their lives into a circus.

Worst of all was the hurt he was about to inflict on those nearest him. His wife and children would be the first to know and so the first to suffer. Then other relatives and friends in an ever widening circle as the word would spread.

It wasn't even that he feared their condemnation. More painful was knowing how they would struggle to understand what he had done. They would close ranks and rally round in support.

He could understand how Lawrence must be haunted by similar fears. Wherever the story was told, Lawrence's role would loom large. There was a sense in which he might become the villain of the piece. The killer would be Richard – no room for doubt about that. But Lawrence would be damned alongside him as the man whose combination of lust and cowardice made him deceive his escort-agency date and so set the whole thing in motion.

He would set the police a dead-line. If they had not arrived by, say, five o'clock then he would ring them and admit to being Philip Thornton's killer. Though he believed it would never come to that. They must even now be working their steady and methodical way towards him.

In whatever time remained, he must make one last attempt to communicate with Claire. It would be unforgivable if she were to learn about his arrest from a column in the morning paper or, even more regrettable, from a friend ringing up to console her when she hadn't even read the paper and so knew nothing.

Who was there among those friends of hers – drawn from their neighbours, old art student pals, the Samaritan and the Amnesty groups she supported, the village gardening group, and whoever else – who might know where he could reach her?

Not Adele certainly: that much had been clear from their encounter this morning. Moira might be his best chance. She had always seemed to keep Claire up to date on the cliff-hanging saga of her own marriage to Roy; perhaps Claire had reciprocated.

Moira was at home and answered his call.

'Richard, hello . . .!'

She sounded pleased to be hearing from him. He wondered whether it was a bad sign. Did it mean she had no more idea where Claire was than he had himself and she was counting on him to tell her?

'I have to get in touch with Claire,' he said. 'It's really quite urgent.'

'Oh, dear.'

'You probably know that she's gone away for a few days –'

'I gathered something of the sort, yes.'

He decided to be bold about it: 'Do you know where she is?'

'No, I'm sorry, I don't.'

Should he believe her? 'Moira, this is important, otherwise I wouldn't be asking you.'

'I really don't,' she said firmly. 'I'm not saying I'd definitely tell you if I did. But actually that's not a problem because I really and truly don't.'

Her statement had the depressing ring of truth about it.

'Do you know anybody else who might know where she is?'

He knew he was leaving himself open to all manner of speculation on Moira's part as to just what had been going on in the Gillow marriage, but what did that matter now? It was thin gruel compared to the rich meat he was about to throw to them all, friends, neighbours and closet enemies alike, with his forthcoming confession to murder.

'No, I can't think of anybody,' she said. She went on quickly, as if fearing that, having found her useless, he would cut her off: 'I do know she was very upset because she felt you weren't being honest with her. Richard, you may feel this is none of my business but, believe me, my only wish is to see you two happy together.'

'Thank you,' he said. 'That's all I want too.'

'So why don't you come clean with her about this other woman and I'm sure that'll be an end to it.'

He felt there was nothing he could say in reply and so remained silent. His wife had clearly confided more or less everything to Moira: he had been right to suspect that. But he wasn't in the mood to put her straight. Nor was he going to launch into the kind of explanation of events that he should be giving to Claire and Claire alone.

Moira said: 'Richard, I'm only saying this because I care for both of you.'

It would have been churlish of him not to have responded. 'I know you do, Moira. But things are nothing like so simple as you seem to think.'

'When have things between a husband and wife ever been simple?'

'Well, no –'

'D'you think I don't know that?' She laughed bitterly.

Even then, he wasn't annoyed at her for her persistence in relating their problems to her own and Roy's. That was only natural. Why he felt sorry for her and wanted to end their conversation was because he foresaw how mortified she would be when she learnt the truth. She would read the newspaper head-lines and remember with embarrassment her banal prescriptions for putting things right.

'Moira, I'm sorry but I've got to go. I've got to try and find Claire, all right?'

'When you do –'

'Yes.'

'Remember – in the long run, honesty is best.'

He thanked her, said goodbye and rang off.

He abandoned the notion of ringing any of Claire's other friends. They would only react in the same way. It would be even worse if they attempted to sympathize with him.

Besides, the more he thought about it, the more it seemed unlikely Claire would have contacted any of them. She had always been notoriously self-sufficient. Over the years it had been her friends who had contacted her, not she them.

He decided to write her a letter. Something not unaffectionate, not chiding her because she hadn't been there when he had most needed her, but a letter that would simply spell out what had happened since she had left and why it was that her husband was currently languishing in jail.

He took a piece of notepaper from his desk drawer, thought about it for a moment and then began to write.

'My darling Claire. I am giving this to Diane and asking her to hand it to you as soon as you return. Since we last spoke, there has been a succession of unhappy events that have conspired to –'

He stopped, thinking he heard voices from below. Had someone been calling him?

Was this the police arriving at last? The prospect threw him into a small panic. Would they allow him to finish the letter? What might they be saying now, at this moment, to Diane?

He left his desk and opened his study door. The voices from below were now clear. He heard Diane laughing and then – and how his heart leapt at this! – he heard Claire's voice, so low he couldn't make out what she was saying but unmistakably it was the voice of his wife.

'Claire . . .?' he called.

Her voice rose to him in response: 'Yes, hello, I'm back!'

There was a moment when he was sorely tempted to respond with bitter accusations. Why had she ever gone in the first place? Why hadn't she at least communicated with them – if not with him, then with her children? Why hadn't she come back earlier? Why, in short, had she done nothing, not a jot, to help him try and extricate their marriage from the badlands into which it had wandered?

But none of these were for now. First he must welcome her, and then explain as gently as he could the terrible events that were about to explode across their lives.

19

She looked as if she were back from a holiday, tanned and rested. 'Darling,' she said, opening her arms to him, 'how are you?' She was smiling and composed, not at all what he had expected.

He put his sudden doubts behind him and went to embrace her. 'It's wonderful to see you,' he said. The familiar perfume she was wearing and just the feeling of her in his arms was overwhelming and made him conscious of all he had squandered. He hugged her tightly.

'It's all right, I'm here,' she said, surprised by his passion.

Diane stepped forward and clapped her hands gleefully. 'Right, we're going to go out and leave you two,' she said. 'Come on!'

The call was to Will, who was lurking in the kitchen doorway. He slipped past them, muttering about it being nice to see Mrs Gillow again and followed Diane towards the door. Richard knew he ought to warn his daughter that these scenes of reconciliation were dangerously deceptive. All was *not* well. Her mother's return would mark not a resumption of their old life but the beginning of fresh horrors.

'We won't be back for *hours*,' Diane called, and then they were gone.

Still holding her, Richard gazed down at Claire. 'You look wonderful. So well.'

'I went to the Lakes. Did some walking and quite a lot of thinking.'

'Yes, I did wonder –'

'And now I'm dying for a coffee. I feel as though I've been sitting on that motorway for a week!'

She stepped away from him, leaving her bag in a heap on the floor, and headed into the kitchen.

Following her, he felt oddly disappointed, frustrated that they hadn't seemed to make real contact. It wasn't just that she *looked* as though she'd come back from an enjoyable, little holiday; she was behaving like it too, giving him a quick embrace and then occupying herself around the kitchen. Even allowing that she was still unaware of how serious events had become, he had expected something more. He sensed an awkwardness about her, an unwillingness to meet his eye, as she made coffee and gathered some fruit and cheese for a makeshift meal.

' . . . Everything looks in good order. I suppose Diane's been doing most of the catering, has she?'

'Sit down,' he said.

'Yes, I will in a minute –'

'Please!'

She stared at him, resenting his insistent tone. 'Darling, I'm just getting something to eat. Surely you don't begrudge me that? And then we will talk, I promise you. Why do you think I've come back if it isn't that I know we have to talk and I want to do that just as much as you do?'

Of course he could have grabbed her attention immediately by announcing that he had killed a man. But that would have been almost as brutal as the killing itself. She believed she had returned to a world which was much as she had left it. She would be horrified to learn how much had been devastated during her few days' absence.

He forced himself to remain patient until the coffee was made and she had settled at the table, across from him.

'Can we talk now?' he asked.

She sighed, then said, 'Of course we can.'

'Well, then –'

'No, please, can I just say something first?'

He waited.

'It's just – I know we have to say *something* about those damned letters and everything they said about you and Melissa. But I don't want us to go on and on about it –'

He tried to interrupt. He must let her know that they were well beyond the stage of choosing what they wished to talk about. The agenda had already been set, by events of which she knew nothing.

'What you don't understand –'

But she put up a hand to silence him.

'No, wait. I have to say this. You know why I went away. It was because we'd got to a stage where all we could talk about was Melissa and those letters. Well, look . . .' She paused, took a breath, then continued: 'I don't care whether she exists or doesn't exist or what might or might not have gone on between the two of you. All I'm concerned about is that she doesn't destroy our marriage. So can we just put all that behind us. Can we *burn* the bloody letters or, I don't know, do whatever you want with them. But what I'm saying, I just don't want to hear that name *Melissa* again. I don't ever want to see those letters again. Can we please, please just put the whole rotten, stupid thing behind us. Yes?'

So this was the message she had brought back with her, one that contained not a word of retraction or apology. Two days ago he would have been bitterly disappointed. Now his disappointment registered only as something that might once have been important. He marvelled how they neither of them had been able to handle the challenge of the letters. The accusations they contained now seemed venial and puny compared to those he would shortly be facing.

'I'm afraid it's not as simple as that,' he said.

She looked at him in surprise. She had expected him to agree and welcome her willingness to forget the past. Now here he was sounding like he was about to throw her offer back at her.

'Please, Richard,' she said. 'I just can't stand it if we're going to start all over again –'

'No, no, we're not,' he said quickly. 'It's just that . . . those things aren't important anymore.'

Now she was puzzled. Was he rejecting her or not? He saw he must begin the difficult explanation.

'Things have happened,' he said.

'Yes?'

'While you've been away, various thing have happened which have, well . . . changed everything. What you're saying about Melissa, all that's really not important anymore. Whether we talk about it or not I don't mind.'

'You don't?' Now she was suspicious, trying to see where this might be leading and mindful of the lengths he had gone to before to try and discredit the letters. Was this going to be another of his clever manoeuvres?

'No, I don't,' he said. 'Oh, she exists. I'm not denying that. Melissa exists, though I've never had any sort of relationship with her.'

'You're still saying that the letters are a lie?'

'I am, yes. If you're asking me that question, of course they're a lie.'

He saw her expression harden as she set herself to oppose him. Stop this, he told himself. This was not what he had intended. It was barely ten minutes since Claire had walked in through the door and here they were drifting back to their entrenched positions, digging in for another bout of hostilities.

'It was Lawrence,' he said, trying to make progress.

'What?'

'Lawrence Nevison. He was the one who'd been seeing Melissa.'

She looked at him as though he had taken leave of his senses. 'Lawrence had been seeing . . .?'

'Yes.'

'I'm sorry, but I don't understand.'

'Well, no, you won't. Let me explain. He met her through an escort agency. They used to get together every couple of weeks or so at that hotel, the Queens. Only, because he didn't want to use his real name, he used mine instead.'

She stared at him, stupefied. 'But why?'

'Why didn't he want to use his real name?'

She nodded.

'Oh, because he was scared of being blackmailed. Which is a bit sick when you think about it. *He* was scared of being blackmailed – and so I ended up being blackmailed in his place.'

'But how do you know this?'

'Mainly thanks to that private detective you might remember me going to. He put me in touch with Melissa. And, fortunately, she was able to give me Lawrence's real name.'

'And what does Lawrence say to all this?'

'Oh, he's admitted it, yes.'

'He has?'

'Yes. And, when you see him, he'll admit it to you too.'

Knowing Lawrence, it might not be quite as straightforward as that, but he didn't feel like wasting time warning her of Lawrence's mood-swings. They were still thrashing around in shallow waters; he had yet to show her the real depths ahead of them.

'That's how I came to get the letters,' he said, wanting to get this part of the account over and done with. 'Because he'd been seeing this young woman, but using my name.'

'Richard, is all this is true?' she said.

'Of course it's true. Would I be telling you if it wasn't?'

He could see she was still resisting him. Presumably she was finding it difficult to admit just how far she had been in the wrong.

'Look, I can understand why you didn't believe me,' he said, trying to make it easier for her. 'From your point of view of course it looked as though the letters had to be telling the truth.'

'Well, yes —'

'But that was only because Lawrence had been using my name. That's what's at the root of all this.'

She frowned. 'You're saying that Lawrence pretended to be you when he was with this woman . . .'

'Yes.'

'So I can see how the woman might have believed he was you. But how did the blackmailer manage to do the same?'

Of course, he hadn't yet explained that.

'Because the blackmailer was a barman at the hotel where they used to meet.'

'The Queens?'

'Yes. He saw them together and knew she was from an escort agency. So he went to the hotel records to get Lawrence's name with the intention of blackmailing him.'

'Only it wasn't —'

He nodded. 'It wasn't Lawrence's name, no. It was *my* name. My name and this address and so that's how I came to get the letters.'

She seemed stunned by all he had to tell her. At the same time he sensed she was at last beginning to accept the truth of it.

'And so it really was Lawrence . . .?' she said slowly.

'Yes. Only, wait, there's more. There's a lot more that's happened since —'

The doorbell rang, stopping him.

'Oh, Christ,' he said, and started to his feet, though without any clear idea of whether he was about to answer the door or go the other way in an attempt to evade capture.

'What's the matter?' said Claire, startled. 'Who's that?'

He cursed himself for not having prepared her.

'I think . . . it might well be the police.'

'The police . . .?'

'Yes.'

'But why?'

It was the one question he should have been answering from the minute she walked in. Instead, they'd wasted precious time talking about Melissa and Lawrence and where they met and how they'd been spotted, all stuff that was pretty well beside the point now anyway.

He said: 'I'm afraid things are a lot more serious than you think.'

'Richard, I don't understand –'

'No.' He took her hands. 'Darling, let me go and talk to the police and then afterwards I'll tell you everything.'

Surely they would allow him to have some time alone with his wife before they took him away? They would have to. He couldn't blurt everything out to her now. The doorbell rang again.

'I'd better go –'

'Yes.'

'I'm sorry,' he said, seeing her confusion and fear. 'I'm most dreadfully sorry you've had to come back to this.'

It was Detective Inspector Beresford who was waiting on the doorstep, the same young man with the curly, ginger hair to whom Richard had taken the letters. It was fitting that he should turn up again now for the final reckoning.

Richard ushered him quickly into the lounge, fearing lest Claire might overhear anything said on the doorstep. Though, in fact, Beresford said little beyond a reference to their earlier meeting. The uniformed policeman who had arrived with him remained outside in the car.

'Please . . . sit down,' said Richard, feeling himself caught between the two roles of host and prisoner.

Beresford said, 'Thanks,' and perched on the edge of one of the armchairs. It surprised Richard, who had expected him to remain standing. It left him with no option but to sit down himself. He sank onto the sofa, thinking all right, go ahead, get it over with.

Beresford seemed in no hurry to get anything over with. He sat further back in the chair, settling himself as though for a long stay. It made Richard wonder whether he was going to sit there in silence until Richard confessed. Until finally he began to speak.

'Well, Mr Gillow, it seems you were right and I was wrong.'

It wasn't what Richard had expected. 'Pardon?' he said.

'When you came down to the station and showed me those nasty, little letters you'd been getting.'

'Ah –'

'And I refused to believe you when you said you knew nothing about what they were saying.'

'Well –'

'Sorry about that. I was quite wrong.'

He seemed genuinely apologetic. Richard caught himself about to insist that it was quite understandable – after all, his wife hadn't believed him either. He stopped himself in the nick of time.

What game was this man playing? This polite gorilla of a policeman, in his sports jacket, twill trousers and desert boots, wasn't he just amusing himself by toying with his prey like this? Courteous and apologetic, admitting to his own earlier shortcomings ... where was all this leading but to a moment when, having put Richard at his ease, he would move in for the kill?

Richard said: 'Inspector, why don't you just tell me what it is you've come to say?'

'Yes, why don't I,' said Beresford, unperturbed. He studied his finger-nails, then looked up and said: 'The Queens Hotel ...? I think that featured in those letters of yours, didn't it?'

'You know it did.'

Beresford smiled and gave a nod of his head. 'I also know that last night a man who worked as a barman at the Queens Hotel – a Mr Philip Thornton – was found unconscious at his home. He'd been assaulted.'

Richard said nothing. He was prepared to confess at the right time and in the proper manner. He wasn't going to respond to this kind of taunting.

Seeing that he was getting no response, Beresford went on: 'Somebody rang for an ambulance. We don't know who because they wouldn't give their name. Anyway, Philip Thornton was taken into hospital where he died at nine-fifty-five this morning. I don't know whether you know this . . .?'

Richard sighed. 'Yes, I do as a matter of fact.'

'Well, let me tell you something you certainly won't know. Before he died, Philip Thornton did, in fact, regain consciousness.'

Richard couldn't hide his surprise. 'He did?'

'Yes.'

Now he understood Beresford's casual approach. Thornton had said enough before he died to identify Richard as his assailant and so had handed Beresford the kind of sewn-up, no-room-for-doubt case that policemen must dream of. No wonder he was relishing every minute of it.

'He wasn't able to say much,' Beresford went on, 'but he did name his attacker.'

There was a pause. Richard was conscious of a clock ticking in the room. It was the carriage clock that the children had bought them on some earlier anniversary. Through the window he could see the garden. Claire came into his line-of-vision. She was doing a tour of the flower-beds.

'He said that his attacker was you. Richard Gillow.'

It was delivered at last, the *coup de grâce*. Richard felt it almost as a relief after the tortuous route they had taken to reach it.

He began to say, 'Yes —' but Beresford was speaking again.

'I'm not asking you to say anything to that. Philip Thornton cited you as his attacker. It doesn't mean that we believe him.'

Richard stared, not knowing what to make of this new detour. Or was it only a continuation of the game, a prolonging of the suspense?

'See, when he gave us your name . . . and that was about *all* he said, all he could say . . . well, it rang a bell with me. I remembered you coming to see me with those letters. Oh, and of course by that time we'd done a check on our Mr Thornton and found he already had a record for this kind of activity, blackmailing guests at another hotel. So it all sort of tied up you might say.'

'Yes –'

But still he wasn't being allowed to speak, as Beresford continued.

'Meantime we searched his flat, and that was when we hit the jackpot. Because he was something of a photographer was Mr Thornton. Very keen too. There was a whole stack of his . . . well, you might call 'em candid camera shots I suppose. Mainly people in the hotel bar, couples.'

'Yes.'

'But none of you.'

'No, well –'

'Which struck me as odd because I remembered that the letters you'd shown me had talked about photographs of you with some lady. And yet, among all these photographs of other people, there were none of you. But what we did find . . . and this was the key to it . . . we found a bunch of photographs of *somebody* else with your name and address written on the back.'

'Yes.'

'And you know who that somebody else was?'

Richard hesitated. Was he being invited to identify Lawrence for them? If so, then why? Had Lawrence been wrong then in assuming he'd be instantly recognizable by every copper in Greater Manchester?

'Oh, don't worry, we know who he is,' said Beresford, as if in answer to his unspoken questions. 'Your neighbour, isn't it, Mr Nevison?'

'Yes,' said Richard.

What harm could there be in agreeing to what they knew already? What harm, anyway, since Thornton had regained consciousness and named Richard as his assailant?

'Of course I know Mr Nevison,' said Beresford. 'I've come across him many a time in court, so I was able to recognise him straight away.'

So Lawrence could come to no more harm than he had already. It freed Richard to speak about him. He might as well fill in what gaps there were in the police knowledge. Get this phoney interrogation over with and onto the real point of Beresford's visit.

'He was using my name because he didn't want the woman he was meeting to know who he was.'

'Was he now. Yes, I thought it must have been something like that.'

'Inspector, there's really no need to prolong this.'

'And I'm not doing, sir, I can promise you. I just didn't know how much you were aware of.'

'Oh, I think I'm aware of a great deal,' said Richard bitterly.

'Well, then you'll understand how we came to the conclusion that it was your neighbour, Mr Lawrence Nevison, who made the assault on Philip Thornton that was responsible for his death.'

Richard stared, wondering if he could have heard correctly.

'You're saying that Lawrence Nevison killed Philip Thornton . . .?'

'Oh, yes, no doubt about it.'

Richard gave a groan of dismay and shook his head. So must he now argue the case for Lawrence's innocence and so prosecute himself? What kind of bizarre conspiracy was going on here that the police seemed determined to turn their backs on a truth that was staring them in the face? It surely couldn't be that they were repaying old scores? Trying to set up Lawrence as revenge for whatever courtroom victories he'd had over them? Whatever the motives, it was a grotesque misreading of events that must be swiftly put right.

'You said that Philip Thornton had regained consciousness,' said Richard.

'He did.'

'And he named me – *me* – as the man who'd gone to his flat and assaulted him.'

'He gave us your name, yes.'

'Well, then –'

'But wait. Sorry to interrupt. To begin with, we certainly did think that Thornton was naming you. Richard Gillow, yes. It was when we saw the photographs of Mr Nevison with your name on the back that we realized that Thornton believed Nevison to be you.'

Richard glimpsed an outline of what was to come. 'And so you believe –'

Beresford was nodding. 'We believe that when he named his assailant as Richard Gillow . . . it was actually Lawrence Nevison he had in mind.'

In different circumstances Richard might have enjoyed the crazy logic behind this bit of police thinking, and even the element of nemesis it brought with it. Lawrence had donned the identity of Richard Gillow for his own nefarious purposes; in doing so, he had unwittingly set himself up to be the fall-guy for Thornton's murder.

He was even tempted to agree. After all, this was the police version of events, one they were keen on getting him to subscribe to. All he had to do was act dumb and go along with it . . . And he would be free for as long as it took them to find Lawrence and charge him.

He could imagine the ruckus Lawrence would create. He would leave them in no doubt that it was the Richard Gillow, the *real* Richard Gillow, who'd beaten up the blackmailing barman and killed him. In his final utterance on this earth, Philip Thornton had been speaking the literal truth.

'No,' said Richard. 'I can't let you go on believing that.'

'Oh, I know you'll find it difficult to accept. Your neighbour . . . a solicitor . . . a man of some reputation . . . and now he goes and does a thing like this —'

Richard shook his head. 'It's not a question of whether or not I accept it —'

'We couldn't believe it ourselves. Till we went to find Mr Nevison, see what he had to say.'

They were words that stopped Richard in his tracks. So they had already spoken to Lawrence . . .? What could he possibly have said that had left Beresford still thinking he was Thornton's killer?

'You've been to see him?'

'Oh, yes. He was our first port of call was Mr Nevison.'

'And what . . . what did he say?'

'I'm afraid he wasn't able to say anything. Mr Nevison committed suicide, some time earlier this afternoon.'

His last sight of Lawrence had been of him walking away along after he had all but ejected him from his study. He had promised him he would try and keep his name out of the disclosures that were to come. Lawrence in reply had said something like, 'Thanks, but I don't think that'll make much difference.' Looking back, Richard could now see this for the admission of defeat it was. Lawrence knew that his secret life was about to be exploded over the tabloids and knew also that he wouldn't be able to live through the exposure and humiliation. He had refused to live through it.

'I'm sorry to be the bearer of bad news,' said Beresford.

'How did he die?' asked Richard.

Not that he had any particular curiosity. It was one of those questions that had to be asked.

'Carbon monoxide poisoning. He shut himself up in his garage and attached a hosepipe to the car exhaust. It was his wife who found him.'

Richard winced at the thought of what Adele must have gone through. Finding Lawrence dead in circumstances that spoke unambiguously of suicide ... then having the police arrive showing compromising photographs and telling her of assignations in hotel bars. As if his death weren't enough, she had then to learn how he had betrayed her when alive.

'He left a note,' said Beresford. 'Some of it was to his wife ... personal ... but the last part might interest you.' He pulled a notebook from his pocket, thumbed through the pages, then began to read in a solemn monotone: 'I have behaved terribly, using the name of a friend and almost destroying his marriage in the process. The responsibility for everything that has happened is mine and mine alone.' He flipped the notebook closed. 'Taken along with everything else, that's as clear a confession as I've ever come across.'

It was only as Beresford read from the suicide note that Richard suddenly saw how all this offered him the chance of freedom. It was no longer necessary that he be hauled out and paraded as a murderer. Fate had conspired to protect him. It had done so ruthlessly, sacrificing poor Lawrence in the process.

Beresford hadn't come to the house in order to charge or arrest him. He had come only to explain, to reassure Richard that he was not to worry. Even though his name had come up in the course of their investigations, they discounted this as a result of Thornton's continuing mis-identification of him.

Beresford said: 'He certainly wrote the letter himself. His wife has identified the handwriting.'

It was as if he were searching around for more details to

demonstrate to Richard how futile it would be even for him to attempt to question their version of events.

'And, of course, it's not just the letter. It's the way everything else corroborates it. We have the photographs of him. We know that this man, Thornton, was out to blackmail him. All right, he got you instead but it was Mr Nevison he was after. And then – what really seals it – Thornton identified him. Oh, he gave us your name, yes, but it's clear enough who he meant. The man he saw as you was, in fact, your neighbour, Lawrence Nevison.'

He spoke with an exaggerated clarity, as though explaining to someone of poor hearing or concentration.

Richard knew that he could still jolt Beresford with the truth. Any time he chose he could force him to abandon his neat and tidy version of events in which all the pieces fitted and there were none left over. An honest confession was what he had intended all along; even now his conscience gnawed at him, prompting him to speak.

But there was another voice, almost drowning it out, asking what good could possibly come from such a sacrifice. Lawrence had escaped forever the pointing fingers he had so feared. Let people believe what they chose about him. None of it could touch him now.

While for Richard this was a heaven-sent reprieve which only a fool or a saint would reject.

'I know it's hard to believe,' said Beresford. 'But that really is what happened. As far as we're concerned, the case is already closed.'

'I see,' said Richard. 'Well, then of course I accept what you say. Of course I do.'

20

Adele's reaction bordered on the heroic. She was stoical and dignified in the presence of other people, revealing nothing of whatever she might have been suffering in private. She stuck to the routine of her life much as if Lawrence were still alive. She could even be seen working vigorously in the garden, breaking off to receive the next in a stream of visitors come to offer their condolences.

Richard went round to see her on the evening of Lawrence's death. It was a visit he was dreading but which he knew he must make.

Though first, of course, he had to explain things to his wife. Once Detective Inspector Beresford had driven off, he sat Claire down and gave her the full story – or anyway the authorized version, the one that Beresford had given him. He told her that it was Lawrence who had gone to Thornton's flat to demand the photographs from him and Lawrence who had ended up assaulting him. After that, distraught at the news of Thornton's death, he had gone home and killed himself.

Claire was horrified, almost literally struck dumb as she struggled to come to terms with this turbulent world to which she had returned.

Richard marvelled at his own new-found expertise in lying. If he could convince Claire, who knew him better than anybody, then who couldn't he convince? Though he wondered, too, if it would be possible to sustain the lie through the difficult days ahead and then for the years beyond. Wouldn't he one day find the temptation to confess irresistible?

The immediate test was in facing Adele, the real victim in all this.

Her sister, Miriam, had already arrived to stay with her and answered the door. She recognized Richard, who asked if he might speak to Adele – 'Though only if she'd like to see me.'

'Oh, I'm sure she would,' said Miriam. 'Please come through.'

He had expected to find Adele propped up among pillows, as though physically stricken by events, but no, she was standing by the French windows in the lounge, gazing out into the garden. She turned at his approach and he saw that, although her face was sad and drawn, she was composed and even quite calm.

'I'm so sorry,' he said, and took her hand.

'Thank you. I think you probably understand more about this than I do.'

'I know a certain amount of what's happened,' he admitted, hating himself because it was this woman who was paying the true price for his freedom. She had to grieve for her husband while believing him to be a murderer.

'This man was blackmailing him, is that it?'

'More or less, yes.'

'Because of some woman he was seeing?'

Here he would have liked to have lied to her but He couldn't. She already knew too much and so he did the best he could: 'She didn't mean anything to him, you mustn't think that. She was just . . . somebody he spent some time with.'

She slowly nodded, then said, 'I did sometimes wonder. I'm afraid there wasn't too much love between us. Well, not of that sort anyway.'

He searched for some shred of consolation that he might offer. 'One thing I do know for a fact,' he said. 'He had already stopped seeing this woman when the blackmail started.'

She turned her dark, sad eyes on him. 'Really?'

'Oh, yes. So you mustn't ever think of him as having somebody else in his life, I mean apart from you. Because he didn't.'

There was a long pause. The room had become shadowy as dusk had swiftly descended outside.

'There is one thing I can't understand,' said Adele.

'What?'

'He was supposed to have *assaulted* this man? I mean just with his bare hands he beat him up so badly that the man later died . . .?'

Richard improvised. 'I think that just shows how desperate he was.'

But it didn't satisfy her. 'Richard, Lawrence did not have one ounce of aggression in his body. Not *physical* aggression. We

275

used to joke about it. That if anybody was ever going to throw a punch in this house, it was going to be me!'

She tried to laugh but couldn't quite manage it. She had kept hold of his hand, gripping it so hard that he felt her nails digging into his skin. He took her other hand and pulled her round so that she was facing him, their faces close.

'We're all of us capable of quite extraordinary things,' he said, 'especially when they're done to protect those that we love.'

She gave a small, tearful smile. 'He was a good man. Basically he was a good man, I always knew that.'

'And that's how you must remember him,' said Richard. 'As a good man who was destroyed by those who weren't fit to hold a candle to him.'

She gave him smile of gratitude. 'You know he always looked up to you.'

'Well, I can't think why.'

'Oh, he didn't say so, not in so many words. But that was the impression I got.'

'He had no need to look up to anyone. Lawrence was a very fine man, and that's how you must remember him.'

'I will,' she said. 'Thank you.'

He was shown out of the house by the sister into a blue-black darkness. He took a deep breath, relieved to have got that over with. The lights were shining in his own house. He passed by the hawthorn hedge and turned into his drive.

Perhaps, after all, he was a better liar than he'd ever given himself credit for. Or perhaps it was simply that he'd spoken more of the truth than he'd been aware when he'd sought to reassure Adele by telling her how we are all of us capable of quite extraordinary things.

The newspaper coverage was mercifully discreet. A couple of reporters came, had a few drinks in the George and went, but there was no large-scale press invasion of the kind that Lawrence had always feared would follow the breaking of the story. It may have been that the police had held back on what they had released. Certainly there was a coyness about some of the reporting. All the papers made it clear that Lawrence Nevison had killed the man who was blackmailing him, before taking his own life. But the particular grounds for blackmail, as well as the specific circumstances of the killing . . . these were left hanging in a journalistic fog.

Diane, of course, had to be told everything so that Richard once again sat down at the kitchen table and went through the full story. Of course he gave her the version that Beresford had insisted on and which he had already told to Claire.

Then he telephoned David. Telling him took even longer since he knew nothing of what had happened since the anniversary party. Richard took him through everything step by step, trusting that this would be the last time he would have to repeat the lie. He didn't relish this slandering his dead friend and neighbour, feeling he was each time perjuring himself afresh.

The testing time was still not over. Each of the deaths would require its own inquest, one on Philip Thornton and a second on Lawrence. Richard was called to be a witness in both.

The first inquest turned out to be the easier of the two. It was held in Manchester. Richard attended alone, going straight from the office. He nursed a secret worry that some unexpected witness might have come forward, someone who had seen him at Meredith House say. In fact, the court room was virtually deserted. The only people present, apart from the court officials, were Richard, Detective Inspector Beresford and a doctor who had treated Thornton at the hospital.

Proceedings were low-key but brisk. Clearly this was one among several cases to be got through this morning. Beresford ran quickly through the authorized version of events. He was listened to and thanked by the Coroner.

Richard was called and was asked about the mis-directed blackmail letters. He was able to give an honest account of how they had arrived and his later discovery as to why. Then he, too, was thanked by the Coroner, who declared that he fully accepted the police account of events and saw no reason to do other than record that Philip Conway Thornton was unlawfully killed by one Lawrence Nevison.

The second inquest was tougher.

It was held locally and this time Claire came along with him. They sat beside Adele, who was with her sister, Miriam. Detective Inspector Beresford was there again, and also a number of other people who seemed to be relatives of Adele.

There was a tense, unhappy atmosphere to the gathering which put Richard on edge. He had the feeling that anything might happen, that any of these people present might stand up and denounce him or even that he might stand up and denounce himself.

He had been called as a witness this time because he was the last person to have seen Lawrence alive. He felt himself sweating and tense as he took the stand. He knew that he must concentrate on the Coroner alone and not look across the courtroom to where Adele was sitting close to his wife.

'Mr Nevison called to see you early in the afternoon of the seventh,' said the Coroner, who was a mild-mannered man with black-rimmed glasses, more presiding clergyman than inquisitor.

'Yes, he did.'

'And why did he do that?'

'Mainly because he was still worrying about the blackmail letters. Well, I say the letters ... actually his real concern was the photographs that they referred to.'

The Coroner probed gently, wanting to know just what had been said and what Lawrence's manner had been. Richard responded with an edited version of the truth, one that he hoped wouldn't be too distressing for Adele or, for that matter, raise any problems for himself.

The verdict, short and simple, was that Lawrence had taken his own life. The Coroner expressed his sympathy for the family of the bereaved, which drew a murmur of sympathetic agreement from around the courtroom.

Afterwards, they went back to Adele's for some tea. Claire was adamant that she shouldn't be left alone or have to rely solely on her sister. Once again, Adele displayed a surprising degree of self-possession. She waited on them, refusing to let Claire or Miriam take over as hostess. She talked about the inquest and her own feelings as she had heard the piecing together of her husband's final hours.

'I think it's probably helped me,' she said. 'At least I feel I understand something of what he must have been going through.'

Richard marvelled that his own performance could have contributed to such an effect. For him the day had been a terrible ordeal. Many more like it and he doubted he would have the will to go on supporting the lie that it was Lawrence who struck the fatal blows.

And now Adele had turned to him. 'Richard, could I ask you a favour?'

'Anything,' he said. And then waited with bated breath.'

'Would you mind if, some time in the future, I wanted to talk to you about Lawrence? I mean about what he said during that last meeting you had with him? I know you told us today, but if I could just go over it again with you . . .?'

He managed a tight smile. 'Of course.'

'I'm sure Richard will talk to you any time you like,' prompted Claire.

'I will, yes,' he said. 'Any time.'

'I found his novel,' said Adele, with a sad smile. 'The one that I told you about —'

'Yes.' He wondered for a desperate moment whether he should offer to read it, or even whether she would expect him to publish it as some kind of memorial.

'I don't think it's very good. I suppose you might say it's about himself when he was young.'

'Is it finished?'

'I don't know. I think I need to read it again but not for some time.'

For the meantime he had escaped having to take Lawrence's manuscript home with him. Even so, he felt it to be another warning that his ordeal was going to be a lasting one. There was no prospect of Lawrence's death slipping quietly into history. It would remain with them, to be gone over and analysed.

The funeral was in the village church on what might have been termed the first proper day of autumn, with a gusty wind tugging at the plane trees in the churchyard. Adele refused to hide behind a veil but wore a black suit and matching broad-brimmed hat. The pews were moderately full with friends and neighbours and then a whole row of men in city suits, who must have been Lawrence's law-practice colleagues.

They sang 'The Lord Is My Shepherd', then said some prayers, before the vicar mounted the pulpit. He spoke — rather well, as general opinion later had it — of the need to consider a man's life as a whole and not to allow their inevitable and proper grief at

Lawrence's tragic death to blot out the memory of what his life had been. There were more prayers, then they sang 'Abide With Me' as the coffin was carried out with the mourners following.

Richard and Claire – and Diane, who was with them – were towards the back of this line of mourners as they silently filed out. It was a relief to Richard, who wanted only to lose himself in the crowd.

There were three black funeral cars to follow the hearse to the crematorium. The Gillows went in Richard's own car, giving a lift to Roy and Moira.

'Actually I didn't know him all that well,' said Roy, as they took their place in the queue of cars.

Richard felt called upon to respond. 'He was the last person you'd expect to get involved in . . . well, in something like he did.'

'And nobody could want a more loyal or faithful wife,' said Claire.

It was as though she had issued a challenge which none of them felt like taking up and so they sat in silence until they arrived at the crematorium.

Here there were more prayers and solemn music as a curtain closed over the coffin. In no more than ten minutes they were back out in the trim gardens that surrounded the crematorium building. There was an instant lightening of spirits, in which even Richard shared. People lit cigarettes and stood talking, as though reluctant to tear themselves away.

Most of those present repaired to the George, where a buffet lunch was provided. The numbers dwindled as the afternoon wore on till there was only a small number of close relatives and friends left to escort Adele home.

'I'm glad she's staying in that house,' said Claire, when they were home in the evening.

'You mean next-door?'

'Yes. It means we'll be able to keep an eye on her. After all, I do think we bear some of the responsibility.'

Did she mean for Lawrence's death? He waited for her to elaborate.

'I mean if we'd reacted differently when those dreadful letters first arrived . . . Oh, I'm not sure what we should have done so don't ask me. I just think it needn't have all ended as it did.'

'Possibly not.'

'But anyway we must look after Adele. Even have her round here to stay if she's finding it impossible to be on her own in that house.'

So now, it seemed, Lawrence's widow might even end up living with them. It was fortunate he wasn't superstitious or he might have begun to imagine that this was Lawrence's own doing. It was his spirit pursuing Richard, determined on sooner or later forcing a confession out of him.

'I just don't think he trusts me anymore,' Claire said. 'After all, why should he?'

Moira sought to reassure. 'You've both had a bad experience. It's bound to take a while to get over it.'

They were in Claire's workroom, the day after the funeral. They had opened the windows as wide as they would go to allow the smoke from their cigarettes to escape and were halfway through the bottle of White Bordeaux that Moira had brought with her.

'But I refused to believe him, didn't I. When he swore to me that he wasn't seeing this Melissa . . . that he'd never been seeing *anybody* . . . I refused to believe him.'

'Which you were perfectly within your rights to do.'

Claire looked at her in surprise.

'Well, all the evidence was against him. I wouldn't have believed him either. There isn't a woman in this village would. And Richard is intelligent enough to realize that.'

Claire shook her head, not because she disagreed but because, obscurely, she felt things weren't that simple.

'He doesn't seem to want to talk about it.'

'No, well, I can understand –'

'Or for me to talk about it. I mean I've tried telling him I'm sorry that I didn't believe him and sorry that I went away like I did. I've even tried doing what you've just said – getting him to see it from my point of view.' She gave a gesture of despair. 'It's like he shuts off. He just doesn't want to know.'

'And what about sex?'

'What?'

'You're doing that again, are you?'

Claire hesitated, then admitted, 'No, we're not. At first I thought it was those inquests he had to attend, and then the funeral. I mean those kind of things don't exactly –'

'Don't put you in the mood for it, no.'

'Only now I feel there's more to it than that. And all I can think is that he can't forgive me because I didn't trust him when he most needed me to.'

Richard wondered what rumours must have gone round his staff. No doubt he had been the main topic of conversation since the story had appeared in the newspapers, naming him as the friend who was blackmailed in error.

Now, trying to immerse himself in his old routine, he caught one or two of them looking at him oddly, as though trying to assess whether the experience might have left its mark on him. Few were bold enough to raise the subject openly. When they did, it was as a sympathetic enquiry – 'I read about that blackmail business. It sounded awful . . .?'

He gave a short, non-committal reply, making it clear that the subject was out of bounds. It was torture enough that he had to continue to lie to his wife and family and that he had Lawrence Nevison's widow living next-door and regarding him as the sole authority on her husband's final hours. The last thing he wanted was for the whole wretched business to pursue him to the office and infect his life there too.

It was late afternoon on the day after the funeral. Richard was in conference with Simon, catching up on the backlog of paperwork that had grown during his absence. The telephone rang, even though he had instructed Lynne that they should not be interrupted.

He picked up the receiver. 'Yes?'

It was Yvonne. She must have caught the irritation in his voice. 'Sorry to disturb you, Mr Gillow, but I've a lady on the line who says she must speak to you.'

He sighed. 'And what's her name, this lady?'

'She said to tell you Melissa. I asked her her second name but that was all she'd say – just Melissa.'

He realized immediately how much he had been longing to hear from her. Not that she had been constantly on his mind;

but he had wondered from time to time what she must be thinking and whether they might ever meet again.

Of course he was aware of the dangers she brought with her. She had been with him on that fateful night when he'd set out to deal once and for all with Philip Thornton. She must have heard since about Thornton's death. She was an intelligent woman. She would surely have seen through the version put out in the press and worked out for herself what must have really happened.

He asked Simon to leave, then spoke into the receiver, 'Hello?'

'Richard?'

There was no mistaking the voice. He found himself smiling.

'Yes. And how are you?'

'Very well. Still retired.'

'I'm glad to hear it.' He was conscious of how easily there might be others listening in. He must stop her incriminating both of them. 'Look, I'd rather not talk on the phone. Can I meet you somewhere? What about lunch tomorrow – would that be possible?'

'Tomorrow?' She didn't affect the slightest hesitation. 'Yes, that would be very nice. Where did you have in mind?'

21

He arrived early at the Riverside Restaurant, where they had arranged to meet. A waiter showed him to a table and brought him a campari-and-soda. He moved his chair round so that he could keep an eye on the door.

As he waited, it occurred to him that he was simultaneously in great jeopardy yet untouchable. He had killed a man and would be hiding from that for the rest of his life. But where he was absolutely safe was in doing what he was doing now, having lunch with a strange woman. Alone among married men, he had no need to fear news of this getting back to his wife.

Melissa appeared at one o'clock. He saw her enter and look around. Then she spotted him. She waved and smiled and made her way through the tables towards him.

He rose to meet her and they shook hands.

'So you got here all right,' he said.

'Oh, yes. I told you – name the place and I'll be there.'

He remembered her as an attractive woman, with a kind of slow-burning sensuality that was quite unlike Claire's quicksilver charms. He now saw that his memory hadn't done her justice. It wasn't only the wide, brown eyes and the olive complexion that gave her a Mediterranean beauty, but there was a gleam in those eyes that he hadn't noticed before and which excited him now.

Perhaps it wasn't surprising that he should now see her differently. When they had last met, he had been preoccupied with clearing his name and saving his marriage while she had been the girl from the escort agency who was costing him ninety-five pounds a time.

They concentrated on the menu and ordering drinks. The waiter took their order and scuttled off. Richard sat back, giving her the chance to speak first.

'So what really happened?' she said.

He had thought himself prepared for anything but her direct-ness took him by surprise.

'You mean . . . after I left you that night?'

'Yes. When you were going to follow that barman and force him to give you the pictures he'd taken? By the way, where are those pictures? Do you have them?'

'No, I, er . . . I assume the police have. Have they not been in touch with you?'

'No.'

'Even so, I assume they've got the photographs. But I shouldn't worry. I don't think they're interested, not anymore.'

'So go on then – what did happen?'

There was something teasing about her manner that suggested she had never believed the version in the newspapers, so he needn't bother trying to sell her *that*.

Instead, he told her the truth. He knew there was a certain risk in doing so. After all, she could be here because she was being paid money by some newspaper to approach him. She could be miked up with a miniature recorder in her pocket. She could have already gone to the police and been urged by them to try and get him to talk. There were all kinds of possibilities . . . though, looking at her, he couldn't seriously believe in any of them.

He said, 'I followed him home, and tried to get him to give me the photographs. But he wouldn't. He wanted money. And I lost my temper and hit him. He went down. I called an ambu-lance. Then I got out fast. They took him to the hospital . . . and he died.'

She didn't seem surprised. 'So it was you and not Lawrence Nevison?'

'It was me and not Lawrence, yes.'

'So why did the police get it so wrong?'

He told her how Thornton had regained consciousness and given the police the name Richard Gillow. And how the police had seen the mis-named pictures of Lawrence and assumed that Thornton had similarly mis-named his assailant.

She smiled. 'And you didn't like to correct them.'

'Well, I intended to,' he said, not minding whether she be-lieved this. He wasn't even sure how far he believed it himself

285

any more. 'But then, when they told me Lawrence had committed suicide, there didn't seem a lot of point.'

'Poor Lawrence,' she said, her smile going.

'I know.'

They maintained a few seconds of silence in honour of his memory, then she asked, 'And what about your wife? She's back I imagine?'

'Yes.'

'So have you told her all this?'

'No. Oh, no.'

Their first course arrived, holding up conversation. They began to eat.

'Why haven't you told her?' she asked.

'Why . . .? Oh, because I don't think it would be fair. I mean to put her in that position.'

'Surely she wouldn't go to the police?'

He considered, then gave his honest opinion: 'I'm sure she wouldn't, no. But then I'd be asking her to shield me for the rest of her life. And I don't think I've a right to do that. Anyway, why tell her? What would be the point?'

There was a pause, then she said, 'But you don't mind telling me?'

'You knew anyway.'

'I didn't know for sure.'

'You'd a pretty good idea. Or else why would you have rung?'

'Perhaps I just wanted to see you again.'

The smile and the teasing manner had returned. He didn't quite know how to respond.

He said, 'I was certainly delighted to hear from you.'

She met his gaze. 'You mean that?'

'Of course. Why shouldn't I?'

'Well, I thought you'd want to put this whole business behind you –'

'Which I certainly do.'

'Yes, but I'm part of it, aren't I. So I thought you might want to put me behind you as well.'

'No,' he said quietly. 'Definitely not.'

'I'm glad to hear it.'

On an impulse, he reached out a hand and placed it over hers for a moment.

'You see,' he said, 'part of me still wants to confess. Or at least to be able to *talk* about the whole rotten business. But I can't. Quite the opposite. I have to be constantly on my guard —'

'Except with me,' she said.

'Yes.'

The waiter arrived to ask if everything was all right. When they said it was, he whipped away their empty plates.

'I told you that I couldn't tell Claire, my wife, about any of this —'

'Yes.'

'Which I can't. And never will be able to tell her for the rest of our lives together. The trouble is that, in the past, we've always told one another everything. We've always been very *confiding*. But now I have to live with this monstrous secret, the biggest secret of my life, and I can't ever share it with her. I think that's going to be very corrosive. I think it's going to slowly eat away at us.'

This time it was she who took his hand. 'I think it's a good thing I rang when I did.'

'I think it is,' he said, heartfelt.

Their main courses arrived but neither paid them much attention.

'We seem to be talking all about me,' he said.

'That's because you know so little about me,' she responded. 'Which I think gives me the advantage. I'm not sure whether I should relinquish that.'

'I don't even know your name, not your real name.'

'Do you want to?'

He considered. 'Perhaps not yet.'

'Only I'm rather fond of *Melissa*. And now I've no opportunity to use it except for when I'm with you.'

'When you're with me . . .?' Earlier than he had expected, he found they had come to an important turning-point. 'So you think we should meet again after today?'

Diane was packing for her return to university. Claire had begun to work again and supervised the gardener as he gathered in the apples and pruned the roses in preparation for winter.

Yet Richard sensed that she remained ill-at-ease. Perhaps she was still in something of a state of shock. After all, she had believed herself to be returning to a home that wasn't much different to the one she had left. Then, once back, she had found herself in a maelstrom of violence and suicide.

He tentatively broached the subject of London. His regular visits had been suspended since the day he had arrived home and found the first of the letters. Now he wondered aloud whether it was time he reinstated them.

'Oh, but of course you must,' Claire insisted. 'There isn't the slightest reason why not.'

'And you wouldn't be . . . worried?'

She looked at him. 'I'm only worried because . . . because we don't seem very close anymore. And that might be my fault. It probably is. I just don't know what –'

'Come here,' he said, and went and folded her in his arms.

'Darling, I do love you,' she said, looking up pleadingly.

'And I love you,' he said, and kissed her.

'You do still? I haven't spoiled everything because I didn't believe –'

'No,' he said, stopping her. 'You haven't spoiled anything at all. It's just that we've both needed a bit of time to . . . to get over things.'

She gave him a tearful smile. 'I know. You're right. We just need to get back to normal. Oh, but of course you must go to London . . .!'

He marvelled at how easy it was to say the right thing. He must take care to pay Claire more attention in future. He must let her feel that they were back on their old, intimate footing.

It struck him that anyone could maintain peace within a marriage providing they had a strong enough motive for wanting it.

Later, she was filling in the calendar. 'So, your trip to London . . .?' she said, sounding more cheerful than at any time since her return. 'What day is it going to be – Thursday, staying over till Friday?'

'Yes, I think so,' he said. Melissa was to join him for the Thursday night. 'That'll be all right, will it?'

'Yes, of course. And I'll do us a special dinner for when you come back.'

He knew, of course, that somewhere along the way he had sold his soul to the devil. Having got away with murder, he was about to embark on what was surely the much simpler task of deceiving his wife.

He remembered the night at the Midland Hotel when he had forced Lawrence to confess and Lawrence had counter-attacked by accusing him of not knowing how lucky he was. 'Life's easy for you,' he had said. 'You get things right instinctively, without even trying.'

Perhaps there was more truth to that than Richard had been willing to admit. Certainly now, as he waited to begin a new life neatly divided between Melissa and Claire, it would be difficult to deny.